THE PRIORY
by
DOROTHY WHIPPLE

✳✳✳✳✳✳✳

with a new afterword by

DAVID CONVILLE

PERSEPHONE BOOKS

BATH

for Amy and Rodney Stone

THE PRIORY

CHAPTER I

IT was almost dark. Cars, weaving like shuttles on the high road between two towns fifteen miles apart, had their lights on. Every few moments, the gates of Saunby Priory were illuminated. Every few moments, to left or to right, the winter dusk was pierced by needle points of light which, rushing swiftly into brilliance, summoned the old gateway like an apparition from the night and, passing, dispelled it.

The gates were from time to time illuminated, but the Priory, set more than a mile behind them, was still dark. To the stranger it would have appeared deserted. It stood in dark bulk, with a cold glitter of water beside it, a cold glitter of glass window when clouds moved in the sky. The West Front of the Priory, built in the thirteenth century for the service of God and the poor, towered above the house that had been raised alongside from its ruins, from its very stones. And because no light showed from any window here, the stranger, visiting Saunby at this hour, would have concluded that the house was empty.

But he would have been wrong. There were many people within.

At the top of the house, in what was still known as the nursery, though the occupants had passed the nursery age by ten years or more, two girls pored over a paper-dress pattern spread out on the floor. They crawled on their hands and knees about the pieces, fitting them together with great seriousness, their short

7

hair hanging over their eyes. In the room, the red glow of the fire gained on the white light of day from the windows.

Christine threw down her scissors in disgust.

"It's no good," she said. "I can't see."

"Where *is* father?" said Penelope in exasperation.

They sat on the floor, waiting. Christine, cross-legged, gazed upwards at the sky, her mind, in spite of that flash of irritation, a comfortable blank. Penelope, leaning backwards on her hands, whistled.

Three storeys below in the drawing-room their Aunt Victoria sat in the dark, her white stockings alone betraying her presence.

In their own quarters behind the green baize door, the servants lolled round the fire. They had, if they had needed it, the excuse that they couldn't see to do anything else. But they didn't need excuses at Saunby. No one questioned them.

The whole house waited for Major Marwood and light.

The electricity plant was old and out of date. It was on its last legs, but it must be made to do, because, as the Major frequently pointed out, he could not afford to replace it. It must be spared, he decreed, as much as possible. Since he was very economical in everything that did not directly affect his own comfort, the household had to wait for light until he wanted light himself.

He was now approaching the house by way of the elm avenue. As he walked under the old trees he made irritable cuts with his stick at nothing. Rough, the Golden Retriever, kept close at heel, careful not to offend. He felt his master's mood.

Half-way up the avenue the Major halted to survey the cricket field, which lay to the left. Empty, with its little black sodden shuttered pavilion, it was typical of winter and he hated winter. He would have liked to blame somebody for winter. And for the fact that Spencer at Top Farm was bothering him for gates again and Wilkinson's roof was leaking.

Somebody was always wanting something. Always wanting something, he repeated aloud, for he talked to himself. Though how the devil, he continued, they have the nerve to ask for repairs with the rent they pay . . .

He struck a fallen tree, peeled of its bark, bleached like a bone, so sharply with his stick that Rough trembled, but stood his ground. Rents. When he took over Saunby he'd been getting two pounds an acre ; now he got ten shillings.

It goaded him to think of it. He walked on. He'd thought he was in for a good thing when he inherited Saunby, but he'd been wrong. Beautiful though it was and proud though he was to own it, he wished he'd never taken it on. He wished to God he'd never left the Army.

He wished this every winter. In summer he was too taken up with cricket to wish for anything else. But it was winter now and he was too sunk in depression to remind himself that summer would come again.

He decided, suddenly, not to continue up the avenue, but to cut across the field and get to the house as quickly as possible ; to his room and the fire and tea and *The Times*. The thought of these spurred him to haste. He struck across the field to a gate in the yew hedge, and striding past the antic stumps of brussels sprouts which were all that remained in the kitchen garden, past the greenhouses fogged with cold and disuse, he took a path that brought him to the circular sweep of small sandy gravel before the main entrance to the house.

9

"Kennel," he said briefly to Rough, and Rough padded obediently to the stable-yard and put himself to bed.

The Major opened the door and felt for his switches.

A single light bloomed slowly in the hall, revealing stone walls hung with skins of leopard, lion and tiger and bristling with the heads, horns, tusks, teeth, brushes and pads of other animals. All were grey with dust, and the highest buffalo heads had beards of cobweb in addition to their own. An immense elephant tusk was laid as it were negligently upon a littered table, and beside it in a pot, a lily with brown edges struggled upwards.

Major Marwood threw his hat to join a collection of other hats, all his own, on the chest and strode through the hall, making for his fire. But when he reached his room, he halted on the threshold. The fire was out. He stood staring at the place where it should have been and his eyes hardened with anger.

"Damnation," he whispered. "Damn it all, this is the last straw."

Why on earth couldn't Victoria see to things ? Why couldn't she see that the servants did their work ? The house was full of servants, but it was kept like a pigsty, the food was abominable, he'd had indigestion ever since lunch, and now when he came in frozen to the bone and depressed like hell, his fire was out.

In two long strides he reached the bell. He jerked the handle down with such violence that when it fell back, the white china knob flew off. The Major let it fly. He did not even look at it. His eyes on the door, his well-shaped hands spread fanwise at the small of his back, he waited.

'Now I'll let 'em have it,' he promised himself.

§

Miss Victoria, unaware of the crisis, rang for tea to be brought to her in the drawing-room. She had thought once of going up to have it with the girls, but inertia and the pleasure she always took in her own company made her decide to stay where she was. Besides, she was thinking about a picture and did not wish inspiration to be dispelled by conversation.

She had decided to re-do the stormy sea-scape she had done in Cornwall in the summer and put a boat in the middle of it. That was what it needed. Human interest.

"A little barque," said Miss Victoria, biting into a tough scone. "Tossing in the waves. The whole thing rather dark. The shades of night are falling. And at the prow a lantern—a mere point of vermilion and gamboge. And I shall call the picture : 'Lead, Kindly Light.'"

It was a noble conception, she thought, and her eyes watered as she took another scone. Victoria's eyes watered for her pictures, but for nothing else.

When her brother complained about her house-keeping, Victoria reminded him that she was an artist.

"I am an artist," she said with dignity. "I don't care about material things."

Yet she had a large, undiscriminating appetite. She could eat great quantities of almost anything.

She sat now under the inverted funnel of light from the standard lamp beside her, a bulky figure in a shapeless coat and skirt and white stockings. Her nieces were puzzled by their aunt's stockings. No matter what colour they were when she bought them, sooner or later they went white.

Although she had not been out and was not going out, Miss Marwood wore a hat. She generally wore a hat when out of bed, except at dinner and then she arranged a coloured scarf on her head. Her hair was thin on the top. The girls wondered if she wore a hat because she was bald, or if she was bald because she wore a hat.

Apart from possible sensitiveness about baldness, Miss Marwood was indifferent to other people's opinion.

She painted in oils. Not mildly as befitted a maiden lady of fifty-three years, but boldly and badly. In her pictures there was neither background nor foreground ; everything was presented on the same hard plane with no detail missed. Her landscapes were composite ; she put in or left out whatever she fancied, such as trees without shadows and shadows without trees, smoke blowing one way and washing on the line another, so that the beholder was filled with irritation and spent much longer than he wished in trying to find out exactly what was the matter. The pictures could well have been reproduced in the competition corner of a children's paper with prizes offered for those who could point out what was wrong.

Miss Marwood, however, was pleased with her work, and no matter what criticism was passed upon it, she continued to be pleased. She put adverse criticism down to ignorance and merely smiled at it. Upon ambiguous criticism she put a construction favourable to herself.

" He said my pictures were highly personal. That was splendid, wasn't it ? " she said to her nieces. " Very complimentary, wasn't it ? "

" I don't know," said Christine. " It depends on the person, I suppose."

" I could tell from the way he spoke," said Miss Marwood coldly, " that he thought my pictures were excellent."

" Good," said Christine politely.

"But what a marvellous get-out," she said afterwards to Penelope. " ' Highly personal ' ! It's the sort of thing Talleyrand might have said. I wish I could think of things like that."

There was a collection of *bons mots* in an old reader on the nursery shelves and from that Christine had formed her admiration for Talleyrand.

The attics of Saunby were stocked with Miss Marwood's canvasses, although she gave them very freely to Conservative fêtes, bazaars in aid of the District Nurse, Jumble Sales for the Women's Institute and so on. She also sold a picture now and then to the farmer's wives. They liked the pictures she painted of their farms and paid five shillings, sometimes ten for them.

The Major was disgusted that she should take money from his tenants, but she told him she liked to turn an honest penny and that people only valued what they paid for. Besides, what was ten shillings for one of her pictures ? Not a tenth of its value. She was indignant with her brother. But what, she asked, could one expect of one whose sole interests were war and cricket ? Certainly not appreciation of art.

Miss Victoria now took a large piece of cake that resembled an extinct volcano, being dark with a cracked crust, high at the sides and sunk in the middle and strewn with exploded cinders that had once been currants. She settled herself more comfortably in her chair and extended her white stockinged ankles.

' Lead, Kindly Light,' she reflected. ' Beautiful.'

§

In his room, Major Marwood sat over his newly-lit fire, watching with a mixture of rage and resignation a maid fiddling with a folding table for his tea. He suffered obscurely because he hadn't been able to let fly when this girl appeared in answer to the bell. She was obviously new and obviously terrified of him, so after the first burst he had to keep back the rest and wait as best he could for her to finish and go.

Bessy Palmer fluttered under his gaze. Everything she did seemed to go wrong. She made a noise with the table and bit her lip and blushed. A curl escaped from her cap and dangled over her cheeks ; she felt untidy and hot and helpless and feared he would fly out at her again any minute. She kept glancing apprehensively first at him and then at the fire. What if it should go out and make her have to build it up again with him looking at her ? At last, she got the table up and the tray on it, and with a final glance at the fire, she escaped with relief.

Left to himself, Major Marwood leaned over the arm of his chair and considered his tray with distaste. Cheap earthenware teapot, cup and saucer of fine porcelain, papier-mâché tray and Georgian silver spoons. Since the tray had come in like this for years, he should have been used to these incongruities. But to-day he saw everything anew. To-day he was taking stock. Mostly he drifted. He drifted because there was not much else he could do. Saunby had proved too much for him.

He could have sold it when his father died. The place was not entailed and he could have got rid of it then and remained in the army, sticking to a job he knew. But he had inherited Saunby at a psychological crisis in his life.

During the war, while serving as a very junior captain with his regiment, he had been seconded for service with one of the battalions of Kitchener's Army and was promoted a temporary major. When the war ended, he found himself back with his Line Regiment on the Curragh and back to his substantive rank of captain. This galled him ; especially as in spite of his distinguished war service he was not even given the command of a Company. His father, at this moment, died. Francis Marwood sent in his papers and removed himself with his wife and three children to civil life and Saunby. He was allowed to retain his wartime rank of Major.

Arriving at Saunby he plunged at once into a sea of troubles. His father's financial affairs proved to be chaotic and the estate itself was crippled by heavy mortgages. Encouraged by the after-war boom, however, and in the first flush of inheritance Francis felt he could tackle everything. He furnished the room he now sat in as an office and set about managing the estate for himself.

Unfortunately he was no manager. He over-estimated his in-comings and underestimated his out-goings, and at the end of every year failed to understand why things hadn't turned out better. He was in a state of perpetual indignation at the demands of income tax, insurance, repairs.

The boom passed, the slump set in. He was obliged to reduce his rents again and yet again. All the dice, he felt, were loaded against him. His land was poor, almost pure sand. There was no coal under it. Coal had been found under almost all lands but his, and he was an increasingly poor man among increasingly rich neighbours. He was always wishing coal could be found under his land or that an aunt would leave him money. Something ought to happen, he thought indignantly. By God it ought.

When the sea of troubles threatened to engulf him, he sold a farm. By selling a farm, he received a lump sum and cut down his income. He was relieved from present embarrassments and committed to worse embarrassments in the future. But they *were* in the future and needn't be faced yet. And before time brought them up, something might happen to disperse them. Coal ; or a legacy ; or something.

For the rest, the Major considered himself extremely economical. His coverts were without game, his stables without horses, his green-houses without heat, his woods without a woodman, his gardens pretty well without gardeners. He'd cut down outdoor expenses to a minimum. The only thing he spent money on was cricket. Cricket might cost a certain amount but a man must have something.

As a matter of fact, cricket cost a great deal, but the Major preferred not to reckon that out too closely. He ran a team of his own. He held a cricket fortnight every year in August, during which he entertained a special holiday team in the house, spending money like water for their reception. He provided lunches and teas for visiting teams and teas for all spectators. It was a rule at Saunby that anyone who came to watch a match should be able to go into the tent for tea. But the most considerable item of expense in the name of cricket was the Major's maintenance of an ex-professional named Thompson. He paid Thompson all the year round a wage he could ill-afford and the amount of which he concealed as if it were a vice, as indeed in the circumstances it almost was. But, he told himself, he couldn't do without Thompson. In the winter, Thompson drove the car, collected the rents and attended the Major generally. In summer, he kept the ground and played for the Priory team. And he was always on hand to do the donkey-work about cricket fixtures and all that. The Major himself did not do donkey-work, as he frequently pointed out. Besides, the Major enjoyed Thompson's company. At Saunby, in the winter, it was the only company he had.

16

In the summer, while there was cricket, the Major was happy enough. But in the winter he had too much time to think and thinking depressed him. He was depressed to-day.

To-day he felt his fifty years. He felt, not old, but as if he would in time be old. That surprised and saddened him. Somehow he had never been able to believe that old age would reach him.

He poured out another cup of tea, considered the cake, rejected it, and leaned back with a sigh.

Behind him in the room, his past was spread out. Regimental groups on the walls, photographs of Company cricket teams, pen and ink caricatures of himself and his brother officers, his medals in a little glass case, his sword over the mantelpiece, and on his desk a photograph of his wife in her presentation gown. She had died in their first year at Saunby.

Against one wall, under their dusty japanned covers, stood the two typewriters in which he had enthusiastically invested when he furnished this room as an office for the management of Saunby. It was typical of him that he should have bought two typewriters where one would have done. Even one was superfluous. Only Thompson took a cover off now and then to type out, with one finger, a cricket notice or two.

The Major sighed. The demands from the farms this afternoon had reminded him that Saunby was a mill-stone round his neck ; a beautiful and honourable mill-stone, a mill-stone conferring great distinction, but a mill-stone.

He often felt bitter towards his son, but he was obliged to admit, to-day, that Guy had shown more sense than he had shown himself. Guy had firmly refused to succeed him at Saunby. Guy, having also refused to go into the Army, was at the Bar and doing well. He showed a more urgent desire to do well than a gentleman, in the Major's opinion, should. Pleading hard work, he rarely came home. Had his father known it, Guy thought it best to keep out of the way. He considered his father's financial behaviour fantastic and had no wish to be involved. The Major was hurt by Guy's behaviour. He was always hurt and astonished if the measure he meted out to others was meted out to him.

Having finished his tea, the Major got up to rummage in his desk for cigarettes. The desk was full of bills. The Major in his depression looked at several. All had entreatments on them : ' We respectfully beg to draw your attention . . .' ' Fear you have overlooked this account.' ' A cheque will oblige . . .'

He threw them back into the desk and closed the lid on them. Those were household bills. Those were bills run up by Victoria. Of all the wretched, incapable housekeepers, Victoria was the worst. She spent an immense amount of money and no one got any benefit from it. She kept a great staff of servants and they never did any work. She mismanaged everything. Look at the mess she made of cricket fortnight year after year after year, said the Major, talking to himself. Last year it was worse than ever. Nobody could get a bath after a match because the water was never hot. The meals were appalling. Never would he forget that cold fruit pudding that fizzed from fermentation in the mouth ; and the chickens that oozed pink when they were carved ; and all those wet vegetables. Worst of all he had discovered, to his everlasting shame, that some of the guests had actually to make their own beds before they could get into them at night. The servants simply overran the house like flustered fowls and got nothing done.

Victoria was hopeless. She did nothing for the girls. Never had done anything. Thank heaven the girls were good girls and didn't bother him, but the fact remained that they existed and something would have to be done for them sometime. Somebody would have to see about getting them married, and he didn't see how he could do anything about that himself.

And look at his fire to-day. Out. Simply another proof of Victoria's appalling slackness. The fire was the last straw. Positively the last. He would stand no more.

The Major was whipping himself up to his decision. He lashed out at Victoria, the bills, Guy, the dead fire, the demands of Spencer and Wilkinson, the winter weather, but it was all part of coming to the point.

The point was that he was going, at last, to propose to Anthea Sumpton. He was going to marry again. Things couldn't go on as they were. The household expenses must be cut down. The servants must be looked after. The girls must be looked after. He must be looked after. And his friends must be better entertained. Anthea, he was sure, would do all this, because she was devoted to him. Doted on him, in fact. He knew it.

She was in every way suitable for a second wife ; sensible, devoted, and no longer young. Thirty-six or seven, must be. But that was all to the good. She wouldn't want to start having a family at that age and he didn't want another family. It took him all his time to keep the one he'd got. Besides, young children, babies, at his age, would be ludicrous. Ludicrous. His mind boggled and turned tail at the thought of them.

He hurried to dwell on something more pleasant. Anthea took a great interest in cricket ; that was another point in her favour. It was at a match that he had first noticed her and she had been at almost every match he had played in since. She would appreciate the importance of his cricket fortnight, he was sure.

She *might* have a little money. If so, it would come in very useful. But she might have none at all, because he thought he remembered having heard somewhere that old Sumpton lived on an annuity. It didn't matter, though, whether she had money or not ; he would marry her with or without. She was so suitable. In a second marriage you thought of suitability, not of romance.

Anthea was, if not attractive, at least presentable. Strange that with her height, her strong hooked nose, her big bones, she should still seem schoolgirlish and diffident. He supposed it was because she hadn't got married and felt on the shelf. Well, he thought benevolently, he was going to change that for her and there was no knowing how she would blossom out when she was a married woman.

He rose suddenly from his chair. His mind was made up, and now that it was made up, he felt clear of his troubles. A wave of optimism washed over him, bearing them away. Everything was going to be different. Everything was going to be much better.

He stretched to the full height of his six feet two inches and smiled round at the room. He was fifty, but he was spare and graceful and all his movements were easy. He was as good looking at fifty as the extremely good looking young subaltern on the walls had been at twenty. In fact, the slight recession of his grey hair gave him a look of intellectual beauty that might have been missing at twenty ; and time had been kind in merely modelling more finely the fine bones of his face. He often looked as if the world had offended him, but when he smiled, his smile endeared him to people.

He smiled now. He was going to get it over. He

would go over to Brockington at once and propose to her.

He strode to the door. But there he paused. He came slowly back to the hearth-rug. He'd feel a fool, proposing. And suppose she wouldn't have him? It was extremely unlikely, but you never knew with women. It would be a nuisance if he went over all that way, ten miles on a cold night in the old car, getting Thompson out too, if she refused him when he got there.

He stood, turning the plain ring on the little finger of his left hand, debating with himself. Then his eyes fell on the telephone beside the chair. It gave him an idea. He would ring up and find out how the land lay. That would save trouble for everybody concerned.

He sat down and looked up the Sumptons' number in the directory. Then he took up the receiver and asked for it. He extended his long legs comfortably to the warmth of the fire as he waited. The telephone clicked in his ear.

" Hello ? " he said.

CHAPTER II

TEN miles across the dark fields in another large cold house, Anthea Sumpton sat at the round table in her sitting-room, reading. The book was entitled : *Be Happy*.

She was cold where she sat, far from the fire, but as the only light in the room hung above the table, there perforce she had to sit to read. The drawn blinds sucked slowly in and out behind her, for though Anthea suffered from the cold, she had been hygienically brought up and always had the windows open.

Beyond, through curtains looped back from an archway, was her bedroom. The bed there was a grim leggy affair of iron, as hygienic, again, in appearance as a bed in a hospital. But on the pillow was displayed a girlish nightdress-case of frilled muslin ornamented with pink bows.

The nightdress-case struck a contradictory note, and Anthea in herself, struck several. As she sat at the table with her large-boned frame, high-bridged nose, clumsy knot of dark hair, she seemed mature and full of latent power. But when she looked at people her eyes were diffident, rather lost, and her smile was almost apologetic. The expression of Anthea's eyes in her strongly marked face was as incongruous as the muslin nightdress-case on the stern virgin bed.

She read eagerly. The title of the book had halted her as she was about to pass the bookseller's window that morning in the town. *Be happy*. Anthea longed to be able to obey such a command. She bought the book, as she had bought others of the same kind. On the shelves in her room were several such books, with the word ' happiness ' or ' joy ' common to the titles. From which it could be gathered that Anthea made a determined, even desperate, pursuit of this fugitive state.

She doubled her cold hands under her armpits for warmth as she read. She would have been more comfortable downstairs in the drawing-room, but her parents were there. They would be sure to ask what she was reading and she would have hated to reply : " A book called *Be Happy*."

They would be amused and a little contemptuous that anyone should have to be told to be happy. They were both happy. A handsome, well-preserved pair, they had brought up their family of three, launched two in the world, and had now turned to outside interests of great variety and number. They were, between them, on almost every committee formed in the county.

If Anthea was not happy it was, in a world full of committees, entirely her own fault, they felt.

As the eldest of the family, Anthea had been devoted to her brother Henry and her sister Evelyn. She had played with them, read to them, taught them. She felt it was she who had brought them up, not their mother or the nurses and governesses who had followed each other in such rapid succession because Mrs. Sumpton was so exacting.

But both Henry and Evelyn had married early and hardly ever now, she knew, gave her a thought.

It was Henry's wife, not Henry, who wrote to her from India at Christmas and sent her beads and bracelets Henry must have known, if he had troubled to glance at them, that she would never wear.

Evelyn was the wife of Seton Craig, a Wimpole Street specialist, and Anthea rarely saw her, because she could not go to the house after the terrible affair of the baby's bottle.

When Evelyn's daughter was born, Anthea flew on the wings of love to London. She greeted the baby ecstatically. Now at last here was her opportunity. How she would cherish this child, how she would look after her when Evelyn was away, have her for the holidays, nurse her through measles and that sort of thing, help her when she went to school—do anything, everything, for this tiny, defenceless, enchanting creature ! As she held the baby in her arms, dedicating herself to the child, a passion of maternal love showed in her eyes such as had never showed in Evelyn's lovely glances.

But Evelyn was kind.

" Let her help you with baby, Nurse," she said. " She'll love it."

So Anthea helped, loved it, but was also filled with alarm. Susan was so thin, so light. Evelyn nursed the baby herself because her husband insisted. But Susan wailed incessantly, turning her head from side to side in what seemed to Anthea a heartrending appeal for food.

" I'm sure she's hungry," she kept saying.

But Seton said sternly that she was all right ; Evelyn must persevere. The nurse remarked coldly that Mr. Craig must be supposed to know better than Anthea.

" Oh, I *know*," Anthea hastened to assure her. " It's only that Susan always seems so hungry."

The baby's crying irritated Evelyn, so Anthea often bore Susan out of hearing, and it was when she had the baby to herself that Anthea suffered most. Whenever she lifted Susan up against her face to comfort her, Susan's lips fastened at once on Anthea's cheek,

24

sucking desperately. For a moment silence fell and over the baby's head Anthea's eyes filled with tears. Then the thin wailing broke out again.

One afternoon, when the nurse was out and Evelyn sleeping, Anthea could stand this no longer. She called the housemaid, a pleasant girl who had said as openly as she dared that the child was not getting enough food.

"Take her," said Anthea briefly, and rushing out hatless to the nearest chemist's shop, she bought a feeding bottle and a tin of the most highly recommended food.

Rushing back as if she had an incendiary bomb concealed in her arms, she prepared the food according to the instructions, urged to a frenzy of haste by Susan's desperate cries and by the fear that someone would discover and stop her before she could give the child the bottle.

"Now," she said at last with a fanatic light in her eye. "Give her to me."

A blessed silence fell at once. Susan, restrained by her aunt at intervals, drained the bottle, and as soon as she had done so, fell asleep. She slept all afternoon and woke rosy and contented. Anthea, proud and nervous, confessed to the returned nurse what she had done.

It was the end. After a dreadful interview with her brother-in-law Anthea left the house that night and had never re-entered it. No one had any sympathy with her. All were amazed that she should set herself up against a specialist. A *specialist*, they repeated. Anthea never knew that shortly after her departure the baby was given supplementary feeds of the very food and from the very bottle she had provided.

Seton Craig was an ungenerous man ; moreover, the less he saw of his wife's relatives the better he was pleased. It suited him that Anthea should continue to think herself in the wrong and ban herself from his house.

So Anthea saw Susan only on her annual visit to Brockington. Evelyn, quite kind, but too indolent to oppose her husband, sent snapshots of Susan to Anthea from time to time, over which Anthea, in secret, wept.

It was after this unfortunate affair that Anthea took to buying books on being happy.

But about eighteen months before this January day she had found another object to set up in her empty heart.

One summer afternoon, because there was nothing better to do, she accompanied her father to a cricket match and sat, by fate, on the seat adjoining the pavilion gangway. When Major Marwood brushed her skirts on his way out to bat, she felt nothing more than a vague interest in a man she had seen about almost all her life. He was a contemporary more of her father than of herself.

But when Major Marwood returned to the pavilion, everything was changed. Not that he had acquitted himself with brilliance. On the contrary. He was out for a duck, but a man out for a duck is not only lovable, but vulnerable, and as Major Marwood, smiling but discomfited, approached the pavilion, he noticed, with the eyes that were momentarily anxious to escape other eyes, that a scarf had fallen to the ground behind the woman occupying the outside chair. More to give himself countenance than anything else, he bent to pick up the scarf.

" Is this yours ? " he said, and his eyes sought hers in refuge.

Her eyes received him. She took him in and comforted him in the space of a second. They smiled at each other. She received her scarf and he went on into the pavilion. But it was a moment of significance for both of them. From that moment, Anthea's floating devotion became fixed upon him, and every time the Major thought of taking a second wife, he thought of her.

But nothing much had so far come of it. He sought her out at cricket matches, Conservative fêtes and county affairs of all kinds. He stood with her for several minutes when they met in the streets of the town. He kept saying vaguely that he wished she would come over some time. His courtship seemed to continue but not to progress, and poor Anthea took to buying books on happiness again.

And as she sat reading the one she had bought that very morning, she heard footsteps running down the corridor towards her room. Someone was coming to summon her. She felt intuitively that something was going to happen ; some change was coming into her life with those running footsteps. Holding her book, she turned to the door.

" Come in," she called.

A breathless little maid with cap askew panted out :

" Telephone, Miss Anthea, please. Major Marwood, he said."

The book was so hastily thrown aside that it slid over the table and fell to the floor. Anthea rushed to the mirror to smooth her hair, as if he were going to be able to see her across the miles that separated them. Then she sped from her room. The little maid, enjoying herself, rushed after her, but Anthea threw out an imperious hand.

" I'll go," she said.

When she reached the back hall she was breathless, not so much from haste as from excitement. He had never rung her up before. She controlled her breathing with difficulty and took up the receiver.

" Hello," she said.

" Is that you, Anthea ? "

" Yes, but didn't you want to speak to father ?   He's in somewhere.   Shall I find him ? "

" No, I don't want your father.   It's you I want."

" Oh, do you ? "   What a beautiful voice he had ! It was more than ever noticeable when disembodied.

" Yes, it's you I want," said the Major.

There was a pause during which Anthea thought he must hear her heart beat.

" I say, Anthea, I thought I'd have a word with you on the telephone before coming over.   Of course I'll come over at once if it's all right, but I thought it would save us both a lot of bother and embarrassment if I got the worst over by telephone, don't you agree ? "

" Well," said Anthea with a nervous laugh.   " You see, I don't know what it's about . . ."

" Well, I want to say . . ." the Major paused again. " I want to say . . .   Damn it, I must get it *out*. It's this, Anthea.   Will you marry me ?   I know it must seem sudden to you and all that, but it isn't sudden to me.   I've been thinking about it for a long time.   Yes, I have.   I've been thinking about it for a very long time.   And now I want to know if you feel you could.   Eh ?   If you think you could, I'll come over.   But it's not much good if you don't feel able to, is it ?   You see my point, don't you ?   What do you feel about it ? "

A long-drawn breath was his only answer.

"Are you there? " he inquired anxiously.   "Hello? "

" Yes, I'm here," she said in a low voice.   " Oh, Francis . . ."

At the other end of the wire the Major smiled broadly.

" Well ? " he said.

" Oh, Francis *darling* . . ."

" It's all right then, is it ? " he shouted jovially.

28

" Good. By God, it's splendid. I'll come over now, shall I ? "

" Oh, yes," cried Anthea, her voice ringing light and high. " Come. Come now."

" Or would you rather I waited until after dinner ? " suggested the Major.

" No, no, come now," Anthea besought him. " Come quickly."

" Right you are. I'll be over within the hour. Good-bye, Anthea. Good-bye, my dear."

He put down the telephone and reached for a cigarette. That was settled. Regret and relief mingled in his mind. He hoped it would work out all right. He hoped he hadn't taken a false step. But she was a nice girl. She'd behaved sensibly from the start ; taken him straight off without shillyshallying and never tried to hide the fact that she was glad to get him. A very promising beginning.

He picked up *The Times*. He thought he'd have time to glance through it before he need start. He rang the bell and ordered Thompson to bring the car round in twenty minutes.

Anthea, meanwhile, was back in her room standing beside her table, bemused, with a look of ecstasy on her face.

CHAPTER III

DOMESTIC life at Saunby had run for many years on strange lines. When death removed the mistress, it removed the retaining pin of the household. The pieces fell apart and so far had never been re-assembled. The occupants of the house were divided up and lived in the places they had made for themselves, with but little communication between the separate camps.

The Major and Miss Victoria met at meals. For the rest, when they were indoors, he kept to his room across the hall and she painted in her studio and sat in the drawing-room.

The servants lived their own lives in their own quarters, emerging to do the minimum of work as quickly as possible so that they could get back to the fun. They looked upon the family as a nuisance to be put up with for the sake of board and wages.

Bertha Siddle said as much and Bessy Palmer, the new girl, was shocked. She showed it in her pretty round face.

" I knew you was one of the buttery kind as soon as I saw you," said Bertha mockingly.

Bessy blushed. She was not homesick, no one could be homesick for such a home as hers, ruled by such a man of iron as her father, but she felt very new and strange and tears were not far off during these first days at Saunby.

" Let her alone," said Thompson good-naturedly from behind his paper.

And Bertha, who took notice of Thompson if of no one else, for the time being, did.

Thompson was a privileged person. He moved with equal ease and friendliness on either side of the green baize door. He was as comfortable in the Major's company as he was in the servants' hall. Everybody liked Thompson. In fact, there was almost always some girl in love with him. Thompson, if he could not manage to be in love himself, nevertheless let himself be loved with the good humour he displayed towards life in general.

The third camp at Saunby was at the top of the house. Christine and Penelope Marwood had been in the nursery as babies when their mother died, and at twenty and nineteen years of age were in the nursery still. No one, through the years, had suggested that they should come down, and they themselves had never wished to. It was much more fun upstairs.

Their set of rooms was quite complete ; a little world of its own shut off from the downstairs adult world by a stout oak door at the top of the stairs. Behind this door was a small hall with a deep cupboard for coals. The hall gave into a big room that had once been the nursery, was afterwards the schoolroom and was now the living-room. From this, three bedrooms opened off.

All the rooms were papered alike in an old-fashioned paper of white with a trailing pattern of stems and flowers in blue and green and red ; a placid paper with clear spaces in it. The paint was a placid pale green. The carpet was shabby, the chairs were much kicked about the legs. There was an old doll's house —it had been Victoria's—in one corner, and tottering piles of books and papers in all the others. Before the fire there still stood the high guard over which their childish combinations used to air. There was an upright piano with keys as yellow as old teeth. A sewing machine was a recent addition ; they had bought it between them second-hand. The room contained evidence of their entire progress from babyhood to young womanhood.

The views from the nursery windows were at first sight all of the sky. But when you stood against the panes, you saw the gardens immediately below with the pattern of the Park beyond, the elm-tree avenue with the cricket field alongside and the lake to the left of the house ; the other lake was hidden in a wood. The narrow river that made the lakes ran very clear at Saunby, but ten miles farther on it was dark and evil-smelling. It gave its name to one of the worst quarters of a city and people drowned themselves in it.

In this little world from which nurses and governesses had departed, Christine and Penelope Marwood lived in happy isolation. They did not concern themselves much with what went on downstairs. When they wanted anything, they rang the bell, and Bertha Siddle, albeit reluctantly, appeared.

Since Bertha had to climb three flights of stairs to wait upon the young ladies, it was perhaps not surprising that she did it with an ill grace, and on this January day when she had set out the two plates of cold beef, the salad, the dish of potatoes in their jackets, she looked round to see that nothing was missing, not from a wish to oblige, but to save herself the trouble of coming back.

Daft idea, she thought, carting food up to the top of the house like this. Why couldn't they all eat together ? But in her opinion the whole family was cracked. Like most of the gentry. Bertha despised the gentry. They were feckless ; they couldn't do a hand's turn for themselves. And the way they spoke and what they talked about made her want to laugh. She had a lot of fun in the servants' hall taking them off. Even Bill Thompson had to laugh at her sometimes.

At the thought of Thompson, Bertha looked pleased with herself. The outer corners of her long eyes and long mouth slanted upwards in a smile. Two deep dimples showed in her thin cheeks, and her small pointed teeth gleamed. She looked pretty, but wolfish. On her way to ring the brass bell she pinched up her permanent waves at the mirror. Then she lifted the bell, clapped it carelessly and went out.

The girls came in from their bedroom, their hands red from washing in cold water. They sat down at once to the table, and the winter sunshine, striking a strong light upwards from the white cloth, made them look like young illuminated saints with pure, grave faces and downcast eyes. They were in fact contemplating nothing holier than the extremely undercooked beef.

" I don't like it as bloody as this," complained Penelope, looking to see if Christine's beef was as bad as hers or better.

" Would you rather have this ? " asked Christine. " I don't mind."

Penelope changed plates. As the younger sister, she was used to having things made right for her by Christine. She helped herself to salad while Christine hunted among the potatoes for one to her liking.

There was a strong likeness between the sisters. They were cast in the same mould ; they had the same slender length of limb, the same shape of face— oval squared at the chin—the same fine straight noses, feminine replicas of their father's. But Christine's hair was dark, Penelope's very fair ; they both wore it, curling naturally, to clear their shoulders. Christine's eyes were grey, Penelope's blue. Penelope attracted attention, but Christine held it by some subtle quality in herself; a response or awareness that Penelope lacked, or did not wish for.

In spite of the fact that their checked skirts were skimpy and their woollen jumpers shrunk from washing, the girls looked charming. Their figures were so youthful it did not matter what they wore, and their hair shone with youth and health, their teeth showed perfect when they laughed, which was often.

" My goodness," said Penelope, sawing at her beef. " It's as tough as old boots again."

" Never mind," said Christine. " The pommes de terres are all right."

" How pleased Rosie would be if she could hear you," said Penelope with her mouth full. " Keeping up your French."

" 'M, she would. We must write to her this week."

" You must, you mean. I shan't. It takes me half-an hour to write a page looking up spellings in the dictionary, so she won't be ashamed of me."

" I use words I don't have to look up," said Christine. " So I'm developing a nice simple style."

" You can practise it then. One letter will do for both of us."

" Don't be mean. Poor Rosie," reproached Christine.

" Well, perhaps I'll add a few words at the end of yours," conceded Penelope.

Miss Rosewarne, their last governess, had left to be married. Her anxiety for her late charges had spoilt the honeymoon. Whenever her husband clasped her in his arms, she dissolved into tears and wanted to know what those poor children would do without her. When the unfortunate man repeated with some impatience that he was sure they would be all right, she thought him unfeeling and turned from him. For weeks she wrote letters full of advice and affection almost daily, but the girls wondered why she bothered. Left to themselves they got on very well.

" Although our education is appalling," Christine told Penelope.

" No worse than anybody else's round here," said Penelope.

" You wait. We shall make nice fools of ourselves when we get out into the world," said Christine darkly.

" Lots of other people will be making fools of themselves, too," said Penelope comfortably.

" But I don't want to be a fool," said Christine.

When Penelope was caught out in a mispronunciation she laughed, but when Christine made a mistake, she blushed and felt humiliated. It was fortunate for her peace of mind that she did not know how many she made. As is usual with the ignorant, long words had the fascination for both girls that obstacles on the road have for a bad driver ; instead of avoiding them they ran into them.

The girls had, however, a natural intelligence, and their education was, as Penelope said, little worse than that of the rest of their female acquaintance. They belonged to a class and a circle which sends its sons to preparatory and public schools and to universities, but keeps its daughters at home during their most receptive years under the instruction of, for the most part, uninstructed governesses and sends them too late to finishing schools at home or abroad.

The Marwood girls had not even been sent to one of these establishments. Miss Victoria had once gone so far as to lay in a few prospectuses, but when she showed them to the Major he was so outraged at the

35

fees that Miss Marwood returned to her painting and the subject was not broached again.

The girls were relieved. They didn't want to leave home. Their life seemed odd and undesirable to the matrons round about, but the girls were happy in it.

" But what do you *do*, dear? " a matron, outwardly sympathetic, inwardly disapproving, would inquire.

" Do ? "

The girls were puzzled by such a question. There was always plenty to do.

They spent most of their time out of doors. Fresh air was their natural element and unless the weather was very bad they could not remain in the house for long.

They knew where to go for the first of everything : the first snowdrops, the first catkins, primroses, violets, forget-me-nots, wild roses, honeysuckle. These flowers appeared in turn on the nursery sills almost as soon as they appeared in the woods and fields. The girls liked to make miniature gardens in bowls too, and to grow trees from acorn and plum stones. They took no interest in the real gardens round the house. They were only interested in what was theirs, in what they did themselves. This egotism, normal to youth, was perhaps prolonged in them because they had been left to themselves so long.

They were kept busy making their own clothes. They knitted, successfully, their own jumpers, caps and scarves, and they made, less successfully, their own dresses.

They read a good deal. They dipped without discrimination into the bran pie of a circulating library in the town, and were often very disappointed by what they brought out ; the more so because a bad draw meant having nothing to read until they could afford to take the bus back for another book.

" Why do people write such rot ? " they inquired indignantly of each other.

" It costs us a lot of money," complained Penelope.

Their allowances were small and had to be carefully laid out. The size of the bus fare prevented their going often into the town. When they felt in need, as they often did, of bars of chocolate they walked the two miles to the village. They walked, too, to their favourite farm. They had an affection for Mrs. Spencer there, based in childhood on excellent currant pasty.

Altogether their days passed pleasantly and so long as they kept to themselves they were contented, at times soaringly happy, but when they made excursions into social life, they were disturbed. When they looked round at the lives of other people, they wondered what waited for them. Was life going to be no better than this ? they asked themselves with apprehension.

The female society of their acquaintance was split into two. Into the sheep and the goats, Christine said. The goats—the beautiful, the smart, the gay—broke away early and were seen, in photogravure, in the illustrated papers, at balls and restaurants, and in the flesh out hunting, very well groomed and brilliantly made up. They were heard, too, using strong fashionable language in the lanes. The Marwoods, following the hounds on their bicycles, gazed wistfully at these young Dianas and wished they could afford to be like them. They wished to be like them when they saw them, but when they were back at home together, they forgot to wish to be anything.

The other set, the sheep, stayed within the fold and gave mild tennis parties in the summer and afternoon card parties in the winter, to which Christine and Penelope went. At these parties the company was always the same. It was made up of elderly presiding matrons and of girls whose ages ranged from seventeen to forty.

Except for the meteor-passage of some gay young creature who strayed in on leaving school but who soon went over to the goats, these girls seemed all to be of the same type, and even at forty were still girls in outlook and behaviour. They seemed never to have left the sixth form of some school where the pupils were not encouraged to know too much, but where the tone was nice. They seemed to have been put on their honour at an early age and never to have come off it.

Girls and matrons were full of good works and their talk was mostly of bazaars, girls' guilds and activities to raise money for the heathen. For these, they were always trying to sell something. The Marwoods were embarrassed by being asked to buy such things as woollen buttons and sealing-wax ornaments for hats. They had little money to spend, and Penelope was at last driven to explain that what they had, they needed for themselves.

Christine, to make up to Rosamund Hunter for not buying her raffia purses, listened to a long account of her bazaar where the stall-holders had dressed as Japanese ladies with paper chrysanthemums in their hair. Six months later she found herself listening again to an account of a bazaar where the stall-holders had dressed as Japanese ladies with paper chrysanthemums in their hair.

" You dressed up like that twice then ? " she inquired politely.

" No—only once," said Rosamund.

" Then you're still talking about the same bazaar ? " asked Christine.

" Oh, yes, the same bazaar," said Rosamund.

' Fancy talking about the same bazaar for six months,' thought Christine.

The Marwood sisters were no more approved of by the sheep than the sheep were approved of by the sisters. The sheep thought the sisters very slack because they refused to be drawn into the bazaars, and the matrons considered their upbringing disgraceful, though they blamed Victoria for that. In spite of the general disapproval, however, Christine and Penelope were included in the parties, because this social circle felt obscurely a need to reinforce itself, to keep itself together.

Things were breaking up. Everything was changing. It no longer seemed to matter who one was. Daughters of good families were breaking away in all directions. They went to universities, they went on the films, sometimes they just went. There was hardly anybody left to play cards and tennis in the afternoon, and those that were left were precious. So the circle clung to Christine and Penelope, however unsatisfactory.

For their part, Christine and Penelope went to the parties because they were the only entertainment. If they had not gone to the card and tennis parties, they would have gone nowhere. Besides, whatever the company, the food was good. The Bennett-Gow's cook, for instance, made the most delicious cream buns. When Penelope saw the plates of plump buns on the Bennett-Gow's table, she winked surreptitiously at her sister and once managed to eat nine without detection.

But whenever they had been to a party, one was sure to clutch the other's hand going home and say passionately : " We must *never* be like that."

In their youth and intolerance Christine and Penelope only saw effects, which they disliked ; they made no allowance for causes.

It was in reaction from the drab dress of the sheep that the sisters were moved to send for patterns to the fashion papers and make their own clothes. They considered that Rosamund Hunter and the rest dressed abominably.

"Artificial silk," they scoffed. "And old furs handed down from their mothers and woollen suits with the skirts bulging at the back."

They did not pause to reflect that their friends at forty were still dressing on the allowance allotted to them at eighteen. Few parents thought it necessary to augment their daughters' allowances with the years, and it is much more difficult to dress cheaply at forty than at eighteen. Christine and Penelope, however, did not yet know this and were scornful.

Their own dressmaking did not altogether satisfy them. As with everything else, conception was exciting and execution disappointing. The dresses were always going to be wonderful, but somehow they generally turned out slightly wrong. The girls had a good eye for colour, but little skill. There was almost always something in the finished dress that had to be covered up by a sash or a knot of flowers or even hidden altogether by a little jacket that was itself also slightly wrong somewhere.

The girls thought they were successful in hiding these defects, but the truth was that their clothes caused some amusement among those whose clothes they themselves despised. Before a party there was often some speculation as to what the Marwood girls would turn up in.

They were about to make new dresses now and planned to cut them out after lunch before the light went.

"Tough though this beef is," said Penelope, "I'll have some more."

She rang the bell that would bring Bertha up the three flights of stairs, and in due time, Bertha appeared, her face pinched with the effort to keep her tongue civil.

" More beef, please," said Penelope.

The girls did not like Bertha and were therefore callous about her having to climb the stairs. Christine was a little less callous than Penelope.

" It's a long way up," she said.

" Well, let her leave," said Penelope. " She's got a face like a ferret."

When lunch was over they went to perch on the rim of the high fireguard.

" We ought to cut out," said Christine. " But I feel like a walk. What do you feel like ? "

" Full," said Penelope.

They laughed and rubbed against each other like young colts.

" Let's go," said Christine. " We can cut out when we come in."

§

In old coats and knitted caps they ran down through the house. They ran past the case of wholly un-remarkable sea-shells set up on the second landing, past the stuffed rat, embalmed because he was so big, past the illuminated addresses presented in other days to other Marwoods, through the hall and out into the fresh air, where both drew a long breath of pleasure and snatched off the caps they had just put on.

They went to the stable yard to unloose Rough. They pitied Rough for having to be so much with their father. He liked obedience in his dogs and poor Rough when out with him walked sedately at his heels. If he met the girls when he was with the Major he made no attempt to leave him and follow them. He gazed after them mournfully, but he knew where his duty lay and he did it.

As soon as they loosed him now, he leapt at them with delirious gratitude and stood on his hind legs to embrace them in turn.

"Go on now, go on," they urged him, and in a moment he was plunging through the broken-spined bracken in the open park, rising and falling like a rocking-horse.

The girls went down into the elm avenue. The trees here were three centuries old and still magnificent. The walk beneath was grass-grown and kept close by countless rabbits. Rabbits and bracken, if nothing else, flourished exceedingly at Saunby.

Under these elms, monks must have walked in the old days, and hunting-parties ridden, lords and ladies taken the air and coaches rumbled, but now nobody came but the Major and the girls and courting servants, and in the cricket season the spectators to the matches which were played in the field alongside.

The elm avenue ended in a pair of gates with a lodge beside them, but in these days the lodge was empty and no lodge-keeper ran out when the girls went through. Beyond the gates a lane led to Top Farm.

Mrs. Spencer was bustling about in her great kitchen.

"Come in, come in," she called heartily as they approached. "And how d'you find yourselves this week?"

"We're very well. How are you?" they called back.

"I say, Mrs. Spencer," said Christine. "There's someone in your top field."

Mrs. Spencer poked her cheerful face out of the door to look. Then she laid her hand on Christine's arm and bent almost double to laugh.

"Well, I told our Johnny somebody'd be taken in and it's you! That's his new scarecrow, bless you!"

"Well . . ." Christine looked as if she couldn't

believe that it wasn't a woman in a bonnet and coat with an umbrella in the crook of her arm and a dog at her feet.

" What's it guarding ? " asked Penelope.

" Winter wheat," said Mrs. Spencer. " Now come inside and let me get you a piece of my cake while we're talking."

Christine took her piece to the door and continued to gaze at the mock woman in the field.

" She's more than real," she said to herself.

She suddenly wished she could write poetry. She didn't know what she wanted to say, but she wanted urgently to say something about the woman walking for ever in the field of winter wheat. And that great shoulder of the hill should come in, and the colourless sky. When familiarity and warmth suddenly drained away from a scene, how miraculous it was. Christine, standing at the farm door with her unbitten piece of cake, struggled to reach her thoughts. But kind Mrs. Spencer came to see what she was doing.

" You'll get your death standing at that door. Come in to the fire, love.

" I hear you've got Bessy Palmer up at the house now," said Mrs. Spencer when she had satisfied herself by getting both girls into chairs by the hearth.

" Have we ? " said Penelope.

" I don't suppose we've seen her yet," explained Christine.

" Fancy," said Mrs. Spencer in surprise. She meant fancy not knowing who's in your house and who isn't. She wouldn't like to live like that, she thought.

" She's a nice girl, is Bessy," continued Mrs. Spencer. " She comes of ever such nice parents. Her mother was a schoolmate of mine, but they left this part and went over into Beesley and I never see her now."

Beesley was not more than ten miles away, but it

might have been the other side of the world to Mrs. Spencer, who never went five yards beyond her own farm.

"Anyway, if you do happen to come across Bessy in the house any time," Mrs. Spencer was speaking now as if Saunby was some sort of vast labyrinth, thought Christine. "If you *do* happen to fall in with her, I'd be much obliged if you'd just say I'd be glad to see her on her day out—for her mother's sake, you know. Just say that, but don't put yourselves out over it, of course."

The girls did not stay long. They knew how busy Mrs. Spencer always was. On the way down the lane they met Johnny Spencer, a tall lad with a thatch of fair hair. His face was as kind as his mother's, but quieter. He had a gun under his arm and a ferret in his pocket.

"I've been trying to get a rabbit for the pot," he said, "but this chap won't do his duty."

He brought the ferret out of his pocket and it looked in mild inquiry at the girls and Rough.

"He hasn't got a ferret's nature somehow," said Johnny, stroking the little animal.

"I like him all the better for that," said Christine.

"Aye, may be," said Johnny. "But if you've got a ferret's job to do you'd better have a ferret's nature, hadn't you?"

"I suppose so," Christine acknowledged.

They left Johnny and went on, through the gates again and into the elm avenue.

"We've time to go home through the wood," said Penelope.

They struck through the wood, amusing themselves by fording the stream in apparently impossible places. Their shoes were soaked when they burst through the thorn hedge into the back meadow and came face to face with Thompson. They were surprised, but Thompson was startled. His eyebrows shot up at the sight of them.

" Hullo, Thompson," said Penelope. " What're you doing out here ? "

He didn't seem to know what to reply, so Christine hastened to help him.

" Can't he go for a walk, poor chap, if he wants to ? "

" That's right," said Thompson, recovering himself. " I've got to keep my weight down, haven't I ? Or the Major'll have something to say."

" He will," said Penelope walking on with her sister.

" You did put him in a hole, asking him that," muttered Christine.

" Well, how did I know he was having another affair ? " protested Penelope. " Who is it this time, I wonder ? "

Thompson had had affairs before. A handsome housemaid had lately left in tears, and it was said that the head gardener's daughter had married another man merely out of spite. Neither spite nor tears seemed to affect Thompson. He remained imperturbable, cheerful, good looking, vigorous.

" Father's best friend," said Christine.

" Not his *friend*," objected Penelope. After all, she thought, Thompson's a chauffeur.

" His friend," insisted Christine. " Don't you notice how comfortable father is with Thompson ? His face clears when Thompson so much as comes in sight."

They reached the porch and had to take reluctant leave of Rough. They always hated to leave him outside.

" Kennel, Rough, kennel," they said, smoothing the dog's head. " Poor old boy, it's a shame."

Rough stood on the drive, looking mournfully over

45

his shoulder at them, but when they said kennel again, he padded off.

When they reached the nursery, they found Miss Marwood sitting there in the dark.

" Hello, Aunt Victoria, have you come to have tea with us ? " asked Christine.

" Anything up ? " asked the cruder Penelope.

" Yes to both those questions," said Miss Marwood. " Try the light, one of you."

" It's too early," said Christine.

" No, your father's in," said her aunt.

When the light was on, Miss Marwood was seen to be twitching, so the girls knew she was upset. When Miss Marwood was put out, she twitched in every limb.

" Anything up, indeed," she said. " I should think so. I'll tell you and you won't like it."

A threatening triumph was in her tone, as if she looked forward to disturbing them as much as she herself had been disturbed.

" What is it ? " asked Christine.

" Wait," said Miss Marwood, raising an imperious hand. " I hear Bertha coming with tea. If the maids get wind of this affair, they'll leave in a body, and though they can leave *afterwards* for all I care, I'm blest if I'm going to have the bother of getting a new lot before."

" Goodness, what can it be ? "

" Hush ! " commanded Miss Marwood.

The door opened, but it was not Bertha who appeared. It was a maid the girls hadn't seen before, a girl with a sweet rounded face and very blue eyes. She looked nervous.

" Oh, you must be Bessy Palmer ! " exclaimed Christine.

" Yes, miss," said Bessy blushing.

46

" Where's Bertha ? " asked Miss Marwood, sharpened by anger into noticing the servants.

" She slipped out for half an hour, miss," said Bessy, anxiously. " She asked me to see to her tray for her if she wasn't back."

" Tell Bertha from me to do her own work," said Miss Marwood.

" Yes, miss," murmured Bessy, setting out the cups and saucers.

" We've seen Mrs. Spencer at Top Farm this afternoon," said Christine. " And she said would you go and see her sometime on your afternoon off."

" Thank you, miss," said Bessy, blushing again.

As soon as she had gone, the girls turned to their aunt.

" Now," they said. " Tell us. Tell us."

" Your father," announced Miss Marwood, with great deliberation, " is going to marry again."

The girls' faces changed. They had not expected anything in the least like this.

Miss Marwood sat twitching triumphantly, letting them take it in.

" Marry again ? " said Christine. " *Marry ?* "

" Who is it ? " asked Penelope.

" Anthea Sumpton."

" Anthea Sumpton ! "

" You mean the Sumptons who live at Brockington ? We've seen her. She was at the Berrys' once. You remember, Penelope. She's one of the sheep. She's just like all the rest . . ." said Christine, with wide incredulous eyes.

" She's old," said Penelope. " She's long past thirty. I should think she's even forty."

" And father's fifty," said Christine. " What do they want to get married for ? "

The sisters gazed with amazement into each other's

eyes. To marry at forty and fifty. It shouldn't be done. It was awful. Such bad taste . . . their own father . . .

The girls had never had much to do with their father, but he had always been there. He was part of their background and they had taken it for granted that he would always be the same. When he met them in the house he said hullo and gave them a fleeting smile. When they asked him for extra money he either said : " Good God, I can't afford it. What d'you take me for ? " or else he gave it to them without demur. They never knew which it was going to be. What amazed them now was that he was going to be different, he was going to be connected with somebody else, with a *wife* ? It was incredible. It was stupefying. They gazed with bewildered eyes at each other and at their aunt.

" Will she come here ? " asked Christine.

" Of course she'll come here. Where else do you think she'll go ? " said Miss Marwood tartly.

" Will she make us go downstairs and live with her and father ? "

" She'll be our step-mother. We don't want a step-mother."

" No," said Miss Marwood. " I should think you'd almost rather have me."

The girls were so preoccupied that they did not reassure her on that point, and Miss Marwood, sore from the plain-speaking of her brother who had implied that had she kept house properly he might not have had to take a wife, now felt sorer still.

" Blow, blow, thou winter wind," said Miss Marwood, bitterly, but the girls did not even ask her what she meant.

She wondered if it would be better to call her picture that instead of ' Lead, Kindly Light.' Only how, she wondered, could she work ingratitude in? She must lay that problem aside for the present. An artist, she thought resentfully, should not be subjected to these disturbances. An artist should be protected in society. But she was being violently upset, and who cared? This affair would spoil her work for weeks, perhaps for ever. Getting the house ready for a bride! What a task! It filled her with fatigue and nausea even to think of it.

"Well, I just shan't do it," she decided. "Why should I? I've done enough and what thanks have I ever had?"

She was so upset that for once she forgot to eat. She forgot that tea waited until Penelope said: "What about tea?"

Miss Marwood moved to the table then.

"Your future step-mother's coming to tea to-morrow," she announced.

"Oh . . ."

Apprehension and distaste showed in the girls' faces and they bit reluctantly into their bread-and-butter. But as soon as Miss Marwood sat down to table, habit reasserted itself and she ate as heartily as ever.

§

Night fell and at night the ruins came into their own. The past dwarfed the present. The ruined Priory regained the noble significance of its origin and aspired still, while the house crouched low beside it, to shelter its little company of human beings.

In her strange bed, Bessy Palmer was thankful the day was over, thankful to get away from the others, to have a room, though very small, to herself. This room to herself was about the only advantage of this queer place, she thought. What a house! You couldn't clean anything up properly. And no proper mistress to go to for orders. That Miss Marwood was so funny, always painting pictures and wiping her hands down the front of her dress. Never answered your questions so you could understand what she wanted done. If she wanted anything. The Major was a lovely man, but she wouldn't like to cross him, thought Bessy. He was a gentleman and his language was something awful. She did dislike that Bertha Siddle. You never knew where she was going to jab at you next.

But she must stay at Saunby. She mustn't leave, or her father would be on to her. At the thought of her father, Bessy decided that strange though Saunby was it had at least the advantage of being ten miles from her home. Her father couldn't get at her here. Her last place had been outside their village, and her father used to humiliate her by fetching her on her nights out, or sending one of her brothers for her. He wouldn't trust her out by herself. You never knew what mischief a girl would get into, he told them. Bessy had to spend her time off sitting in the home kitchen under his grim eye. If the family in whose service she was had not moved away, she didn't know how she would ever have escaped. But she had escaped ; and she wasn't going back if she could help it.

Anyway, she could go and see Mrs. Spencer on her afternoon off. She wondered what Johnny Spencer was like nowadays. He used to be a nice lad, she thought sleepily.

In the adjoining attic, Bertha Siddle smiled, thinking of Thompson.

Mrs. Nall, the cook, snored with her man's cap hung on the bed-post ready for morning. The house was so cold that she always wore her deceased husband's cap in winter to go about the kitchens first thing.

Thompson, care-free, was sound asleep in his room up the wooden stair in the stable yard.

The Major, in his vast cold bedroom, wished it was summer again and his team in the house and the days meaning something. Above him, his daughters talked far into the night, astonished and indignant still.

CHAPTER IV

THE following afternoon the Sumpton car turned
in at the Priory gates. In it, behind the chauffeur,
sat Anthea, alone.

The fact that she was alone in the car was enough
to mark the significance of the occasion. As a rule,
when Anthea wanted to go anywhere, unless her
parents were going too, she travelled by bus. To-day,
the car had been given up to her as a matter of course,
and her parents had seen her off with as much fuss
as if she had been Henry or Evelyn.

Since her engagement, everything was changed ; the
attitude of her parents, of everyone she knew, changed
overnight. Life itself was changed entirely. The
future was full where before it had been so empty.
She had had to buy books on happiness to give her
the courage to advance into it. Now she need never
open them again. Her future was filled by Francis
and his interests and his family.

And upon her who had felt only last week that
nothing had ever happened or would ever happen,
excitements crowded thick and fast. Here she was,
after choosing rings yesterday, now being borne down
the drive towards her future home.

She had been to Saunby before for cricket matches,
but then she had eyes only for the Major. Now she
must look at Saunby itself, because she was going to
share in it. She was so eagerly interested that she
almost called out to Bastow to go slowly so that she

could take everything in. But Bastow was going slowly of his own accord. He didn't want to throw up any more than he could help of this red sand which was making such a mess of his car.

They passed between the banks of rhododendron bushes, their leaves glittering like knives in the sun, and came out into the open park. On either hand the land rolled gently upwards to the sky-line. Trees, the glory of Saunby, stood singly and in groups in winter beauty. The dead bracken on the slopes was threaded with green paths like little streams.

Anthea was full of happy anticipation. She kept smiling at the thought of meeting her new family. Francis said they needed her so badly. How lovely to be needed ! Her life, she thought, with a backward glance at it, had been so lonely, empty and futile for so many years that it would be happiness to have people depending upon her and looking to her for help.

The girls were so pretty. They would perhaps confide in her about their clothes and their young men. She herself, she thought, wasn't so old that they couldn't all be friends together. She saw herself going about with the girls and hearing people say : " That's Mrs. Marwood with her step-daughters. They're *devoted* to her. She's wonderful to them."

And Miss Marwood. She might be a bad housekeeper. Francis said she was. But perhaps she couldn't help it. She painted pictures, and those artistic people, Anthea knew from books, were rather unpractical and needed to be understood and humoured. Anthea was quite prepared to understand and humour Victoria.

She felt qualms about the housekeeping. She had no experience of it ; her capable mother had seen to that. Mrs. Sumpton kept the housekeeping reins in her own hands. But Anthea felt she could learn. She would do her very best. She would draw upon the resources of strength she always felt were hidden in her somewhere. No one had needed this strength until now ; it had always seemed that no one wanted what she had been ready to lavish with both hands. But now everything was going to be different.

The car rose and dipped and rose and dipped again and the house came into view. Anthea, her heart beating fast, threw one end of her stiff fur over her shoulder to be ready to get out, and as the car swept round the circular space before the door, she saw that the Major stood on the steps.

' Waiting for me,' she thought with a rush of gratitude, love and excitement.

The Major was, however, talking to Thompson. He had not expected Anthea so soon. He continued to talk to Thompson as the car approached, and when it drew up and he had to go forward to open the door for his eager betrothed, he still talked to Thompson, who was by this time respectfully receding.

" Right you are," he called after Thompson, with his hand on the car door and Bastow now hovering beside him. " Do that, will you ? I'll be free again by and by. Well, Anthea, my dear," he said, turning his attention to her and letting her out at last. " How are you ? Cold day, isn't it ? Come in to the house. I think they're in the drawing-room."

Anthea steadily kept her smile as she went in with him. It was foolish to have expected him to say something in welcome, to have recognized this as an occasion. Men, she had always read, never showed their deepest feelings. She should have remembered that.

The size of the hall and the multiplicity of the objects with which it was crammed amazed her. But before she could receive more than a fleeting impression of jungle and jumble sale, she was hurried out at the other side and precipitated into the drawing-room by the Major.

"You've met Victoria somewhere, haven't you?" said the Major shortly. "This is Christine and this is Penelope."

He felt an obscure irritation in having to perform these introductions, so he showed what he felt. He and his sister Victoria were alike in the transparency of their behaviour.

Having performed the introductions he murmured something about being back soon and went out of the room.

Anthea was astonished. It was as if a child leaping from a wall into outstretched arms found the arms withdrawn at the last moment. Anthea fell hard among the stones of her new relatives. She had to pick herself up and give no sign that she was hurt.

They all sat down.

When Anthea was nervous, she talked too much. She was as full of gush as a schoolgirl and she chose schoolgirl topics now. She talked about the Berrys' party where she had met the girls. Wasn't it a long time ago and didn't time fly? Had they seen the Berrys lately? No, she hadn't, either. She always thought Muriel Berry was so sweet. Anthea clung to the Berrys as if they were a lifebelt she shared with the girls adrift in an unknown sea. At last she let the Berrys go and snatched at the lovely views from the windows.

"I must just look out," she said apologetically, and hurried to the windows one after the other. The eyes of her prospective relatives followed her and she felt them and wished she had never left her seat.

She came back to it and talked with determination about the weather. The Marwoods made suitable, if guarded, replies.

55

The little battery of small talk rattled hollowly in the great room where the random chairs and sofas seemed to have been arrested in the act of skating over the polished floor. It all looked so neglected, thought Anthea.

She wondered if her future sister-in-law had some nervous illness. She twitched so ; eyes, thumbs, feet all twitching. Anthea hardly dared to look at her in case she should seem to be noticing some affliction about which Victoria must surely be very self-conscious. Anthea wondered what she could do for Victoria ; what treatment she could recommend or give. Massage or something like that.

The girls were prettier than ever. They did not talk much, but probably they were shy. She had been shy herself at that age. In fact she was shy still. She wished this visit was over and threw back her fur because she felt hot, though the room was inadequately heated by the little fire in the big basket grate. All the fire was falling through it.

Was that a portrait of Francis's first wife over the mantelpiece ? She hardly dared to look at it, but she was conscious of youth, beauty, blue gauze and pearls.

' And I'm so sallow,' she thought. ' My bones are so big.'

Panic invaded her. She wished she could keep hidden in her spinster state.

' It will be a dreadful ordeal, marrying him,' she thought.

Tea was brought in and made a welcome interruption. The great silver tray unearthed for the occasion was pink with plate powder in the crevices and iridescent with stubborn tarnish.

" Will *you* pour out ? " asked Victoria with ungracious significance.

" Oh, no," protested Anthea. " Please."

The Major came in for tea. But he would not sit down. He stood, cup and saucer in hand, against the mantelpiece with the four females ranged on chairs below him. He gazed rather gloomily over their heads. From time to time he joined in the conversation sufficiently to emit a brief laugh and say in absent agreement : " By God, yes. Yes."

This was what his daughters called his Army manner ; all ha-ha and by God. It tickled them, but it both impressed and depressed Anthea. It made him seem such a *man*. So male and therefore so remote. She knew little of men, and it made her hopeless to think that he was a man living in a man's world where she could never follow him. And he looked so beautiful standing there, she thought desperately, that she felt more than ever plain and unworthy of him. She felt humble. She looked humble.

She brightened when the Major suggested that she should go over the house with Victoria and the girls. The Major brightened himself when he had thought of this. He clapped his hands to his pockets as if to make sure of important papers and said he would be in his room when Anthea had finished.

Victoria led the way upstairs, her stockings showing thick white cylinders at every step.

" Nuisance," she grumbled to herself. " Why can't he show her about himself ? "

The girls came some distance behind, observing Anthea's unfashionable felt hat, her unfashionable coat and skirt, her fur.

" Where do they get these furs ? " asked Christine when Victoria and Anthea had turned the corner of the first landing. " Do they come off stuffed badgers ? "

" They must," giggled Penelope. " Miss Harter's is just like that, and Miss Felicity Marshall's. It must prick to wear them. You see," she said darkly to Christine, " we're going to have to live with the most sheepy sort of sheep."

"I know," said Christine dismally.

They trailed hand in hand down the corridor. They wished Anthea would go. She seemed to have been with them a very long time. They could have been out in the park this afternoon, or getting on with their dresses.

What a house, thought Anthea in dismay, stepping in and out of rooms, surveying shrouded beds, rolled-up carpets, an incredible confusion of furniture of all periods, but mostly nondescript. The wallpaper in some of the rooms was terrible ; embossed in plush. And somebody seemed to have had a passion for fretwork or a Moorish type of decoration.

Victoria at last opened the door of a room that seemed to matter to her.

"I paint here," she announced.

"Oh, do you ? " cried Anthea, hurrying in.

"What lovely pictures ! " she exclaimed before she had time to see them. "What's this one ? " she asked, halting before Victoria's latest standing on an easel in the middle of the room.

"The subject is a storm at sea," said Victoria with dignity. "The small boat is bringing help. The picture is entitled : 'Lead, Kindly Light.' "

The girls pinched each other's hands.

"Oh, I see," cried Anthea. "I see why. It's rather a lovely idea, isn't it ? "

"*I* thought so," said Victoria.

At the door, she said frostily :

"I hope I may be allowed to keep my studio ? "

"Oh, of course." Anthea was shocked that anyone should think she would take anything from anybody, or make any difference at all in the house. She

58

wished she could reassure them on this point. But she didn't know how to broach the subject.

Bertha was on the stairs as they went down. She flattened herself against the wall to let them pass, and Anthea smiled at her in acknowledgment.

"Well," said Bertha, going back to report to the others ; Victoria need not have troubled to take precautions to prevent their knowing anything ; they always knew everything. "We don't need to bother about her. Proper helpless like the rest. She were frightened of me, I could see. She smiled like this at me as she went by."

The cook and parlour-maid went into fits of laughter. Bessy, melting butter before the fire, did not laugh. She disliked Bertha more and more.

"Come and sit down," invited Mrs. Nall, hitching her chair aside to make room for Bertha. "Doris is just mashing tea. Tell us a bit more."

"Oh, well, she's old fashioned," said Bertha with scorn. "Looks as if she belongs to the year one. One of them costumes with too much stuff in the skirt and a hat like a bird-cage. She looks as if her hair's coming down all the time. "

"But you don't think she's the sort to come poking her nose about after us ? " asked Mrs. Nall.

"Not she," said Bertha confidently. "She's too soft."

"I'm glad to hear it," said Mrs. Nall with relief. "Doris," she called out to the kitchen. "Are you bringing that there tea ? Or 'ave I to get up for it meself ? "

The Major was in a better mood when Anthea came into his room. He put aside *The Times* and rose with a smile.

"Well ? Seen everything ? "

"I don't know, but I've seen a great deal. What a huge place it is ! "

59

His smile brought her to his side. He put an arm round her waist, lightly, negligently, but happiness came flooding back to Anthea. She leaned against him.

Everything was all right really. The failure of the afternoon had been her fault. She expected so much of people that what she got fell short and chilled her. It was silly to keep on expecting. She must stop. See how precious this moment was, when she hadn't expected anything.

Francis's room was warm and intimate. The queer chaotic house with its problems was shut out ; at any rate for the present. And when she had to start on it, he would be there and all she did would be for him, so why worry ?

" When shall we be married ? " said the Major suddenly. " March ? "

She exclaimed, startled :

" So soon ? "

She was hardly used to the immense pleasure and novelty of being engaged yet.

" There's nothing to wait for," said the Major.

As far as he was concerned, the sooner the better. Then the honeymoon, he supposed there would have to be one, would get over and Anthea could get settled before the cricket season started.

" Let it be March," he said, with another smile and a light pressure of her waist.

Anthea's heart beat fast.

" Very well, darling," she said in a low voice. She lifted her mouth to his. He kissed her. Her eyes closed, but, his lips imprisoned longer than he wished, his eyes looked in some alarm sideways at the room. He hoped she wasn't going to turn out to be intense.

Anthea opened her dark eyes. Her mouth still close to his, she murmured :

" I do love you, darling."

" Your hat's crooked," remarked the Major.

" Oh," gasped Anthea, her hands flying to straighten it. How awful ! How awful to be brought down from heaven by a crooked hat ! Nothing could have brought her down quicker. She fell like a stone.

" I'm so sorry," she said, fumbling with her hat, her eyes on him in distress.

" It's all right, my dear," said the Major, as if she was making far too much fuss. What did it matter about her hat, anyway ?

" When shall I see you again ? " he asked.

Anthea felt better. He could restore her so quickly.

" Mother told me to ask you to dine on Wednesday," she said, smiling self-consciously because it was still so new to her to ask a man to dinner.

" I shall be delighted, thanks," said the Major. He had dined several times at Brockington by this time and had always had an excellent dinner.

" I wish you could bring your cook with you when you come," he said.

She laughed.

" Well, I can't. Mother would never part with her."

" Seen my sword ? " asked the Major, lifting it down.

She took it into her hands with reverence. When she had admired it as much as she could, he replaced it and showed her his medals and she admired those. She had been expressing her admiration all afternoon, saying how lovely, how beautiful, how interesting, how nice, and she said it all again now, wishing she could find something else to say, something not so ordinary.

She easily picked him out in the regimental groups ; there was no one else half so good looking.

" You were a very beautiful young man," she said.

If only she had known him then ; if only she had been his age then ; if only she had been as beautiful as his first wife ; her photograph was on his desk and she had a good look at it. If only she had *been* his first wife . . .

When she had seen everything he had to show her in the room, she came back to the fire and stood there with one foot on the fender.

" Well, my dear," said the Major, after a moment. " I don't want to hurry you, but don't you think perhaps you've kept Bastow waiting long enough ? "

She removed her foot from the fender at once.

" Oh, I have. I really must be going. Poor Bastow, I'd forgotten all about him. Where are my gloves ? Oh, thank you."

" Here's your fur," said the Major, wrapping it round her neck for her.

She blushed to feel his hands at her neck, but she did not offer to kiss him again. She remembered her hat. The Major, however, of his own accord put his lips to her cheek.

" Good-bye, my dear, and let's fix things up for March, shall we ? "

" March it shall be," said Anthea, showing her large, excellent teeth in a smile.

He put his arm through hers and led her out to the car.

CHAPTER V

ON a gusty day in March, towards half-past one, the people of Brockington village, wiping their mouths from their dinners, began to emerge in twos and threes from the cottages lining the single street to collect at the gates of the church.

Cars drove up and wedding guests alighted. Unheeding of the warnings of mortality in the shape of grave-stones in the yard, they went into the church. Everybody seemed to have a casual air. The sense of excitement, radiance, risk, hope, pathos of the marriage of youth was missing from this occasion.

"They ought to have been married where nobody could see," said Christine, going up the path with Penelope.

"I don't think we ought to have been expected to come, anyway," said Penelope. "Guy was very sensible to say he couldn't get off."

The girls felt that there was something almost indecent in this marriage ceremony and in their participation in it.

Miss Marwood came behind them, an odd figure for a wedding. She was muffled to the eyes in old clothes and topped by a red velvet hat like a tea-cosy.

The group of village people at the gates greeted Evelyn Craig, arriving with her solemn husband, and murmured sentimentally over their little daughter who, a posy in her hand, danced up the path to be a bridesmaid.

The group swayed with interest when the bridegroom appeared. He was no longer young, but he was tall, straight, handsome, indifferent, and entirely their idea of a gentleman.

At last the guests were all gone into the church and a hush of expectancy fell. A few rooks blew like burnt paper about the tops of the gaunt trees. A swift wraith of sharp white dust passed up the street.

At one end of the village the bridal car appeared and simultaneously at the other end, the figure of a girl on a bicycle.

The bicycle reached the gates first and the girl, a healthy, hearty creature with rough hair, alighted.

" What's up ? " she asked. " A wedding ? "

She sniffed cheerfully and reared her head above the crowd to see.

The bridal car drew up, the door was opened. The bride's father got out and stood aside. A mass of white satin train was transferred from the car to the arms of a waiting attendant, followed by a mass of white tulle, followed again by a sheaf of white lilies, and at last, the culmination of expectancy, came Anthea.

" My God ! " exclaimed the girl with the bicycle so clearly that everyone, including Anthea, heard. " She's left it a bit late, hasn't she ? Fancy putting a physog like that into white satin."

With a yelp of laughter and no further interest, she threw her leg over her bicycle and rode off.

Anthea continued to smile as she went on into the church. But above the music of the wedding march, above the Vicar's words, the bridegroom's vows, the voices of the boys singing ' O Perfect Love,' she heard the loud, free comment of the girl on the bicycle. The girl spoke the truth, the rest was farce.

She smiled throughout the wedding breakfast, sitting

64

beside her husband with her veil thrown back. Sitting among the white icing, the pink flowers, the pale gold champagne, she smiled, but her eyes were ashamed. She felt everyone must be thinking what the girl on the bicycle had thought.

She had longed for this day to come. She had felt that something would happen to snatch from her the ineffable happiness of being married to Francis. But nothing had happened. The day had come : but the girl had ruined it. She had destroyed Anthea's confidence, never, where Francis was concerned, very great. Love is happy only when it is confident. When it is humble, it is full of pain and misgiving ; there is hardly any happiness to be had out of it at all.

It was a relief to escape from the company, to discard the white satin for her customary sober brown. She felt more herself in that, with her godmother's gift of pearls, her new fur coat and an expensive but still unbecoming hat. Her hair was so heavy no hat became her.

She went down the familiar staircase and braved the guests again. She kissed her parents.

' No matter what the future is like,' she thought suddenly, as she kissed her mother's cheek, ' It can't be worse than the past. I'm *glad* to be leaving all this.'

She threw all her childhood and girlhood from her and fierce tears stung her eyes for a moment. The guests were wrong in attributing them to filial affection.

She passed through the farewells. There was no joking ; everyone felt it would have been out of place. She got into the Major's car and was wrapped in rugs by Thompson while the guests looked on from the gravel.

Christine and Penelope, in suits of spring green for once not made by themselves, had a young man between them. His name was Paul Kenworthy and he lived at Brockington Grange with his mother. He was an amiable, pink, plump young man with fair curling hair and rather embedded eyes. He reminded Christine of a well-mannered pig. One of the new pigs that are kept very clean. He seemed to get on best with Penelope, but he looked after them both very well, and the girls, contrary to their expectation, had enjoyed their father's wedding. The only blot upon it was the thought that they would later have to live with the bride.

Anthea's own relations were experiencing unaccustomed feelings. Her parents and her sister were vaguely remorseful, as if they had not valued enough what they would now have no longer. She was going, and they had thought she never would and had treated her accordingly.

Her brother-in-law was uncomfortable. He had behaved badly to her and it had turned out to be a mistake. Here she was, married into a good family. Seton Craig, who had made his own way in the world, had a respect for good families. This one had no money, it appeared, but was probably connected with people who might have been useful to him. He blamed himself deeply, and as he looked at Anthea words of apology were almost visible on his lips. He kept trying to direct the attention of his small daughter to the aunt who had loved her so much and was now about to depart. But Susan was entirely taken up with jumping on and off the steps and only raised the posy absently in the air when spoken to.

At last, set in motion it seemed by the waving of hands, the car left its moorings under the porch and moved off down the drive. The guests waved after it until it rounded the last laurel and was lost to sight. Then they turned and hurried out of the wind into the house.

" *So* nice for her," gushed a matron to the bride's mother.

" Thank God that's over," said the Major. " Now
you can drive like hell, Thompson. I've had more
than enough."

Through the driving mirror Anthea saw Thompson's
smile of amusement. She wished it hadn't been
necessary to bring Thompson on their honeymoon.
It made it so unprivate. But Francis had said that
with things as they were, there was nowhere fit to go
to abroad. No one had come forward with the offer
of a house ; the simplest thing therefore, he decided,
was to take Thompson and the car and travel about
the south coast of England.

So they set out on a journey none of them, in secret,
wished to take. Thompson didn't want to leave
Bertha ; just when things were getting interesting.
Anthea had always suffered from car-sickness on long
journeys and waited in apprehension for the first wave
of nausea. She dreaded having to be sick in the
presence of the Major and Thompson. The Major
himself was irritated at having to go about in bad
weather and spend money in doing things he didn't
like. He hated hotels and thought them extremely
and unnecessarily dear.

Still, he told himself, he was in for it now. He
must make the best of it. And for sixty miles or so,
he did make the best of it. He sat at the back of the
car, holding Anthea's hand dutifully under the rug for
sixty miles, and then he said he thought he would go
in front with Thompson because there was more room
for his legs.

" Do, dear," said Anthea, who wanted to get out
the little tubes of aromatic vapour with which she had
armed herself.

The Major got in beside Thompson and looked

relieved. He and Thompson fell into the desultory, easy talk of men who have known each other a long time and get on well together.

Anthea behind them crushed the fragile tube of silk and glass and inhaled the sharp scent with relief.

As the honeymoon continued, the gloom of the travellers increased. It rained almost incessantly. For miles there was no sound inside the car but the monotonous whirr of the windscreen wiper, a rustle from Anthea as she crushed another phial, or an audible yawn from the Major.

He was long past hiding his feelings now. They were too strong for that. He was so used to doing as he liked that he could not bear the constraint of considering anybody else.

The hotels were as dull and as dear as he had expected and Anthea's bridge, when they could make up a four, was very poor. She apologized so much for it that he was ashamed of her. One should never apologize, he felt.

He did not like to find himself at close quarters with a woman. It had been different with Viola. She was lovely, he was young, they were both in love. But now he had none of these alleviations for close proximity. He hated dressing and undressing in the same room as Anthea, but if you took a bathroom or a dressing-room, which you could rarely do in these places, the price was appalling.

The Major admitted to himself that the mild attraction he had felt for Anthea did not seem to be standing the strain of intimacy. She still remained suitable and he did not regret his marriage, but the sight of her lying with her heavy hair spread over the pillow and her dark eyes beseeching him made him very uncomfortable. It put him off, he complained to himself. He wished he could go to bed by himself. He wished he was at home in his own room. He found it irksome to pretend to ardours he did not feel. In fact, he couldn't pretend.

And in the mornings there was salt rime on the windows, or rain, and a dismal view of a leaden sea and a length of empty, wet promenade. The Major sunk deeper each day into gloom and dragged Anthea and Thompson after him.

One morning when they were setting out for Torquay Anthea said suddenly :

" Let's go home."

The change in the Major's face would have been laughable if Anthea had been able to laugh.

" Good God," he cried. " D'you mean it ? "

Then he leaned over from the front seat and laid a hand on her knee.

" Would you really like to go home, my dear ? " he inquired with what sounded like deep solicitude.

" Yes," said Anthea.

" You're sure ? I hear Torquay's a nice sort oι place. Are you sure you don't want to see it ? "

He went through the little farce while Thompson slowed down the car to a crawl. No good going any farther in the wrong direction, thought Thompson, though it wouldn't do to stop altogether until he got the word.

" You know we thought of going on for another ten days or so," the Major reminded his bride.

" But the weather's so awful," said Anthea.

He was delighted with her.

" It is. Perfectly dreadful. Well, Thompson, turn the car. She wants to go home and go home she shall."

Anthea, smiling, accepted the implication that she was a capricious female and he an indulgent lover gratifying her whim.

Thompson turned the car and sped for Saunby.

"You all right, dear?" inquired the Major from time to time. "Warm enough?"

Anthea received these crumbs of consideration with gratitude ; although, in her heart, she recognized them for what they were, mere mechanical expressions of his own satisfaction at getting what he wanted, which was in this case to end the honeymoon, to get home and be done with it.

CHAPTER VI

THE bedroom prepared for Anthea and the Major at Saunby was almost symbolic. An extra bed had merely been put up, and even this was odd. Two beds that did not match now stood where one had been before. One bed was low and the other so high that daylight showed beneath as well as above it. Anthea had the high bed and the Major the low.

Anthea, dressing in this room on her first morning at Saunby, looked about her regretfully. Brides, as a rule, had everything new. They chose what they wanted. She wished she could have chosen the furnishings and decoration of this one room for herself. She would have had pink. She loved pink, although she never dared to wear it. But to sleep among pink would have been lovely. Fleecy pink blankets, she thought, and a rosy bedside lamp, drawn silk curtains, warmth, intimacy. She supposed it was because Francis had been a soldier that his room had this bare, camping-out look.

Still, there were so many old things in this house she supposed they had to be made use of. She knew it had not occurred to Francis to buy anything, and why should it, she asked, obliging herself to be reasonable, when there was already far too much?

Her eyes fell on her girlish toilet silver, a twenty-first birthday present, set out on the dressing-table. The fact that her brushes and bottles used to be set out on her table at Brockington and were now set out in the room she shared with her husband was significant. She was a married woman. It gave her a feeling of solid satisfaction, it restored her, to remember that.

She hurried over her dressing. Her husband had disappeared some time ago and she wanted to join him as quickly as possible. The Priory felt like an unknown hotel to her and she shrank from going down to breakfast in it by herself.

The Major was in the middle of a boiled egg and *The Times* when she reached the dining-room. Victoria was also at the table.

" Good morning, Victoria," said Anthea brightly, still supported by the satisfaction she felt in being married. " You are an early bird."

" An early bird ? " repeated Victoria in what anybody else would have taken for an insulting tone. Victoria had a way of forcing their words back into people's mouths. They either swallowed or repeated them according to their nature.

" Well, I see you've either been out already or are just going out," explained Anthea, beginning to blush.

" But nothing of the sort," said Victoria, staring her out of countenance.

" Oh," mumbled Anthea, plunging to the sideboard to hide her confusion among the dish-covers. " I was only judging from your hat."

" What's this ? " inquired the Major, rising from submersion in *The Times*.

" My hat surprises her," said Victoria.

" Victoria always wears a hat," said the Major, sinking again.

" I beg your pardon," said Anthea to Victoria.

" Why ? " asked Victoria with an unkind smile.

Anthea didn't know, and bent lower over her bacon.

Victoria was one of the hardy people who like rudeness to be met by rudeness. Then rudeness becomes a sport in which the players belabour each other to their mutual satisfaction. But if rudeness is met by shrinking, the rude one becomes brutal, possibly from disappointment, and seizes every opportunity of hitting the shrinker over his wretched unprotected head. Unfortunately, Anthea, unused to Victoria, shrank.

She was relieved when Victoria, having finished a large breakfast, stumped out of the room.

The Major remained deep in *The Times*, feeling round it now and again with an absent hand for toast. Anthea did not disturb him. She sat with her back to the fire and her face to the four long windows. Through them the world showed very cold. It was March, but lines of old snow still lay under the fences ; and close at hand in the garden there was no sign of Spring.

As she drank her coffee, Anthea's eyes took in the room. She had not had much chance to observe it, unobserved, before. There was a path worn in the dark red carpet all round the table. The chairs were very fine, though their seats sagged and were covered by very worn leather. The portraits on the walls were so dark you could scarcely make them out, though the Marwood face persisted in most of them. From one black canvas there glimmered only the white hand of a woman, but it was the same hand, thought Anthea with a thrill of discovery, as Christine's. No one could help noticing Christine's long slender hands. Anthea looked at her own. They were strong, sallow. Someone had once said they looked as if they were firm on the reins ; and that was funny, she thought, because she didn't ride.

" Well," said the Major, folding up his paper. " I must go."

" Where to ? " asked Anthea.

" I must go round to see what's gone wrong while I've been away," said the Major.

"Oh," cried Anthea. "May I come?"

"It's a very cold day," said the Major.

"I can wrap up."

"It's a long way round," he said.

"I love walking," said Anthea.

She left her coffee and rushed upstairs to get ready. New energy and hope possessed her. The honeymoon, she admitted suddenly, as she rummaged in her luggage for her strongest shoes—no one thought of unpacking for you in this house, it seemed—the honeymoon had been a failure. Well, admit it. Let it go. Think no more about it, she counselled herself, remembering the maxims of the books on happiness. Life renews itself every day and if happiness cannot be found in one direction it can be found in another. Here was another direction. She would go over the estate with Francis and get to know his life so that she could share it. She must show that she was deeply interested in all that he did.

She looked doubtfully at the sky. Flocks of clouds, like sheep with heavy, dirty fleeces were jostling across it. She could hardly bring herself to risk one of her new hats. Hitherto she had always been careful of her hats, but now, she told herself, she must be careful of her appearance.

She put on a new brown felt hat, a brown scarf and a brown raincoat. Anthea, brown-haired and sallow, always dressed in brown and sallow clothes.

The Major was waiting in the hall. He lifted his eyes to watch her coming down the stairs and looked like a martyr in a church window. He had the expression of one who had waited so long that he has given up all hope.

"I haven't kept you waiting, have I?" asked Anthea in alarm. "Not more than five minutes, have I? I couldn't find my shoes . . ."

74

He opened the door on her explanations, and she hurried out.

" Please wait," he said. " I must get my dog."

He didn't want Anthea with him. He was used to walking alone. Almost every day, except in the cricket season, he walked alone over the estate.

" Oh, Rough," cried Anthea as her husband approached with the dog. " Rough, Rough, Rough."

She patted her knee and clicked her fingers, but Rough would not leave his master. Anthea ran off a little way in invitation and the Major averted his eyes. Why did she run ? She never should. She was too big to throw herself about like that.

Since Rough could not be persuaded to join her, Anthea, breathless and slightly dashed, returned to her husband's side. She took his arm and that was another mistake. He did not like his arm to be taken. He stalked stiffly with Anthea hanging on his arm, and his daughters saw him from the nursery windows.

They were so astonished that they watched the trio out of sight. Later in the morning they saw them again. Rain was blowing like smoke over the scene when the trio passed on the skyline, this time in single file ; the Major in front, Rough dodging at his heels, and Anthea behind, holding her hat on.

" The start and the finish," said Penelope. " Stories without words."

Christine, folding over her fingers the smooth white linen of a cuff she was making, paused to consider Anthea. She seemed to be making a lot of mistakes, thought Christine. Behaving like a sheep trying to get into the wrong field, trying with misplaced determination to get through the hedge in impossible places. A sheep was a poor thing. It had no independence, no dignity. Her father might be selfish ; in fact, he was. But there was a kind of dignity in his very selfish-

75

ness and detachment. Christine believed in dignity for the elderly and in detachment for everybody. Having decided this to her satisfaction, she began to embroider a rather crooked line of blue crosses on the white cuff.

Anthea came back from the morning's walk, tired in body and spirit. It had seemed a long way round, battling with the wind and her hat. At every farm someone had some request to make, and Francis got very cross. His irritation made her ashamed, and to mitigate it, she made herself far too amiable. She smiled a great deal and sympathized too much. She forgot that the tenants were much more used to his ways than she was. Her sugary behaviour annoyed him as much as his bad temper upset her, so the morning together was a failure, and Anthea went upstairs wearily to take off her ruined hat.

§

If only the weather were better, thought Anthea. If only the sun would shine in the afternoons so that she could be out-of-doors, instead of trying to find a place in this house where the places seemed to be already occupied by people who resented her intrusion. The occupants of Saunby looked at her when she came into a room as people in a railway carriage look at a traveller who gets in later on the journey. The Marwoods, she was beginning to find out, were the sort of people who like a carriage to themselves.

Victoria had glared when she came into the drawing-room after lunch. Anthea had tried Francis's room first, but he had said he was having Thompson in to discuss some cricket business.

" D'you mind ? " Francis had said, holding the door open.

"Oh, not at all, dear," apologized Anthea, withdrawing swiftly from the hearthrug.

She hung about the hall for a moment before going into the drawing-room.

Victoria, settling her hat against the back of a chair for her usual nap, raised her head.

"Are you coming in here?" she asked.

"Well, yes, I think so . . ." faltered Anthea.

"I was going to sleep," said Victoria.

"Do go to sleep," said Anthea. "I won't disturb you. I'll just sit by the fire. There isn't a fire anywhere else, except in Francis's room and he's busy with Thompson this afternoon."

"There's a fire in the nursery," said Victoria, twitching.

Anthea did not reply. She felt a slight, but sustaining dawn of obstinacy which enabled her to continue, though unwanted, to sit.

Victoria, however, could not sleep in company. For a while she tried. She frowned heavily and kept her eyes shut. But the lids twitched and exasperation got the better of her. She sat up with a loud sigh, and together, though very much apart, the sisters-in-law stared, each from her place, into the fire.

There was silence for some time. Then Anthea spoke.

"If you really aren't going to sleep," she said, "may I ask your advice?"

"Advice. What about?"

"About the house. I must begin to get ready for the cricketers, but I hardly know where to begin. I don't know who to ask to help me, among the servants, I mean."

"Oh, that's your affair now. You must please yourself what you do," said Victoria. "It's nothing to do with me, thank heaven, any more."

" I just wondered what you used to do," said Anthea.

" I didn't," said Victoria. " I told the servants to see to it. I don't believe in keeping dogs and barking myself. Besides, I am an artist. For years I've had to fritter my time away on things connected with the house and the children. But now you've been installed I don't intend to do it any more. I must be free for my art. Did I tell you I'd sold my picture ' Lead, Kindly Light ' ? "

Victoria, though annoyed by Anthea's presence, could not resist imparting this information.

" Oh, have you ? " cried Anthea, responding at once to what seemed an approach at last. " How splendid ! I'm so glad."

Victoria had sold the picture to Mrs. Pink, the recently widowed proprietress of the ' Three Pigeons ' in the village. Mrs. Pink had bought it to hang above her lonely bed. She told Victoria that every time she looked at it, it put her in mind of her late husband. The connection might to some have been obscure, but Victoria was gratified by the sentiment and by the pound note she received in payment.

After silence had reigned for some time again in the drawing-room, Victoria sighed.

" Well," she said. " I suppose I'd better go and do some work."

' If you insist on staying,' her tone implied, ' then I must go.'

But Anthea did not take the hint. She stayed ; and so Victoria went.

§

One evening later, she tried the girls.

The girls had determined their attitude before the return from the honeymoon, and when Anthea opened

78

the door and said : " May I come in ? " Penelope flashed a reminding look at Christine.

" If we're nice to her," Penelope had pointed out. " She'll like us and then she'll either want us downstairs or she'll want to be up here all the time, and we couldn't stand that."

" No," agreed Christine. " We couldn't. But we must be fairly decent all the same. We can be decent without going too far."

The atmosphere of the nursery was warm and intimate. It was the best place in the house, thought Anthea. The fire glowed deeply behind the old guard. Christine was reading, her feet on its brass rail. Penelope sat under the light, sewing.

Although Anthea, refusing Christine's chair, hurried to sit on the hearthrug so as not to disturb the comfortable atmosphere, intimacy evaporated. Penelope put down her sewing and Christine her feet.

" I wish you'd sit here," said Christine.

" Oh, I love sitting on the floor," said Anthea girlishly, clasping her large ankles with her large hands.

' She shouldn't,' thought Christine. ' It isn't the place for her.'

" How cosy you are up here," said Anthea.

The girls looked guarded.

" In the nursery at home . . ." began Anthea.

The girls listened, but they were not interested in the doings of Henry and Evelyn when they were small. If Anthea had been able to tell in an interesting way, they might have been interested. But Anthea had not the art of narrative. Her sentences began with a gush and fizzed out. She talked like damp squibs. She had no confidence in what she was saying. She started with enthusiasm and then doubted.

The girls were keeping back their yawns with

79

clenched teeth when Bertha brought in two glasses of hot milk and had to go back for a third.

At last Anthea prepared reluctantly to withdraw.

" It's so nice up here," she said, looking in at their bedroom.

" You're lucky to have each other," she said.

Christine and Penelope smiled. They knew.

" Why do you share a room when there are two others empty ? " asked Anthea.

" So we can talk in the night."

" Ah, yes," said Anthea. " That's what I've always longed for—someone to talk to in the night."

The girls accompanied their visitor to the nursery door.

" Good night," said Anthea.

She hesitated in the gloom at the top of the stairs ; then she plunged forward and kissed Christine. Having kissed Christine, she had to kiss Penelope.

" *Good* night," she said again.

" Good night," responded the girls, and withdrawing, they closed their door.

" Fancy kissing us," exclaimed Penelope. " I nearly collapsed ! "

Anthea, feeling her way down the stairs, wished she hadn't.

' They didn't expect me to kiss them,' she worried.

She went into her cold, cavernous room. Her husband had not come up yet and she hurried to undress before he should. His dislike of bedroom intimacy was beginning to affect her in the same way.

The rubber hot-water bottle was like a toad in her bed.

' It's no good,' she thought, removing it. ' I shall have to tackle the servants.'

She hadn't wanted to start off by complaining. But

things were too bad to be any longer ignored. She must complain.

"At least, I won't *complain*," she said to herself, drawing the blankets high to keep out the cold. "I'll try to get them on my side. I'll *appeal* to them."

She was relieved when she had thought of that. In spite of the many rebuffs she had met with at Saunby, she still had these recrudescences of hope and optimism. They kept her going. The mere thought, now, of winning the servants round to do their work properly gave her as much satisfaction as if she had already done it.

Such satisfaction, unwarranted though it might be, induced a certain amount of detachment in Anthea. It lifted her a little above her circumstances and let her look at them. It was only a mood and it would pass, but as she lay in her bed waiting for her husband to come up, she could think quite clearly about him and about herself.

"Why do I love him?" she asked herself. "He doesn't love me."

She could bear to acknowledge this to herself for the moment.

"I don't think he's worth loving," she said. "He's absolutely selfish."

Her husband came in as she reached this stage in her summing-up. She watched him move about the room ; remote, thinking about his own concerns.

'But I'm infatuated with him,' thought Anthea. 'I am. Everything he does and says, every movement he makes fascinates me still. My love for him has changed. I don't hope for much response or understanding now. I don't think I shall get anything from him at all. But I love him. I'm mad about him. I am. I can't help it.'

"Francis !" she said suddenly, holding out her arms.

CHAPTER VII

IN the room down the stone passage, behind the green baize door, the midday meal was being concluded by the customary cups of tea. On the table stood a great suet pudding from which a single portion had been scooped. The portion stood on a plate halfway down the table, rejected too. The staff had 'made out' with tinned peaches.

Mrs. Nall had a contempt for weights and measures. She cooked on the hit-or-miss principle.

"I don't need no scales," she said. "I can guess."

And guess she did, but mostly wrong. Her mistakes, however, did not upset her.

"Me oven must 'ave been a bit 'ot," she would say, blandly surveying a batch of burnt cakes. "Never mind. I'll make another lot to-morrow."

"I must've missed the baking-powder," she would say. "Somebody must've been talking to me. But never mind."

The servants didn't mind. They preferred food out of tins to hers, and she saw to it that there were always tins to fall back on.

"Funny about that pudding," she ruminated aloud now, putting a handful of sugar lumps into her cup. "The water must have gone off the boil. More tea, Bill?"

"I don't mind if I do," said Thompson, passing his cup. Waiting for it to come back, he whistled a tune, and Bertha, crossing the room, danced to it. Their eyes met over the heads of the others and they smiled.

Funny sort of smile, thought Bessy Palmer, turning her head away.

" Ooh, I have got a headache," complained Richards, the parlour-maid.

" 'Ave another cup of tea," counselled Mrs. Nall. " That'll chase it."

Richards, in the act of passing her cup, paused. Someone was coming into the room. It was the new mistress. They rose, astonished.

Anthea, who had a clumsy courage and made herself do what other people would not dream of doing, had come to beard the lions in their den.

" Do sit down," she besought them. " I don't want to disturb you.

" Er . . ." she began.

Servants, she thought wildly. If we could only do without them. They don't like us, but do we like them any better ? They live on us and we put up with anything rather than wait on ourselves.

" Er . . ."

When you met a servant singly and gave an order, it seemed all right, quite natural. But when you faced them in a body on their own ground, you felt their hostility.

Anthea saw the unconcerned gooseberry gaze of Mrs. Nall and Bertha's sly slanting eyes and hurriedly abandoned the opening she had planned.

" I just thought I would look in and see how you were getting on in here," she said. " I'm finding my way about, you see. Now are you all comfortable ? Have you everything you want ? Or is there anything you would like to say to me ? "

She waited. They stared.

' Plenty we'd like to say,' thought Bertha, smiling at her own thoughts. ' Such as " Get out." '

" No ? " said Anthea.

She must say *something* of what she had so carefully worked out.

" Well," she plunged, resting her fingers on the littered table. " You know I always think the kitchen department is the most important in the house. If things are wrong in the kitchen, they're wrong everywhere, aren't they ? And Cook carries a great responsibility, don't you, Cook ? Our digestion depends on Cook." To her horror, Anthea found herself looking down with a significance she did not intend on the suet pudding. " Our digestion," she floundered, " and therefore our health and therefore our happiness, all depend upon Cook."

She made it sound as if that must be so nice for Cook, but Mrs. Nall did not take it like that. She looked put out. Very put out indeed, and Anthea felt suddenly that she couldn't go on ; in case she put them all out. She had intended to go round the table, reminding each one of the dignity and importance of her task. She had begun with Cook because she was the head of the kitchen. But Cook's reaction made it impossible to go on to the others. Anthea abandoned her project. She changed the subject.

" I'm going to begin to clear out some of the things in the yellow room to-morrow morning," she said. " There are lots of small things I shall have to go through myself, but I should like someone to come and help me."

Her eyes roved the table. There was only one face she could appeal to.

" Will you come ? " she said to Bessy. " About half-past ten."

" Yes'm." Bessy blushed and rose.

"Do sit down," said Anthea.

"I'm going now," she said, flashing a bazaar-opening smile round on them all. "Do drink your tea. I hope it hasn't gone cold."

Her steps receded down the stone passage, and the green baize door clapped softly to and fro behind her.

"Well, my hat," said Bertha when it was safe to speak. "What d'you think of that? *Do* sit down. *Do* make yourselves comfortable. Don't mind me. I'm only a lady, I am. I've never done anything but ring bells in my life. Soft thing, blushing at her age."

"She was shy," said Bessy, with sudden courage. "I were sorry for her."

"Oh, you," said Bertha dismissingly. "You'd be sorry for ducks on a wet day."

"I don't know what call she had to talk at me like that," said the aggrieved Mrs. Nall. "What did she pick on me for? I never done her no harm. What was she getting at? I'm blowed if I know."

"She doesn't know herself," said Bertha. "So don't bother."

§

Anthea had been like a retriever : anxious, eager, but rather slow in finding out which track its master wanted it to follow. She had tried several, but now she had found the right one. Now she was following it for all she was worth. She was reorganizing the house and getting ready for the cricketers, and Francis showed his approval.

Before Bessy was due to arrive in the yellow room, Anthea went to inspect it.

She lifted the dust-sheets on the bed, so large that it looked as if it could hold a whole family. A head-piece was revealed, stuffed and buttoned into a reps

85

of bilious yellow patterned in brown and magenta.
This stuff had evidently given great pleasure to some
woman long ago, for it was lovingly repeated wherever
possible : at the windows in curtains and canopies
with ball-fringe, fastened to the mantelpiece in fes-
toons, covering the ottoman and armchairs and every
little box and buffet. Every piece of furniture had
been hunted down and subjected to the yellow and
magenta reps.

Anthea let the dust-sheet fall back over the bed and
walked to the hearth. Above the fire-place there was
an overmantel like a Swiss chalet. It was of fretwork
and glittered and glimmered with looking-glass and
mother-o'-pearl insertments. It was covered with
little shelves and on every shelf something stood, a
basket of china moss, a dancing girl with broken skirts,
a leaden dog with no tail, vases of all sizes and no
value.

Anthea stared helplessly and then went to look into
the cavernous wardrobe. One side was stuffed with
old fur capes and parcels wrapped in yellowed newspaper. The other side was ranged with shallow
shelves on which lay a miscellaneous litter. Anthea
stirred up tarnished silver brooches, brass bed-knobs,
spilled pearls, a supple gold necklace like a serpent,
ornamental hasps of knives, old purses and prayer
books, silver chatelaines, pearl penknives. How could
she sort out all those things ?

She shut up the wardrobe and wandered round the
room. She wondered if Victoria had painted the
pictures on the walls : a cow with a body like a block
on castors, a stiff waterfall falling all of a piece down
a glen, a dog with every hair of his coat painted
separately and a mean face such as no dog ever had.

There were steps in the corridor, and Anthea looked
towards the open door. The girls passed it, going out.

They looked in at Anthea standing helplessly in the room and smiled and said hello and went on.

Anthea turned back to the room. She tried a drawer in the chest. It stuck at first and then fell out, spilling its crammed contents at her feet ; more little boxes, lids, buttons, bottles, brooches. Anthea stared down at them, too exasperated to pick them up. This was only one room. All Saunby was like this, and she had to go through it all. The prospect appalled her. It was so dull. It was dreadful. And it would take such a long time.

Leaving the overturned drawer on the floor, she went down to her husband. She must have a few words of encouragement from him to enable her to begin.

He was writing cricket letters in his room and gazed at her, pen poised, with bland unseeing eyes. Then he realized what she was saying. She was saying that cupboards and drawers were stuffed with things and she didn't know what to do with them. He looked shocked that she should have applied to him about cupboards and drawers.

" Do as you like with them, my dear," he said, as if that ought to have occurred to her. " Do exactly as you like."

He moved restlessly in his chair. She felt him mentally pushing her out of the room. She sighed and left him, and he pinched his lower lip between his finger and thumb and found his place again.

When Anthea returned to the yellow room Bessy was there.

" I don't know what to do with it," said Anthea despairingly. " We ought to make a clean sweep of everything and start again."

" Let's 'm," said Bessy with energy. " Let's have everything out."

" How can we get the things out ? " asked Anthea, heavily.

" Well, I seen Thompson in the yard, doing nothing special," said Bessy with a faint blush. " He might give me a hand. Shall I run down and see, 'm ? "

" Do," said Anthea, and Bessy was off, her starched skirts rattling like sails in the wind.

In a moment she was back with Thompson. She was happy because she was eager to help the new mistress who seemed to be as lost in the house as she was herself, and because Thompson, who had stuck up for her against Bertha, was here to help too.

Anthea was also glad to have Thompson. There was something about Thompson that made people glad to have him.

" Now then," he said, standing vigorous and handsome in the room. " What's first ? "

" What about this ? " suggested Bessy, her hand on the chest of drawers, her eyes on him.

" Right you are," said Thompson.

Between them they trundled it into the passage, and came back for the wash-hand stand.

" I think I'll begin on the wardrobe," said Anthea, galvanized into energy by their presence.

They all began to enjoy themselves. Wholesale destruction can be invigorating. Anthea dealt ruthlessly with all that came to hand, Thompson prized off the overmantel and the bed-head, plucked down the curtains, hauled out the carpet, and Bessy darted here and there, chattering happily as she worked.

Thompson observed her. Her neck was like milk and her eyes were like blue flowers or stars or something. He liked her for championing the new mistress and he liked the way she rushed about, enjoying her work. As he helped her out with an armchair, he looked deeply at her, not with one of his smiling, male, appraising glances, but with a serious, different look, and Bessy, meeting it, became serious too.

Bertha came in at the door.

"I could give you some help now, madam," she said as if it went against the grain to offer.

"No, thank you, Bertha," said Anthea cheerfully. "There's really no need. We're getting on very nicely."

So Bertha, to Bessy's satisfaction, had to go away again.

CHAPTER VIII

A ND now the spring, which had been lurking so long under cover, only daring to show in the sheltered places, ran out into the open with all her banners. The trees were proud with gold and silver buds, and at the edge of the wood bounding one side of the cricket field the wild cherry suddenly sprayed into blossom.

Thompson, guiding the motor-mower over the cricket ground, felt the sun very warm. The motor-mower shook him so hard that it looked as if the machine worked the man instead of the man the machine. Thompson's bare arms jerked, his cheeks jerked, his high crest of dark hair jerked fantastically and his cheerful whistle was shaken out of him in spasms. As he mowed, he thought, looking round : 'Thank God I can play cricket.'

For Thompson, before he became a professional cricketer, had been a miner, and on such a day as this his heart swelled with gladness at the change in his lot. To be above ground instead of below—what luck it was ! The thought of it sometimes made Thompson almost light-headed. It made him, as he said, so damn cheerful that he did things he regretted in soberer moments ; such as running after the girls. Then he found himself embarrassed. As at present. Bertha was certainly making herself awkward, he reflected. Forcing him to go on longer than he wanted to. Thompson, thinking of Bertha, ceased to whistle.

He strode behind the mower, unaware that the Major followed him with a letter in his hand and Rough at his heels. Rough hated the motor-mower, but the Major liked to be attended. At last Thompson caught sight of the Major and switched off the machine. Rough brought up his ears and felt better.

" By God, Thompson, we're in luck's way," called the Major. " Bellinger writes to say he's got young Ashwell for August."

" Ah," said Thompson, with satisfaction, all thought of Bertha dispelled. " That's nice. That's very nice, sir. We ought to make the Ramblers look sick with Mr. Ashwell to bat for us."

" Yes, and we'll beat Barwell's side too, or I'll be damned," said the Major.

" Well, I hope so. It was a bad business last year," said Thompson.

The battle of the year was against Lord Barwell's team. The rivalry between this side and the Major's was fierce and not entirely without bad feeling.

" By God, though, Thompson," said the Major with a satisfaction so great as to be solemn. " I'm pleased about this."

He flicked the letter from Bellinger.

" So'm I, sir, I am that," said Thompson.

The Major offered Thompson a cigarette, and by common consent they moved towards the pavilion. The piece of luck in getting young Ashwell for August had to be talked over and savoured to the full.

Young Ashwell was an asset. He had played for his county second eleven in the minor counties competition. He was considered by some to be worth a trial in the county first team, and Bellinger wrote that he didn't get it only because the committee were disinclined to disturb the side, all-professional except for the captain, at a time when they hoped for the championship.

Young Ashwell, who had no business ties and could always get off, was in great demand. Clubs and scratch and country house teams vied with one another for his company, and the Major felt extremely fortunate to get him. He must be one of the best of good fellows too, he was sure, since he was a member of the Free Foresters, a club for which the Major had the liveliest admiration.

In the pavilion, the Major seated himself in an old deck-chair that threatened to give way at any minute. Thompson sat on his hands on the table. His hands swelled and went dark from his weight, but he continued to sit on them. When he had to take one out to attend to his cigarette, he replaced it immediately beneath his thigh.

" Yes, it's a bit of good luck us getting Mr. Ashwell," he resumed, as they both gazed across the field to the avenue of elms up which the spectators would later come to the matches. " I saw him play last year, you know, sir, when you was away. Against the Regimental Depot. He knocked up a jolly fine innings. Hundred and three."

" Let him repeat it here against Barwell," said the Major, " and I shan't complain."

" Let's see, his father's a knight or a bart, isn't he ? " mused Thompson.

" Something of the sort," said the Major with indifference. Whatever young Ashwell's father was it was something very recent.

" Sir James Ashwell, the cotton prince, he is. Or was," amended Thompson. " There aren't any cotton princes now, I don't suppose. They say he was clever enough to get out in time. Anyway, he's got pots of money. I saw him at the Depot match, you know. He takes an interest in his son's play. He's done everything to make him into a first-class cricketer, but it hasn't quite come off, somehow. It's all a lottery. If wanting'd do it, I'd be first-class myself and I daresay you would, too, sir."

"By God, I would," agreed the Major.

They smoked for a moment in silence.

"I ought to have some more marl this week," said Thompson.

"I'm sorry to hear it," said the Major placidly. "This ground costs money. But it's worth it, isn't it?"

"Prettiest ground in England, I'll be bound," said Thompson. "The old house behind and them elms beyond and this wood—it's beautiful. Wherever we go, we never see a place like this. There's no mistake about it, we live a nice life at Saunby, sir."

Bar Bertha, he thought.

The Major smiled. He made his own reservations about his debts and other difficulties, but on the whole, with cricket coming round again, he could agree with Thompson.

"I think things are going to be better for our fortnight this year," said the Major. "I mean in the house. Other years, you know, I've been ashamed. Oh, bloody ashamed, I've been," he said, looking gravely at Thompson.

Thompson had always a warm, tolerant affection for the Major, but when the Major talked to him like this, he positively loved him. Most people reacted to the Major's rare admissions in this way. Poor Anthea was undone by them. After each one, she was spurred to make still wilder efforts to get the house in order before the cricket entertainments should begin, and she alone knew what a Herculean task that was.

"Yes, I think everything's going to be much better this year," said the Major.

"I'm sure it is, sir," Thompson assured him.

" Yes," said the Major. " I hope we'll give them a really first-class time this year. Everything shipshape in the house, and cricket under the best possible conditions. Eh ? "

" That's right, sir," said Thompson.

" Hark," he cried, throwing up his hand. " That's the cuckoo."

They listened. It came again, the sweet round double call of spring.

" First time this year," said Thompson.

From his tight hip pocket he extracted a little diary and among the sports' dealers advertisements made a note : ' Heard the Cuckoo.'

" Well," said the Major, rising from the deck-chair. " I must be getting round. Remind me to ask my wife where she's going to put young Ashwell, will you ? We must look after him well, and then perhaps he'll come again. Rough ! "

The Major made for the gate into the wood, but Thompson did not return to the motor-mower. He had an idea, and he went into the house in search of its mistress.

Anthea was on the first floor with a notebook, a pencil and Bessy. These were nowadays her constant companions. This morning she was concerned with blankets. She wondered how best to inform the laundress that there would be at least fifty blankets to be washed this spring. Anthea still dreaded all dealings with the servants, except Bessy.

To-day she was particularly harassed. It was pay-day and she must give notice to Mrs. Nall. She had shirked it last pay-day, but it could be shirked no longer. The food was appalling and Mrs. Nall must go.

All the time she was inspecting blankets with Bessy, she was rehearsing what she was going to say to Mrs. Nall. How her mother would despise her, she thought.

Once, through the staircase window, she saw Victoria stumping away into the distance with her stool and her paints. Another time, she saw the girls running along the side of the wood, running and leaping and throwing up their arms in an intoxication of youth and joy. Anthea stood, notebook in hand and looked at them.

' I never dared to do that,' she thought.

They were part of the springtime ; as much a part as the leaf-buds in the wood behind them and the new grass under their dancing feet. Young and lovely as they were, all the beautiful things in life were before them and possible to them.

' And I can only be useful,' thought Anthea.

She turned away and went into another bedroom with Bessy. When they came out again, they found Thompson coming down the corridor.

" Something's just struck me, madam," he said in a conspiratorial tone when he reached them.

" Oh ? " said Anthea. " What is it ? "

" Well," said Thompson. " It's this. I've just been having a few words with the Major this morning, and I can tell he wants to treat young Mr. Ashwell rather special. You know, give him the best room in the house and all that, so I thought if you was to ask him to get that room beautified, which you want, don't you ?—he'd probably say yes. I mean, he'd look at it as part of the cricket expenses."

" Oh, Thompson," cried Anthea. " How nice of you to come and tell me. I'll suggest it at lunch."

She badly wanted the yellow room repainted. Dismantled, it presented almost as sorry a sight as before. The furniture had been removed, but its shapes remained, printed on the walls by the suns of long-forgotten summers.

" Well, you'll never do anything with it without it's beautified," said Thompson, propping himself against the wall and preparing to launch himself on one of those conversations which, though they consist mainly of repetition and are mostly about nothing, nevertheless give great satisfaction to those taking part in them. "No, you'll never do anything with it without it's beautified. It's not to be expected."

"Oh, I know," agreed Anthea. "I know, Thompson. But Major Marwood was so firm about not spending anything on the house. This cricket business is so costly."

"That's right," said Thompson with sympathy, and Bessy made a sort of indrawn gasp and shook her head to show that she had sympathy, too.

"Still, it's his hobby," resumed Thompson.

"Oh, I know," said Anthea again, shocked that Thompson should suggest that she would ever grudge anything that gave the Major pleasure. "All I meant was that it's cricket first and the house and everything else—well—where?" she threw out her hands in one of her awkward gestures.

"That's right," agreed Thompson.

Leaning against the wall with his head back, he looked kindly down from his height at Anthea and Bessy. He had fine cleanly-cut nostrils and their slight distention and the set of his lips gave a look of keen pleasure to his face.

He noticed the way Bessy's hair curled up over her cap at the back. Real gold, her hair was. And he was willing to bet that if you pulled one of those curls out straight and let it go, it would fly back like a coiled spring into a curl again.

Bessy smiled all the time Thompson and her mistress talked. She was glad Thompson was conspiring to help her mistress. It showed he had a kind heart as well as a handsome face, and Bessy was glad of that.

This pleasurable meeting might have continued for

96

some time had not the three of them become conscious that they were under observation. They turned their heads and there far down the passage, half in and half out of a bedroom door, was Bertha. She merely stood there, duster in hand, but the group broke up as if dissolved by an invisible ray from her black eyes.

"Well," said Thompson. "I'd better be getting back to the ground, if you'll excuse me, madam."

"Yes," said Anthea. "And we must get back to the blankets, Bessy."

'I don't like that girl Bertha,' she thought. 'I should like to give her notice. But one at a time. I haven't dealt with Mrs. Nall yet.'

She suddenly decided to deal with Mrs. Nall at once. She thrust her notebook and pencil into Bessy's hand.

"You go on without me for a moment, Bessy," she said. "I'm just going downstairs."

She disappeared round the corner of the landing, and Bertha sauntered down the passage to where Bessy stood like a rabbit watching the approach of a weasel.

"Here, you," said Bertha, flicking her duster as she walked. "You'd better stop making sheeps' eyes at Bill Thompson."

Bessy flushed.

"I don't know what you mean, Bertha, I'm not in the habit of making eyes at anybody," she said primly.

"Go on, you can't kid me," said Bertha. "You keep off him, that's all."

"You have got a cheek," said Bessy, suddenly angry. "D'you own him or what?"

"You'd better ask him," said Bertha, sauntering off.

Bessy stood against the wall, watching her go. Her anger ebbed. She felt very unhappy. What did Bertha mean? Was there really anything between her and Bill Thompson? Bertha knew she was safe, telling her to ask him? How could she do such a thing ? But she wished she knew. She did wish she knew.

Anthea, meanwhile, had reached the kitchen. Mrs. Nall was, in her own words, throwing a pudding together. It was literally true. She threw flour, sugar, currants, in handfuls into the mixing bowl, threw in a palmful of baking-powder, cracked in a couple of eggs and dabbled in the mess with her short sausage fingers. Anthea entered in the middle of this operation and from sheer nervousness came straight to her point.

" Mrs. Nall, I'm sorry, but I am obliged to give you your notice to-day. Your cooking is really very unsatisfactory, you know."

Mrs. Nall's gooseberry eyes almost started from her head. She was completely taken aback.

" My notice ! " she repeated. " You're giving me my notice ? Why, I've been here ten year and I've always given satisfaction."

" No, Mrs. Nall," said Anthea shaking her head.

" But I *have*," cried Mrs. Nall, in whom shock was giving place to anger and resentment. " Of course I've given satisfaction, else why haven't I had me notice before ? Ten year I've been here and I've always done me best and this is what I get for it."

" I'm sorry, Mrs. Nall, but please take a month's notice from to-day," said Anthea, escaping swiftly from the kitchen.

Mrs. Nall collapsed into a chair, her floury hands loose on her knee.

" Is anybody there ? " she called out. " Somebody come here, quick ! "

Richards came in from her pantry.

" What's the matter, Mrs. Nall, are you ill ? "

" Yes, I am. I've got me notice," said Mrs. Nall. " She's just given me me notice."

"What?" cried Richards. "I didn't think she'd the pluck."

"Pluck!" cried Mrs. Nall indignantly, wiping her red face with a whitened hand. "It's a coward's trick giving me notice after all I've done for 'em. Ten year have I slaved meself to the bone in this place. There isn't another soul alive would have put up with that range," she said, pointing to it. "Let 'em try to get anybody else to live with it, that's all. They'll be on their bended knees to get me back before they've finished, but no fear. She ought to think shame of herself turning me out at my age. Where am I going to go now? She ought to think shame of 'erself, that's what she ought. Do you know, Ellen Richards," Mrs. Nall leaned with deep indignation over the pudding. "Do you know, I've got very-close veins on my legs as big as apples with standing about in this 'ere place! Simply with standing about at this 'ere table and that there range, and they'll turn me out. But that's them all over. You can wear yourself to the bone for these folks with money and they'll throw you out like an old boot when they've done with you."

"Don't fret yourself," consoled Richards. "I expect we'll all go by and by. Not that I'm expecting my notice," she said. "But anyone can see it's not going to be what it was now she's started interfering. I think I shall begin looking out for something myself."

"You're young," said Mrs. Nall. "It's all right for you."

CHAPTER IX

HER first real test as a housekeeper would come, Anthea felt, on the second Saturday in May. This was the day of the County Club and Ground Match. Like a nervous student before an examination, she conned the notes she had made long before from the Major's instructions :

"Starts 11.30. Cold lunch for both teams in billiard room. Umpires and professionals at small table. Drinks : draught beer and shandy."

Anthea put many anxious questions to Thompson. She found that Francis grew impatient if she did not grasp his meanings at once.

" What is shandy ? " she had asked him.

" Shandy ? " shouted the Major. " D'you mean to say you don't know what shandy is ? What do you know, for God's sake ? "

" Well, I *don't* know what shandy is," murmured Anthea. What was shandy that you had to shout about it and bring God in ?

With another shout of exasperation, he told her what shandy was and she made a note of it and went away to ask about the rest from Thompson.

She did not know what she would have done without Thompson and Bessy. Things were very awkward in the kitchen. Mrs. Nall, under notice, was taking pride in being what she called nasty.

" I can be nasty meself when I like," she informed the staff, and it proved to be true.

Her nastiness affected the food, and Anthea found herself on the horns of a dilemma about the County Club and Ground luncheon. If Mrs. Nall prepared the food, Anthea would save money, but the lunch would be bad and Francis would be angry. If the food was sent ready-cooked from caterers in the town, it would cost a good deal and Francis would be angry. But he wouldn't be angry until the bills came in. At the time of the luncheon he would be pleased. It seemed to Anthea, worrying it all out, that it would be better to order lunch from town and postpone Francis's anger. In that way, he would at least be pleased before he was angry. The other way, with Mrs. Nall's cooking, he would be solely and unmitigatedly angry.

Anthea found her new life very complicated. She had always believed in doing things in a straightforward way, or so she thought. But now she was continually making compromises. For instance, she had such difficulty in finding a successor to Mrs. Nall —servants didn't like the country it appeared—that she decided not to give notice to Bertha until the cricket season was over in case she could not replace her. She disliked Bertha, and to put up with someone you disliked to suit your own convenience seemed to her unadmirable, but it also seemed unavoidable, so she did it.

On the morning of the match, Anthea went early to the billiard-room, where the cricket luncheons were always held. While the painters were at work on the yellow room the Major had decided that they must do the billiard-room as well, and now with its clean stone floor and spotless white walls rising to the old wooden roof it looked as it might have looked centuries ago when it was, perhaps, the refectory for the monks, since some parts of the ancient priory had certainly been incorporated in the house. It was a good room, thought Anthea, now that the plush wallseats, the marking boards, broken table, and pieces of old felt carpeting had been moved up to the attics.

At the thought of all that had been moved up to the attics she sighed. The disposal of rubbish in this house was like a nightmare sum that would never come out. You could only move the quantities from one place to another. You couldn't get rid of them. And you knew that before long you would have to begin on the problem all over again and again be as far from a solution as ever.

This sort of thing worried her. Everything worried her increasingly. She couldn't sleep for worrying in case she should forget something ; something terribly important, something that would put her to shame before the cricketers and annoy Francis.

She kept her notebook under her pillow so that she could look into it when she thought of something in the night. If the notebook wasn't at hand, she would worry until the morning. This notebook was a revelation, if anybody had looked at it, of Anthea's anxiety, inexperience and lack of self-confidence.

On this May morning, she felt quite sick with nervousness. It seemed impossible that luncheon for twenty-odd men should ever be achieved ; impossible that the tables should ever get put up, set out and the food arrive upon them. She felt she must rush about and do everything herself, but she forced herself to watch, to superintend without interfering.

Whatever else went wrong, she thought, at least the flowers were lovely. She had done them herself. She had been standing for nearly two hours this morning doing the flowers for the house as well as for this room. Perhaps that was why she was so tired. Still, the flowers were worth it. She hoped Francis would notice them. Suddenly, as she admired them, they swam together in a mist of nausea.

Anthea leaned against the wall.

' I do feel queer,' she thought.

The nausea passed, but she was afraid it might return. She decided to go in search of her smelling-tubes.

The girls, coming down to go out, passed her on the stairs.

" What a sight she looks," said Penelope, when they were out of hearing.

" She looks kind of haggard," said Christine. " She's worried about the cricket lunch, I suppose."

She thought about Anthea for quite a few minutes. Anthea seemed to be changing somehow. She didn't seem to be trying to get in any more. She seemed to have given it up and to be looking at them all from rather a distance. With the perversity of human nature, Christine felt slightly sorry not to have shown more friendliness to Anthea while Anthea wanted her to be friendly. But this feeling was transitory. Once out-of-doors, Christine forgot Anthea.

The morning was lovely. Under the high blue sky, house and ruins lay together in unity. To-day they were merged, grey, peaceable, the old with the comparatively new, the religious with the secular.

Beyond the yew hedge the cricket field was like a lawn, with a white figure, Thompson, going about giving the pitch a last inspection.

Beyond the field the elms were in young leaf and the cuckoo called so incessantly that Thompson damned the bird.

Before the house another white figure paced the sandy sweep : the Major waiting for his team. By half-past ten they began to arrive in cars, and Anthea.

down from her room again, watched her husband greet his friends.

How different he was with men! How easy, friendly, charming he could be!

' He'll never be like that with me,' she thought.

Where had she gone wrong, she wondered. She couldn't think of any mistake. Except the mistake of loving him too much. Perhaps that had been it. But what a storm of love he had roused in her. Looking back she wondered how she had come through it. She still loved him, she said to herself, but not like that. She had too much to do. Also she was too tired.

She looked at the long, lithe figure of her husband. Not a man there to equal him in looks, except, in a different way, Thompson. She looked at him as if he were going away—not merely to the cricket ground for a match—but away from her. And she let him go. She gave him up to himself, since that was what he wanted.

She stood on at the window after he had gone. She felt so strange. The empty sunlit scene trembled, the lawns, the trees, the old wall trembled like reflections in water. She clutched the window-jamb, trying to keep a hold on reality.

But as a large red bus full of men swung into the dissolving scene, Anthea fainted.

§

Skirting the house to avoid the arriving team, the girls found a young bird on the path. They had almost stepped on it and stood poised in horror at what they might have done. Then Christine stooped swiftly and picked it up.

" He's not dead," she said. " He's very much alive."

" Where did he fall from ? " said Penelope.

They looked about. There was only the blank blue sky above ; not a tree, not an eave.

" It's a mystery how birds and eggs come to be in places like this," said Christine. " But do look at him ! "

The bird was bald, blind, with a mouth like a nigger minstrel and a paunch like a balloon. He had a slight grey down all over him like a mould.

" Goodness, he looks like something ante-flood ? " said Penelope. " Isn't he hideous, the darling ? "

" I adore him," said Christine, unconscious of extravagance. " And I think we could rear him. He's so strong."

" There's Thompson. Let's ask him." Penelope darted after Thompson, who knew all about birds.

Christine followed more carefully, bird in hand.

Thompson shot a swift glance at it. He was in a hurry to return to the field.

" You might," he said. " It's a starling. Chop worms up and feed it."

He was gone.

The girls hurried up to the nursery. Penelope took the squawking bird into her hands, while Christine rummaged for a cardboard box and a piece of flannel. They were already full of love for their foundling and when they put him into the box and leaned above him, their faces showed the smiling tenderness of young mothers.

The object of their devotion worked about on his paunch and squawked without cease.

" He's hungry. We must go down and get worms."

Carefully arranging the lid half off and half on the box so as to provide shade and still allow for air, the girls flew off down the stairs, loving the bird for depending so entirely upon them and making them so busy.

" I say," said Penelope, flying after her sister. " Perhaps we can bring him up to be like that pheasant chick Johnny Spencer had. D'you remember how it used to stand on the rim of his plate while he was having his dinner ? Think if we could get ours to do that ! "

" M'mm," said Christine fervently.

They ran to the sheds in the kitchen garden and got a fork each. They turned over the soil in the flower gardens with reckless vigour. They must have young and tender worms.

" Good red-blooded ones," said Penelope. " Not these great pale flabby things with joins in them." She threw one back to earth with disgust.

Once they had felt a solicitude for worms, but not now. Not when their foundling needed them for food.

" Funny how you can't go on being sorry for *everything*," observed Christine. " As you go on, you get quite willing to sacrifice things to something you like better."

When they had worms to their choice, they threw down the forks for someone else to find and replace, and went back to the house.

As they climbed the stairs, Bessy came out of Anthea's room, closing the door carefully behind her.

" The doctor's there now," she said reassuringly.

" Doctor ! " the girls exclaimed. " Who's ill ? "

" Why, the mistress fainted," said Bessy. " She came all over useless in the billiard-room, didn't you know ? We couldn't get her round for ever such a long time. Miss Marwood sent for the doctor in the end and he's just come. She's been doing too much and it's that hot to-day."

The girls stood with worms in their palms, looking at Bessy. They weren't used to illness.

" D'you think we need to go in and see how she is ? "

asked Christine, and was secretly relieved when Bessy said not yet, because the doctor was there.

" I suppose Aunt Victoria's looking after her," said Christine, providing another reason for not concerning themselves.

" Well, she knows about it," was all Bessy would admit.

Victoria's efforts in first aid had consisted in pouring brandy over Anthea's chin and of urging her repeatedly to come.

" Come, Anthea ! Anthea ! Come. Come now," she kept saying sternly.

Since Anthea remained unconscious, she gave up and telephoned for the doctor.

" You don't think we can do anything then, Bessy ? " suggested Christine.

" No, miss. I'm just going down to get a cup of tea ready for her for when the doctor goes. I'll look after her. She's used to me," said Bessy with pride.

The girls lingered no longer. George—they had decided to call their fledgling George, which was the name for almost everything at this time—George was hungry. It was a matter of more concern to them that George should be hungry than that Anthea should have fainted. Unconscious of any lack of proportion, they hurried upwards.

§

Anthea lay on her high bed, her face turned to the wide-open windows. The soft spring air came in and she smiled to feel it on her brow and eyelids.

Dr. Carter had gone. She felt quite well now. She felt more than that ; she felt supremely happy, relaxed and unworried.

The luncheon for the cricketers was going on downstairs, the lunch for which she had made such anxious preparations and she no longer cared what happened to it. Probably everything had gone wrong with no one to superintend, but it didn't matter to her. All the fuss and worry she had felt that morning had drifted off. Cricket affairs now seemed to her quite unimportant.

The door opened and she turned her head with delicious langour towards it. The Major came into the room, with his cricket cap on his head.

'A silly little cap,' thought Anthea in her detachment. She had hitherto felt much respect for it, a symbol of masculinity.

The Major squeaked over the parquet in his rubber shoes. He was not disturbed about Anthea. Women had all sorts of ailments which never seemed to make any difference to them in the long run. It was a pity she'd chosen to-day to faint, but on the whole the lunch had been much better than usual and the match was a good one. The other side was in and doing well enough to make a close finish, but not too well to make a win for the Priory team impossible.

He reached Anthea's bed and stood beside it. He looked, however, not at her, but at the view of the field through the windows directly beyond her.

"Well," he said affably. "Better? Been doing too much, I suppose. You should get more out of the servants, my dear. What do we pay 'em for? Lunch went off quite well. Sorry I didn't see Carter before he went, but of course I didn't know he was here. What did he say was wrong with you?"

Anthea flushed and lay mute. She suddenly didn't want to tell him.

"Eh?" said the Major, continuing to look out at the field. He hoped Thompson would get Waters's wicket before long. "What did Carter say?" he repeated. "Come on, if you want to tell me. The men are going out again I see."

He rubbed his hand comfortingly over his bare chest inside his open shirt and thought about the possibility of Thompson's getting Waters out for quite a moment before he realized that she was not telling him what Carter had said.

"I say," he said, looking down at her now. "You're not really ill, are you? You're not starting 'flu or anything like that, are you?"

"No," said Anthea. "I'm going to have a baby."

His face hung above her, blank, incredulous. She looked up at him, watching how he took it.

"Going to have a baby?" he repeated after a long pause.

His jaw dropped. A slow flush rose over his cheeks and a vein stood out on his forehead. He seemed to sag above her. Then he straightened up from the bed.

"You're going to have a baby?" he said, staring down at her.

"Yes," said Anthea.

"It's—it's incredible," he said.

Anthea said nothing. She who had been propitiatory was not propitiatory now. He didn't want the baby. She did, she thought, fiercely protective.

"Have you known long?" he asked suspiciously.

"I knew nothing until to-day," said Anthea. "I've been overdoing things so much the symptoms were confusing, so Doctor Carter says."

"Good God, it's awful," said the Major, turning away. "I've got three children already."

"But I have none," said Anthea.

He turned round and stared at her, but he hadn't heard.

"Think of the expense," he said. "If it's a boy,

think how much it will cost. I simply can't afford any more education."

Anthea was stung.

" Don't worry too much," she said. " We might both die and cost you nothing."

He stared at her in astonishment. Imagine Anthea saying a thing like that.

" That's too bad," he protested.

He seemed distressed. Anthea put out a hand in contrition, and he took it. He held her hand, her large, well-shaped, sallow hand, looking down at it in deep dejection. For a moment they stood in an entirely new relationship to each other. It was a significant moment. Anthea waited, her eyes on his face. If he responded now, her devotion was his for ever. She longed for him to rise to this occasion, to allow her to love him more than ever as the father of her child.

But the Major dropped her hand and strode gloomily to the windows.

" This has damn-well ruined the day for me," he said. " We've only to lose the match now to put the lid on it."

Anthea flushed deeply with resentment. Fancy comparing the start of a new life with a cricket match ! The anti-climax was ludicrous. He had not responded. On the contrary he showed up very badly ; very, very badly, she thought. He was behaving in a way she would find it hard to forgive. Not that it would matter to him. And perhaps, she thought with sudden elation, it wouldn't matter to her either. His behaviour was after all unimportant. The baby would arrive just the same.

This thought made her so happy and excited that she smiled.

" Well, I must go," said the Major turning from the

window and speaking in a cold voice implying blame. " I can see them on the field."

" I think they'll manage at tea," said Anthea briskly. " I'm not coming down again to-day, of course."

He stared at her. The tone of her voice surprised him. He was, for some obscure reason, affronted by it.

" I should go," Anthea urged him. " You're probably keeping them waiting."

He strode to the door, but there he paused and stood for a moment with his back towards her. Then he turned round, came to kiss her on the brow. He supposed that was expected of him. After that, he went from the room.

Anthea sighed with relief and sank more comfortably into her pillows. She closed her eyes again. A baby. At last someone to belong to her, someone to whom she could belong. A baby.

The Major hurried to the ground. All his pleasure was gone. He couldn't give his mind to the match. As he took his place at mid-off, he thought what a shame it all was. He'd meant this season to be such a good one. He'd brought Anthea in to lessen his troubles, but instead she was adding to them immeasurably. He bit his nails and a ball got past him. Curtis, who knew the Major couldn't run, sped after it, and the Major watched, cursing himself.

When they changed over, he walked round to point. A baby !

" I can't *afford* it," he said, talking to himself.

Another ball shot past him and he shouted at it. Then he pulled himself together.

" This won't do," he admonished himself sternly.

' By God, it's ruining my game,' he thought, blaming Anthea, blaming everything.

§

Once again Victoria was the bearer of what she considered bad news to the nursery. She was quite pleased to do it. She had prophesied trouble and trouble had come. That is always gratifying to the prophet if to no one else.

But Victoria did not derive the satisfaction she had expected from her communication to the girls. After an exclamation or two, they said nothing more. They would not show their feelings to her. They could hardly show them to each other. They felt a peculiar distaste, a shame, even. Their father had always been aloof, remote, unserious in his paternal relationship to them, but, unconsciously, they had liked him like that. They were used to thinking of him like that, and they suffered obscurely from having to see him in this new light as the husband of Anthea and the father of someone not themselves.

They did not speak of this ; but they discussed other aspects of the subject.

" We shall have to give up the nursery when it comes," said Christine, " and go down and live with them."

" Oh, dear," groaned Penelope. " I hadn't thought of that. Oh, what does she want to go having a baby for ? At her age. Doesn't she know its dangerous ? Christine, I hope I never have a baby," she burst out suddenly. " I hope I never do. I think it's awful. Every time I see a woman who's going to have a baby, I think have I got to go through that ? Every time I read about it in novels I think I never, never could."

" M'mm," agreed Christine. " It's an awful prospect. But if I got married I should want some children. Married people without children look so aimless, wandering about. Children do make you important where you otherwise wouldn't be. Unless you *are* important in yourself; then, perhaps, you don't need children. I don't know what I'm going to be yet; whether I'm going to be important in myself or just married. Of course," she chattered on. " The worst of being married and having children is always having to be bothering with *other people*. I like to be free. Not to be tied up to man, woman or child. Except you," she conceded.

" And George," Penelope reminded her.

" Yes, George," agreed Christine. " We've had him nearly a fortnight now, you know. We'll rear him all right."

" We'd better go to sleep," said Penelope. " Half-past five will be here too soon."

At half-past five every morning they had to get up and go down into the garden to dig up fresh worms for George. They were slaves to George. They tried to do for him everything his natural parents would have done. In consequence they were very tied. He had to be fed every hour, and they would not go anywhere that took them away longer than that hour. It was quite a relief, they agreed, when he was settled for the night. When they took a last look at him before going to bed themselves, he had always got himself into a far corner of the box, where, with his back turned and his beak propped vertically upwards, he slept sitting. His back view was touching.

" So *young*," said Christine.

One morning it seemed to them that he squawked less urgently.

" Perhaps he's growing," suggested Christine.

His eyes were open now, and he had a few spines of feathers on him. He was less ugly too. He knew their voices and greeted them with distended mouth, but some of his squawks became soundless and the girls were worried.

They consulted Thompson, who came to look, shook his head and suggested a drop of olive oil now and again. The girls went down to the kitchen to get some from Mrs. Nall's successor, Mrs. Green.

" Are all cooks widows ? " Christine asked Penelope. " It seems a bit omnious to me."

She meant " ominous, " but the joke served. It was their last joke for days. George worsened. He became quite silent. They could not prevent themselves taking the lid off the box every few minutes to pore over him and beseech him in tender voices to be better. He could not swallow the smallest piece of worm now. When they put one into his mouth, they had to take it out again.

One morning when it was just beginning to be light, Penelope woke to find Christine standing beside her bed with a piteous face and George in her hand.

" He's dying," she said. " He's so cold."

" Oh, bring him into bed," said Penelope, making room swiftly. " Let's warm him in our hands."

They crouched together under the covers, Christine held the bird and Penelope folded her hands round Christine's.

" It's no good," said Christine, suddenly clambering backwards out of the bed. " We can't let him suffer like this. I'm going down to ask Thompson to put him out of it. I can't."

" Oh, Christine . . ." faltered Penelope.

" It'll have to be done. We're being cruel to keep him alive. Put my dressing-gown on for me. Pass my slippers, will you ? Don't you come."

With George in her careful hand, Christine went down through the house. The door leading to the stable-yard where Thompson slept was unbolted, but she did not notice she had no bolts to draw. She went out into the dawn where the birds were singing. As she reached the foot of the wooden stair to Thompson's room, George gave a sudden convulsion, and Christine halted. He died, and she stood there, weeping over him.

The door at the top of the stair opened and Bertha came out. At the sight of Christine, she gave a loud exclamation and withdrew her foot from the step. Thompson appeared behind her, in pyjamas.

Christine looked up at them, her eyes full of tears.

" I was coming to ask you to kill him, Thompson, but he's just died," she said, turning away and going out of the stable-yard with the dead bird in her hand.

The two at the top of the stair stood transfixed, looking after her. Then they turned on each other.

" Now we've done it," said Thompson angrily. " How many times have I told you it's not safe to come up here ? You're going to lose me my job and your own as well. And what'll she think of us—a young girl like that ? It makes me sick. Keep out of my room," he said furiously. " I can't keep myself to myself any more. You're always after me."

Shock drove him to speak the brutal truth.

" That's right, you swine," said Bertha. " Blame it on me."

Thompson turned back into his room and made to shut the door, but Bertha pushed it back and followed him.

" Don't be so soft," she taunted. " That girl's too daft to think anything. She were too taken up with blubbing over that bird. Besides, you'll never lose your job, Bill," she said more propitiatingly. " The Major's too fond of you. *You're* safe, whatever happens."

" Oh, not I," said Thompson. " But stop this,

Bertha, for the love of mike. And get out now before anybody else comes. Go on, go."

Bertha went. She went noiselessly back to the house and up to her attic. She was more perturbed than she had let Thompson see. That girl might be daft, but then again she might not. The worst of those people was they didn't let you see what they were thinking if they didn't want to. If the girl told the new mistress, Bertha would have to go. She would not only lose her job, she would lose Thompson as well and Bessy Palmer might get him after all. Bertha reflected with bitterness that her misconduct would cause the mistress to dismiss her, but Thompson's would have no effect on the master.

" It's the woman that pays," she said to herself, getting into her own bed.

She lay thinking, her thin lips set with determination to get herself out of this corner.

Her first conjecture, had she known it, had been right. Innocence, or inexperience, is blind. Christine thought nothing of seeing Bertha come out of Thompson's room at that hour. She was too grieved for the death of George to think consciously about anything else, but the idea passed at the back of her mind that Bertha had gone to tell Thompson it was time to get up.

When she had given the pair the fright of their lives, she went into the garden, and scooping a hole in the ground under a bush with her fingers, she laid George in it, covered him over and went back to the nursery. She got into her bed, pulled up the sheet and wept again under it. Penelope was weeping under hers. He had been such an engaging bird.

CHAPTER X

THE girls were astonished when Anthea asked them to accompany her to the city to interview the nurse recommended by Dr. Carter.

" A queer thing to ask us to do," complained Penelope. " Why doesn't she take Aunt Victoria, or even Bessy ? "

" Oh, well, so long as she pays our bus fares," said Christine. " We can change our books and have ices, you know."

No one asked for Thompson and the car during the cricket season, so, on a hot summer afternoon, they took the bus into the city. They found Nurse Pye's rooms in a little house in a narrow street up the hill by the Castle.

Nurse Pye was a highly efficient nurse, it appeared, and so much sought after that she could pick and choose her patients. She had detached herself from the private nursing service to which she had belonged and now lived in rooms, drove a baby car and nursed as she felt inclined. She would not take many maternity cases, and Anthea, on Dr. Carter's advice, was making a special journey to plead her cause.

The crested notepaper on which she had written to ask for an appointment had pleaded for her already. Nurse Pye was impressed and decided to receive her visitor with tea. She went out, and laid in three penny-worth of scones, an iced cake and a bag of mustard and cress for sandwiches. A nice, refined little tea for two, she considered, and was taken aback when she opened the door in answer to the knock and found three people instead of one on the steps, and two of these young girls with, in all probability, healthy appetites.

The girls were, however, only accompanying Anthea inside for a moment " for fun," and after the moment in the little front room entirely filled, it seemed, by photographs of naked babies, the fun, as far as the girls were concerned, was exhausted and, arranging to call back at half-past five, they crushed together down the oilclothed passage and reappeared in the street.

" Whew ! " blew Christine. " The atmosphere of obstetrics was too much for me. What a funny little woman ! What shall we do ? "

They stood in the street, looking about them. They wore white linen dresses they had made themselves. The dresses were simple and for once had no mistakes in them. They wore cheap wide-brimmed straw hats. Their slender brown arms were bare. Paul Kenworthy coming up to his office wondered who these lovely young creatures could be, standing in the sunlight and transforming the street. They looked free, untouched, and as if they might move away, like young does, not afraid but indifferent, if you spoke to them.

They stood hand-in-hand, as was their habit, wondering where to go.

" Good afternoon," said Paul, confronting them. " Do you remember me ? "

Grey eyes and blue surveyed the plump young man, who was even pinker, from the heat, than he had been in March.

" Oh, you were at the wedding," they cried.

" Anthea was getting married then and now . . ."

Christine's voice tailed off. "We're waiting for her. She's making a call here," she finished with dignity.

"Have you time for tea?" asked Paul eagerly. Work waited at his office, but it must wait.

"We were just thinking about ices," said Penelope.

"Good," said Paul. "Excellent. May I lead the way?"

"Do," said Penelope.

He went proudly down the hill with them. He hoped he would meet all his acquaintances. Two such beautiful girls. And they were not only beautiful, they were kind. They did not laugh at him. Paul, pink and podgy, was always searching the faces of girls to see if they were laughing at him. He had met with such ridicule at school, where he was known as "Porker" that he had looked for it ever since, and frequently found it. Especially when he was in Boy Scout uniform. It was all right so long as he remained with his troop in Brockington where everybody knew him, but when he had to bring his boys into the city, he suffered from the exposition of large dimpled knees and quivering thighs. Nevertheless he continued, with courage, to be a Scout Leader.

A man, no matter how fat, can always get a girl of some kind to go about with. But that would not do for Paul. He was attracted only by the best, and hitherto the best had not been attracted by him. Now, however, he was with two lovely girls. He had been enraptured by their looks, especially Penelope's, and their kindness at the wedding, and had always hoped he would meet them again. Now he had met them and had found them as lovely and as kind as ever. He beamed happily and felt very light and springy in spite of his weight and the heat. At every lamp-post, he sprang aside to let the girls pass and altogether behaved with the greatest gallantry and agility.

The girls were happy too. They didn't know they were being kind, but it was a lovely day and everything was very interesting. It was fun going out to ices with a man. And not having to pay.

" We've had a lovely time," they said, returning to Anthea.

Anthea had had a lovely time, in her way, too. Nurse Pye had put her at ease at once. Anthea had dreaded this interview. For thirty-seven years she had lived reticent to the point of shame about all bodily functions and now she had to plunge into discussions of the most intimate nature with strangers. First a strange doctor and now a strange nurse.

When she found Nurse Pye so comfortable and sympathetic, Anthea's relief was extreme. In an access of intimacy, she took off her hat, accepted several cups of tea from Nurse Pye's beaten pewter teapot, and made all sorts of confidences, discreet and indiscreet ; she felt there was no need to discriminate between them.

" I do hope I'm not too old to have a baby," she said wistfully.

" Not a bit of it," said Nurse Pye briskly. " Look at the baby on the gramophone and the one on the piano. They were first babies and their mothers were turned forty."

" I don't think my husband really wants this baby," said Anthea, leaping comfortably from one subject to another.

" He'll have to put up with it," said Nurse Pye, who had small sympathy with husbands.

Anthea told Nurse Pye how happy she was to be having a baby, how she loved babies, how she had loved Susan, her small niece, but had never been able to see anything of her while she was a baby. She told Nurse Pye about the feeding-bottle.

" You were quite right," said Nurse Pye.

" I felt I was," said Anthea. " But it's nice to hear you say so."

Anthea had never talked so much in her life or been so listened to.

Nurse Pye was a small woman, hardly more than five feet high, but she was both pugnacious and protective. She was plain, with a snub nose, a red face, a firm mouth and small lively blue eyes that missed nothing. When out of uniform she dressed as severely as if she were in it, in navy blue or grey. She wore mushroom hats, felt in winter, straw in summer, so that she looked like a little police-woman and children up to mischief often ran when they saw her coming.

She was a north-country woman and believed in calling a spade a spade. She had her weaknesses. She was a snob. She liked good families, fine houses, large cars. She liked people who owned such things to come seeking her in her little house. It increased her appreciation of herself, never low. Strangely enough, this snobbery did not affect her behaviour. She was as outspoken to the rich as to the poor. It was as if she admired breeding and wealth in the abstract ; the possessors of these had to pass the same test, when Nurse Pye came to deal with them, as those who had neither.

Before she saw Anthea, she decided to nurse her. She saw already in imagination an addition to the gallery of naked babies in the shape of a portrait of an aristocratic-looking child, sex undefined, to whom she would be able to point and say : " That's the Marwood baby. Lovely old place Saunby Priory, isn't it ? "

If she had disliked Anthea, she would nevertheless

have nursed her for the prestige of staying at the Priory. But she liked Anthea at once, as Anthea liked her. Anthea was exactly the sort of patient Nurse Pye liked best ; inexperienced, looking to Nurse Pye for help, physical and moral. Nurse Pye liked to be looked to, she liked to help, to manage other people's affairs for them.

When Anthea had gone, having given Nurse Pye a warm invitation to come to see her at Saunby as often as possible, Nurse Pye put on her mushroom hat and went to the pictures to round off the day. She had to go through a slum district to reach the picture house, and as she walked through the hot, narrow streets, she looked about her with lively disapproving eyes.

If she could have had her way, she would have managed those children off the streets and into their beds. She would have managed those gossiping slatternly women off their doorsteps and the men out of the public houses. She would that, she said to herself. And why hadn't those men got the covers drawn up over the dust-carts ? She'd a good mind to write the Medical Officer about them. Thus she walked, silently exercising her powers of management. She was born for management. She could, she felt, have managed anything.

§

In the kitchen at Top Farm, Bessy and Mrs. Spencer and Johnny sat on at the table after tea, enjoying one another's company and the interval from work.

The great black kettle, off duty too, puffed gently on the hob. Hams and clean clothes airing on a pulley hung from the ceiling. On the table stood remnants of the tea : cold-meat pie, beetroot in vinegar, jam, cake. The door into the yard was open and, from the dimness of the kitchen, it was like a little stage, strongly lit by the sun. From time to time a hen appeared upon it to strut and peck about before going off again.

Bessy, her bare arms folded on the table, smiled dreamily. The Spencers, mother and son, looked at her.

' Suppose I could come in every day for my tea and find her here,' thought Johnny.

' She's just the wife for him,' thought his mother.

The grandfather clock struck once. Bessy looked round at it.

" Half-past five," she said. " I've to be in at six. I'll just wash these pots up before I go."

" Nay, you won't," said Mrs. Spencer. " You've enough to do at the house without washing up on your afternoon out."

Bessy smiled and began to carry pots to the sink.

" Nay, leave them, leave them," protested Johnny, trying to intercept her.

" Out of my way, like a good lad," said Bessy. " Or you'll be breaking something."

" Nay, he won't," said Mrs. Spencer. " Johnny doesn't break things. And if you're so set on washing up, he'll dry while I finish in my dairy."

Good chance to leave them together, she thought.

Bessy washed the pots quickly and Johnny dried them slowly, turning each pot carefully in his strong red hands. He took the pots very seriously. He was stiff in his big farm boots and leggings, his hands were stiff, his fair hair was stiff like thatch. When Bessy had finished washing, she scoured the sink, rinsed the dish-cloth, seized a towel and began to dry the pots, diminishing the pile rapidly and darting to the cupboards to put them away, while Johnny revolved slowly, pot in hand, to keep her in his eye. She was so pretty in that pink frock with little blue flowers in the pattern. Her cheeks were pink to match and her eyes a deeper blue than the flowers.

She went to the square of looking-glass hanging beside the window to put her hat on, and Johnny was entranced to think her face was reflected in the glass he shaved at every day. Every time he shaved now he would think of her face.

" I'll just pop in to say good-bye to your mother," said Bessy.

When she came back, he had thought of a way to keep himself a little longer in her company.

" I might as well see you to the lodge gates," he said. " Seeing I've nothing else to do."

" Right," said Bessy. " Come on."

He walked with her to the gates, but he had to let her go there because he didn't know how to keep her any longer. She parted from him with a friendly smile. Nice lad, she thought, and forgot him.

As soon as she was through the gates, her eyes flew to the cricket field. It was empty and her spirits fell. It was a long time since she had seen Thompson. Now that cricket was on he hardly ever came to her part of the house. All day, she had counted on catching a glimpse of him on the field when she passed it, either going out or coming back, but she had been disappointed both times, and now there was no other chance to-day.

Subdued, muted, Bessy entered the avenue of elms. She went under the trees, heavy with their summer canopy of leaves. She walked disconsolately, her eyes on the ground. Then she lifted them and her heart gave a leap. Thompson was coming down the avenue towards her.

Bessy had an impulse to turn back or to run sideways across the field, but she managed to keep on her way, biting her lip and blushing and looking anywhere but at him. Thompson came steadily on, staring at her.

Thompson had kept away from Bessy. He had broken altogether with Bertha after that morning in the room over the stable, but he could not pass straight from her to Bessy. It wasn't decent, he felt. For the first time in his life he wanted to be decent—to Bessy, not to Bertha. He had no compunction for Bertha. She was as hard as nails and he wasn't the first, he knew. She had gone after him with her eyes open ; and it was she who had gone after him, not he after her.

But Bessy was different. He felt he must do something to himself, make himself decent before he courted her. Bessy had destroyed his cheerful self-confidence ; she had made him humble and anxious. He wanted to be the sort of man she could love. He knew she was strict in her ideas and he was frightened she would never approve of him.

He meant to keep up his self-discipline for weeks ; he meant to keep his distance. That afternoon he had posted himself in the pavilion to watch Bessy pass by on her way to Top Farm, and he meant to watch her come back in the same way. But when he saw Johnny Spencer with her at the gates, he could not stop himself coming to find out at once what Spencer was to her.

" Good afternoon," he said sternly, reaching her. His nostrils were distended and he did not smile.

" Good afternoon," faltered Bessy, wondering what was the matter.

He turned and walked beside her up the avenue.

" I've been to see Mrs. Spencer," volunteered Bessy, since he did not seem to be going to say anything.

"Yes, and I see Johnny Spencer brought you to the gates," said Thompson.

"Yes," said Bessy.

"Are you and him walking out then?" Thompson fired at her.

Bessy's blue eyes flew wide with amazement.

"Me and Johnny Spencer!" she cried. "Why, I've known him all my life. I'm not walking out with anybody," she offered.

Thompson turned round to her and smiled, a smile of vast relief and satisfaction. Bessy laughed up at him, and they walked on, lurching a little into each other as if each was a magnet for the other.

It was obvious from the way they walked that they were in love. It was obvious to Bertha, who had followed Thompson out and was now following him in again, dodging from tree to tree to do it.

At half-past six, Bessy rushed up the back stairs to change into her black and Thompson sauntered across the stable-yard. With one of his quick changes of movement, he clapped his hand to the wooden rail and sprang up the stair to his room in two bounds. Whistling, he went in and left the door open.

Bertha came in so noiselessly that he did not know she was there until he turned with a pair of shoes in his hand that he was going to whiten. At the sight of her he stood still. She closed the door and planted herself against it, her head back, looking at him with a smile that made him hate her, a sneering insolent smile as if all the tricks were in her hand.

He dropped the shoes and came towards her. He pulled her aside and opened the door.

"I'd like this place to myself," he said.

"I daresay you would," said Bertha. "So's Bessy Palmer could come up."

Thompson's brows came down in a hard frown.

"You shut up about her," he said.

"I'll say what I like about her," said Bertha. "Who's going to stop me?"

Thompson flushed with anger.

"You've got to blushing about her now, have you?" said Bertha. "Well, there's something else you'd better blush for instead. Stand away from that door. I've got something to say to you, Bill Thompson, that you won't want anybody to hear no more than I do."

She wrenched the door from his hand and shut it. She planted herself against it as before.

"You've got me into a nice mess, Bill Thompson. I'm going to have a baby."

Thompson stood stock still. Slowly the colour ran out of his face. He stared at her.

"Well?" she asked, her head quivering.

"It's a lie," he said.

"Is it?" she smiled.

He stared at her, transfixed.

"It's a lie," he repeated.

"Say it a few more times, and you'll happen believe it," taunted Bertha.

Someone clattered through the stable-yard below. The two fantails that Thompson fed appeared hopefully on the window-sill.

"Well?" said Bertha. "What're you going to do about it?" she said.

He did not speak.

"I suppose you'd like to let an innocent child suffer so you can run after Bessy Palmer and bring another illegitimate brat into the world?"

"You shut up about her, d'you hear?" said Thompson. "Or I'll put you out."

He walked to the table and took a cigarette from a packet with shaking hands. But he could not go as far as finding a match ; he sat down on a stool turning the cigarette in his fingers.

" Sorry for yourself, aren't you ? " taunted Bertha. " But what about me ? What about the shame I've got to stand ? When I tell my dad about you, Bill Thompson, he'll come up and give you such a thrashing as you've never had in your life and you'll deserve it. I hope he kills you. Getting me into trouble and off after another girl before I've even had time to tell you about it."

" Oh, shut up, for God's sake," said the goaded Thompson. " And let me think."

" Think ! " she burst out. " You've no need to think. You know what you'll have to do, Bill Thompson, if you've any decency left. You'll have to marry me, that's what, and straight off, if our child's going to get born without a stain on it. You don't want people pointing at your kid, do you, and calling it a bastard ? You can't let an innocent child suffer all its life because you wanted your bit of fun. You've got to face up to this, Bill, whether you want to or not. If you don't, you're the rottenest cad that ever walked, that's what you are, and I'll tell Bessy Palmer and everybody else."

" Shut up," said Thompson.

He sat on at the table, while the fantails cooed gently for their supper from the sill. After a time, Bertha moved from the door and came to stand by his side.

" Well ? " she began again.

CHAPTER XI

BESSY was bewildered. She couldn't make things out. Since their meeting in the avenue, Thompson had never so much as looked at her. Something had gone wrong at once, because when she crossed him in the hall that very night, he turned his face away with his jaw clenched as if he'd got the toothache. She only wished he had had the toothache ; it would have been a reason for his strange behaviour. But he was out playing cricket next day and nobody said anything about toothache.

What had she done ? she was for ever asking herself. Was there something about her he found he didn't like ? Why had he changed towards her ? Why ? Why ? And why was Bertha going about like a cat full of cream ? Day after day went by and brought no answer to these questions and Bessy was very unhappy.

The days were bad enough, because she couldn't get to herself anywhere. She had to look cheerful, because if she didn't someone would ask what was the matter. She had to keep her trouble to herself all day and that was bad enough, but at night when she could give way, it was worse. Until now, night had never been long enough for Bessy. No sooner, it seemed, had her head touched the pillow than the alarm clock went off and it was time to get up. Night had been something she did not know about. But now she knew how long the night was, lying through the hours, wondering, worrying, crying into her pillow. When she should have been getting up, she fell asleep and came down late, pale and heavy-eyed.

In spite of her attempts to look cheerful, it was clear that something was wrong. Anthea asked her at last, but Bessy said there was nothing. She blushed so painfully as she said it that Anthea did not ask any more questions. Whatever it was, it was something Bessy wished to keep to herself.

Bessy served Anthea as devotedly as ever, bringing her tea at all hours. A cup of tea was Bessy's remedy for everything ; for other people. She did not administer to herself. She brought tea to Anthea and listened patiently to all Anthea's talk about her baby. As the eldest of a large, impoverished family Bessy was used to babies. They were to be put up with rather than rhapsodized over. But she listened to Anthea and smiled responsively.

Then, on a Wednesday afternoon, when she was cleaning the windows of Anthea's bedroom, Bessy saw Bertha and Thompson going up the drive in their best clothes. Going to catch the bus and go to the Pictures most likely, she thought, clasping her wash-leather in anguish.

She watched them out of sight, her face pressed to the pane.

" He's no good," she said to herself. " On my day off he's out with me. On her day off he's out with her. He's after everybody. He's not worth bothering about."

For half an hour she despised Thompson with fierce joy. She was angry with him and anger is a grand cure for love if you can only keep it up. Bessy kept it up for half an hour, during which she cleaned windows with great vigour. But when they were done, she wept. It didn't matter whether he was worth bothering about or not. It didn't matter what he was. She loved him.

§

After this excursion with Bertha, Thompson sought an interview with the Major.

"You *fool*, Thompson," said the Major, deeply perturbed.

He sat with his arms collapsed along the sides of his desk, and stared at Thompson as if he could not believe anyone could commit such folly.

In a matter of this kind, the Major had no scruples. He did not believe in making respectable women of women who had hitherto not been respectable. And in this case his sympathies were fiercely with Thompson. A good fellow like Thompson tied up for life to a little shrew like that! Worse than a shrew. He wasn't at all sure she hadn't tried to make eyes even at him once or twice.

"Why didn't you come to me first?" he said sternly. "Why didn't you come before you married her? I'd have made you see sense then, man. But what can I do for you now? I can't do anything. It's too late."

Thompson said nothing. He stood at the desk, silent.

"And you want to leave the house?" asked the Major.

"There's nothing else for it, sir," said Thompson.

"But how the hell can you go in the middle of the season?" cried the Major, recovering sufficiently from the shock of Thompson's disclosure to think about cricket. "How the hell do you think I can manage without you?"

"I wasn't thinking of leaving you, sir. Only of

131

leaving the house. I wondered if there was anywhere I could go, sir, round about?"

The Major considered this, while Thompson waited, sick at heart. Fancy having to go like this. To go with Bertha.

"The only thing I can think of, Thompson, is that you should move with—what's-her-name," an expression of distaste crossed the Major's face and Thompson winced. "Move into the empty lodge. You'll have to clean it out and paint it up. But if it's any use to you, you can have it."

Thompson began to thank him.

"Ah—don't," said the Major, getting up from his desk.

Poor Thompson, taken from the life he liked and made to live *her* sort of life. His freedom was over. Women, he thought. A man had no chance against them.

He walked to the door with his hand on Thompson's shoulder.

"The old days seem to be over," he said heavily.

§

Bessy, in her turn, sought an interview with her mistress. She arrived with tea in her hand to help her through it.

"Please, 'm, I want to give my notice," she said proffering a shaking tray.

Anthea dropped her knitting into her lap.

"Bessy," she cried. "Your notice! You can't mean it."

"I do mean it, 'm, please."

"But why?" cried Anthea. "Bessy, you can't leave me. I can't possibly do without you. You've done so much for me ever since I came and now I need you more than ever."

Bessy put her apron to her face and gulped.

"What's the matter, Bessy?" said Anthea. "I know something's been wrong lately. Tell me, and let's see if we can't do something about it."

"You can't do anything, 'm," sobbed Bessy. "Nobody can."

"Is the work too much for you?"

"Oh, no," Bessy repudiated such an idea.

"Are you homesick? Would you like to go home for a few days?"

"Oh, no." Bessy shook her head more vigorously than ever.

Then she dried her eyes with sudden resolution and smoothed down her apron.

"It's just that I want to go," she said.

"But, Bessy," pleaded Anthea. "I can't bear to lose you. Not only for my own sake, but for the baby's. I'm relying on you to help me with the baby. You know I am."

Bessy twisted her apron in her hands and looked in distress at Anthea.

"I can't stay, 'm. I can't stay here with Bertha and Bill Thompson, 'm. That's what's the matter. You see, 'm, I thought . . . I thought . . ." She took refuge in her apron again and shook her head speechlessly.

"So did I, Bessy," said Anthea. "I thought so too. It was a great shock to me when I heard about him and Bertha. I don't like Bertha. I never did. I was going to give her notice the moment the cricket season was over. I only wish I'd given it to her weeks ago, when I meant to first. Then this would never have happened."

Poor Bessy, she thought. I could have saved her from this. If only we could see what was going to happen; what depended on us.

133

" I can't bear to see them about, 'm," Bessy said from behind her apron. " She keeps flaunting herself about and saying ' Me and Bill ' and ' Same as I said to Bill ' and she looks at me every time she says it. And I can't bear to see him, neither, he looks that wretched and as if he's done something he didn't ought to."

" So he has," said Anthea, sternly. " He was carrying on with her all the time. I've been completely deceived in Thompson and I shan't forgive him."

Bessy, sobbing, shook her head in protest.

" I can't stop here with them," she brought out.

" But, Bessy, they're going," said Anthea.

" Going ? " The apron dropped from Bessy's face, revealing her red eyes. " Going ? Where to ? "

" They're leaving the house, anyway. They're going to live in the empty lodge."

Bessy turned away. He was going to live in a house with Bertha. He was married all right. No good thinking it wasn't really true. No good thinking it would somehow come right. It wouldn't. It was all over. Finished.

" So you see, Bessy, there's no need for you to go," said Anthea pleadingly. " You need hardly ever see either of them again. And you'll be far better with me than with strangers, because I know about it and I can help you."

" I'd rather go right away, 'm, please," said poor Bessy.

Anthea caught Bessy's red hand in hers.

" No, Bessy, I won't hear of it. Sit down and let's talk it over. You'll be happy again sometime, although you think now that you won't. I know, because I've been unhappy myself. So unhappy I thought I'd never get over it, but I did. I'll help you to be happy, Bessy. You trust *me*."

In the end, she persuaded Bessy to stay. She meant to be kind.

CHAPTER XII

WHERE once the Major had high hopes of this year's cricket fortnight, he now had no hope at all. Everything was going wrong. First it was Anthea. Then it was Thompson. He wouldn't be at all surprised, he thought gloomily, if Ashwell wrote any day now to say he couldn't come.

He considered that Anthea was very half-hearted in her preparations for the entertainment of the team. She seemed to him always to be consulting the layette list drawn up by Nurse Pye, instead of the cricket notebook he had once been so pleased with her about. In fact, once when he suggested she should make some further notes in it, she said she didn't know where it was and wouldn't a bit of paper do? And she didn't say this with her old anxiety that he would be angry. She said it with the new calmness that secretly amazed her husband.

He was frequently amazed, nowadays, by Anthea's behaviour. It was changing visibly, rapidly and not for the better. In the early days of their marriage, he had been irritated when she followed him about, humble and adoring, like a dog. Like a bitch really, he amended secretly, and he had never cared much for bitches. They were too affectionate. He could not bear to be fawned upon. Anthea had certainly got on his nerves in those days.

But surely there was a happy medium for a wife's behaviour? He resented the progressive withdrawal of Anthea's interest in all that concerned him. She

had not only downed tools, she had turned her back ;
and she seemed to think of nothing now but the baby.
This wasn't fair. It wasn't what he had married her
for. She wasn't doing her duty by him. He felt
considerably aggrieved.

It was true that Anthea's behaviour was changing.
So was her appearance. The heaviness of her figure
suited her. It gave her a dignity she had hitherto
lacked. She could no longer sit on the floor or make
any of her misguided attempts at running or being
girlish. She moved about Saunby with a gait like
Juno's, and the household was impressed and modified
its behaviour accordingly.

Most people are taken at their own valuation, and
Anthea's valuation of herself was altered. She no
longer felt humble and unnecessary. She felt important ; vitally important as the mother of her child.
Much more important than cricket or indeed than
anything or anyone in the house. If other people did
not think her important, it didn't really matter. She
would look after herself. But they must also look after
themselves and not bother her to do it.

It was this attitude that secretly staggered the Major
and Victoria and the girls. It cut the ground from
under their feet and enabled Anthea to do with them
what she would once never have attempted.

For one thing, she brought the girls downstairs for
meals.

When Bertha left to live at the lodge with Thompson,
Anthea did not replace her in the house.

" We can't afford to," she told her husband. " We
must cut down expenses. Babies cost a good deal, you
know, and must be provided for."

" Don't I know it," said the Major grimly.

She looked briefly at him. She did not forgive him
these digs at the baby.

There was no maid now to wait on the nursery, Anthea pointed out to the girls.

"So you must please simplify matters by coming down for meals," she said, bringing about by a few words a thing she would once never have dreamt of doing.

The girls hated this arrangement. After their long isolation in the nursery they positively suffered from having to sit at table with their father, their step-mother and their aunt. The dining-room seemed dark and red and dreary after the high, light nursery. It seemed to take a very long time to get food brought in and taken out again. Their Aunt Victoria ate a great deal and took ages over it, so that they had to sit waiting for her to finish, which they did restlessly, their eyes on her plate. They couldn't talk, since there was nothing they wished to say in such company. Nobody else said anything much or worth listening to ; the Major was generally put-out about something, Anthea was preoccupied and Victoria as usual indifferent.

"A party in a parlour all silent and all damned," said Christine. "Even Bessy is miserable waiting on us."

After every meal the girls made swiftly for the door and ran all the way upstairs to the nursery, muttering, "Good Heavens, wasn't it awful . . . worse than ever . . ." and giggling to think what they had been through.

The day Nurse Pye came to lunch, the Marwoods, rarely united in anything, were united in surprise. They sat almost stupefied while Anthea and Nurse Pye carried on their conversation, talking happily and ceaselessly together, behaving in fact as if the Marwoods *weren't there*. This feeling of invisibility annoyed the Major. Though it was absurd to be annoyed, he told himself, because he didn't care about the behaviour of two silly women. Why should he? He didn't care ; and yet they made him wild.

He was annoyed, too, that Anthea should expect him to eat with a midwife. He hated strangers at the table, unless they were also cricketers. But to have to eat with a midwife who behaved as if she had known him all his life and didn't think much of him, as if she'd brought him into the world, dammit, as if he wouldn't have existed but for her, it was too much. And what would it be like when she was installed at Saunby for a month or five weeks or whatever she was coming for ? The Major tapped his fingers on the arms of his carving chair in irritated protest at the presence of Nurse Pye. But Anthea and Nurse Pye did not notice ; they chatted on.

Their talk veered round to the coming cricket fortnight, and the Major was horrified to hear it discussed by Nurse Pye as a nuisance. A nuisance for Anthea ; and Anthea smilingly accepted it as such ! Most disloyal, fumed the Major inwardly. He would never have thought it of her. He glared sternly at her from under his lowered brows and fiddled furiously with his knives and forks.

" I'm afraid I shan't be able to do much towards it now," said Anthea.

" You mustn't," said Nurse Pye firmly.

" Somebody must be prepared to take my place when I have to rest," said Anthea. " What about you, Victoria ? "

" No, thank you," said Victoria with a rude laugh. " Since my efforts failed to give satisfaction in the past I am certainly not going to renew them now."

Nurse Pye observed Victoria with the greatest interest.

" Then it will have to be Christine," said Anthea.

" Me ? " cried Christine, in astonishment.

Nurse Pye turned her attention to Christine.

" What could *I* do ? " asked Christine.

" What I would otherwise do," said Anthea.

Christine looked and felt unwilling. She could also feel Nurse Pye disapproving of her and she stiffened. She wasn't used to being disapproved of and who was this little person to disapprove of her ?

" What would I have to do ? " she said to Anthea.

" I'll tell you when the time comes," said Anthea with a dismissing smile. She wasn't going to waste time talking to Christine when she could be talking to Nurse Pye.

When lunch was over Anthea and Nurse Pye sat in the drawing-room and Victoria had to take her nap elsewhere.

" And no apology," said Victoria furiously as she stumped through the hall, passing her brother on his way to his room.

The Major banged his door on all these women. All these women and none of them willing to do a thing for him. He kept them all. Victoria had a little money of her own, but she spent it all on paint as far as he could see. Otherwise, she lived on him. They all lived on him.

He strode to his open windows and there before the majestic ruin of the West Front stood Nurse Pye's baby car.

" Typical ! " exclaimed the Major. " That woman's like one of those damn little things herself. And she'd calmly put herself in the wrong place too and never know it."

Thompson appeared at that moment round the side of the house.

" Hi ! Thompson ! " shouted the Major. " Can't you move that car ? Take it round to the yard."

"Certainly, sir," said Thompson in surprise, starting towards it.

"Oh, never mind," groaned the Major before he could reach it. "Leave it where it is."

Anthea was so queer nowadays, she might take it as an affront. Besides, if that woman didn't know her place, it was no good showing it to her; she wouldn't recognize it.

"What're you doing this afternoon, Thompson?" he shouted.

Thompson came within speaking distance before he replied.

"I'm going over the ground with the mower, sir."

"Right you are," said the Major. "I'll come down with you."

He stepped through the windows into the relief of Thompson's company.

Thompson's company, however, was not so good as it used to be. He was changed. He was no longer the cheerful, confident young man he had been; he was quiet. He went about with a set face, like a man keeping to his duty.

Life had changed abruptly for Thompson. Not only had he to live with Bertha without love for her, but he had to live alone with her. Both he and Bertha were used to the servants' hall with plenty of talk and company and now they were shut up alone together at the lodge where all around was quiet, even deserted.

Bertha had no complaint to make about the change in her life. She had come out on top. She hadn't lost her job as she feared she might; she had left it. She was no longer at the beck and call of the gentry or anybody else. She had a husband and a house, which she had very much enjoyed furnishing out of Thompson's savings.

The handsome three-piece suite in the parlour gave

her special satisfaction. Bill had let her buy as she liked. She wished he had behaved better in the furniture shops. It looked bad in front of those young men with permed hair and patent leather shoes for Bill not to be taking any interest. But never mind, she told herself. She'd got what she wanted. That was the main thing in life, to get what you wanted. You had to put up with the little things on the side so long as you got the big things you wanted. That was why she could put up with Bill's behaviour now. Let him sulk. He'd have to come round in time, and there was plenty of that. All his life, in fact.

She was wrong about Thompson. He was not sulking. He felt heavily responsible. He had no feeling for Bertha. She was the last woman he would have chosen to be the mother of his child, but since she was to be the mother of his child, he would do his duty by her.

Thompson's great friend in boyhood had been illegitimate. He lived in poverty with his mother and nobody knew who his father was. This boy's sufferings at school had made a deep impression on Thompson. He had championed his cause as he was championing the cause of his unborn child now. He had stuck up for Jim against all comers and he would stick up for his child. He would see that his child didn't suffer as Jim had suffered.

So long as he kept his mind on the child, he could go on. But when he could not, he was wretched.

He had to live with Bertha, but he loved Bessy. He rarely saw Bessy now, but she was hardly ever out of his mind. Miserably he wondered what she thought of him. She must think badly of him and he had to let her go on thinking badly of him. He couldn't explain without giving Bertha and his child away.

He had to fight against a constant longing to set himself right in Bessy's eyes.

It was a strain living with Bertha. The more he saw of her the less he liked her. She was too sharp ; her face, figure and tongue too sharp. Her cleverdick talk got on his nerves. He couldn't think how it had ever amused him. She seemed to have no liking for anybody. She was always pointing out mean motives and shabby tricks in other people. Thompson wouldn't let her talk about the Major or Anthea.

" They've been very decent to us and you know it, so shut up," he told her.

Sometimes, as he sat with his paper in the lodge kitchen, with Bertha passing to and fro before him, a wave of such bitter realization would come over him that he almost groaned aloud.

" I've got to live with her for the rest of my life."

But by riveting his attention on the cricket scores and refusing to let it wander he managed to keep quiet and to keep on.

The strain, however, told on his spirits, on his health and finally on his game. The Major besought him to pull himself together before the cricket fortnight started. Thompson said he'd be all right soon, but he worried about his game and the more he worried the worse he played.

August and the cricket fortnight approached. Under Anthea's direction beds used at no other time were aired and made up, rooms were arranged and allotted. There was no question who was to have the best—the yellow room. It was to be given to Nicholas Ashwell.

The Major had talked enthusiastically for weeks of this young man, but he had roused little interest in his daughters. They had been disappointed too often in their father's swans and had come to take it for granted that the people who appealed to him would automatically fail to appeal to them.

They took little interest in cricket. They were too used to it and it was too slow, they complained. They took almost as little interest in the men who came to play it. These men were mostly married and a married man to a young girl is like a book she doesn't want to read. After one glance at the title, she doesn't even bother to open it.

During the cricket fortnight, the girls hardly saw their father's guests. The team had meals in the billiard-room, and although the drawing-room was supposed to be given up to them at night, they did not use it. They sat on at the table after it had been cleared or strolled about out-of-doors.

The girls heard the men in the house ; they heard voices and whistling and coughings in the mornings and sounds of vigorous ablution from the bathrooms. A cloud of cigarette smoke hung bluely in the well of the staircase and pairs of white shoes stood perpetually outside bedroom doors. But for the rest, the girls avoided the cricketers and were glad when they had gone.

This year, however, Christine, deputizing for Anthea, was to be obliged to see something of them. She didn't like the prospect. The life of isolation led by the girls in the nursery had encouraged in them the family tendency to detachment. They didn't like to be asked to do anything, they didn't like fixed hours or fixed appointments, they didn't like taking part in other people's affairs at all.

Christine thought Penelope ought to support her in this tiresome business of seeing that the cricketers were properly entertained, but Penelope refused.

" No fear," she said. " She didn't ask *me*."

" Well, I jolly well hope she will," said Christine.

The third of August arrived, and before night-fall the Major's team was complete at Saunby. All day long they had been coming in and he had been receiving them with a pleasure he felt at no other time. He grasped their hands and smiled into their faces. He took them to their rooms himself and came down again, whistling soundlessly, to wait for others. At last Nicholas Ashwell arrived, and by his arrival and the fact that he turned out to be a fine upstanding young man of modest behaviour he completed both the team and the Major's satisfaction. They were all in now, the good, the excellent fellows, and everything was set for enjoyment. The Major's geniality spread to include Anthea, and he was so charming to her that she almost fell in love with him again ; but not so much as to be uncomfortable about it.

CHAPTER XIII

SAUNBY, so quiet in the winter, now buzzed with activity. In the mornings the drive was alive with tradesmen's vans bringing meat, bread, beer and cleaned flannel trousers for the guests. In the afternoons or earlier, bee-lines of spectators for the matches wavered down the drive from one direction and up the elm avenue from another. Large vivid buses brought visiting teams from far and near. The boot-boy was like a flour-miller from daily whitening so many pairs of boots. The laundry-maid had to wash every day, and Mrs. Green, the cook, stood continually on the brink of giving notice. It was an Army cook that was wanted, she kept saying. She'd never have taken the job on if she'd known, she said. She was very cross, hot and important all day long and every-body, including Anthea, listened meekly while she spoke her mind :

" There's no sense, 'm, in providing tea and scones for all as chooses to come for it," she said. " No sense at all. And I've too much to do with all the break-fasts, lunches, teas and dinners for the 'ouse without bothering meself with urns and scones for outside."

" I quite agree with you, cook," said Anthea sooth-ingly. " But what can we do ? It's one of the rules of Saunby that everybody who comes to watch a match can have tea. But another year it will have to be done away with. I tell you what we could do," she said. " We could buy iced buns that don't need buttering and have them cut up before they're delivered. Would that be better ? "

" It might," conceded Mrs. Green, wiping her hot face.

Summer was at its peak. On the day for the match against Lord Barwell's side a small sun burned down from a dull sky on a scene where there seemed to be too much of everything : the bracken too thick on the slopes, the trees too dark and full with leaf, the grass too long, the gardens too massed with over-blown roses. The flies were a pest and all the cricketers were anointed with an anti-fly cream supplied by the Major.

The billiard-room, however, was cool. Christine, who was supposed to be supervising the preparations for lunch, walked about conscious of the coolness of the room and of herself. The servants were putting up trestle tables and shaking out starched white cloths, but Christine hardly looked at them. She was there to please Anthea, who felt the heat and was lying down for the day ; she was there, but the servants knew what to do better than she did and she merely walked about, humming, her thoughts wandering happily.

She felt very light to-day, as if she could run and spring. Her bare feet in white sandals walked joyfully on the smooth stone floor. She felt her feet could do anything ; dance marvellously. If the servants had not been there, she would have let them dance.

In the long room with the white walls and high wooden roof and all the windows wide open, she moved in her yellow dress. The dress was like the white linen one. She had made several dresses from the same pattern and had sought to vary them by what the fashion papers called the ' accessories.' One dress, for instance, had no sleeves, but it had cuffs ; like pie-frills out of place. This yellow dress was differentiated from the others by the addition of a very large bow of stiff white muslin at the neck. The bow was crooked and it pricked her chin, but Christine bore with it because the fashion paper said it was " amusing." It was amusing, but not in the sense that the fashion paper or Christine intended. As she walked about she occasionally wrenched the bow into place.

Penelope looked in at the door on her way out. She was taking a book and Rough and a picnic lunch to the Lake Wood.

" Bye-bye," she called heartlessly.

" Mean pig," responded Christine, more from habit than because she really minded being in the billiard-room.

She put the bowls of flowers on the tables herself, because she had arranged them and was proud of them. She stood off to see the effect. Lovely, she thought. The tables were beginning to look nice, with bowls of salad and jugs of beer and dishes of bedewed butter ; and to the side tables huge cold pies were being brought in, and high ribs of beef and low-lying shoulders of lamb. A very masculine lunch, thought Christine, smiling and walking about heel and toe, heel and toe in her sandals.

To her surprise, Bertha arrived, dressed in her former uniform.

" I didn't know you were coming, Bertha," said Christine.

" The mistress sent for me to wait on," said Bertha.

" Oh," said Christine. " She didn't tell me."

Anthea had also forgotten to tell Bessy, and when Bessy came in with bread, she stood stock still staring at Bertha ; then with a dull flush mounting in her pale cheeks, she moved on and put down the bread. She went out of the room again and was a long time in coming back. Meanwhile Bertha was going about the room, being the married woman to the other maids and telling them they could come to tea now she'd got her curtains up.

" They'll be coming soon," Christine called out. " It's nearly half-past one."

She wondered how the match was going. The rivalry to-day was not so much between the teams as between Lord Barwell and the Major. These two men lived in acute consciousness each of the other. They irritated each other to the point almost of exhilaration. They had been at the same school and in the same regiment. Now they ran rival cricket teams.

For the past few years, Lord Barwell had been engaged in writing his memoirs, but he rued the day he had told the Major about it.

" How's the book ? " was always the Major's first inquiry as he proffered his long indifferent hand to his enemy. " Got anybody to publish it yet ? "

" No, but I will," said Lord Barwell, with a slight distension of his nostrils.

At which the Major laughed.

" Don't drag me into your bloody memoirs," he said. " Or I'll sue you for libel."

" My dear fellow, you'd have to be a damned sight more interesting than you are to appear in my book," said the nettled author.

The Major spoke of Lord Barwell's literary activities as : " Barwell making a fool of himself."

What riled the Major more than anything else was Lord Barwell's invariable habit, when he lost a match, of explaining why he had lost it.

" We should have won, if only . . ."

The infuriated Major, after such a remark, went about among his team hissing : " Of course he would have won if he hadn't lost, the ass ! "

" If we win the match to-day—and we ought to with

Ashwell to bat for us," the Major had said—"if we win and Barwell begins any of his explanations as to why they've lost, by God, I'll shoot him."

When Christine heard this, she smiled. She found her father's extravagance amusing, stagey. As children, both she and Penelope had been disappointed when their father's exciting threats came to nothing. Once they had believed in them.

"Daddy's going to shoot Uncle Dick," they went about saying, with wide eyes. "Yes, he is. He's going to *shoot* him."

But as the years went by and their father did not shoot Uncle Dick or anybody else, did not, in fact, carry out any of his frequent threats, the children came not to believe in anything he said. They still did not believe in anything he said.

Every morning during cricket fortnight Anthea and the girls had to wait for their baths until the cricketers were out of the way. Saunby possessed only two bathrooms, although the Major seriously thought of putting in a third for the convenience of his cricketers. So far, however, he had not been able to find the money. Every morning the girls sat unseen on the top step of their stairs, ticking off the guests from the list of bathers.

"That's Mr. Palliser in and Mr. Bennet out." "That's Captain Parr done." "There's only Mr. Bellinger now."

One morning they had ample opportunity of observing Nicholas Ashwell. He could not get into the bathroom so he paced the corridor outside to make sure of it as soon as it was free. The girls peered through the banisters at him. He was tall, young, with thick tawny hair, a blue silk dressing-gown and a towel round his neck. He prowled about the passage like a panther.

" Not bad," whispered the girls in surprise to each other.

Nicholas Ashwell paused in his prowlings to read the illuminated address presented to the Major's parents on the occasion of his birth. He read it, threw back his head and laughed soundlessly. The girls looked at each other in mute inquiry. What was there to laugh at ? They decided to read the address again at once to see. They looked down in indignation at the young man who dared to laugh at something at Saunby. Nicholas Ashwell turned away, smiling at his slippers as he resumed his pacings. Then the bolt of the bathroom door shot back and sundry grampus-like blowings preceded the appearance of red-faced Mr. Vyner, who had come to every cricket fortnight that the girls could remember.

" Sorry to have kept you waiting, Nick," he said.

" It's all right. All right," breathed Nicholas, leaping into the vacancy. He slammed the bathroom door and at once broke into exuberant whistling, expressive of his satisfaction at having got in.

The girls played catchers with their sponges to while away the time.

So far, the girls had seen little more than this of their father's guests, and when she heard them coming up now from the field for lunch, Christine obeyed her usual instinct to avoid them. She called out to the maids : " They're coming ! " and ran swiftly, as excited as if she was escaping from some pursuit, across the room and into the passage leading to the kitchen. She would have to come back in a moment, but she would not be there for them all to see when they came in.

She stood in the darkness of the passage, unseen but able to see. Voices and laughter approached, and suddenly the room was full of big men in white. They threw their legs over the benches and sat down at once. There was no hesitation, no attempt to sit by so-and-so as at the tennis and card parties, thought Christine. The men sat solidly down to feed. The tables were filled with broad white backs interspersed by the red and brown faces of their opposites. The Major sat at the head of one table with Lord Barwell at his right hand ; they looked as acutely discontented with each other as ever and were engaged in hot argument.

The maids began to go about asking : " Veal-and-ham pie, pigeon pie, cold beef or lamb, sir ? "

Thompson, to answer the question, had to look right into Bessy's face ; Bessy's face, pale with trembling lips, so close above his. He looked up at her with misery in his own. Who would have thought, to look at them, that she was only asking him what he would have to eat ?

A moment later, Bertha came behind him and to show he was hers, laid her ringed hand on his shoulder as she reached over for the beer jug. Thompson winced under her hand. He hated her to touch him. Bertha went away with a complacent expression on her face. She ran her eyes efficiently over the table and gave a sharp order to Bessy who was coming back with Thompson's plate. Bertha flourished at the expense of the other two.

Christine came back into the room and placed herself just inside the door. There were so many men. She felt isolated, self-conscious. She leant against the wall and looked at her own feet because she didn't know where else to look.

Nicholas Ashwell saw her and all he noticed at first was the huge white bow on her dress. It surprised him. And even as he looked at it, it fell off. Christine had wrenched at it once too often. It fell off and fluttered to the floor like a toy aeroplane.

Christine was startled. She clapped a hand to her denuded neck and looked round to see if anyone had noticed. Yes, there was that Mr. Ashwell laughing again. He laughed at illuminated addresses on the walls and now he laughed at her. She picked up the bow and stood looking down at it in her hands, her short curling hair hiding her face, the picture of youthful embarrassment. Then with sudden dignity, she threw her hair back and looked again at Nicholas Ashwell. You may laugh, her expression said. It doesn't matter to me.

But this look, begun in amusement on his part and dignity on hers, changed ; their eyes became grave, questioning. For a brief space of time they really saw each other. They were divided by the room and surrounded by other people, but their essential selves stood together alone and were supremely aware of each other.

Then Christine turned her head away. The look was too much. It made her heart beat too fast and sent the blood to her cheeks. Christine hated blushing ; it was such a betrayal. She knew she was going to blush now, and so, bow in hand, she walked out of the room, and Nicholas Ashwell watched her go.

Christine ran swiftly up to the nursery, glad for once that Penelope was not there. She burst into the room and began to search for her work-box so that she could re-fix the bow on her dress. She searched busily, almost wildly, for the box, but she was not thinking about it. She was disturbed, startled. Something had happened that she could not account for. She found the box and carried it to her battered white chest of drawers with the little swing-mirror on the top. But when she came face to face with herself in the glass, she forgot the bow she was going to stitch on. She leaned upwards to look at herself. Would anybody think she was pretty, she wondered. Would *he*?

She considered her face. She put the bow under her chin and took it away again. She looked better without it. Her hands and eyes were busy again, but, underneath, the sense of disturbance and of singing exhilaration persisted.

She put the bow and the box away and stood poised in the nursery. She wanted to go back to the billiard-room, but was afraid to. There was something significant about going back, like taking an irrevocable step forward, away from all she had known so far. But if she didn't go now, lunch would be over and he would go back to the field and she might not see him again. She stood for a moment in her familiar girl's life where she had been untouched, unconcerned, free. Then turning her back on it, she went down-stairs.

It was with an effort that she entered the billiard-room again.

" But after all," she reassured herself, " I'm *supposed* to be here."

She put herself against the wall and watched Bessy carrying things about. For some time she did not allow herself to look towards Nicholas Ashwell, but at last looked. He was talking to his neighbour, she was relieved to find, and she could examine his face without embarrassment.

' He looks nice when he smiles,' she thought. ' He looks kind and lazy mostly and then suddenly he doesn't look lazy. He looks mixed. He's very brown ; he must be out-of-doors all the time. Oh, when he laughs he's nice . . . what good teeth . . .'

She was considering him with frank interest when he turned and looked at her. This was their second

secret meeting, as close, as aware, as disturbing as the
first. Christine turned her head away from it again,
and suddenly the men were all getting up from the
tables and she was in the midst of them, lost in a forest
of large white figures. As she tried to get out, her
father took her by the elbow and she had to speak to
Lord Barwell. While she was speaking to him,
Nicholas Ashwell came up and from looking at him
across the room she now came to putting her hand
in his and saying, " How-d'you-do ? "

Lord Barwell and her father were moving off, and
the Major put a hand on Nicholas's shoulder and said :
" Come on, Ashwell, back to it."

Nicholas made a desperate attempt.

" Are you coming to watch ? " he asked her.

" Oh," she said, her eyes wide because she hadn't
thought of such a thing. " I don't know. If I can
find Pen . . ."

" Who's Pen ? " he asked, consumed with curiosity
now to know everything.

" My sister," said Christine.

During this time they were receding from each other
as he was being drawn out with the rest through the
door.

" I should come and watch," he said. " It's quite
a good match."

" Perhaps I will," said Christine.

He smiled and nodded to her, collided with an
umpire, apologized and stumbled out into the heat.

Paul Kenworthy who had come to the match, but
not from interest in cricket, saw them later sitting
together on the benches. He saw the dark girl, but
where was the fair one ? Where was Penelope ? He
sat on the hard little bench all afternoon, unrewarded.
And when he went away, the only satisfaction he had
was in the fact that it was Christine, and not Penelope,

who had been sitting with a young man. Better far
that Penelope should be absent, than present with a
young man, a young man, too, who was handsome
and not fat.

CHAPTER XIV

THAT same evening, after the visiting team, van-
quished, had gone home, Thompson sat in the
kitchen of his lodge, feeling himself an exile. Up at
the house the rest of the Priory team would be collected
in the billiard-room after dinner, discussing the game.
Other years he used to be sent for to talk it over with
them. The discussion of a match after it was over
was almost the best part of it. But now he had to
come home.

Home. It wasn't the right word. Thompson,
behind his paper, looked round him. It was a nice
enough little place ; it wasn't that there was anything
wrong with the *place*. From where he sat he could
see up the side of the elm avenue between the trees
and the fence of the wood alongside ; it was very
pretty. The grass-plot beside the house was pretty,
with a tree-stump in the middle of it. The tree-stump
made a platform where the fantails sunned themselves
all day long.

The fantails had found him out at the lodge. Every
morning they came wheeling over the wood to alight
at this back door and coo for their breakfast. Every
evening towards set of sun, they rose into the air, flew
once round the cottage and wheeled back to the
Priory. Thompson was pleased and touched that they
should come to him. They were almost all there was
of his happy past that continued into his unhappy
present and he forgot some of his misery when they

came to stand on his hands, spreading their strong, nervous, red-kid feet upon his palms.

It had taken him a long time to train them to do that ; much longer than it would have done if Bertha hadn't been there. When he stood at the back door with wheat on his outstretched hand, Bertha, who had no patience with such foolishness, used to pass in and out to the coal-house or the dust-bin, and frighten the birds off. Thompson knew she did it on purpose, but he kept his mouth tightly shut so as not to swear at her and he went on waiting for the birds. They came in the end.

Bessy wouldn't have frightened the birds off, he thought. Once when he had been with her in the stable-yard, the birds had appeared, hovering above them, their wings high.

" Aren't they beautiful ? " said Bessy, almost awed.

He remembered how she had stood there, in the old grey yard, her blue eyes lifted to the birds, white against the blue sky. Every time he saw the fantails now he saw that scene again.

Sitting behind his paper on this August evening, he thought of Bessy. She had looked poorly, he thought, at the lunch. She looked about as bad as he felt. It was awful, when you loved a girl, to see her look like that.

He watched Bertha from behind his paper. She was clearing the supper-table, carrying pots from kitchen to scullery. She looked pleased with herself. She'd had a good time to-day, digging at Bessy and flaunting herself about as a married woman among a lot of spinsters. She was still flaunting about between the kitchen and the scullery.

As Thompson watched Bertha, a thought began to form in his mind. It formed of its own accord, generated by nothing that he had thought before.

' She looks very well,' he thought. ' Does a woman who is having a baby look as well as this ? '

It struck him that there were no signs of having a baby about Bertha.

She came through the door into the kitchen again.

" I don't see much signs of this baby," he said suddenly.

Bertha had reached the table and was about to pick up the bread-board, but her hand fell away from it. She looked as startled as if he had struck her. Her mouth dropped open and she went white. Then her face changed ; she looked like a sharp animal trapped. Her black eyes glinted round for a way out. She took up the bread-board and went into the scullery.

Thompson crashed his paper together and went after her.

" Here," he said, spinning her round by the shoulder so roughly that the bread-board clattered to the floor. " What's this mean ? "

" What's what mean ? " said Bertha. " Let me alone, you great brute. You've no need to hurt me."

" What about this here baby ? " asked Thompson. He could scarcely get it out, he could scarcely breathe.

" Let me go," said Bertha, wrenching herself free.

She went to the cupboard and got between its doors, her back to him. Her hands clattered among the pots. He stood stock still behind her.

" Well ? " he said in a choked voice.

Bertha arranged the pots, taking cups from hooks and hanging them up again.

She made her voice casual.

" It were a false alarm," she said.

There was silence. Bertha kept her hands on the pots, waiting. Thompson stood behind her, his head lowered like a bull.

159

Then with one stride forward he banged the cupboard doors back and brought her out with a twist of his hand. He brought her to face him and held her there. His lips were drawn back tight against his teeth.

"You don't think you're getting away with that, do you?" he said.

Bertha scratched unavailingly at the iron hand on her shoulder.

"You let me go," she shrilled. "What d'you think you're doing? I can't help it if it were a false alarm, can I?"

"It was a lie," said Thompson. "It was a bloody lie. You trapped me. You knew I didn't want you, you bitch, and you got me that way."

He threw her violently from him and she fell back against the cupboard. She stood there, panting, white, vicious, rubbing her shoulder.

"Don't you dare to lay a hand on me, Bill Thompson," she said, "or I'll fetch the police. You come near me again and I'll run screaming up that avenue to the house and bring them all out."

"You bitch," said Thompson, his face brilliant with hate. "I could kill you."

He took a step towards her as if he would do it. She faced him unflinchingly.

"Don't you *dare* to touch me," she said in a low, steady voice.

Her eyes held him off. He dropped his arm. But every filthy word he had heard applied to women in the pit as a boy rose to his lips. He used them all for her, and if he had not been able to frighten her, he shamed her. Her eyes fell. When he had finished, he walked into the kitchen. But in a moment he was back.

"I wouldn't touch you again," he said, his face

twisted with contempt. " Not if you was the only woman left in the world. Not with a barge-pole."

He snatched his jacket from the hook and went out of the door, across the grass-plot, thrusting his arms into his sleeves as he went.

Bertha watched him go. Her lips curled in outward bravado, but she was white and trembling. Her mind was frantically busy, like a spider trying to repair severe damage to its web. As fast as she covered the damage to her pride in one place, it broke down in another. What if he didn't come back? What if he deserted her and everybody got to know? What if everybody got to know why? She'd have to leave this house and her furniture and go back into service. People would pretend to pity her, but they'd laugh up their sleeves. Everybody despised a deserted woman. To be put into a position where people could pity or laugh at her was intolerable to Bertha.

She stood at the window. Dusk thickened. She could hardly see up the avenue. Would he come back or not? If he came back, let him act as he liked. It wouldn't matter what went on inside the house so long as he was *there*. She felt herself a match for him all right ; but not for other people. Not for other people.

§

In the servants' hall, the tired maids sat down at last to their supper cocoa, but Bessy, though as tired as any of them, drank hers standing. She said she must go out and get cool before she went to bed. She gulped her cocoa, looking at it in distaste between the gulps. She realized suddenly that she didn't like cocoa, had never liked it, but had drunk it every day for years.

"Don't make me no more cocoa," she said. " I'm fed up with it."

The maids stared at her in surprise. It wasn't often that Bessy broke out like this. Bessy put down her cup, snatched off her cap, shook out her hair and left them staring.

If she didn't get a bit of peace and quiet, she thought, making for the stable-yard, she'd go crazy.

The yard was grey in the evening, deserted, the stalls empty, the doors closed, the cobbles clean, the mounting-block offering mute help no longer needed. The stable-yard at Saunby had meant little for years, but now that Thompson had left the room up the wooden stair, it meant nothing at all. Except to Bessy ; to her it was still the place where he had been.

Bessy leant against the wall, pressing her aching back to it and moving her tired head from side to side on the rough stone as if it were a pillow. The day had been too much for her ; her nerves still jangled from its bustle and confusion. All that running backwards and forwards with Bertha bumping into her and getting into her way at every turn. She was sure Bertha did it on purpose. She had never been able to get away from Bertha. Bertha hung over the whole day, darkening it. Then Bill—looking so miserable. And in the middle of it all, Johnny Spencer coming to the back door to ask for her.

" You're wanted," someone had said to her at the height of the rush. She was too busy to pay attention at first, but in the end she got tired of being called out to as she ran from kitchen to billiard-room and back again : " You're wanted, Bessy, at the back door."

When she rushed out at last, serving-cloth in hand, there was Johnny Spencer, looking queer and stiff in his best blue suit with a red tie clashing with his complexion.

" Oh, it's you, is it ? " said Bessy in an unwelcoming tone. " What d'you want, Johnny ? We're that busy . . ."

He was so slow in getting out what he wanted that she fidgeted in impatience on the step, looking at him with an exasperated expression that did not help him to hurry.

" I just thought, seeing as I was coming up to the match, as I'd just inquire how you was," he said. " You haven't been up to see us for a long while and Mother and me was a bit worried in case you was ill or something . . ."

" No, I'm all right, thank you," said Bessy, putting her hand to her head in a distracted fashion and wishing he would go. " But we're very busy in the house now and I've no time for visiting. How's your mother ? Is she all right ? "

Johnny admitted that his mother was all right. " But how's yourself, Bessy ? It seems to me as you're looking poorly."

He looked unhappily at her. She was pale and much thinner. She had a driven look. They were working her too hard, it was plain to see. Rage at those who would work her too hard filled him. If only she would marry him and let him look after her. He gazed at her, beseeching her mutely to help him to say this. But all he could get out was : " Will you come Sunday ? "

" Sunday ? " said Bessy distractedly. " No, I'm sorry, Johnny, I can't. I don't know when I'll be able to come again, and I've got to go now. We're right in the middle of serving the gentlemen's lunch."

At the impatience of her tone, Johnny reddened. She thought he oughtn't to have come, he could tell, and that was hard after the torture he had gone through to present himself at the back door of Saunby and ask for her. Worse still, she held out no hope of letting him see her again.

He looked deeply at her. Then he turned away.

" Well, I'll be going," he said, accepting it.

Through her own misery, Bessy was suddenly conscious of his.

" Good-bye," she called wistfully. If only you could want the one you could have instead of the one you couldn't. " Good-bye, Johnny."

" Good-bye," said Johnny. But he did not look round. Discarding the fiction of having come to see the match, he went home. His mother, busy with her baking, looked at him shrewdly across the kitchen but said nothing. Johnny went upstairs and took off his best suit. He came down in his farm-clothes and went out to get ready for milking. The cows took no notice of summer-time and were already standing at the field-gate, waiting.

Bessy thought of Johnny again as she leaned against the wall in the stable-yard in the evening. He was a good lad ; so kind. She wished she could be better to him, but she didn't seem to be able to *remember* to think of anybody but Bill.

She raised her eyes to the window of the loft where she used to be able once to see him. Where was he now ? Sitting with Bertha, she supposed.

She turned her head slackly on the wall and saw him coming into the yard. Startled, brought to vivid life by the mere sight of him, Bessy pressed herself against the wall. She thought he must have come to get something from his old room and she hoped fervently that he wouldn't see her and hoped equally fervently that he would.

He came straight towards her.

" I've been looking for you," he said, holding his coat together over his white cricket shirt and speaking in a strange, excited way. " Come out. Come with me a minute. I want to say something to you."

Bessy stammered. " How can I ? How can I get off ? "

" Just come," urged Thompson. " Come on. Nobody'll know at this time of night."

" Where shall I come to ? "

" Come to Lake Wood. I'll be inside the gate, waiting. I'll go there now. Come quick after me."

Bessy, with a thudding heart, sped into the house and up the back stairs. She snatched off her betraying white apron and put on her coat. Her chalk-white face glimmered at her as she passed the glass. She sped, swift, secretive, down the stairs again, out of the lighted house full of talking people, into the quiet evening, running—breathless, fearful, wildly happy— to the wood.

She opened the gate and peered, holding her heart, through the dusk.

" I'm here," said Thompson. His strong warm hand clasped hers.

Bessy went with him. With her hand in his, she would have gone anywhere. They went along an overgrown path where everything seemed to conspire to hold her back. Roots caught her feet, brambles her dress, the trees her hair. She kept laughing apologetically and saying, " Oh dear." Thompson kept freeing her, saying nothing. At last he picked her up in his arms and strode through the tangled wood to the place he knew of ; a place under the boundary wall, hung over by a tree and protected on the three other sides by thick brambles and bracken. He knew this place as he knew almost every square yard of Saunby, but he had never brought a girl to it. If he had, he would not have brought Bessy.

He put her down against the wall and, propping his

hands against the stone, looked gravely down on her. Shy, wondering, she waited.

" Kiss me, Bessy," he said.

" Oh, no," she said, putting her hands swiftly to her face. " I mustn't, Bill. It wouldn't be right."

She must try to do right. She must remember all she had been taught. Her father . . . sin . . . shame. She could hear her father's harsh voice going on and on as it used to in the evenings at home, going on and on about the wages of sin and girls going out with married men or going out with men at all.

"You're married, Bill," she reminded him falteringly.

" Listen," said Thompson, drawing her into his arms in spite of her resistance. " You listen and then tell me what sort of a married man I am."

He told her, while she gazed into his face with amazement, anger, pity, relief showing in turn in her own.

" What are you going to do, Bill? " she asked breathlessly. " Are you going to leave her? "

" First go off, I thought I would," he said. " But when I came to think, I didn't see how I could go straight away. I can't leave the Major in the middle of his fortnight or till the end of the season. I've no money. Bertha took it all to furnish with. I couldn't get another cricketing job. I'm not as good as I was, and gentlemen who'll pay a cricketer the whole year round, or even at all, aren't as thick as flies in summer. I couldn't get a job of any kind except in the pit."

" Oh, you mustn't go back to the pit," cried Bessy, putting her arms round his neck.

" I'd go back to the pit all right if I'd got you to come home to," he said, holding her closer. " If you could come with me, I'd go. But I know you, Bessy. You're good. You ought to be married decent and proper and have kids and a home. You'd never be happy with people pointing their fingers at you and sniggering."

"Oh, Bill," she said, forgetting her father. "I'd be happy with you."

He kissed her suddenly and desperately and she kissed him in return. They held each other close and forgot Bertha. They forgot everything but each other.

It grew dark under the tree. The water from the lake flowed quietly, continually, down the race near by. An owl hooted. From a tall tree a strange, prolonged, toneless trilling began.

"What's that?" asked Bessy, lifting her head from Thompson's shoulder.

"The night-jar," said Thompson, kissing her.

Her head fell back into its place. Caught up to him, held up off her own tired feet by his strong arm, she leaned happily against him, smiling. He could just make her face out, pale in the darkness, so sweet, so near. He stroked the curve of her cheek with his finger.

"Bessy, darling," he said, moved to a passion of protectiveness. "I'll never hurt you. I'll never do anything to harm you. You're too good. I'd never make you ashamed or have to hang your head about me. I've been wild enough, I daresay. I've believed in having a good time. But you see how I've got to pay. I can't have you, I can't marry you—but I love you and I mean to treat you straight. I'll never hurt you, Bessy."

She lifted her lips to his. She loved him, and if she could go on loving him without the fear of doing wrong, how wonderful it would be! She was filled with trust and happiness. She seized his strong rough hand and pressed her lips to it.

"Don't do that," said Thompson, shocked.

" I shall," said Bessy, kissing his hand again and holding it with both her own hands to her breast.

" Oh, Bessy."

Hard though it was, he determined to put his good resolutions for the protection of Bessy into immediate practice.

" You must go in," he said firmly. " You've been out long enough. We don't want any talk. Kiss me just once more."

He carried her through the brambles and took her to the gate. With more promises and kisses, they parted, and Bessy sped across the field like a shadow.

Thompson was left at the gate. And now that he was alone, bereft of Bessy, his previous anger and hatred flowed back upon him. He had to go back to the house where Bertha was. He looked towards it, and a glimmer of light shining high told him she had gone up to bed. He swore softly. If only there was somewhere else he could go ! But his old room over the stables was locked up, the pavilion was locked up. There was only the wood or the field, and he dared not lie down there. There was a drenching dew and he could not risk being stiff for the match to-morrow. He would have to go back to the house in the morning, in any case, he told himself. To shave. The necessity of having to lie down to sleep, of having to shave, irked him. A man kidded himself that he was free, but he was nothing of the sort. He was bound—bound by things like shaving and beds.

Well, he'd have to go back. He'd sleep on the couch in the parlour. He had been angry with Bertha for buying such an expensive upholstered three-piece suite from the city, but it was going to come in useful after all. To-morrow he'd tell her to get the house divided up so that he could eat and sleep by himself. He'd live in the house for the time being, but he'd make it plain that he was living in it for his own convenience.

Bertha heard him come in. She had been just about to give up hope and blow out the light when she heard his step on the path. She held the candle in her hand, and the looking-glass mirrored the change in her face from pinched anxiety to triumph. Her black eyes slanted upwards in a smile.

' He's come back,' she thought.

She waited. He did not come upstairs. She heard him shut himself into the parlour and guessed what he intended to do. She smiled again, with scorn that he should think he could punish her.

" As if it matters to me," she said, blowing out the light.

CHAPTER XV

LYING in her bed, Christine waited for Penelope to stop talking. The sisters had always talked before going to sleep ; most nights they fell asleep talking. But these last nights, Christine had come to think it was a dreadful habit. She had waited with feverish impatience for Penelope to stop. To-night, the waiting seemed longer than ever.

This was the last night that Nicholas Ashwell would spend at Saunby. To-morrow morning he would go. He would be gone and they had not said anything to each other. They had hardly been alone together for more than five minutes at a time and that was her fault. Whenever she had seen him approaching, she had escaped. Whenever she had found herself actually with him, she had called Penelope or pretended that she must go. It wasn't coyness that made her behave like this ; it was more like cowardice. Whatever it was, she was ashamed of it.

She wrenched her mind from the painful consideration of her behaviour to listen to Penelope. But Penelope had paused, and in the silence the tick of the nursery clock made itself heard and the sound of the waterfall from the garden below. Night in the room was tranquil, with the dim familiar shapes of furniture and her sister's voice running idly on again now. Only Christine was different, torn out of it all.

" Here—are you asleep or something ? " Penelope inquired.

" Nearly," murmured Christine.

" Oh, well," yawned Penelope. " I'm pretty sleepy myself. Night-night."

" Good night," said Christine, feeling guilty.

She waited, taut, to see if Penelope would break out again. But the silence continued and Christine's thoughts stole pleasurably, painfully back ; back to all that had happened since she had first met his eyes in the billiard-room.

As soon as she looked into her memory, it was all there. The room, the men, the white clothes, the salad with the tomato-quarters showing as red as ever, Bertha and Bessy passing to and fro, Thompson looking queer, and she herself leaning against the wall— carelessly, with no idea what was going to happen within the next minute. And then it happened. She saw him and he saw her and that was the beginning.

Her memory presented her with another scene, intact again. The heat quivering over the cricket ground, herself on the narrow bench watching him bat. Seventy-three he had scored. She had applauded him when he came in to the pavilion and the next moment he arrived on the bench beside her.

" Oh," she said, and smiled at him. Then she turned her head and clasped the edges of her big straw hat together under her chin. It looked like a gesture that meant nothing, but it was done to hide the blush she felt coming into her cheeks. This blushing, she had thought furiously. It spoils everything.

Moreover, she could think of nothing to say. Nothing. ' I knew it would come to this,' she said to herself. ' Pen and I haven't been about enough. We don't know what to talk about. I want to talk, but I can't think of *anything*,' she thought wildly.

When she did think of something to say, how stupid it was ! Far better to have kept quiet.

" Who's going in now ? " she had asked him.

" Thompson," he replied.

" Oh, of course."

Fancy not knowing Thompson ! He must have thought she was half-witted or short-sighted. Short sight was almost as bad, in her opinion, as mental deficiency. She was at an age when no physical imperfection can be tolerated. Things like spectacles and false teeth appalled her ; she could hardly think how people who had to have them could bear to go on living.

The conversation had, however, gone better ; it had improved.

" There's Thompson out for five," exclaimed Nicholas. " Oh, that's bad. That's a back-set for us. What's the matter with Thompson ? " he asked, turning a corrugated brow towards her. " Everybody's saying how he's gone off this season."

" Oh ? "

Christine was concerned. She liked Thompson. Thompson was part of Saunby and anything that affected him affected them all. She didn't like to hear that people were saying Thompson had gone off. She looked in anxiety at poor Thompson carrying in his bat and looking sick with himself.

" You know," she said, turning impulsively to Nicholas so that her big hat covered both him and her like an umbrella, " I wonder if he's happy with Bertha ? He went off suddenly and got married to her. She's a sharp, bitter kind of a girl, and perhaps they don't get on. But you wouldn't think that would affect his play, would you ? "

" It might," said Nicholas.

Under the hat he was so near. His eyes looked into hers. They talked about Thompson, but their eyes had nothing to do with their words. They looked deep, searching each other out.

" Ashwell ! "

They started and Christine turned her head so quickly to the voice that her hat-brim grazed Nicholas's cheek. It was the Major calling from the pavilion, and Nicholas had to go. For the space of half a minute, Christine remained where she was. Then she got up and hurried away to the house.

That was what she had been doing ever since. Hurrying away. And why? Since she wanted so much to stay? She seemed to herself to have behaved idiotically the whole time. She was learning things about herself she had not known before. She had thought she was a calm, cool girl, but now it seemed that she was nothing of the sort.

And to-night she had given the worst sample of idiocy possible even to her. In the afternoon, he had asked her to go to the pavilion with him after dinner to collect his things. But in case he hadn't really been asking her, or in case he hadn't meant it, or in case he should think she was attaching any importance to going to the pavilion with him, she had taken Penelope with her. They had stood about in the pavilion for a few moments ; then he collected his things and they all walked back to the house together. Under the porch, she and Penelope shook hands with him and said good-bye.

" Because," said Christine, " we may not see you in the morning."

She had actually said that, though what possessed her to say it, she didn't know.

He looked strangely at her, she thought, when she took his hand.

' But perhaps he didn't,' she said to herself. ' Perhaps I'm only imagining that.'

That was the worst of it all. Everything had to be examined now and interpreted ; and she could never be sure if she got the interpretation right. She had never had to pay such attention to her own behaviour or anyone else's before. She had left her world of calm certainty for confusion, and whenever she was alone, her mind worried at its new problems without solving them.

" Oh, dear," she sighed, letting herself go now that Penelope was sound asleep.

" I can't stop in bed," she said, throwing back the covers.

She went to the wide-open windows, over which the curtains were never drawn at night. Moonlight lay like snow over Saunby. The scene was still, lovely, dreamlike. But it was not what Christine wanted to see.

She wandered into the nursery and stood at the windows there. Another scene as lovely lay before her, but she turned from that, too.

At last she gave in and did what she had been wanting to do all the time. She opened the outer door and went on to the landing. She leaned over the banister-rail and looked down into the black pit of the staircase. He was down there. But to-morrow he would be gone. She would probably never see him again.

' He might come next year,' she told herself. But in her youth next year was almost the same as never to her.

She sighed and her sigh drifted down the hollow stairs. The darkness and silence forced themselves upon her consciousness. In the night and the silence the house felt old ; it smelled old. It was as if the past put out its cold hand and touched her. Christine shivered. What if all the people who have lived and died in this house could come together now and stand on these stairs, she thought. Peering down, she could almost see them thronging there, pale faces turned up towards her. 'And some day I shall be among them,' she thought. She turned and ran into the nursery with a fluttering nightgown. She shut the door on the ghosts and took a flying leap into bed.

'Besides, he's asleep,' she said to herself. He must be tired after the match, peacefully tired as she was when she and Penelope followed the hounds on foot. He was asleep and not thinking about her. She must sleep and not think about him. She must be prouder.

§

But she was wrong. Nicholas was not asleep. He was not even in bed. Islanded in a chintz armchair on a sea of blue carpet, burning the electric light for a length of time that would have considerably upset his host, Nicholas was thinking.

At first his thoughts had been only of Christine. Why hadn't she allowed him to see her alone on this last night? Why had she brought her sister to the pavilion? Was she being deliberately cruel, or was it that she didn't *like* him? He was afraid that it must be that she didn't like him. And yet at times he thought she did.

'But I may be imagining that,' he thought.

He might be imagining it, because he wanted to think it was so. Her behaviour, he thought, trying to make himself get at the truth, had been consistent the whole time. She had avoided him. There was no getting away from it ; she had avoided him. And on this last night, their last chance of being alone together, she'd brought her sister with her to their pre-arranged meeting at the pavilion.

Well, he must accept it. He must take his medicine.

Nobody had said anything about his coming back to Saunby. He would probably never see her again.

" And it's just as well for her," he said bitterly.

His thoughts passed to a review of himself. He looked at himself as he imagined she would look at him and was ashamed.

He saw a young man, now the only son, living with his prosperous parents in a large red-brick villa on the front at Mansbridge-on-Sea. Looked at from Saunby, Mansbridge seemed very new, hard and glaring, with its blocks of hotels and villas cut into sections by asphalt pavements.

Mansbridge was quite flat and bare. You had to go far inland to come to a tree. To make up for this deficiency in incidence and natural vegetation, the corporation had constructed gardens on the front, where residents and visitors could make a little variety for themselves by climbing up one side of the cement hills and going down the other and twisting and turning along the cement paths and being surprised, if they had not done it too often, at coming out where they started from. On gala nights, these gardens were illuminated by red and green lights cunningly placed to show cement elves fishing under the cement bridges.

The sea at Mansbridge came very thinly in over miles of sand and went thinly out again. But the air was good.

Nicholas thought he would have preferred Christine to see his former home at Birchley ; the old begrimed house standing above the valley where the Ashwell mills used to belch thick plumy smoke all the week long. There had been some meaning in Birchley, thought Nicholas ; there was none in Mansbridge. But it was at the very gate of the Birchley house that Rupert had been killed on his motor-cycle and no one passed through it without remembering that.

176

Also when the mills were sold and afterwards closed, Birchley became too depressing to live in. The Ashwells, even Sir James who kept asking everybody, including himself, what else he could have done, the Ashwells had not enjoyed seeing their former mill-hands standing at the corners of the streets, idle and increasingly desperate. They had not enjoyed seeing tight-lipped women and children with pinched faces. They knew many of these families intimately, the Arkwrights, the Greenhalghs, the Steads, the Blackledges, and it wrung their hearts to see them sink.

But when you couldn't do anything to mend matters, said Sir James, better get out. He gave a huge lump sum to the Birchley relief fund and removed his family to Mansbridge.

Nicholas hated this desertion of Birchley.

"You and your friends," he said to his father with youthful scorn. "You've thought of yourself as Captains of Industry. But as soon as the ship shows signs of sinking, you behave like rats."

"Don't talk like that to me, sir," shouted Sir James. "And don't be such a fool. And rats show sense. What good does it do the ship or anybody else if the rats go down with it? Does it save the ship? Answer me that? And where'd you and your mother be without my money? You can't even earn your own living."

"That's your fault," said Nicholas, white with anger. It was like his father to taunt him with that. "You should have let me go when I wanted to. I'd have been earning my living now all right, instead of having to come to you for every penny."

Every time he had a row with his father, Nicholas brought up his grievance that he had not been allowed to go to Canada or Australia or South Africa when he left school. He longed for a free, open-air life, but when Rupert was killed he had to take his place in the mills and at home.

When he went to the mills his father pointed out that he was worth nothing as an employee and could be paid nothing until he was worth something. He said he would pay Nicholas's bills as before and give him pocket-money. As this pocket-money was a considerable advance on that he had received as a schoolboy, Nicholas was satisfied. For the time being. He gradually became very dissatisfied, but before he could make any headway in his struggle for a salary, the mills were sold and the family moved to Mansbridge.

Nicholas again broached the subject of his going to the colonies, but his parents were so distressed, he gave it up again. He did not bargain then with his father as he might have done, because he would not take advantage of his father's distress. Sir James, however, had no such scruples. He kept his son dependent upon him and taunted him, in moments of anger, with his dependence.

Nicholas tried, surreptitiously, to get a job. He tried surreptitiously because he would not use his father's influence. He was sensitive about applying for work as the son of a man who had turned hundreds of men and women out of employment. But cotton was the only job he knew. He discovered, to his chagrin, that outside cotton he was practically unemployable.

He tried to turn his prowess at cricket to account. He had captained his school eleven with such distinction that his head master, when Nicholas came to leave, said with some emotion that he hoped to see him captain England. He was chosen to play in the minor counties competition, he was a member of the Free Foresters, he was from time to time considered for the county first eleven, but he found he could turn his cricket to no practical purpose. He should have been a Blue, they told him, if he wanted to become a master in a Preparatory School. And to come, in his opinion, from the sublime to the ridiculous, he should have passed School Certificate. School Certificate! He could hardly believe his ears. He had hardly heard of the thing. As captain of the school eleven, he had not concerned himself with swotting for an *exam*. But here it was, cropping up now to keep him from getting even the smallest kind of job. He felt resentment against those who had been in charge of him because they hadn't seen to it that he was better equipped for the economic fight.

He saw, as time went on, that his friends, whose families had mostly been in cotton too, were in much worse case than he was. They were doing work that he could not have stood for a single day, or so he told himself. They were travelling in things like sardines and flour and neon signs. Or they were trying to run poultry farms or inns, or they walked the floors of ladies' stores, handling stays and stockings; or else they had no jobs at all and avoided Nicholas in the streets of Manchester, whither he often went to the first night of a revue or to dine at the Midland Hotel by way of a change.

Compared with his friends, Nicholas began to think himself rather lucky than otherwise. He decided to ' hang on for a bit ' until things improved. If they ever did. There would probably be a war before long and then he, with the rest of his generation, would be employable again; as soldiers. When most of them were killed off, competition for jobs would be lessened, he thought cynically. The uncertainty of the times affected Nicholas adversely. He had a secret feeling that nothing was worth doing, because nothing would last. He felt he might as well have a good time while he could, because to-morrow, or the day after, the good times would be over.

He drifted from one cricket season to another and filled in the winter by playing golf. There was an excellent course at Mansbridge and he fell in with a set of people who also believed in having a good time. Their good time consisted in getting together at the club-house, playing golf on fine days and poker on wet, having food together at intervals and drinks together most of the time. When they were tired of the club, and they were apt to tire suddenly, they got into cars and went in a body to the hotel in favour at the moment.

"Let's go," somebody would say, and by common consent they got up and went to the Splendide Hotel, if it was the Splendide they were affecting at the time. They would frequent the Splendide every night for a fortnight and then change abruptly to the Grand.

From time to time someone would discover a new place for them to go to ; an inn on the moors or in a village. The first time they came, the landlord would be astonished at the descent of so many new, lively, and obviously rich clients. When they came a second, third, fourth, fifth time, he began to think his fortune was made. But before he could complete the improvements he had inaugurated for their entertainment, they had wavered off, like bees in swarm, and clustered on some other inn somewhere else.

Nicholas went about with these people and did as they did. At times he was consumed with boredom ; but so were they, and when they had told each other about it, they felt better.

Nicholas's chief confidante was Cicely Hoyle, a smart, rather hardbitten young woman a year or two older than himself. Cicely drove a long ball, played a rash game of poker, and on wet afternoons drank as much as any man there without turning a hair. She was the type of girl who looks best in a vivid sweater and a coat and skirt. Cicely hardly ever took her coat off, but hardly ever wore a hat on curls dark by nature but bleached by fair art. She had a hard, bright, nervous attraction, and Nicholas had spent some week-ends with her at one stage in their acquaintance. If he had been charged, he would have said that it was nobody's business but theirs, that they weren't doing anybody any harm. But he had a misgiving that the week-ends had been a mistake. He didn't know why. It wasn't that they were *wrong*, but that they were meaningless and preferably forgotten.

Cicely had given him to understand that she felt the same about them. He was relieved and grateful and admired her the more for it. Women were always supposed to make such a fuss when they found you didn't love them, but Cicely made no fuss, and he thought of her as a very good sport.

In his summing-up under the Major's electric light, Nicholas hardly included Cicely. He hardly thought about her. He was much more concerned with his dependence upon his father.

Nobody would believe him, he thought, if he disclosed the fact that at twenty-five years of age he had to go to his father for everything he wanted. Not that he didn't get what he wanted. He did ; and more. But he had to ask for it and his father had to know what it was.

The silk dressing-gown worn by Nicholas at this moment, the ivory brushes on the dressing-table, the leather cases in the corner of the room, could not have been matched by the dressing-gown, brushes or cases of any other guest in the house. Nicholas was provided with the best of everything by his father. Sir James would only tolerate the best. " Only the Best," materially speaking, of course, could have been the motto for the family crest Sir James was always hankering after.

Nicholas's mother, a woman of simple tastes, had diamonds and furs heaped upon her by her husband. Yet she had hardly a penny-piece in her pocket and, like Nicholas, no banking account.

Their situation was incredible. People simply wouldn't believe it if they were told, thought Nicholas. But they wouldn't be told. Mother and son kept this idiosyncrasy of Sir James's as dark as if it had been a vice. They were ashamed of it and deeply embarrassed by it. But they could not move him. He would keep his hands on the money ; he would give to them, either to keep them helpless, or to let himself feel benevolent, they didn't know which it was. Either way it irked them. But they could do nothing to change him. Sarah sighed and put up with him. Nicholas rebelled, rowed, but gave in. He gave in from disgust, affection, amusement, but he gave in.

Now, he decided, getting out of the chintz chair, he would give in no longer. He would go home, have it out once and for all with his father, insist on a loan and go to the colonies.

Half-way to the door to turn off the light, he paused. He couldn't go to the colonies. If he did, he would never see Christine again. His situation was now worse than ever.

Suppose he managed, it seemed impossible, but suppose he did manage to get a job of some kind, of any kind, who was going to pay him enough to enable him to marry Christine ? It would be years before he was in a position to propose to her, and in the meantime someone else would get her. Someone would certainly come to Saunby and fall in love with her. Who could help it ?

He stood sunk in gloom. After a time, he turned

out the light and carefully opened his door. To-night they were under the same roof. To-morrow they would be miles apart. If only he could speak to her. Explain. She was up there. Only a stair divided them, but it might have been Everest so impossible was it of ascent. Nicholas yearned towards her in the darkness.

The closing of a door somewhere in the house alarmed him and sent him back into his room. He couldn't be found hanging about on the landing, he told himself.

There was nothing for it but to give up and go to bed.

And the next morning, though neither he nor Christine could believe it would really happen, he had to go. He got into his car, and Christine, again with Penelope, stood on the steps to see him off.

" Good-bye," called Penelope cheerfully.

" Good-bye," called Christine rather wildly.

Nicholas raised a hand, smiled a queer tight-lipped smile and drove off very fast in a cloud of reddish dust. The roar of the car diminished up the drive and died away.

" Now," said Christine brightly, " what shall we do ? "

She was very bright to deceive Penelope. She must deceive everybody, even herself, and never show that she loved a man who had gone away without saying a single word about coming back.

CHAPTER XVI

THE Major watched the last guest go with regret, Anthea with relief. Thank heaven, she thought. Thank heaven the house was clear of strange men. Thank heaven she would be able to get to her bath in the mornings, without having to stand indefinitely with her door in her hand, peering through the crack while bulky figures passed to and from the bathroom, taking the precedence hospitality allowed them. Thank heaven she could climb the stairs as slowly as she pleased without having to put on speed because some man waited politely at the top. Thank heaven she needn't bother any more about their food, and above all thank heaven the cost of their entertainment had come to an end. The bills would now begin to come in and would be added to the bills in Francis's desk.

Anthea knew now about these bills. During the cricket fortnight the Major's room across the hall was mostly empty, and one afternoon when Anthea wanted some keys she went to his desk herself in search of them. She did not find the keys, but she found the bills. She meant to be no more than a moment in the room, but she spent the afternoon there, going through the bills, feeling nervous and guilty, starting at every sound.

She read the entreatments written upon them :

" A cheque will oblige." " It is feared you have overlooked this account." " We respectfully beg to draw your attention to the fact that this account is twelve months overdue." " As this was a cut price, immediate payment would much oblige."

She totalled the amounts. Francis owed within a few shillings of five hundred pounds to such various creditors as grocers (fifty-nine pounds to grocers), bakers, butchers, shoe-repairers (seven pounds to a small cobbler), his tailor (two hundred pounds to his tailor), coal-merchants, wine-merchants. The item that made Anthea most indignant was a bill for nine pounds for petrol from a little man who kept two pumps along the main road not far from the Priory gates. That was altogether too bad, she thought.

There was a demand notice for payment of income tax, a threat to cut off the telephone. Heaven alone knew what he owed besides, for none of the estate accounts were here.

Anthea closed the desk and crept away appalled.

To owe so much and yet to keep on spending so lavishly and unnecessarily on cricket and the entertainment of his friends ! It was madness. Anthea was extremely disturbed by this revelation of her husband's unpractical, or careless, nature. She had married him with the blind trustfulness of a woman in love. He would look after her, she felt. But now she knew that he would not. Not he. He had no thought of looking after her. Saunby was heavily mortgaged and she didn't think Francis was even insured. He was considerably older than she was and in the ordinary course of nature she would outlive him by many years. Her child would outlive him by many more. But he had no thought of providing for them. His indifference to what happened to them was the measure of his feeling for them. He simply couldn't care about them at all, Anthea concluded.

While his guests were in the house, Anthea saw her husband only in their bedroom. She watched him moving about it, pleasantly preoccupied. He was thinking about what had happened or what was going to happen during the day, but she was nursing her resentment, looking at him deeply, wondering at him.

She had forgotten that she had once been so in love that when he mentioned casually that he was hard up, had always been hard up and would always be hard up, she assured him with fervour that money didn't matter at all so long as they had each other. If he was poor, then she would be poor too and never mind. And he must always spend his money just as he wished without thinking of her. She needed very, very little, she told him.

But all that was changed now. The baby had changed it. The baby must be provided for. Anthea's will and energy were now bent on securing provision for the baby. She saw that she would have to fight to do that. The baby's natural provider, his father, was going to be no good to him. It would all fall on Anthea. Silently she made herself resolute to do it. And she pushed her husband, although he was unaware of it, a little farther still out of her consideration.

This readjustment, however, made her feel lonely. She felt in need of support, of a friend, and her thoughts turned to Nurse Pye. She couldn't discuss money troubles with Nurse Pye, she warned herself as if she had almost thought of doing it, but a little of Nurse Pye's cheerful, common-sensical company would do her a world of good. She telephoned to Nurse Pye to ask her to come for lunch or tea.

Nurse Pye was on a case, but she said she would take a half-day as soon as possible and would drive out to Saunby for tea and be glad of the change. Anthea put down the telephone with a smile, feeling supported already. It was good to have Nurse Pye for a friend. Anthea was moving towards the greatest experience of her life, and Nurse Pye was the only one who would share it with her.

Strange, thought Anthea, that those closest to you should be the least in sympathy with you in the big moments of your life. Neither her husband nor her mother gave her any help at present. Mrs. Sumpton had never been any good in illness. She didn't like it ; she had no time for it ; it was too interruptive. She rushed in to see Anthea now and again between committees, expressed her satisfaction that all went well, said, " Send for me, of course, if you need me," and was driven off again, having done her duty.

It was people like Nurse Pye and Bessy, thought Anthea, who helped.

Bessy seemed quite to have got over her unfortunate love-affair.

' I knew she would,' thought Anthea complacently, glad to think that love did not endure, since it was almost unbearable.

Anthea did not ask Bessy if she had got over it. You couldn't ask Bessy such things. Bessy was simple, warm-hearted, generous, but she had a reserve nobody attempted to force. Anthea was glad Bessy was happy again, both for Bessy's sake and for her own. She wanted to make a cosy circle consisting of herself, Nurse Pye, Bessy and ultimately the baby. If Bessy had been as unhappy and restless as she once had been, the circle would have been threatened by a breach. As it was, Anthea was very content.

Summer seemed suddenly to end at Saunby. There had been a long drought and autumn was coming in thin and withered after the full-bosomed summer. The grass was like straw in the fields and the dry leaves rattled on the trees. The girls slid over the hard ground on the slippery soles of their shoes when they went for their walks.

Every other autumn, the girls had played at " Happy Days." For every leaf, a governess had once told them, that you catch betweeen the tree and the ground, you have a happy day. When the girls saw a leaf coming down, they shouted to each other and ran for all they were worth. But this year, only Penelope ran for the leaves. Christine said she couldn't be bothered. Secretly, with the despair of youth which can see no end to what it suffers, she thought that without Nicholas she would never have a happy day again. Penelope ran for the first few leaves, then gave it up. It was no fun without Christine. She walked, both sad and cross, beside her sister and let the leaves fall unheeded.

The weather turned cold and windy ; the leaves came off in droves and bowled down the avenue as noisily as if they had been stamped out of tin. The day Nurse Pye came to tea, Anthea ordered a fire in the drawing-room and one in the morning-room too.

When Christine and Penelope came to the drawing-room in search of tea, Anthea raised her chin to look at them over Nurse Pye's head.

" Is it anything you want ? " she asked.

" Tea," they said, standing in the doorway with surprise on their faces.

" In the morning-room," said Anthea.

Shortly afterwards Victoria came into the room but halted abruptly at the sight of Nurse Pye sitting where she herself always sat.

" There's a fire in the morning-room," said Anthea, lifting her chin again.

" I'm glad to hear it," said Victoria ambiguously.

" The girls are having tea there this . . ." Anthea was saying, but the door closed on Victoria before she could finish.

" She's always rather rude," Anthea explained, in

case Nurse Pye should think Victoria's rudeness was meant for her, as, of course, it was.

" Is she ? " asked Nurse Pye with interest. " What for ? "

" Oh, I think she resents my being here," said Anthea.

" I like that," commented Nurse Pye, passing her cup for more tea. " The boot should be on the other leg. It's generally the wife who objects to the sister-in-law being in the house, not the sister-in-law to the wife."

A look of surprise came into Anthea's face. She had never thought of objecting to Victoria. She had accepted her as part of Saunby.

" You don't seem to have thought of that," said Nurse Pye.

" No," admitted Anthea.

" Well," said Nurse Pye. " Fancy."

After tea, or as much of it as they could get—they did not like having tea with their aunt because she always ate everything—after tea, the girls went back to the nursery.

It was a melancholy kind of day, thought Christine, wandering from window to window, looking out at the woods resigned to winter, the sad quiet fields, the ungleaming water. And this was the most melancholy time of the day, when the light was going. An indeterminate time, a time between an ending and a beginning, like towards the end of a voyage when the ship is nearing the shore and you are waiting to land.

' Though no one is coming to meet you,' thought Christine.

That was what she felt like always now. That no one was coming to meet her.

Penelope had tried the switches, but no light resulted.

She put a record on the gramophone and the nursery was filled with the music of " Fingal's Cave."

" How lovely the sea is ! How lovely the sea is ! " sang Penelope.

Miss Rosewarne had told them this was what the music said.

Underneath her hair, Christine surreptitiously closed her ears with her fingers. She daren't stop the gramophone, though she felt it would drive her crazy. She always had to remember to be careful, so that Penelope should not ask her what was the matter with her.

The record came mercifully to an end, and the light came on.

" Thank goodness," said Christine, and reached for a book.

Penelope got out her sewing and sat down on the low rocking-chair. She rocked as she sewed, and hummed : " How lovely the sea is." Christine's eyes followed the print with determination, striving against the distraction of Penelope's rocking and humming. She felt the thought of Nicholas had worn a painful furrow in her brain, and her mind ran up and down in it like a trapped mouse. She held the book higher to shut Penelope out and frowned at it.

The door opened and in came Anthea with Nurse Pye. The girls stood up in surprise.

" Don't let us disturb you," said Anthea graciously. " I just want Nurse Pye to look at the nurseries while she is here."

Nurse Pye surveyed the room with the girls' eyes upon her, Penelope's aghast.

" It's a good room," admitted Nurse Pye. " Pity it's so high up. Of course, all this stuff will have to be cleared out," she said, indicating the furniture, the piles of books, the old doll's house, everything in the room. " It's not healthy. The carpet'll have to come up. I should have a good lino put down. What about the fire-place ? Chimney doesn't smoke, I hope ? "

Anthea turned to Penelope.

" No, I don't think so, does it ? "

Penelope couldn't speak ; she was dumb with indignation. Christine answered for her : " No, the chimney doesn't smoke."

Anthea and Nurse Pye went into the bedrooms.

" Our room . . . the cheek . . ." whispered Penelope furiously.

" Sh," warned Christine.

Anthea and Nurse Pye went in and out of the rooms, Nurse Pye like a Napoleon surveying the field of battle, Anthea an eager lieutenant at her heels.

" Well, that's what I should do," said Nurse Pye when they returned to the nursery. " Let's be up here. We'll be out of the way, we'll be self-contained and the baby can have a room to itself from birth, which is as it should be. I always like to start my babies in the right way. I'll be able to have a room to myself instead of having a bed in yours and that'll be better for both of us. Couldn't have been better arranged. Three rooms and a day nursery. It's like a little clinic on its own," said Nurse Pye with satisfaction. " Or will be when it's cleared out and cleaned up."

She threw another look round, smiled absently on the girls like a matron of a hospital on two probationers and left the room with Anthea.

" Well," Penelope burst out. " Looking over our things as if they were a lot of old rubbish ! Our things, our rooms where we've lived all our lives ! Why should we be turned out ? Saunby's ours. It's our home. Anthea's an outsider. Why can't the baby be born downstairs in her room ? Why does it have to be born up here ? I can't bear the idea of it being born up here. The whole thing makes me sick."

She looked sick as she spoke, and Christine was startled.

" But, Pen, this has always been the nursery, the children's part of the house," she said soothingly. "We shall have to give it up to the baby. It's only natural."

" Oh, *you* don't care," said Penelope bitterly. " You don't care about anything now. Not about me or anything. You're in love with that man. Don't think I don't know, because I know all right."

Christine recoiled. She pressed back against the wicker chair she sat in and stared at Penelope.

" Oh, Pen," she faltered, white herself now, exposed, defenceless. " I didn't think you knew. I didn't want anybody to know."

" Why didn't you tell me ? " said Penelope harshly. " Keeping secrets. You've never done that before. And what did you take me for ? Some kind of a fool ? It's you that's the fool. Falling in *love*," she said scornfully, walking to the table and flicking at a book. " A nice mess it's made of you. You do nothing but mope, and your hair's all out of curl. Good heavens, you look awful," she said, turning on her sister. " You look like the Lady of Shallot or some such idiot."

Christine spread the fingers of one hand over her face.

" Oh, don't," she said weakly, " I'm so miserable."

" It's your own fault," said Penelope.

" It isn't."

" Of course it's your own fault," repeated Penelope.

She stood at the table, flicking over the pages of the book. Christine huddled in the wicker chair, her fingers still over her face, trying not to let go, not to cry. But it was Penelope who burst into tears. She flung herself on her sister with such impetus that the wicker chair plunged backwards and Penelope had to right it, grimacing wildly through her tears to see to it.

" Oh, Christine, what did you go and fall in love for, spoiling everything ? " she sobbed. " You'll get married and leave me now."

" Oh, no, darling, I shan't." Christine put her arms round her, crying herself. " He'll never come back. He doesn't know. He's no idea."

" Of course he knows, you chump," wept Penelope, wetting her sister's collar with her tears.

" How could he know ? " asked Christine.

" Aw—it's written all over you," said Penelope with a revival of scorn.

" Oh dear . . . if he knows he went just the same." Christine dropped her head to Penelope's curls and wept anew. " I'm so ashamed," she said.

" So you ought to be," said Penelope.

Christine sat up abruptly and put Penelope aside.

" It's no good," she said with resolution. " He doesn't love me. I might as well face it. I must forget him and you must help me, Pen. Only it's so hard here. There doesn't seem to be anything to do."

" Nothing to do ? " echoed Penelope, looking up with a puzzled, tear-stained face from the hearthrug upon which she had subsided. " You've never said that before. That shows what falling in love does to you."

" Perhaps I'll get over it." Christine took her sister's hand and looked with smarting eyes into the fire.

" Perhaps you will. Perhaps it's a kind of illness," said Penelope hopefully. " Like measles."

" Perhaps it is," agreed Christine. " Perhaps it's something everybody has to go through."

"I didn't think much of him," Penelope remarked by and by. "He looked quite ordinary to me."

"Oh, darling . . ." Christine smiled.

"I wish he'd looked ordinary to me," she said, in a moment.

CHAPTER XVII

PENELOPE set to work briskly to cure her sister of love, and Christine submitted with docility, as eager to be cured as Penelope was to cure.

Remembering Christine's wounding complaint that there was nothing to do, Penelope presented one after another the things they had always done together and found pleasure in. Under the rather sergeant-major manner she now adopted, there was pathos in Penelope's anxiety and Christine felt it and tried hard to enjoy what she used to enjoy. A sadness entered for the first time into the sisters' affection for each other. They realized that life, if not now, then later, would separate them. Even if they remained side by side, they knew that life would separate them.

It was blackberry time, and the girls, though indifferent to what happened to them when picked, had always picked blackberries with enthusiasm. The best were to be found on the bushes behind Thompson's lodge and thither one morning Penelope conducted Christine with a command to pick and keep her mind off Nicholas Ashwell.

From her back-kitchen window, Bertha saw the girls at the bushes with their baskets and was angry. Those blackberries were as good as hers. They grew just outside her garden fence. She'd had her eye on them for weeks, waiting for them to ripen. She'd thought of gathering them yesterday, but she'd her washing to do. And now those girls were taking them. They didn't want them, either. What were blackberries to them?

"They might have the decency to leave them things to people as needs them," fumed Bertha. "But they're that greedy, they have to have everything. It's always the same, more they have, more they get. That's all my jam and jelly gone west now."

Bertha was a capable housewife. She and Thompson were as estranged as on the day he had found that she had duped him, but Bertha continued to keep the house spotless and to feed him well. She did this, not to conciliate him, but because she could do no other. It would have been just the same if he had not been there at all.

She worked to time, and though she was tempted to continue to peer at and hate the girls from the back-kitchen window, it was time to start her upstairs work and she must go.

She sent a last black look at them.

"That's right," she said. "Pick every bloomin' berry."

She went up to do the bedrooms, the one at the front where she slept and the one at the back where Thompson slept. When she came to do the back bedroom she could see the girls again and her anger increased the cold contempt she felt for her husband, who seemed to think that by keeping out of her bed he was punishing her.

'We'll see who wants to give up first,' thought Bertha.

She was the kind, without warmth or weakness, who could keep up such a situation for ever. It gave her a kind of fierce pleasure to go about her work, to keep the house as before and be hard and cold and never forget; never forget to keep silent, to show him that two could play at his game and that she could play it best.

As she was sweeping the boxed-in stairs, there was a knock at the back door. With an exclamation of irritation, she went down and found the girls there.

"Would you like these blackberries, Bertha?" inquired Penelope, holding out a full basket.

Bertha looked for a moment as if she was going to refuse them.

"Well—thanks," she said at last, unwillingly. Her anger was not abated by getting the blackberries in the end. The girls were acknowledging her right to them by giving them to her and she didn't see why she should have to thank them. They should have left them alone. She could have picked them herself.

She took the basket indoors and poured the berries into an earthenware bowl.

"You must excuse me not asking you in," she said coldly. "But my dinner wants seeing to."

She looked past Penelope at Christine, listless in the sun, waiting for her sister.

'She's going off in her looks,' thought Bertha with pleasure. She liked to think that these two young creatures would go off, would be diminished by time like everybody else.

"Good morning," said the girls, going away.

"Good morning," said Bertha, and shut her door.

"Funny," said Penelope musingly. "Some people seem to nurse a grievance all the time. You don't know what it is and you've nothing to do with it, but they include you in it and look at you with queer meanings in their eyes and make 'Good morning' sound like a curse. Bertha's like that, and that shop-girl in Powers the other day was the same. She hated me for wanting beige stockings instead of pink. Didn't she? D'you remember?"

There was no answer from Christine. Penelope looked sharply into her sister's absent face.

" Here ! " she said sternly.   " Are you moping about that man ? "

Christine looked guilty.

" I was thinking about him," she admitted.

" Well, don't," said Penelope.   " Come on, I'll race you across the field."

Christine ran obediently.

But it was all no good.   The cure wouldn't work. Christine gradually withdrew herself from it.   She covered her love from Penelope's brisk daily inspection. She wouldn't let it be seen.   Her reserve imposed itself at last upon Penelope, who was silenced and hurt. They talked no more about Nicholas, but Christine loved him and Penelope resented him as before.

They spent their time together as usual, but there was constraint between them.   Each suspected the other's thoughts.   Christine was sorry she was hurting Penelope, but she would not have her heart pried into. She kept going away by herself so that she could be miserable without being watched.

One afternoon she went alone into the elm avenue. It was a golden day and Saunby stood gilded as if with gold paint in a missal.   As if in a missal, the scene was most carefully and distinctly limned.   The west front peaked into a blank blue sky, the house alongside stood neat and complete with its rows of dormer windows in the roof, the whole enclosed by the old stone wall and set with pointed yews and layered cedars.   The little grove of crab-apple trees to the left of the house was burning bright with small fruit, but bare of leaves. Under each tree was a rosy circle of fallen apples. Each separate thing was beautified by the light ; each thing made a claim to notice and wonder, but Christine looked without interest.   Poets made out that everything seemed more beautiful when you were in love, but it wasn't true.   Everything was dull and boring.   Dull and boring, she repeated. Nothing outside her love for Nicholas was of the slightest importance to her.

She wandered down the avenue as far as the lodge-gates and looked at the scarecrow woman Johnny Spencer had moved into the chicken-field now to scare the hawks. The woman still walked with an umbrella in the crook of her arm and a dog at her feet. But she was a little diminished since the spring ; her skirts were less ample and the dog crouched lower in the grass. Christine observed her dully, remembering with what interest she had observed her once.

She went back up the avenue and sat down on the fallen tree. She stared across at Saunby. She just stared, letting herself slump into unhappiness, not attempting to rescue herself.

She sat there a long time. When she heard footsteps in the avenue behind her, she sunk her chin still farther into her cupped hands, refusing to concern herself with the passer-by. Probably Thompson going home, she thought.

She sat with her back presented to the avenue, waiting for the steps to pass. But they halted and Christine, with a pang of fear, knew that someone had come to stand behind her. She turned round.

She rose from the fallen tree, her movements slowed by extreme astonishment. She went pale and her eyes widened as if they could not believe what they saw. Slowly she straightened up, staring at Nicholas.

" Did I startle you ? " he said.

She tried to answer, but nothing would come. She moved round the tree towards him, but she was made clumsy by amazement and hit her foot. Nicholas caught her as she stumbled.

" Oh, Christine."

She knew at once that the separation had been as bad for him as for her. She knew he loved her.

They stood so long, close in each other's arms, silent, rapt, that the rabbits came out of the wood again and ate the grass in the avenue as if they were not there.

At last, Christine laughed and stretched her arms wide and the rabbits fled. She looked so gay and so lovely as she stood laughing and stretching, that Nicholas caught her to him again and they kissed again, but differently this time ; with sheer exhilaration.

They sat down on the tree. Nicholas provided his shoulder for Christine's head and his arm for her back.

" Darling," said Christine. " It's much more comfortable on this tree than when I sat on it alone."

Her face was so near, he could not resist it. He kissed her again.

" Now tell me, tell me," she said with excitement. " How did you get here ? Who told you where I was ? Why didn't you come before ? It's been such a long time. I'd given you up."

A piteous expression came into her face.

" Oh, darling . . ." said Nicholas.

They were so sorry for each other, so sorry for all they had been through. It seemed dreadful to them. They didn't know how they had borne it. And yet it seemed so wonderful that they should have suffered for each other.

Nicholas smoothed Christine's hair back behind her ears with tender hands.

She shook it out again and said, " Don't make me look a sight. I wouldn't like to look a sight to you."

" You could never look a sight," he said. " Without any exaggeration at all, Christine, you're the most beautiful girl I've ever seen."

" I feel like that about you," she said. " But it may have no foundation in fact at all. It's because we're in love."

" No," said Nicholas earnestly. " I'd say that of you in absolute cold blood."

" Would you ? "

" I would," he affirmed solemnly.

In his gravity, he looked very young. She had thought of him as a man, very grown-up ; but he looked a boy at this moment.

" How old are you ? I don't even know how old you are," she said.

" I'm twenty-five."

" Are you ? Are you five years older than me ? I suppose that's about right."

" It is. Everything's right."

They kissed with immense satisfaction in each other and resumed the questions and answers.

" I came by car. I set off at half-past seven this morning, but I had a puncture. Penelope told me where to find you. She didn't seem very pleased to see me. I came as soon as I could, Christine. Just as soon as I could. You see, it was like this."

With his cheek on her hair, he explained.

After leaving her, he had tried to get a job.

" Heavens, how I tried ! "

He didn't know whether she would have him if he asked her to marry him, but at least he must be in a position to ask her.

" Oh, are we going to be married ? " asked Christine, awestruck.

" Good heavens ! " cried Nicholas in alarm. " Don't you want to ? Aren't you serious about me ? "

" Of course I am," said Christine. " But I never thought about getting married. I mean, I hadn't got to that."

" But you'll marry me ? "

" Oh, I will."

" Heavens, what a fright you gave me ! "

They kissed rapturously.

" Fancy being married ! " said Christine.   " Go on."

She took his hand.   She laid it on one of hers and covered it with the other.   She was as much occupied in holding his hand as in listening to what he said.

" I couldn't get a job," he continued.   " Could I hell ! "

What nice strong language, she thought contentedly.

" All I could come within sight of was a miserable little job at four pounds a week, and how could I marry you on that ? "

" No," she said.   " I suppose it would be rather hard to live on that."

She didn't know anything about it.   She continued, undisturbed, to hold his hand in both her own.

" I tried everybody I knew," said Nicholas.   " Without any result whatsoever.   At last I got so desperate I went to my father.   That was yesterday."

" Only yesterday ? " said Christine.

" My father's very difficult," said Nicholas.   " You don't know.   I didn't expect any help from him, but I was wrong.   He's being marvellous about us, Christine.   I suppose it's because you're a Marwood of Saunby—the old chap's a bit of a snob, I warn you—but he's going to give us a very decent allowance, enough for us to be quite comfortable on.   He's going to buy us a house and all the furniture, which you're to choose."

" Oh, am I ? " cried Christine excitedly.   " It sounds like a fairy-tale.   It sounds too good to be true."

" But listen," warned Nicholas.   " He wants us to live near them.   He wants us to live at Mansbridge. Would you mind that ? "

" Oh, not at all," cried Christine.   " Of course I shan't mind."

She would have lived anywhere with Nicholas ; anywhere at all.

" He's going to set us up, while I'm looking round for a job," explained Nicholas. " I would much rather have got a job first and got the house and furniture myself, but I couldn't wait, darling. I must make sure of you. I must marry you. I'd accept any conditions, any at all, to let me marry you. You don't despise me for that, do you ? " he asked anxiously.

" Despise you ? " repeated Christine in amazement. " Darling, how could I ? Why should I despise you for wanting to marry me quickly ? "

" I'm so relieved," murmured Nicholas, burying his lips in her hair. " Now I've only your father to tackle," he said. " Though that scares me to death."

" Oh, you don't need to worry about that," Christine assured him. " He'll be simply delighted to get such a good bat into the family. He'll be overjoyed to think you'll play for his team every summer. Just say, ' Look here, I'll bat for you on condition I can marry your daughter,' and he'll say, ' Right you are,' straight off, and think he's got the best of the bargain."

They laughed and kissed again.

" Christine—I can't believe it," said Nicholas, suddenly serious. " Is it true that you love me ? " He looked with passionate intensity into her upturned face.

" It's true," she said gravely.

The sun had gone ; the evening was suddenly chill.

" What's the time ? " asked Christine, remembering that there was such a thing.

" Good gracious, we must go," she said, looking at his wrist-watch.

They hurried across the field, hand-in-hand.

" I think I'll get it over at once, seeing your father," said Nicholas nervously.

" I should. Then it won't hang over us," advised Christine. " I'll be waiting for you on the stairs."

" If it's all right, I must wire to my parents," said Nicholas as they hurried over the garden-paths. " I promised I would, and if it's all right to your family, they're going to come down by car."

" Oh, dear," said Christine apprehensively. " Suppose they don't approve of me ? "

" They'll love you. Who could help it ? " said Nicholas, snatching one more kiss before they went into the house. " Good-bye. I never went to the war, but going over the top must have been like this."

They parted. Nicholas crossed the hall to the Major's room and Christine ran half-way up the stairs, where she stood poised with her hand at her heart, her eyes on the hall. Penelope, leaning over the nursery banisters, looked down at her. Then, in tears, she turned away. It would never be the same now. Never the same again.

CHAPTER XVIII

IN the great car driven by Gibbs, the chauffeur,
Nicholas Ashwell's parents sped towards Saunby.
It was very comfortable in the car. Sir James sat at
the back with his wife, who had Peke in her lap.
They had cushions at their backs, footstools beneath
their feet and soft rugs over their knees. The windows were closed. Outside the car, the great moors
and fells, first of Lancashire, then of Derbyshire, rose
magnificent and bare in solitude.

Sir James, in conjunction with Gibbs, had plotted
out every detail of the journey. Since his retirement
from cotton manufacturing, he had turned his genius
for organization to such things as journeys and household affairs, carrying his interest in these last so far as
to get out of the car and go into shops to choose the
bacon and the cheese himself. He exasperated his
wife considerably, but she did not show it. She knew
it was necessary for him to have something to occupy
him and she therefore put up with interference in
matters she had managed with efficiency and without
aid for thirty years.

Sir James had decided that this journey must start
at eleven-thirty prompt and eleven-thirty prompt it
was when the car, wafted by the blowing tamarisks,
moved down the drive of Red Lodge, aptly named
because the brick of which it was built was really very
red indeed.

By starting at eleven-thirty and keeping up an

average of thirty-five miles an hour they would arrive at an inn known to Sir James and there they would halt and have a good lunch. Sir James liked good lunches and always arranged for them. After lunch, said Sir James, they would proceed comfortably and reach Saunby at four o'clock.

" That's about the correct time to arrive, eh, Mother ? "

" I should think so," said Sarah.

Sarah and James Ashwell, as they sat at the back of their car, could have been likened to a duck and a drake, or some other ornithological pair. He was the showy one ; she the sober-hued and quiet mate. She was in black with a plain hat and a plain face and sable furs ; he was in pale grey with spectacular white hair and white spats, and on the lapel of his coat a pink carnation in a little holder containing water to keep it fresh. Sarah thought he looked as if he were going to a wedding ; which was premature.

' But let him please himself,' she thought.

He would, anyway.

James was smoking a cigar, and a cigar in such confined space was rather overpowering. But Sarah told herself it would come to an end ; it would finish like everything else. James had similar cigars, his best, ready packed into two pocket cases to offer to the Major during his visit to Saunby. He was sure the Major would appreciate a good cigar, seeing that he probably couldn't afford them himself. Sir James looked forward to giving the Major a treat, poor beggar. Not that he despised the Major for not having any money. Far from it. Lack of money went in a most seemly way with an old name and an old family place, and Sir James was vicariously proud of all three. A marriage between Nicholas and Christine would be in every way satisfactory, since he,

James, would supply the money and the Major the breeding.

James was full of eager conjecture about the visit, about Saunby and Christine and the Major, but Sarah's attitude was that she would wait and see. She would not confess to James that she was nervous of meeting her prospective daughter-in-law. If she was one of the modern girls, like Cicely Hoyle for instance, Sarah knew she would be at a complete loss with her. She would not say to James, either, that she hoped the girl would make a good wife for Nicholas, that she would be a good influence in place of the many foolish, trivial influences with which Nicholas was, in his mother's opinion, beset. That golf club, thought his mother. Those scatter-brained friends of his who did nothing but sit in hotels, drinking. Even the cricket-playing, though healthy enough, she admitted, did not altogether meet with her approval. It made things too easy for Nicholas. People were too nice to him. His whole life was too easy. But that was largely James's fault. Sarah often felt bitter against James for his treatment of Nicholas. She was very fond of James, but he was not a wise man.

Peke was slipping from her lap. She lifted him back into place and kept her hand on his silky head.

When her husband had brought Peke home as a present for her, Sarah was not pleased. She had always thought Pekinese silly little creatures ; the kind of dog that went with rich idle women and men who wore carnations and white spats. She hoped the maids would take to Peke and keep him out of her way. But in no time at all she became extremely attached to the little animal. He was no ordinary Pekinese ; no blue bows or laps (except at a time like the present) for him. He liked to be out walking, and if nobody took him he went by himself. He raced over the asphalt pavements of Mansbridge like a miniature caparisoned horse, and when anything demanded his particular attention, such as a dog across the road, he stood on his hind legs, remaining bolt upright for half a minute at a time, considering the object with insolence. His mistress loved him, and his engaging ways served to distract, as nothing else could, her thoughts which were often heavy.

She had never recovered from Rupert's death, though nobody guessed it. Nobody guessed as she sat in the sun on the promenade, outwardly a placid, prosperous, middle-aged woman with a fancy dog at her feet, that she was living again through the horror of that moment when she had thrown open the front door at Birchley to see Rupert's body being carried by strange men towards her. One hand dragged over the gravel, and crying out, " His hand ! Mind his hand ! " she ran and lifted it up and knew that he was dead.

To this moment, Sarah Ashwell returned again and again. It was as if she had to endure it for a fixed time ; then like a nightmare it passed and released her and she could get up from the seat and move off, calling to Peke.

Rupert's death had implanted in his mother a deep fear of death, the death of others, not of her own, which seemed nothing. It made her demand almost nothing of her husband and her son but that they should go on living, that they should not die. After their shortest absence, she saw them come home with untold relief.

It made her more tolerant of their shortcomings, at least outwardly, than perhaps she should have been. If she had been more exacting, if she had shown them what she really thought, they might have been the better for it. A critic at the family board is not a bad thing, but James and Nicholas went, since Rupert's death, uncriticized by the woman who presided at theirs. When she was happy, she would tell them a thing or two for their own good, but mildly, and as if she had not much expectation of their improvement.

The car moved swiftly on its way, swallowing the miles. It began to climb; it climbed higher and higher with James and Sarah looking wonderingly out of the windows, looking down on the pattern of the fields below intersected by loose white walls and broken through everywhere by craggy white boulders. The skin of the earth was thin here over the rocks. The sheep grazing on the heights were not like the fat sheep of the south; they were lean and limber with wild light eyes and intelligence in their faces, developed in them because they had to use their wits in these high, precarious places. Sarah was exhilarated by the height and the bareness and the solitude. What a relief after the flat, crowded, sameness of Mansbridge!

The car climbed to its utmost height and there at the summit of a great hill was the chosen inn; a mock Tudor place with a man in dress-clothes standing at the door, looking out at the wild scene, or perhaps looking for custom. He had a napkin over his arm and at the sight of the approaching car, he whisked within.

"Here you are," said Gibbs, who as a north-countryman treated his employers with a friendly disrespect. "Up to the minute."

He got out and opened the car door, assisting Sarah to alight, but not bothering with James.

Sarah breathed the pure cold air with deep pleasure and would have lingered to look about her. But James was hungry and hurried her into the dining-room, which was as curtained, carpeted, bepalmed and full of sauce bottles as if it had been in the middle of Manchester. James rubbed his hands. This was what he liked.

They had their good lunch. Gibbs had his and stood ready with the rugs. Sarah would have liked, again, to walk about a little with Peke, but James said they must be off.

"Time we were going, Mother, if we're to keep to schedule."

'Whose schedule?' she thought. 'And if they don't know what time we're going to arrive, what does quarter of an hour either way matter?'

But she said nothing and got in.

They began to descend, to drop into the flat Midlands, which she, who loved hills, had to admit were surprisingly beautiful.

"Such trees," she murmured.

And the villages were so pretty, so different from the stern stone villages she was used to.

"Eh, Mother." When they were alone James often lapsed into Lancashire, though in company he kept up an accent that his wife secretly deplored as lah-di-dah. "Eh, Mother, love's a funny thing. Like the wind that bloweth where it listeth. It's blown our lad to this particular place after this particular girl, you see. Nobody else would do, although he's been all over England. And it blew me to you, from Bolton to Bacup. I'd no choice in the matter. First time I capped eyes on you, I was done for. You were a bonny lass, Sally. If this girl's half as sweet, she'll do."

She always took his compliments in the same fashion. They might have been insults the way she shut her eyes at them and said, "Don't talk silly." Only the pucker at the corners of her mouth showed that she really liked them.

James liked teasing her and laid his hand on hers sentimentally.

"Go on with you," she said, and shook it off.

"That there signpost," remarked Gibbs, with an indication of his head at the post he was rapidly leaving behind, "said 'Saunby.'"

James and Sarah were thrown into a fluster.

"Did it? We must be near."

Sarah powdered her nose discreetly and straightened her hat and her fur. She shook out Peke to make him fluff up and look his best. James adjusted his carnation, smoothed his hair, put his gloves on and got his hat ready.

A nervous flush appeared in Sarah's cheeks. She hoped Nicholas would be at the door to meet them. James looked very alert, not in the least nervous. He was much more used to meeting strangers than she was.

The car approached the gates. A woman came out of the lodge to open them.

"Is this Saunby Priory?"

It was. Sir James threw out half a crown and the car passed through.

"By Jove," said James, looking eagerly out of the windows. "There's a lot of land about here."

"It's a very big place," said Sarah apprehensively. "I don't know what she'll think of our house after this."

The car was getting them there too quickly. They did not feel ready to arrive.

"Not so fast, Gibbs," protested Sir James.

But they were there. The car swept round and brought them to the porch.

"By Jove, Mother," whispered Sir James, looking up at Saunby. "It's a very fine fassayde."

They had hardly alighted and were turning in

bewilderment among the maids and Thompson taking the baggage from the car when Nicholas appeared with Christine by the hand.

" Mother," he said.

Sarah hurried round the car towards them. Relief flooded her heart at the sight of Christine, smiling and shy.

' She'll do,' she thought with sudden happiness.

" Well," she said, shy herself but managing to take Christine's hand into both her own. " Well, dear ? "

Her eyes beamed the approval her tongue could not utter. James was more articulate ; too articulate in Nicholas's opinion.

" Well, well, well," he said, putting both hands on Christine's shoulders. " So this is the young lady ! By Jove, Nick, you knew what you were doing ! Dear me, I didn't expect anything like this."

He gave her cheek such a paternal pinch that it showed a white mark for several seconds. Nicholas was annoyed. He also felt like a crab bereft of its shell ; he felt wincing, vulnerable.

Major Marwood had appeared, waiting, cool, smiling, imperturbable as was his way, until people should become aware of his presence. They always did in the end and were apologetic, as he intended them to be.

" My dear sir," cried James, leaping at him. " Excuse me. I didn't see you. How are you ? A great occasion this, eh ? Allow me to present Lady Ashwell. My wife. You have a very fine place here, Major," said James, craning up at the West Front again. " A very fine place. Is it safe ? A lot of history behind this, I'll be bound. Christine must tell me all about it. I always had a weakness for history, hadn't I, Sarah ? "

The Major smiled and led them within, James making a great to-do of stamping his feet and striding to take as long steps as the long-legged Major. Sarah didn't know why James, on meeting new people, always made himself ridiculous. He wasn't ridiculous, really, at least only a little now and again, and later he would settle down and stop showing off and let his native quality appear. But at the beginning of an acquaintance it was always a little embarrassing for everybody, and she knew Nicholas would feel sensitive about it. For herself, the more James showed off the quieter she became.

'Dear me,' she thought on entering the hall. 'What a place this must be to turn out! It's like the Birchley Museum, where I used to take the boys on wet afternoons.'

Anthea came to greet them.

'Dear, dear,' thought Sarah again. 'Poor woman, she's near her time. She can't possibly want visitors just now.'

Anthea took Sarah upstairs, apologizing, but proudly, for being so short of breath.

"It is trying, isn't it?" said Sarah. "But never mind. It's worth it."

"Oh, I know," smiled Anthea, secure in her knowledge.

She left Sarah in her bedroom, and Bessy came in with cans of hot water.

Drying her hands, Sarah looked out of the windows and saw that James was out at the front of the house again, striding with the Major. He was talking hard, she could see. He was probably boasting. But she had decided long ago that a husband was not only for public occasions, he was for private life, and in private life James, apart from his idiosyncrasies about allowances and bank-books, was a good husband. With all his faults, he suited her and she loved him, and if he did behave a bit wrong with other people, what did it matter? She soothed herself thus and hoped Nicholas would have the sense to do the same.

For her part, she realized that she would have to keep an eye on her own behaviour. So many things astonished her already. This bedroom, for instance, and that hall. So full of old junk. And though there might be a piece or two here and there that was good, most of it was fit for nothing but the auctioneers and the dust-bin, in her opinion. But she must keep her opinion dark. She mustn't look round and she mustn't look surprised. She thought with some complacency of her own spotless, comfortable home replete with the newest labour-saving devices and the best of everything. 'Funny,' she thought, 'nobody has everything. I know I haven't got what they've got : this lovely old place and their looks and the way they speak, but they haven't got what I've got, either. I mean,' said Sarah, struggling to find out what it was she did mean, 'I mean that with all they've got, they seem to have *no idea*.'

She knew then what she meant, though perhaps nobody outside Lancashire would have known. Simply no idea, she thought compassionately, and replacing upon her damp fingers the diamond rings James liked her to wear, she went down to tea.

Tea was in the dining-room, which surprised her. At Mansbridge the drawing-room was considered the correct place for tea ; the drawing-room with embroidered napkins on the knee and the parlour-maid to hand round the toasted tea-cake, the many varieties of sandwich, the cakes bulging with cream and jam, the iced fancies so pretty in mauve and pink and pale yellow decorated with crystallized fruits and so on. But at Saunby they sat up to a very plain tea at the table, with Anthea presiding at the head. Just a large fruit cake and a sponge cake, Sarah noted, and a few plates of scones and some jam. The table looked half-spread to her. But she was very happy, because the second sight she now got of Christine reinforced her first impressions.

' So wholesome,' she thought gratefully.

Christine, across the table, would not have been pleased. No girl likes to be called wholesome ; she likes to be thought something much more interesting than that.

When her aunt came into the room, Christine held her breath. She was used to Victoria's rudeness ; it was part of her, like her habit of wearing a hat in the house. Christine had always felt that people accepted the rudeness with the hat though both might surprise them at first. But to-day she was apprehensive. She felt it really would matter if her aunt was rude to Sir James and Lady Ashwell ; it would be a breach of something more than manners. So she held her breath when Victoria was introduced.

Miraculously, Victoria was not rude at all. She was unusually genial. Eating heartily—Sarah was careful not to look surprised—Victoria told the listening Ashwells all about her art, and impressed them considerably.

" You must come and see my pictures after tea," she said firmly.

" We certainly must," agreed Sir James.

It was Penelope, after all, who gave Christine the most cause for anxiety. She arrived late, apologized, murmured quietly in response to introductions and thereafter took no part. She turned a cool appraising glance on the visitors from time to time, and though it was such a glance as Christine herself might once have given them, she was wounded now. Penelope sat at tea almost as if she were alone in the room, and when she had finished she got up and went away. Where to, wondered Christine. Somewhere alone. She felt a pang of sadness for her sister, but Nicholas, seeing her face change, took her hand under the table and the sadness fled before the strong joy she always felt at his touch.

Tea ended and the Marwoods and the Ashwells moved out of the dining-room. At the door Sir James fell back to Nicholas.

" These chairs," he said with an indication of his head towards the dozen Chippendales. " They're worth about eighty pounds apiece, you know."

This information was conveyed to Nicholas in an aside more apparent than real. Sir James, in his eagerness to display his recognition of a good thing when he saw it, was not at all averse to being over-heard. He was overheard, but he did not produce the effect he wished for. Nicholas gave him a deep scowling look and the others continued into the hall without a flicker on their faces.

" Come and see my pictures, Sir James," said Victoria blandly, and led the way to the stairs.

Sir James, conscious that Nicholas and Sarah were not pleased with him, followed her with alacrity.

Nicholas and Christine hung about in the hall. A curious embarrassment had fallen upon them. Nicholas's happiness had, in fact, been undermined by the arrival of his parents. They were his parents, he was very fond of them, he wanted them to see Christine, it was their right to come, but all the same the radiance had been dimmed by the sight of them. He had felt that life, now that he had Christine, was henceforward going to be new, splendid, different. But the sight of his parents brought him to earth ; they reminded him —although they were innocent and they couldn't help it—they reminded him that life would be very largely the same, the background, the life he and they had made for him would be the same and the old irritations would very probably continue. Nicholas looked and felt considerably dashed as he hung about the hall. He felt separated from Christine, and she, sensing his mood, felt separated from him. After the close, rapt communication of the last few days this was painful to them. They passionately wanted to be one, and the reminder that they were two chilled and depressed them.

Christine moved vaguely round the table, and from window to window, pulling up her checked skirt at the waist, pulling down her yellow jumper, restless, lost. Nicholas lit cigarettes and pressed them out again in the plant-pot that now held a huge mop-headed chrysanthemum. Their talk was unsatisfactory to both of them. Everything that Nicholas, albeit half-heartedly, proposed that they should do—a walk, ping-pong, pictures in the city—Christine made some objection to. Because he had held her off a little she, with feminine thoroughness, had gone farther away ; she was now almost unreachable.

Victoria reappeared on the staircase with Sir James. He turned off into the drawing-room, but Victoria continued through the hall.

As she was about to pass out at the other side she made an announcement.

" Sir James has bought two of my pictures," she said triumphantly.

Christine whipped round from the window.

" Oh, it's disgusting ! " she cried, screwing up her face and shutting her eyes as if she could not bear the back view of her aunt.

Nicholas pulled her into the billiard-room and they fell into each other's arms, laughing so hard that their teeth clashed tightly as they kissed. They laughed and laughed and then they mopped their eyes and went out into the garden, at peace with their relations and each other.

CHAPTER XIX

THE visit passed off very well. The weather was perfect and Saunby showed at its best, tranquil, mellow, seeming to smile on the activities of the little human beings who went about it.

Sir James enjoyed himself enormously. His days were spent in a glow of boastfulness and benevolence with the Major.

The two men got on well together. Each admired in the other what he himself had not. The Major had looks and breeding, James money and business acumen. There was therefore no competition between them. Neither knew anything of the world the other lived in, and though the Major was silent about his, James admired it perhaps all the more for that. He himself expatiated largely upon his own world and boasted happily about his deals and his friends. What characters his friends seemed when he told the Major about them ! He had hardly realized it himself until now.

When the talk turned upon their young people, the Major was silent perforce again. James enlarged upon all he was going to do for them, but the Major could not afford to do anything. So he kept quiet while James did the talking, and it was one of the most pleasurable experiences James had known to be listened to by and to make an impression upon this gentleman. That was how James thought of the Major and how he spoke of him to Sarah in their room at night.

" He's a gentleman," he said, making his tone extremely gentlemanly to say it.

While James was talking, the Major sometimes wondered if he should broach the subject of a marriage settlement. But he came to the conclusion that there was no need to. Sir James was very well off, Nicholas was his only son and would in due time be very well off too. In the meantime, Sir James was treating the young couple handsomely and the Major shrank from asking for more.

It was perhaps as well. In Sir James's world, marriage settlements were unheard of. Sir James and his kind married more romantically than that. A young man fell in love with a young woman, married her and provided for her and her children as best he could. They were so romantic in Sir James's world that they never faced the fact that love might die and marriages go wrong, and Sir James could not have borne such an idea now.

Also he liked to give of his own accord ; he did not like to be made to give. In such a case he was quite capable of refusing to give at all. This was his idiosyncrasy ; thus he treated his wife and son. Leave it to him, he told them, and he would always treat them generously. But let them try to pin him down to allowances and such and they would find themselves a sight worse off, that's all.

The Major and Sir James would not have seen eye to eye on the subject of marriage settlements, nor did they see eye to eye on another matter. Sir James was inclined to be apologetic and explanatory about the fact that Nicholas had no job, but the Major thought nothing of it. In his world young men otherwise well provided for frequently did no work at all ; some went into the Army for a few years, others occupied themselves with their fathers' estates, but many were entirely idle, and the fact that Nicholas did not work for his living did not seem anything out of the ordinary to the Major, who did not work for his.

The trace of wistfulness in the Major's manner as he listened to James's past, present and future financial deals went to James's head and made him boast. James knew he boasted. He knew he shouldn't, but he couldn't help himself. He boasted to his son and his wife, and when he had overdone it and felt, from the quietness of their manner and from his own internal misgivings, that he had made a fool of himself, he gave them a few pound notes by way of asking them to excuse him. But he could not do that to the Major, and though he told himself in the uneasy hour before sleep that he must really stop, he was at it as hard as ever the next day.

James's benevolent heart was touched by the Major's situation. It was obvious from the look of the whole place that he was in dire financial straits. James was touched too by the Major himself, by his very helplessness. He would have despised this helplessness in another man, but in the Major it only touched him.

" It's a damn shame," he said with indignation against he scarcely knew what, to Sarah as he disrobed at night. " By Jove, it's a damn shame that he has to let a place like this go to pieces because he has no money to keep it up. I sometimes feel I'll have to offer to lend to him. But I really mustn't," said James, bending to undo his sock suspenders and coming up red in the face. " I must not, because not only do I know that he'd never pay me back, I know he'd never even pay the interest. Mother, the cord's come out of my pyjama trousers," he said, helpless himself in this contingency.

" Give it to me," said Sarah, already in bed, " and pass me a safety-pin out of that pin-cushion."

She fixed the pin to the cord and began to push it through the hem, while James waited beside her in his under-pants, looking like an elderly boy.

"What I can't understand," said Sarah, who could always talk more freely to her men-folk when she was doing something for them. "What I can't understand is the fecklessness of these upper-class people when they've lost their money."

"Eh, Mother," said James. "You've got hold of the wrong end of the stick. They're feckless before they lose it, that's why they lose it. D'you think I'd let a place like this go if it was mine? Not I! I'd fight for it tooth and nail, by God I would."

"James," protested Sarah. "That's very strong language."

"Huh," said James. "It's nothing to what the Major uses."

"You're not the Major," said Sarah, handing him his trousers. "It doesn't suit you."

"Thank you," said James, taking them. "But I'd find a way, by Jove, I would."

"I'm sure you would," said Sarah, and she *was* sure.

At this word of praise, James began to swell a little, and as he brushed his teeth at the wash-hand stand, he boasted about what he would do if he were in the Major's place. He boasted and foamed with tooth-paste at the mouth while Sarah lay back on her pillows and thought of other things.

"They're very happy," she murmured.

"Who?" asked the surprised James. "The Major and his wife?"

"Oh, no," said Sarah. "I mean Nicholas and Christine. Oh, no, I should say that other was a marriage of convenience, but I should say it's going to turn out very inconvenient for him."

" Oh ! " said James with interest.

" Well, nobody might have had a baby before, the way she goes on," said Sarah : " You can see it means everything in the world to her and nothing to him. As far as I can see all his interests pull one way and hers another. There's bound to be trouble in a house when it's like that. Are you ever going to get to bed to-night, James ? You might be a society beauty the time it takes you."

The Major and Sir James got on well together, so did their wives. Anthea liked Sarah so much that she asked Nurse Pye out to meet her.

" I like you to see the people I see," confided Anthea, leading Nurse Pye by the arm from the baby car to the house. " So we can talk about them better afterwards."

Nurse Pye sent a smile upwards from under her winter mushroom as if to say you are a caution, and the friends went into the drawing-room together.

Here was another person Sarah could be comfortable with. She and Nurse Pye were both acquainted with Oldham and could discuss it, while Anthea sat smilingly by, delighted that Nurse Pye should have this pleasure.

Christine and Nicholas passed the windows. Anthea rose hastily and opened one to call out :

" Christine dear, Nurse Pye is here. Do bring Nicholas in and introduce him."

Nurse Pye must be included in everything.

The lovers, complaining to each other, nevertheless appeared before Nurse Pye, who suddenly, to Christine's surprise, appeared in quite a new light. She became almost coy with Nicholas. Not exactly coy, Christine amended, but as if she might say something like " My word, if you're not off " at any minute. But she didn't ; and Nicholas, taking Christine by the arm, said they were just going for a walk and so they escaped.

" When are they going to be married ? " asked Nurse Pye.

" Well," said Anthea, " that's what we must discuss."

Nicholas and Christine wanted to be married as soon as possible. Sir James was on their side, but Sarah thought it would be nice to wait until the Spring.

The deciding factor, however, as soon appeared from the conversation of Anthea and Nurse Pye, was the birth of Anthea's baby. Should the wedding take place before or after ? Before, decided Nurse Pye. Get it over, she said emphatically. Get the bustle out of the house. Let the wedding be in December. Anthea need not appear at all. It would have to be a quiet wedding in any case.

" You see, Lady Ashwell," said Nurse Pye, " Mrs. Marwood must be our first consideration."

Anthea sat smilingly by while Sarah agreed. When one has been of no consideration at all, it is pleasant to be thus spoken of.

" I'm entirely in Nurse Pye's hands," she said.

So Sarah was deputed to report that Nurse Pye thought the wedding ought to be in December.

" It doesn't give us much time to find a house and furnish it," demurred Sarah.

" You'll manage it," said Nurse Pye.

She could have managed it herself.

§

Christine and Nicholas were together ; Sir James and the Major ; Anthea and Sarah. Only Penelope was alone, and alone as she had never been before. Nicholas and Christine were very kind and always asked her to come with them. They stood before her hand-in-hand and said : " Do come, Penelope." But she made excuses and knew they were glad to go without her.

When the Ashwells went back to Mansbridge, Christine went with them to look for a house.

" I do hate leaving you, Pen," said Christine **at** parting.

" I'd better get used to it," said Penelope grimly.

CHAPTER XX

THE day after the Ashwells' departure, losing no time now that she once more had the house to herself, Anthea followed her husband into his room after breakfast. When she wanted to make him listen to her, she had to do this now. If she spoke to him about what he didn't want to hear in any other part of the house, he simply shook off the subject and walked away.

Once she had been able to say what she wanted to say in their bedroom. Curtain lectures are often the only ones a woman is allowed to give. A man can avoid his wife during the day, but he comes to bed at last and can be talked to. Small wonder that women take their opportunity ; but husbands must often dread retirement.

Since the departure of the cricketers, the Major had slept in his dressing-room. Anthea was sleeping badly and sometimes in desperation turned on the light and reached for a book. This disturbed her husband and gave him his excuse.

When Anthea opened the door of his room he was throwing the morning's harvest of bills into his desk.

" I'm busy," he called out arrestingly.

" I won't keep you a moment, Francis," said Anthea firmly. She knew he wasn't busy. She knew he hadn't anything to be busy with.

She advanced to where he sat at his desk and towered above him. Like a female figurehead of a ship, he thought. He felt dwarfed, diminished, and he didn't like having to look up to her from his desk. So he rose and overtopped her by several inches.

" What is it ? " he asked, from his height.

" I want to have the nurseries papered and painted, Francis," said Anthea. " And I want them done now before the bustle of Christine's wedding starts. There may not be time afterwards."

" Good God," said the Major, sinking to his chair again. " The nurseries ! As if I haven't enough expense to face with Christine's wedding coming off and your affair . . ."

Anthea flushed. That was like him, she thought resentfully.

" Without the nurseries," finished the Major. " What's wrong with the nurseries ? The girls have never complained. The nurseries have been like that for years."

" That's precisely why they must be done now," said Anthea. " Nurse Pye says——"

" For God's sake don't tell me what that woman says," interrupted the Major. " It's bad enough to keep seeing her about the place without being reminded of her when she isn't here. Let me enjoy her absence, please."

Anthea's dark eyes considered him.

" The nurseries must be done," she said patiently, but with determination.

" I tell you I can't afford it," cried the Major. " I can't afford anything more."

" How does the cost of painting and papering the nurseries compare with what you have spent on cricket this season ? " asked Anthea.

" Oh, hell," said the Major.

There was silence while he reached for a cigarette and lit it. The expression of his face, with his lids lowered to watch the flame, was one of great beauty. He was always as good to watch as a man in a play, thought Anthea suddenly.

He shook out the light and threw the match into his waste-paper basket.

"Get your nurseries done," he said in a voice of resignation. "I see you will give me no peace until I agree and peace I must have even at this price. And now may I repeat, my dear, that I am busy?"

"I'm going," said Anthea.

He got up to open the door for her.

"Nurse Pye *says*——" began Anthea, pausing beside him.

"Oh, for God's sake," implored the Major, irritable from defeat.

"Very well," said Anthea with dignity, passing out.

She had tried to tell him. She'd tried to break it to him. On his own head be it, if he wouldn't listen.

Anthea telephoned to the firm of painters recommended by Nurse Pye and asked them to send someone to estimate the cost of papering and painting the nurseries.

"Always get an estimate," Nurse Pye had said.

Anthea then informed Penelope that she must move out of the nursery.

Penelope moved out by walking out, letting Anthea throw away or otherwise dispose of whatever she wished. Penelope would keep nothing. Let it all go, she implied. What does it matter? Christine is going. She's leaving me here. What do I care what's left when she's gone?

She moved down into one of the great bedrooms where Christine's bed was put beside hers. "Just for the last few weeks," said Anthea.

From that time onwards there seemed to Penelope nowhere to sit at Saunby.

Anthea shut her eyes to Penelope's behaviour. She couldn't bother with it. It would be too much waste of precious energy to try to cajole Penelope into acceptance of a new life without Christine. She must look after herself. Besides, what had Penelope, or Christine either, done for her when she first came to Saunby?

Christine came back from Mansbridge, full of excitement.

'Changed already,' thought Penelope, making no allowance for the fact that her sister had plunged into a new world. To Penelope, Christine seemed woundingly full of herself and Nicholas and their plans.

She talked about them most of the day and far into the night, and where once Christine had wished Penelope would be quiet and leave her to herself, it was now Penelope who wished it. But Christine talked on, turning over her new experiences as much for her own enlightenment as Penelope's.

"Lady Ashwell is sweet. But she doesn't talk much and you can't tell what she is thinking, somehow. She gives in to Sir James far too much, and so does Nicholas. To tell you the truth, Pen, I find Sir James rather trying. But I suppose I shall get used to him. He's very kind. He's terribly, terribly kind. But you have to keep thanking him. Of course I *do* thank him," she assured Penelope earnestly. "He's giving us simply everything. But all the same I find perpetual gratitude kind of—I don't know quite what," she puzzled. "It makes me feel kind of false to be always thanking, doesn't it you?"

"I've never had to thank anybody, thank God," said Penelope. "So I don't know."

"And you see," Christine rattled on. "Because Sir James is giving us everything, we had to let him choose. He said I could choose, you know, but it didn't turn out like that. He kept taking us to Man-

chester to look at carpets and furniture and fire-grates
and things, but Nicholas doesn't know much about
that sort of thing, and I felt I couldn't argue with Sir
James when he was paying for everything. He doesn't
like argument, I could tell, and he's very decided in
his taste."

Christine paused to review with some misgiving the
choices of Sir James.

" Oh, well," she said at length. " It can't be helped.
I've got Nicholas.

" Mansbridge is a funny place," she observed.
" Flat and bare. No trees. It makes you feel you
haven't got any eye-lids to your eyes, somehow.

" Our house," she went on. " Nicholas's and my
house, number 19, The Drive, is *rather* like the house
you and I stayed in with Rosie at Hunsworth after
we'd had measles."

" Good Lord ! " exclaimed Penelope.

" Well, I'm warning you," said Christine. " But it
was all we could get, and all the houses in Mansbridge
seem to be the same. The sort of houses that can be
used for lodging-houses if the worst comes to the worst.
I expect the builders when they built them thought
of that.

" Of course, Red Lodge is very nice inside. Very
sumptuous. You sink into everything, carpets, chairs,
cushions, everything. I had one of those new beds
you see advertised. I bounced all night. But my bed
here feels like a sack of potatoes to me now. Funny
I couldn't get used to that, now I can't get used to
this !

" Oh, the food at Red Lodge, Pen. I longed for
you at meals. I wasn't very hungry myself somehow,
but I kept thinking how you would have enjoyed
everything. You never got a plain egg or plain fish
or plain anything. It was always covered with cream

or sauce or something. But I don't like cream in my tea. I used to have early morning tea which would have been very nice, but they only brought cream to put into it, so I couldn't drink it. I used to pour out a cup and pour it down the basin so they wouldn't know. Wasn't it lucky I had running water in my room? Of course they have running water in all the bedrooms. Nicholas and I are having it. I don't know what Lady Ashwell thought of our washing arrangements here."

" What's good enough for us," said Penelope firmly, " is certainly good enough for them."

" Oh, yes," said Christine, equably. " Still . . .

" Nicholas took me to his golf club," she resumed. " It was a wet day and it got rather stuffy and steamy and spirituous. I didn't like anybody much, but that was probably my fault. I don't play golf and poker, so I couldn't talk about them. I didn't like one girl at all. Cicely Hoyle. Her hair's fair on top and dark at the roots. Why *do* they have it like that? Do they think people have no eyes? She's like Bertha. I mean, she's one of those people with a grudge against you, you don't know why. She seemed to be full of insinuations I couldn't grasp. She laughed and sneered a lot, goodness knows why. Nicholas says she's very nice really. A very good sport, he said."

Christine fell silent.

" So on the whole," remarked Penelope with some satisfaction, " you weren't too pleased with your visit."

Christine looked at her in amazement.

" I was," she cried. " It was lovely."

" But you don't really like your house and Sir James chose everything, and you had to keep saying thank you, and you had cream in your tea, and you didn't like that girl," said Penelope.

" Oh, it didn't matter," said Christine dismissingly.
" I had Nicholas."

Christine made a trousseau list and read it out
to Penelope. Anthea was sitting with them in the
drawing-room. Since the nursery had been taken
from them, the girls could not get away from her as
before.

" One dozen pairs of silk stockings," Christine read
out. " Think of having a dozen new pairs of stockings
all at the same time! But do you think I'd better
even have a dozen and a half?" she inquired, looking
round her paper at Penelope. " I don't suppose I'll
be able to wear stockings darned at the heel like this
at Mansbridge."

She extended one slim foot to show the darn above
the back of her shoe.

" I think I'd better put a dozen and a half," she
said, licking her pencil.

" Christine," said Anthea, who had been making
up her mind for some time to speak.

The girls turned.

" I think you ought to remember, dear, that money
is rather restricted."

The girls looked at her.

" How do you mean?" asked Christine. " That
money is restricted? Is it any more restricted than
it ever was?"

" Yes," said Anthea. " It is. Or it's going to be.
We're going to be put to heavy expense. Perhaps
heavier even than we anticipate," she hinted with a
smile that made the girls wonder what on earth she
was smiling at. " After your wedding, there will be
Nurse Pye to pay for weeks. You can't get as good
a nurse as Nurse Pye for nothing, you know. I shall
want to keep her as long as possible, and she has very
kindly arranged to book no more cases until she sees

that I am going to be able to do without her. Then there will be the doctor . . ."

"Do you intend, then," said Penelope, "that Christine should have no trousseau?"

"Oh, no," said Anthea with some of her old haste to reassure. "Of course I don't. What I mean is, will she try to do with as little as possible. After all, she's marrying into a wealthy family. She'll be able to have everything she wants later, won't she?"

"What a hideous idea," said Christine.

Anthea blushed. Once she would have thought so herself.

"Come on, Pen," said Christine, stuffing her list into her skirt pocket. "Let's go out."

"She's terrified we should take anything from her precious child," said Penelope furiously outside the door. "Don't take any notice of her, Christine. You get what you can."

But Christine, from pride, determined to ask for as little as possible.

"I shall have to get my wedding-dress and my going-away suit and one evening dress from Madame Vere, but I shall make the rest," she declared.

She was very worried when she came to buy. Money went nowhere; nowhere at all. She spent a great deal of time figuring out items and costs on pieces of paper, and would get up in the night to look at her list to see if she could manage better some other way. She went into the city to finger *crêpe de Chine* and triple ninon and come away with flowered voile. Her trousseau would have seemed pitiful to the girl who sold her the stuffs behind the counter.

A measure of help came from an unexpected quarter. Guy sent her ten pounds for " trimmings." Christine gazed at the cheque as if she couldn't believe it. They had thought Guy never thought of them, but they had been wrong. A feeling of regret came into her heart. She and Penelope would have loved him if he had let them, but he had never come within their reach. He was being so kind now, though. He was coming to her wedding and he had sent her ten pounds. She wrote warmly to him, telling him that she was sorry they had seen so little of each other and would now, she supposed, see even less. " But I shall always remember how kind you have been to me," she finished, and the letter gave Guy a pang when he read it. He wished he had done more, before.

Victoria presented her wedding gift with a gesture of magnificence. Six large oil paintings. Christine groaned and giggled half the night after receiving them, and Penelope laughed with her, making it quite like old times.

Rosamund Hunter sent linen mats in different sizes embroidered innocently in daisies by herself.

" Typical," said Penelope. " Doesn't she know these things have gone out ? They're as out-of-date as she is. But I suppose they're something that wouldn't sell at a bazaar."

A fur coat arrived from Nicholas's mother.

" I am sending it in good time, dear," wrote Sarah in her old-fashioned Italian hand. " In case you should be thinking of buying one."

" No, I wasn't thinking of buying one," said Christine. " Seeing that I've about two pounds left. But oh, Penelope, isn't it lovely ? And what a multitude of sins it will cover. It won't matter *what* I wear under this. You know, I've had this coat on before. She took me into a very grand fur shop and a man brought this for me to try on. I thought she was looking at coats for herself."

" Well, it was very deep and decent of her," said Penelope.

In order to get married, even in the quietest way, there was, Christine found, a great deal to be done. Things never would get done in time, she groaned. But they did. Journeying backwards and forwards to the city, choosings, fittings, all were done. The sewing was finished except for one or two things Penelope promised to send after her. Everything was folded and packed. Christine came to her last day at Saunby. In the evening Nicholas and his parents and Guy and the other guests would arrive, and the next morning she would be married.

" I think I'll go round and say good-bye by myself," she said to Penelope.

She unloosed Rough and went her round. She went to stand in her favourite places. Under the chestnut tree, bare now and like a many-branched candlestick without candles. Under this tree she and Penelope had always found the best chestnuts. They peeled off the spiked cases, so fierce without and lined so soft within, and picked out with delighted fingers the smooth, highly polished nuts. They took them back to the nursery, saying to each other that you could make the most beautiful doll's furniture out of chestnuts if only you knew how.

She went into Lake Wood. She stood in the avenue and looked across to the grey gables and chimney-stacks of the house, with the towering West Front alongside, pierced with blue sky in place of windows. Lovely, lovely Saunby, she thought. Wherever I go, there'll never be anywhere so lovely.

If only you could have everything ; if only you could keep the best of the old when you pass on to the new ; keep Pen, keep Saunby and have Nicholas and the new life alone with him too.

She went to Top Farm to say good-bye to Mrs. Spencer.

'How quiet Johnny Spencer is nowadays,' she thought, not knowing that Johnny had twice seen Bessy with Thompson. The first time might have been an accident, he allowed, but not the second. He knew now why Bessy avoided him and would not come to the farm.

Christine stood to look at the scarecrow, the mock-woman walking still in the field under the wood. Time had touched her. She stooped as if she was old. She was thin, but she clasped her umbrella in the crook of her arm, kept the dog at her feet and braved the weather.

Christine made her way back up the elm avenue. The short cold day was ending. The rooks were tracking across the sky, making in small companies for Long Wood on the hill. There they would gather in incredible numbers and wheel above the tops of the trees, rising and falling, rising and falling with a great clamour, in some mysterious ritual before they settled to silence and the night.

'I don't want to go,' thought Christine, standing under the trees. 'I want to stay here, as I am.'

Nicholas was a stranger. A few months ago she had never heard of him, and now she was going away with him, throwing in her lot with his. What was love that it made you think you could live with a stranger? You ought to find out first, you ought to be sure.

She sat down at the roots of a tree, clasping her knees. Panic-stricken, she wished she could escape from to-morrow. She tried to look into the future. It held only Nicholas, and what if Nicholas should change or cease to love her?

She had to go back to the house in the end. There was nothing else for it. And there was Nicholas and the end of her fears. As soon as she saw him again, she knew everything would be all right. She smiled at him with such radiant trust that he in his turn felt afraid for a moment. Afraid in case he should ever fail her. Old uneasinesses rose to trouble him.

But soon there was no time for secret speculations. The bustle in the house increased. Guy arrived. They had hardly seen Guy at Saunby since his nursery days and knew little about him, but they all felt that he was an important person and that his opinion mattered. The rooms rang with his name as they called his attention first to this and then to that. As for him, he had left his interests behind in London and was prepared for this short time to take up theirs. He smiled kindly and listened to everything. Christine was glad when she saw that he approved of Nicholas.

Sir James and Lady Ashwell arrived, Sir James coming back like one familiar with Saunby, glad to be on such terms with such a house.

Two great-aunts from Scotland arrived. The Major had insisted that they should be invited, because some of the money he was always looking for might easily come from them.

"They probably won't come," he assured Anthea, but though they were not very urgently invited, they came. "A very quiet wedding . . ." Anthea had written. "Hardly worth while your coming all this way . . ." But they had come and Anthea dealt with them, not without some self-pity, some wondering what Nurse Pye would say if she saw her overdoing it like this, getting no rest.

All spent a restless evening, as if they were collected on a platform waiting to see a train out. Christine was glad to go to bed, and in spite of her excitement she fell asleep at once. It was morning, a fine, clear winter morning in no time, and in no time at all she found herself dressed in her wedding-gown, veiled,

237

holding her lilies, waiting at Saunby with her father to follow the others to the church. It was all like a dream, from which she awoke only when she was driving away from Saunby with Nicholas and turned to see Penelope standing apart from the others, grimacing to keep her tears back.

" Oh, Nicholas," she cried, stretching out her arm to the forlorn figure of her sister. " Penelope's crying."

" Oh, blow Penelope, darling," said Nicholas, driving very fast. " We can't think of Penelope now. Think of us."

Behind them, the group of guests and servants dissolved from the front of the house. As Bessy turned away, she looked at Thompson. ' *They* can be married,' her eyes said, and though he smiled rallyingly at her, she went heavily into the house.

As Guy got into his car to drive back to London, Penelope flew down the steps.

" Oh, Guy," she said, urgently, putting her head in at the window to him. " I don't want to stop here. I want to get away. Could I get work in London ? Do you know of anything I could do ? "

Guy looked at her in amazement, his hands on the wheel.

" Work in London," he repeated. " What an idea ! What could you possibly do ? You aren't trained for anything, and your education, my poor child . . ." He thought of the misspelt letters he occasionally received.

" Oh, Guy, help me."

" My dear, I would if I could," he said. " But there is simply nothing you could do."

Penelope withdrew her head from the window. She stood beside the car, looking forlornly at the gravel she poked with the toe of her shoe.

" What is it ? " asked Guy. " What's the matter ?

Isn't—er—isn't Anthea all right ? She seems a decent sort and all that."

" Oh, she's all right," said Penelope flatly.

Guy was sorry for his sister. But he felt he must not encourage her in any way to leave home. What could she possibly do outside it ?

" I must go," he said. " I'm due out to-night."

Penelope stood away from the car.

" All right," she said. " Good-bye."

He started the engine.

" I tell you what," he called out, putting his handsome head through the window, " I'll try to come over again soon and we'll have a good talk."

Penelope smiled grimly. She knew he wouldn't come. Once he got back to London, he wouldn't come.

" Good-bye," called Guy, moving off. " And cheer up. You'll get used to being without Christine. It's only just at first . . ."

CHAPTER XXI

THE house was free of visitors again at last, and not before time, thought Anthea. Surely she might be entitled to a little consideration now? She ordered a fire in the nursery and withdrew there to knit and be by herself. She had been longing to do this ever since the nurseries were finished, but had not been able to because of the visitors and the bustle downstairs. Now she entered her kingdom and shut the door.

The nurseries were really charming, she thought, looking round happily at everything. The rooms throughout were painted in cream with a faint pink undertone. The paint was glossy, so the walls shone softly in the firelight. A blue cork carpet covered the floors; the curtains at the windows were blue chintz with spotted pink horses scattered over. The rugs were cream with pink and blue borders and made by Anthea herself. Every detail of the nursery furnishings had been lovingly worked out by her and approved of by Nurse Pye.

In the drawers of the blue-painted chest, neatly tied in bundles with ribbon, were the baby-clothes Anthea had also made. She loved to take them out and turn them over and tie them up again. She took pleasure not only in the purpose of these clothes, of a vest, for instance, which would clothe her baby, but she also took pleasure in the vest itself, clean, soft, well-shaped little thing that it was. Her hands found satisfaction in smoothing it out and feeling at it. These satisfactions of hand and eye were coming rather late in life to Anthea, but were none the less pleasurable for that.

She sat by the fire now and unrolled her knitting. Who would recognize the nurseries now? she thought, looking round again. Not a trace of the girls' long occupation was left. She had cleared everything out : the piano, the dolls' house, the sewing machine, the piles of books and music, the framed family photographs, the old table with kicked legs, the white-painted bedroom suites, everything. In the confusion of Saunby, the accumulations of other people's lives, she had made a clearing for her children. *They* should start afresh. Anthea was as satisfied with the nurseries as a cat that has found a good place for its kittens to be born in. She viewed the pretty, hygienic emptiness contentedly. Everything was ready. Everything waited. She knitted by the fire, waiting too.

She was glad Christine had gone. Not that she disliked her particularly, but her going made one less. One less Marwood. Penelope would be easier to deal with without Christine. And perhaps something would remove Penelope before long ; perhaps she would get married too. Anthea hoped so. She wished Victoria would get married and go, but of course there was no hope of that. It was a pity that it was only marriage that moved women about, Anthea reflected. Women moved to men, but otherwise they mostly stayed where they were born. At least, in Victoria's walk of life. Victoria had stayed at Saunby. She had been a little girl in this very nursery, thought Anthea, and what an unpleasant child she must have been.

" She can't come up here now, anyway," Anthea exulted. " These rooms are mine."

She rang for Bessy to bring tea.

'Now I'll have tea in *my* place by *my* self,' she thought, and sent a message to say she wouldn't be down.

"Doesn't everything look lovely, Bessy?" she said when Bessy returned with tea.

"It does, 'm," responded Bessy, smiling.

"Won't it be nice when we're all settled up here together, you and I and Nurse Pye and the baby, in a little world of our own? What more could we want?" asked Anthea, assuming, as mistresses are apt to do, that what made her happy would make her maid happy too.

Bessy murmured non-committally, running about the tea-table with her usual willing haste.

"I'm so glad you got over that Thompson affair, Bessy," Anthea burst out, made rather rash and voluble by her own contentment.

She was sorry at once that she had spoken. Bessy blushed crimson. Evidently, thought Anthea, she can't bear the trouble to be touched upon even yet. She plunged again, to make amends.

"Bessy, go out for an hour or two," she said. "We've been so busy lately with all these people in the house, and by and by we're going to be busier still. So take advantage of this lull and go out. Go up and see Mrs. Spencer. I know you don't mind being out in the dark."

Bessy clasped her hands tight over her apron. If only she could let Bill know, they could meet in the wood. He was probably downstairs still, if she could get to him. Her heart began to beat wildly. She hadn't seen him alone for four days and in a quarter of an hour she might be with him under the tree. She took a deep breath to steady her excitement. If only she didn't feel it was wrong to go to him. She felt wicked and frightened, but she loved him so much, she couldn't keep away. But what if her father found out? She gazed at Anthea in anguish, almost as if she was imploring to be kept in, but Anthea was pouring out her tea and didn't notice.

" Go along, Bessy. Go out until six o'clock," she said kindly.

" I say, Thompson," the Major was saying at that very moment downstairs. " What about that baby of yours? When is it due? "

Thompson, although he had long expected the question, was taken aback when it came.

" Well, sir," he stammered, his eyebrows up in his dilemma. " It—er—it's not coming off. It—something went wrong."

The Major said no more. The marriage had turned out better than might have been expected. Thompson looked well enough, anyway. He was going about again with his old air of being on top of life.

Saunby was sunk in winter silence. Out of doors everything had a dead look. The tree-trunks, the palings were bleached, the coarse grass was almost white. In the house, the occupants were sunk into themselves, wrapped up in their own concerns.

Penelope prowled about the house and park, lonely and bored. There was nothing left, nothing to do, nobody to talk to. And while she was stuck at Saunby, Christine wrote that she was having a lovely time in Paris. Going to the Opera, buying doughnuts hot from a little oven outside a *pâtisserie* on the Rue de Rivoli, peering through the windows of the melancholy deserted pavilions at Trianon, losing Nicholas in the depths of Notre-Dame, buying one neat navy-blue outfit because she dared not go about Paris in the clothes she'd got.

" I never realized how awful my clothes were until

I came here," she wrote. "We've cared too much about colour, my love, and not enough about cut."

'If her clothes are awful when they were all new, what about mine?' thought Penelope indignantly. She thought she ought to have Paris clothes too, visits to Paris, a different life, or at any rate *something* that Christine was having.

When Christine sent her a beautiful little hand-made blouse for Christmas, Penelope dropped it back into its French box.

"I've no skirt to wear with it," she said crossly. "Christine should have thought of that. She knows all my skirts."

Christmas came and went almost unperceived at Saunby. Nobody made much difference for it, thought Penelope. Except the servants. They seemed to be enjoying themselves behind their green baize door. As for her, she sat glumly for most of the day in the drawing-room with her Aunt Victoria, whose Christmas present to her had been a picture, done by herself of course, of the elm avenue with Thompson's lodge in the wrong place to get it in.

"In future I'm going to give you pictures of Saunby on your birthdays and at Christmas," announced Miss Victoria grandly. "So that by the time you come to marry and leave it, you'll have a nice collection of pictures of your old home."

From the way she spoke her pictures might have been pearls, given one by one to make a priceless necklace.

Christine and Nicholas spent Christmas at Red Lodge, but immediately afterwards they moved into their own house, number 19, The Drive, and then, Penelope noted, the gilt began to come off the gingerbread.

"Lady Ashwell engaged two maids for us and they

244

had been in the house for a fortnight, but as soon as we came in they went out. They liked the house to themselves, it seems," wrote Christine. " Or they didn't like us. I am getting two more, but in the meantime we are living on eggs, because an egg is the only thing I can cook. When we want a good meal, we go to Red Lodge or to the Golf Club, but the worst of going to the club is that we can't get away again. Nicholas knows so many people there. They make him play poker with them. I can't play and I don't want to, so I sit beside him and look on. The other night I fell asleep there. I was ashamed to wake up and find them all laughing at me. It was like a night-mare for a minute. Have you been to any card-parties lately ? I hope so. I hope you are going out and getting a bit of fun. And don't despise the sheep too much, Pen. They are better than the people at the club here."

But Penelope did despise the sheep. In fact she had decided to have no more to do with them. After Christine's departure, thinking she would be more amenable by herself, or so Penelope construed it, the sheep renewed their efforts to get her into the fold. They treated her like a stray lamb and baa'd urgently at her to join them at their bazaars, on their platforms, at their guilds and to accompany them on their visits to the poor. Penelope made polite excuses at first, but when Rosamund Hunter, at her card-party, saw fit to read Penelope a lecture, Penelope came out with the truth.

The party was gathered round the huge mahogany table in the Hunter dining-room for tea. This table had once accommodated the Hunter family in their full strength of ten, but now only Rosamund and her parents were left to sit at it. It came in very useful for a party, though.

The thick curtains were drawn ; you could not see the snow outside. You could not feel the winter cold, the fire was so warm. The tea was excellent. You could always rely on the Hunters for food if not for fun, thought Penelope, reaching for first one sort of sandwich and then another. The fare at Saunby was so plain, you were apt to be a bit greedy when you went out. She knew the Hunter chocolate cake of old, and was taking a piece with pleasurable anticipation when Rosamund opened her attack.

"Penelope, you know you *are* a slacker," she said playfully, emboldened by the presence of her mother at the head of the table. Rosamund was more than forty, but she still felt safer when her mother was there. "You're a frightful little slacker ! Why *won't* you sell some tickets for us ? Why won't you take the White Elephant stall with Madeline ? You won't do anything. You're always making excuses. You won't even take over Winifred's families for her while she's away and that's only for a week or two. You might do a little of something sometimes, Penelope. Why won't you ? I do think you're rather selfish."

The faces under the unfashionable felt hats turned to Penelope. How brave of Rosamund ! Of course it was just what Penelope needed, but how brave of Rosamund !

Penelope put down her chocolate cake. Now they should have it.

"You see, I don't believe in what you are doing," she said in her cool voice. " I don't believe in playing with the poor. You've grown out of your dolls, so you take to the poor. The poor are an occupation for you. Getting up bazaars is fun for you. You haven't any affairs of your own, so you go and interfere in the affairs of the poor. You go and visit them in their dreadful houses and portion out allowances for a little food and coal and clothing and then you come back to a home like this and eat a tea like this. Well," said Penelope, looking round at the shocked faces. "I don't believe in that. I believe in 'Sell all that thou hast and give to the poor.' I believe in that," she affirmed. "But I'm not prepared to do it, and since I'm not prepared to do it, I don't do anything. I think it's more honest."

Shocked protests went off like crackers round the table. Mrs. Hunter, from her place behind the teapot, thought it time to intervene.

"Penelope, my dear child, you are talking a great deal of nonsense, and of rather wicked, Bolshevik nonsense too, though you probably haven't the least idea what you mean. When one has not the money to give, as few of us have nowadays, one must give one's time and one's energy and help in any way one can."

"But I don't think you are helping," said Penelope.

"We *know* we are," said Mrs. Hunter, rising like a full-breasted swan from the lake of mahogany. "Come, girls, let us go back to the cards."

Penelope, cramming the last of her chocolate cake into her mouth and regretting that they hadn't given her time to have another piece, thought dispassionately as she went after them : 'I shan't come again.'

The routing of the sheep made an incident in her life and she felt quite cheerful for a few days. Then her mood changed. Nurse Pye arrived to join the household. The birth of Anthea's baby was imminent and Penelope was frightened.

Penelope had a deep fear of child-birth. She could not have told when the seed of this fear had taken root, she only knew that it was now a dark tree shadowing her life. From under this dark tree, she peered unhappily at marriage and the future. She hated to be reminded that there was such a thing as child-birth, and now the thing itself was going to take place in the very house she was in. The arrival of Nurse Pye stirred up all Penelope's morbid fears, and she went about in a nervous, starting apprehension that would have appeared ridiculous to Nurse Pye had she known of it. But no one knew. Normally candid, Penelope concealed this fear, even from Christine. She had spoken of it in passing now and then to her sister, but she had never revealed the dark depth of it. It is a pity that the thing you fear most you cannot tell ; if you could tell it, you might no longer fear it.

Nurse Pye, oblivious of the effect her arrival had on Penelope, parked her baby car beside the Daimler in the garage, mounted to her friend and patient in the nursery and shut the door.

The rest of the household was left to its own devices, to pass the time downstairs as it liked during the short cold days and the long inadequately lit evenings. Upstairs the lights were bright and cheerful, since Nurse Pye's first demand was for stronger electric bulbs from the Major. She must see what she was doing, she told him.

Her demands outraged the Major. But he was helpless to resist them. Nurse Pye would tap briskly on his door, whisk in, her starched skirts rattling like a yacht in full sail, lay her requirements before him and whisk out again, taking it for granted that what she asked for she would get. If she didn't get it within what she considered a reasonable time, she came again. The Major learned to give in at once to save himself from her visits.

In the nursery, Anthea put herself happily into Nurse Pye's hands. It was very satisfactory to her to be able to rely on Nurse Pye, to trust her completely.

All her life, Anthea had been looking for someone to trust, to grapple to her soul with hoops of steel. But until now she had not found anybody. Her parents had not the necessary substance. Henry and Evelyn, though satisfactory when small, had grown up and gone away. And it was unfortunate for Anthea that she had married into a family like the Marwoods, who, more than most people, disliked to be grappled and evaded the grappler. In Nurse Pye, however, Anthea had now found her friend, and happily for her Nurse Pye was as satisfied with Anthea as Anthea was with her.

Nurse Pye admired Anthea. She liked women who bore children with fortitude and without fuss, and Anthea, she knew, was one of these. Nurse Pye was also secretly gratified to be on terms of such friendliness with such a ' lady,' a member of such a very good family. Nurse Pye had nursed many ladies. They were always very nice to her when they were ill ; they were most friendly. But when they recovered they forgot her, in spite of their protestations that they never would. Nurse Pye, although she professed herself too sensible to expect anything else, was always a little hurt. But from the beginning her friendship with Anthea had been different ; it was more real, less of a working hypothesis.

So they were happy talking and knitting and waiting in the nursery. It was Penelope's nerves, not theirs, that wore thin during this time.

All Penelope's alarms had so far proved false ones, but one night she heard sounds of real disturbance. The nursery door, the one she knew so well, banged in the small hours of the morning and steps sounded on the polished stairs. Immediately Penelope was out of bed and at her door ; Nurse Pye hurried past her on her way to the stairs.

"Is it born?" Penelope called out, looking wild with her curls on end.

"Don't be silly," said Nurse Pye, hurrying on.

Snatching her dressing-gown, Penelope went after her. She leaned over the banisters to listen to Nurse Pye telephoning in the hall. She shivered with cold and her fear. She felt sick.

A strange figure appeared beside her on the landing, Victoria in a padded gown, with a frilled boudoir cap on the head no one ever saw uncovered and the old skunk cape she had worn for warmth that night at dinner. One tinned pea, an escape from those they had had at dinner, was spiked on one single stiff skunk hair. At any other time Penelope would have been amused, but not now. She gazed at her aunt, her teeth chattering.

"What's the matter?" asked Victoria. "What's going on?"

"I think the baby's going to be born," said Penelope.

"Well, it's got to be born sometime," said Victoria.

Nurse Pye now reappeared.

"You've no need to stand about," she told them dismissingly. "There's nothing to get up for yet and won't be for hours. I've sent for the doctor and got Bessy up and that's all that can be done for the present."

She continued up the stairs and left them. Victoria stumped off, too, complaining of the draught.

But Penelope stood transfixed. A strange sound had started in the nursery; a low shuddering intermittent whimper. Penelope listened, her eyes distended. Then with a rush, she ran to her room. She shut the door, jumped into her bed, dived under the bed-clothes and stuffed her fingers into her ears. But even then she could hear that sound still; she didn't know whether she heard it in imagination or in reality, but she daren't take her fingers from her ears to find out.

When morning came and she awoke from a nightmare sleep, the doctor had been and gone, but the sound still went on in the nursery.

" Isn't it born *yet*, Bessy ? " asked Penelope in agitation.

" No, miss," said Bessy.

Bessy looked as wan and frightened as Penelope, but for a different reason. All night, as she had been running about doing Nurse Pye's behests, she had been thinking what it would be like for her if she had a baby. No help like this for her, no place to put the child, nowhere to go but home, where her father was.

" Oh, no," she shuddered. " I'd never go home to my father. I'd die first."

But she must never bring herself to such a pass. Never. Never. With a hunted look in her eyes, Bessy hurried back to the nursery.

The doctor returned. Looking very grave, he told the Major that Miss Lattimer must be sent for. The finest gynæcologist in the Midlands, he assured the Major, who could not believe it of a woman. The Major said he would rather a good man was called in, but the doctor was firm, and Miss Lattimer was summoned.

During the day she came. The Major had expected a large manly woman, but a small feminine person with an enigmatic smile came quietly into the hall, offered the Major as cool a hand as, in other circumstances, he might have offered her, and was conducted upstairs with respect by Dr. Carter.

After a long time she came down and went into the garden. She examined the ruins with great interest, came in and went upstairs again.

It was getting dark when Nurse Pye appeared on the stairs and announced to the Major, Victoria and Penelope in the hall that a girl had been born. They had hardly assimilated this news when she appeared again and announced that a boy had also been born.

" Two ! " shouted the Major. " Twins ? "

" Twins," said Nurse Pye triumphantly. " We've thought for some time that it would be twins."

" Then why in heaven's name wasn't I informed ? " cried the Major, who had forgotten, or never realized, that he had rebutted Anthea's attempt to tell him.

" Would the news have been any more acceptable at any other time ? " inquired Victoria. " How is Mrs. Marwood ? " she said to Nurse Pye.

" Very tired, but as well as can be expected. She's been wonderful," said Nurse Pye.

When he had seen Miss Lattimer, still smiling, depart, the Major went into his room.

Twins, he thought. What a catastrophe. At his age. The situation was positively music-hall. Twins. And one of them a boy. It would mean Winchester and Cambridge all over again. Years of expense. But it wouldn't. It couldn't. He simply hadn't got the money.

This reflection in some mysterious way almost restored him. Anthea had produced twins. All right. No doubt she was feeling very pleased with herself. But he hadn't the money to do what she would want for them, and that was that. Let her put that in her pipe and smoke it. As if he could now wash his hands of the matter, the Major reached for *The Times*, the perusal of which had been considerably interrupted that day.

In the bedroom of the nursery, Nurse Pye leaned to Anthea.

" Your mother's come, dear," she said.

Anthea slowly opened her eyes.

" I don't want to see her," she said weakly, and closed them again.

"You shan't, then," said Nurse Pye. "But what about your husband?"

"No," said Anthea.

"All right," said Nurse Pye. "You just rest. The babies are sleeping like angels."

Anthea smiled.

CHAPTER XXII

SNOW whirled white against the grey sky and spattered softly against Anthea's windows. From where she lay she could see only snow and sky, and the sense of quiet that falling snow gives was deepened in her to a profound peace. She had reached harbour. The dreadful struggle was over. She had her babies ; a boy and a girl. It seemed too good to be true. But it was indeed true, and her life was complete.

The room was quiet and warm and very pretty. A fire burned brightly in the grate, and because a fire in her room had been a treat to Anthea as a child, it was a treat still and she kept looking at it appreciatively. Now and again a thin wail rose in the day-nursery and Anthea smiled. She could already interpret the cries of her children and knew which expressed hunger and which sleepiness and which merely temper. Nurse Pye kept coming in and out crisp in her uniform, untiring, efficient, and Anthea's eyes followed her with affection and gratitude. Those terrible hours had bound her to Nurse Pye for ever. She felt that it was through Nurse Pye's will alone that she had survived the exhaustion of bringing the twins into the world.

The only shadow on Anthea's happiness was the thought that Nurse Pye would eventually leave her. Not for weeks, perhaps not for months, but in the end she would leave Saunby.

' I don't need to think of it yet,' Anthea kept telling herself, trying to put the thought aside. But with the tenacity of her nature, she returned to it again and again, wondering what could be done to keep Nurse Pye, wondering how she could get Francis to consent to it.

Before long, Anthea was sitting up in bed in a fleecy pink bed-jacket, with her long dark hair braided into two plaits, brought to the front over each shoulder and tied with pink bows by Nurse Pye, writing letters of thanks to friends and relations. She enjoyed writing these letters. She enjoyed writing to Evelyn :

" How is Susan ? What a pity she will always be too old to companion my two. Though of course they will always be company for each other.
" My son . . ." she wrote. " My son . . ."

Poor Evelyn had no son and Seton Craig wanted one so badly.

The Major paid visits to Anthea twice a day, morning and evening. He came because he thought he had to. He did his duty, but with an ill grace. The sick-room was no place for him and Anthea's plaits irritated him. She looked like a decorated horse, he thought. He averted his eyes from her and looked mostly out of the window.

At each visit, Nurse Pye brought his children to be seen by him.

" Look at your beautiful son. And your beautiful daughter," she would urge him, advancing one arm and then the other, whereon Roger and Veronica, as they were to be christened, lay each on a little pillow. " You ought to be *proud*, Major Marwood," she told him.

But he wasn't ; and he wasn't going to be prodded into pride by Nurse Pye, either. His face assumed an expression of cold hauteur as he looked down at the twins, but Nurse Pye didn't notice it ; she was too engrossed in looking at them with love herself.

When the Major had stood about in the room for what he felt was long enough, he went downstairs with relief, and Anthea, who had tried to include him in her happiness and to give him another chance in her affections, gave him up again. She rejected him. He was beautiful to look at and she had once been mad about him, and but for him, she admitted, she would still be at Brockington with her parents. But he had failed her as a husband, and he was failing again as a father. She turned from him and concentrated the more closely, from his exclusion, on the twins and Nurse Pye.

" What shall I do when you go ? " she said to Nurse Pye. " How can I possibly manage without you ? "

" Well, I think you'll have to engage a trained nurse," said Nurse Pye. " Twins are very hard work and Roger is going to need care. He's not as robust as Veronica. It's always the way. Boys are harder to rear than girls. Men give trouble all their lives to women and they start early. You'll need a trained nurse for Roger for a while. Bessy will be a good nurse-maid for you when I've knocked her into shape," said Nurse Pye, who was driving poor Bessy from pillar to post all day long in the process. " But you'll need a trained nurse all the same."

' If a trained nurse,' thought Anthea. ' Why not Nurse Pye ? '

This surely was an incontrovertible argument to put before Francis, and on her first excursion downstairs she put it. She could not bear to wait, and after fishing delicately, she had ascertained that Nurse Pye would be willing to stay at Saunby.

" Ah—Anthea," said the Major, uncrossing his long

legs to rise when he saw who it was coming into his room. One had to make some show of pleasure, he supposed, when one's wife came downstairs for the first time after the production of twins, and by rising and saying " Ah—Anthea " he thought he had done it.

He put a chair before the fire for her, and she sank into it, feeling rather shaky after her descent of the staircase.

" I want to have a little talk with you, Francis," she said earnestly.

The Major frowned. If there was anything he hated it was little talks.

" About Nurse Pye," said Anthea.

He groaned openly.

" If Nurse Pye goes," said Anthea.

" *If* she goes ! " cried the Major. " What d'you mean, if she goes ? She's going, isn't she ? My God, I hope so."

" If she goes," resumed Anthea patiently, " I shall have to engage a trained nurse."

" Why ? " asked the Major. " I don't see why. The house is full of maids. Why can't they help you ? You're always saying what a nice girl what-you-may-call-her is. Bessy. Why won't she do ? And what about Penelope ? Let her do something. Do her good. She does nothing but hang about the house in the sulks."

" I don't want unwilling help, Francis, and that is all I should get from Penelope. Besides, neither maids nor Penelope can give me the expert help I want. Roger isn't strong and needs care. I shall have to have a trained nurse, Francis, whether you like it or not, so I prefer to keep Nurse Pye."

" Keep Nurse Pye ! " shouted the Major as if he had never heard anything so preposterous in his life. " You can't keep Nurse Pye. Because A : I can't afford her, and B : I can't stand her. So there you are."

Anthea sighed. He was at his most trying to-day.

"Please be serious, Francis," she said, very serious and disapproving herself.

"I am serious," said the Major. "My God, you don't know how serious I am. My dear girl," he said, striding to open his desk. "Look at these bills ! Look at them ! "

He put his hands in and brought the bills out like feathers from a pillow. They fluttered all over the desk and the floor.

Anthea was unmoved. She had seen them before and was, moreover, not to be diverted from her purpose.

The Major looked at her in astonishment. He had expected her to exclaim in alarm at the sight of the bills. Then he put his own interpretation upon her calm demeanour.

"I suppose they don't convey anything to you. I suppose you can't grasp that those bills amount to something like four hundred pounds and that I haven't a penny to pay them with."

"More like five hundred," said Anthea. "Or probably six by now."

"Oh, so you do know about them," said the Major. "Well, how the devil do you think I am going to pay them ? "

"Nobody can tell you that but yourself, Francis."

"I tell you I can't pay them unless I sell another farm. And if I keep selling farms there's going to be nothing left. You don't seem to understand anything. You don't seem to understand where my money comes from or what I live on."

"Unfortunately I understand only too well," said Anthea.

"Then how can you come asking me to keep this

woman on? A woman who costs me four pounds a week? And you come suggesting that I should *go on* paying four pounds a week."

"How much do you pay Thompson?" asked Anthea.

The Major was taken aback. His jaw dropped and he stared at her. Then he recovered and reached for a cigarette.

"What I pay Thompson, my dear girl, is entirely my own affair."

"The children should be your affair too," said Anthea. "But I suppose that is too much to expect from you. But surely you have enough sense of proportion to see that children come before cricket. I ask you, Francis, to dismiss Thompson and let me keep Nurse Pye in his place."

"Dismiss Thompson," said the Major in a voice of anger and amazement. "Dismiss Thompson! I'd never for one moment consider it, so you might as well get the idea out of your head at once. Dismiss Thompson, indeed. How d'you suppose I could run cricket without him?"

"I don't see why you should try to," said Anthea.

"What d'you mean?"

"You ought to give cricket up. You can't afford it."

The Major was so astounded that he was deprived momentarily of speech. He stared at the person who could utter these preposterous, these totally unexpected words. Give up cricket! Had she taken leave of her senses? And how, pray, had she got so far above herself to feel she dare make the suggestion? Recovering from surprise, he mounted his highest horse before speaking.

"My dear girl." He used terms of endearment only when annoyed. "My *dear* Anthea, I must ask you to refrain from telling me what I can and what I cannot afford. I decided those matters for myself for many years without your help and I shall continue so to decide them. Let it suffice that I cannot afford Nurse Pye."

" And I can't do without her," said Anthea stubbornly.

But her legs trembled.

The Major said no more. He implied, by picking up *The Times*, that as far as he was concerned discussion was over. He stood there, reading, his eyes narrowed against the smoke from his cigarette, elegant, aloof, male.

Anthea got up and went out of the room. She wasn't strong yet ; not strong enough to continue the struggle. She must wait and return to it.

§

In the drawing-room, Penelope was trying to write a letter. It was too cold to sit at the Dutch Marquetry writing-table between the windows, so she had a piece of notepaper supported by a book on her knee and sat as close to the fire as possible.

The view from the windows was a wet one. A thaw had set in and everything dripped. The sky was swollen with grey clouds. Penelope found everything profoundly melancholy. The chairs and sofas in the drawing-room were melancholy. Even the fire burned sadly and was more smoke than flame.

' I can't stand it, I can't stand it any more,' thought Penelope.

She dated her letter and gazed at the portrait of her mother over the mantelpiece, wondering how to begin.

She was used to the portrait. It had always been there. As a child, she had been told so often by nurses that her mother was in heaven, that she had thought this was the authentic portrait of an angel. The beauty of her mother's face, her fair hair and the blue gauze round her shoulders had helped the illusion. It was years before Penelope grasped the fact that her mother had been a living woman.

As she gazed at the portrait now, wondering what to write, she realized suddenly that if her mother had lived, she would have had no need to write the letter at all.

" Why did you die ? " she said aloud. " We needed you."

Nobody else had ever cared about her or Christine, she thought. As long as they were together they could manage after a fashion. But now she was alone.

' If I don't do something for myself,' thought Penelope. ' No one will ever do anything for me. I'll simply rot my days away here. I'll be nothing but an elder sister to Anthea's children, and heaven knows how many more she'll have.'

She frowned with concentration and then, in a hand that would have done no credit to a kitchen-maid, she began to write :

DEAR MR. KENWORTHY,

I want to get some work to do, prefferably in an office. Do you know of anybody who needs a secretry ? Do you, perhaps, need one yourself? It would be nice for me if you did. Will you be so kind as to let me know ? I apologize for troubling you, but I know you have a kind nature and will help anybody if you can.

Yours sincerely,

PENELOPE MARWOOD.

She felt much better when she read the letter through. She felt suddenly very hopeful. Surely something would come of that. She put the letter into its envelope, licked it down and stamped it. Then she rushed for her old hat and coat from the pegs in the back hall and in her gum-boots she splashed across the cricket field and down the elm avenue to intercept Pidcock, the postman, who passed through Saunby twice a day on his bicycle, at half-past seven in the morning and at three in the afternoon, threading his way in at the Avenue gates and out at the main gates on the high road. Day in, day out, year in, year out, rain or shine, Pidcock threaded his way through Saunby on his bicycle, making up, by imperceptible, recurrent stitches, his part of the tapestry of Saunby, begun long ago and still unfinished.

Penelope went to intercept him, to place the letter in his bag instead of putting it on the hall table with the others. The letter was private and no one in the house must know about it. Thus does youth send out its ships on secret voyages ; the ships sometimes bring something back, but not often what their sender hopes for.

CHAPTER XXIII

FOR Christine and Nicholas in Mansbridge the honeymoon was over. According to Sarah, they were "settled."

"They're settled in their own home now," she told inquiring matrons. "You can call any time."

Settled was hardly the word. An unsettling process seemed to begin as the honeymoon ended. Everything had been perfect so long as they were alone together, lifted out of their environment. They thought themselves the most perfect companions ; and so, for that time and in those circumstances, they were. It was when they came to Mansbridge and Nicholas returned to live almost the same life he had lived before and Christine began to live a life she had never lived before, that things started to go wrong. The trouble was, though they did not know it, that Nicholas did not want to live the same life and Christine did not want to live a different one. It was what the French call a "deception" to Nicholas to find that, after marriage, his life was so much the same as before, and to Christine to find that hers was so different.

Nicholas dropped back into his club, his friends, his dependence on his father, and the lack of purpose and direction that secretly undermined his happiness.

For Christine everything was new, strange and a great deal of it not what she wanted. Where, in this place, blocked out of concrete and filled, it seemed, with artificial people, where was the peace, the beauty, the solitude of Saunby ? And above all, where was the freedom ? She could hardly do as she liked any more.

At Mansbridge, one seemed to be entirely at the mercy of other people.

Sir James, for instance, called almost every day. Christine felt a deep sense of obligation to Sir James. He paid for everything. But no sense of obligation could prevent her from feeling restive in his company. If she could have come to terms of reality with him, it would have been better ; but she couldn't, because he was so gallant.

" I like to see her blush," he said in one of his asides, which were no asides at all, to Nicholas.

Sir James also did not like to be contradicted, and what sort of a conversation, Christine asked herself, can you have with a person who doesn't like to be contradicted ? You can only put your own views on one side and let him run on, she decided.

James had no idea that she felt as she did about him. He was very proud of her. Such a looker, he thought. Breeding in every line. He liked to walk her about the promenade and come across his friends.

" Look who I've got here," he would say, halting Christine by the arm. " This is my daughter, Nick's wife. Done well for himself, hasn't he ? "

The old men, turning their thin necks inside their wing collars, would willingly admire, while Christine smiled and blushed and strained to get away.

Sarah did not call at all hours of the day as James did. She waited to be asked. But the house seemed always so full of people that Christine mostly forgot to ask her. Sarah rounded up the matrons of Mans-bridge, old and young, to call upon her daughter-in-law. She wanted her to feel " at home." She could not know that she made her just the opposite. Christine wasn't used to company and would much rather have

264

been out with Nicholas on the golf-links than dispensing tea and small talk to strange women.

Cicely Hoyle came with her mother. Cicely had no scruples about visiting Nicholas's bride. Scruples were not in her composition. She snatched at the excuse to observe, at close quarters, the girl Nicholas had married instead of her. She rushed into the torture of seeing Nicholas's wife in Nicholas's house.

The marriage had been a shock to Cicely. It was the last thing she had thought of. It had all happened so quickly too, before she had time to fight. Once, she had schooled herself to be exactly what Nicholas wanted her to be. When he wanted her as a lover, she had been that. When he wanted her as a friend, she had been a friend, beating down her own desires to adapt them to his. But what had been the use of this self-discipline? He had married someone else. She would school herself no longer. She would do as she liked and not consider him any more. So she came to view the enemy and brought her mother as a pretext and a screen.

It was a cold day and Mrs. Hoyle, a mild, bewildered old lady, left, since the death of her husband, to the untender mercies of Cicely, would much rather have stayed at home, dozing by the fire. But Cicely woke her, made her dress up and whirled her through the streets in her open cream-coloured sports car, called " White Lady " after the cocktail.

Cicely, though hatless, entered Christine's drawing-room without a hair out of place, but her mother came behind striving to put away wisps under her crooked hat. She could hardly shake hands for putting her hair away.

" I don't know what you must think of me, dear," she apologized to Christine, " arriving like this. I must be a dreadful sight. Dreadful, I fear."

" Oh, Mother, don't fuss," snapped Cicely.

Christine was startled, but hardly anybody else was. Cicely was always rude to her mother.

Cicely threw herself into a chair and extended her legs. She would not have tea, but she took a box of cigarettes and placed it to her hand. Her eyes coldly followed Christine about the room. Pretty, she admitted. But surely that unsophisticated type would bore him before long ? She remembered how Christine had fallen asleep at the club.

'She'd better keep up with him,' thought Cicely. ' Or she'll lose him. She doesn't realize that Nick has to be kept on the move or else he starts thinking. And when he thinks, he mopes. And after he's moped, he gets restless. I know him. Far better than she does.'

She threw her cigarette expertly into the fire. She spent half the day throwing cigarettes into the fire, so she did it very well. She reached for another and lit it. There might have been no one else in the room now for all the notice she took of the company. She examined the cigarette she was smoking. She gazed out of the window, with her teeth bared in a strange grimace, and there was lipstick on her teeth. She had a very beautiful little arched nose, Christine noticed. She never kept still for a moment. She examined her nails. She kept turning up her curls with her curved hand at the back of her head ; and she kept looking at Christine.

What a queer girl, thought Christine. What queer behaviour.

She would not go. Everybody else went, but Mrs. Hoyle and Cicely sat on. Mrs. Hoyle dared not go until Cicely was ready, so she sat on, keeping up the conversation.

Christine heard Nicholas come in, and saying

"Excuse me one moment, will you?" she ran out into the hall to meet him. She kissed him and whispered vehemently, "That Hoyle girl is here with her mother and she simply won't go." Hand-in-hand they went into the drawing-room.

"Give me a sherry, Nicholas, will you?" said Cicely, cutting short his greeting of her mother.

'How rude!' thought Christine. 'Why didn't she ask me before this if she wanted one.'

Cicely drank her sherry slowly and with deliberation. The torture was fiercer now Nicholas had come in, now that she saw them together. She pressed the sword into her side; she leaned on it.

"Now we'll go home," she said suddenly to her mother, and they went.

"Of all the strange creatures," said Christine, when the sports car had driven off. "What's the matter with her? She's the rudest girl I've ever come across."

"Oh, she's not bad, really," said Nicholas. "I think she has rather a rotten time, you know, alone with that old mother."

"You mean the mother has a rotten time alone with her," said Christine indignantly. "Huh."

Nicholas kissed her, and Christine, for the time being, forgot Cicely.

Nicholas was not pleased to find Cicely in his house, but he reasoned himself out of displeasure. Why should he ban Cicely because she had always been so decent to him? He often reasoned himself out of his instincts.

Cicely began to come frequently to the house. Not alone, but with the "crowd," with Totty Baines and his wife, Gilly Bradford, Doreen Wood, the two Marchants, Bob and Peter, and the rest.

Nicholas had given up going to the club in the evenings, because Christine did not want to go with him. She had tried it; but she didn't like cards, she didn't like drinks, and she didn't like sitting all night, looking over Nicholas's shoulder, or looking at old *Tatlers*. She cried off and tried to persuade him to go without her, but he would not. So they stayed at home, and before long, since they would not go to the " crowd," the " crowd " came to them.

Nicholas's friends were in their way fond of him and liked to be where he was. They revolved round him ; he was their sun, the well-known cricketer, and they were his satellites. He was the only one of their number who showed distinction and they valued him as such and were proud of him. They came to the house and kept on coming. They found this new place of call comfortable and inexpensive. Three or four times a week they parked their cars in the Drive and trooped into the sitting-room with hearty greetings to Nicholas and constrained ones to Christine. The table for poker was got out and the room was soon full of smoke and the smell of drinks ; and by and by Christine had to go and make the sandwiches.

She was often without maids, and when she had them, they were difficult or out, so she mostly had to make the sandwiches herself. She had never cut bread and butter in her life and was amazed that it could give such trouble. The bread was new and crumbly, the knife was new and blunt, and the butter, since it was winter-time, was hard. Christine almost wept with exasperation as she cut sandwiches in the butler's pantry, still so called though butlers had long gone out, if they had ever been in, at Mansbridge.

No sooner had she carried the sandwiches, achieved with such difficulty, into the sitting-room than Nicholas's friends wolfed them up, reaching for them with one hand while they held cards with the other, and she had to go back to the pantry to cut more.

But by and by she hit upon a way to turn these

absences from the sitting-room to advantage. She could escape to get some air. All she had to do was to run down her own steps, cross the road and there she was on the sea-front.

She liked Mansbridge at night when she couldn't see it. And at this time of night and year, there was no one at all on the promenade. From end to end under its lamps it was empty. She could run and leap unseen. When she was out of breath, she could stop and look out to sea. Which was the sky and which the water? Both were merged into the night. How exciting life was, life itself, when you got away from other people! They kept you looking at them, listening to them, doing things for them like making sandwiches. But when you got away from them to be alone, something rose free, like a bird singing. Oh, thought Christine. Oh, oh, oh. She flew again along the promenade. She had no words to express herself; she didn't need them. Running and leaping did it. When she thought the poker-players might be missing her, she turned and ran back to the house.

She brought the cold breath of the sea into the sitting-room. Cicely Hoyle felt it and turned to look at her cold, rosy face and blown curls.

" Ugh," she shivered. " You chill me to the bone. D'you mean to say you've been out? "

" I have," said Christine, taking the empty plates away to fill.

' Meeting some man, I suppose,' thought Cicely, who could not imagine the promenade at night being used for any other purpose.

One night, when the " crowd " had gone, Christine realized with a shock at the heart that Nicholas was drunk. She couldn't think, at first, what was the matter with him. She had not seen a man drunk before. She stared at him in bewilderment as he leaned on the mantelpiece, smiling vacantly. His speech was blurred, his whole face somehow was blurred. He looked so silly, she thought. Then the truth dawned on her.

The fact that people drank whisky and sherry and gin mixtures had never worried her. She had seen trays of bottles carried into the billiard-room summer after summer and thought nothing of it. She had furnished drinks for Nicholas's friends night after night as a matter of course. If the drinks made the friends a little drunk, she didn't notice any difference in their behaviour. They always, drunk or sober, seemed too hilarious by half.

Stories about drunken men were funny. She liked them. Specially the one about the man who was found clasping a pillar-box and heard to say : " Darling, I love you, but you do look different without your teeth." That was a favourite with her and Penelope. The stories were funny, but the fact was not funny at all. When it was your own husband who was drunk, it was different. She stared in horror at Nicholas. It was no use speaking to him ; he couldn't understand. He was changed for the time into an imbecile.

She went upstairs. Thank goodness, she thought, that I have a bed to myself. They had single beds, but so far they had slept crushed into one bed, only parting in the morning when early tea was due.

She was brushing her hair when Nicholas came in from his dressing-room. He went to her to bury his head in her neck as usual. His hands from habit closed over her breast, but she tore herself free and whipped round on him.

" Don't touch me," she cried, quivering with disgust. " You're drunk. You smell. You look hideous, leering like that."

Nicholas steadied himself. His brain, with an

effort, cleared a little. He made her an absurd, courteous bow.

" I beg your pardon," he said, and returned to his dressing-room.

He put his head under the cold-water tap and came back rubbing his hair with a towel.

" What did you say to me ? " he asked.

There was no answer from Christine's bed, and he had enough sense remaining to get into his own and put out the light. In a few moments, he was asleep, emitting, to Christine's horror, a gentle drunken snore. He had never snored before.

She lay in the dark. For the first time, her confidence in life was shaken. She felt fear and distrust of life. If Nicholas fell short of what she had thought him, she could never be happy. He had seemed strong, lovable, dependable, but what if he should turn out to be weak ?

But he wasn't weak, she told herself, trying to get at the truth, trying not to be swamped by childish despair. He didn't drink because he was weak, he didn't associate with these people because he was weak ; he did both because he wanted to. But it was dreadful if he and she were going to want different things, if they were going to have different values. It would mean division instead of union. There would be loneliness instead of the companionship she had taken for granted would be theirs.

The sense of loneliness took the place of anger and disgust, and it was much worse to bear. Christine wept into her pillow, and the steady snore from Nicholas's bed made her weep the more. She cried and he snored, and she thought that might prove to be typical of their married life.

In the morning, she woke to find him kneeling beside her bed.

"Was I a bit drunk last night, darling?" he asked contritely.

"Yes, you were."

She lay like a sad child. He stroked her hair. She lay there, not looking at him, not repulsing him, not welcoming him. He picked up one limp slender hand and bit her fingers.

"Don't take it so badly," he said, laughing. "Most men get a bit drunk from time to time."

"You looked awful," she said, without heat, as if it was something that had happened a long time ago, as if she had travelled a long way since, as indeed she had. "You looked so silly. You slobbered. You slobbered into my neck."

Nicholas reddened.

"I'm so sorry," he said awkwardly. He didn't like the idea of himself looking silly and slobbering.

Christine moved her arm to encircle his head.

"Don't get like that again," she implored.

"I hope I won't," said Nicholas. "Darling, I do adore you."

They kissed. He put his head down beside hers on the pillow. Christine folded his hand to her breast. She lay smiling into his eyes, confidence completely restored. It was all right. Everything was all right. She was so happy.

Suddenly she flung Nicholas's hand away.

"Janet with the tea!" she cried.

Nicholas, swearing, took a flying leap into his own bed. He scrabbled the covers over himself in the nick of time and lay with closed eyes while Janet deposited the tray and the papers, drew the curtains and withdrew herself. Christine emerged giggling from her sheets.

"That was a near shave," said Nicholas.

"It was," she agreed, and sat up to pour out tea.

Life was lovely, and how nice to have morning tea.

" I tell you what," said Nicholas.

" Yes ? "

" When you bring the drinks round in future, bring plain water in a cocktail glass to me. It looks like gin. Nobody'll know. Or you can put a little lime-juice in, then they'll think it's gin and lime."

" Why bother to pretend to drink ? " asked Christine. " Need you ? "

" Oh, well," said Nicholas, taking his tea. " People don't like you not to drink with them, you know. It puts them off."

" Does it ? "

" Yes," said Nicholas. " It makes everything kind of awkward and chilly. You see, sobersides, you've been shut up at Saunby all your life, you don't know what the world's like."

" No, perhaps I don't," admitted Christine. " But I want to learn. I don't want to be always disapproving of everything. It would be awful. Vinegary. But I don't think I shall ever be able to *like* you being drunk."

" Well, bring me water round at nights and I'll not get drunk," he said. " Now let's have a look at the papers."

Nicholas liked to lie in bed in the mornings, smoking endless cigarettes and reading the papers, so Christine lay with him, sharing his bed and his paper.

In his comments, as he read, she could have found many clues to the depression that frequently weighed upon him, and which bewildered her because she did not know what it was about. When the depression was on him, he couldn't talk about it. When it was gone, he wouldn't. He was only too glad to let it go, to be rid of it.

He did reveal himself in flashes, but the inexperienced Christine did not look for clues to his depression in what he said in his normal cheerful state.

"This bloody world," he would say as he read the *Daily Telegraph* in bed in the mornings.

"Is there going to be a war?" Christine would inquire, her chin on his arm, craning to read herself.

"Life to-day," he would say, "isn't really worth living. We're all paralysed. D'you realize that? We're like a lot of rabbits paralysed by what we think are stoats, but which are probably only rabbits, too, paralysed by us. Or else we're all stoats. I don't know.

"You know," he said. "We live from day to day in our time. And that's a bad thing. Man needs to look forward. He needs to hope and to-day he can't.

"Gosh, I wish I could get some work," he would say, suddenly throwing the papers aside. "But I can't hear of anything but little footling jobs that wouldn't keep me, let alone you. Humiliating sorts of jobs, you know, involving boot-licking and back-slapping. I hate boot-licking and back-slapping," he said with scorn.

"Oh, so do I," said Christine fervently. "I couldn't bear you to do anything like that."

And so they talked, stopping late in bed in the mornings, and, if they had but known it, disorganizing the household and piling up trouble with the maids.

Christine had learned for herself that maids were a problem. She had heard people say so before, but the fact had been brought home to her. At Saunby, the servants were segregated; there were so many of them they formed a separate body. But at Mansbridge, Christine found herself living at close quarters with beings who seemed, at first, strange indeed.

Matrons who came to call said sympathetically that she had been unfortunate.

"You *have* been unfortunate with maids, dear," they said.

Christine thought she must have been ; the good maids wouldn't stay and the bad ones had to be got rid of.

There was Willows, one of the earliest ones, who left because Christine was always ringing bells and taking her off her work. Christine thought twice about ringing a bell in future, but Willows' successor left because she couldn't get her upstairs done before lunch. Another left because she was tired of always clearing up the mess in the sitting-room after the visitations of the " crowd." Proper orgies they were, she told her interested friends, making the " g " hard. Another girl left because " there was no consideration " and she " never knew where she was." These good maids left in a state of indignation that sorely puzzled the young mistress of the house. And by and by the place acquired a bad name and good maids did not apply.

Among the bad ones was Catherine, who said " Right-ho " when Christine gave her orders.

"You shouldn't allow her to ' Right-ho ' to you," said Nicholas reprovingly.

"I know. But what can I say to her ? I daren't tell her not to."

"But you must. You mustn't be afraid of your own maids," said Nicholas.

"How would you do it, then ? " asked Christine.

"Oh, I should just say : ' Catherine, don't say Right-ho to me when I ask you to do something. I don't like it.' I should say something like that. It's quite easy."

"I tell you what," said Christine. "I'll ring the

bell now and you ask her to bring some more coal, and if she says ' Right-ho,' you say that to her."

She rang the bell. Nicholas compressed his lips and distended his nostrils as he continued to look at his paper.

Catherine entered. There was a pause. Christine waited. Catherine waited.

" Bring some more coal, Catherine, please," Nicholas brought out at last.

" Right-ho," said Catherine.

Christine kept her eyes expectantly on Nicholas. He kept his eyes on the paper. He said nothing. Catherine, unrebuked, left the room.

" Coward," cried Christine, crashing through the paper on to his knee.

They shrieked with laughter, and Nicholas reproved no more.

But Catherine proceeded from " Right-ho " to green satin slippers in the morning and from those to a man in her bedroom at night. So she had to go.

" I'm too young," Christine complained to Nicholas. " If I was older I'd be able to manage them."

When she engaged girls younger than herself, which was very young, they knew nothing and couldn't be depended upon. When she engaged women older than herself, they took advantage of her youth and inexperience.

She had a disagreeable time getting rid of an elderly woman who came as sole housekeeper. She said she preferred to manage by herself and Christine was delighted to let her. But Mrs. Dunn turned out to be stealthy and sinister. She locked the kitchen door when she was within. She stole about the house in stockinged feet and gave Christine such looks on her own stairs that Christine felt sure she would be murdered some time when Nicholas was out. When the front-door bell rang, Mrs. Dunn opened the door a crack and murmured through it "Not at home." Christine herself rang no more bells, because she could not bear Mrs. Dunn to appear in answer.

At last Christine plucked up courage to give Mrs. Dunn notice. Mrs. Dunn wanted to know why.

Christine didn't know what to say.

"You can't turn a respectable woman away without cause given," said Mrs. Dunn threateningly. "I've my reputation to consider."

She waited, grim, determined. At last Christine furnished the cause.

"It's because I don't like you," she said.

"Good gracious," said Mrs. Dunn dismissingly. "Is that all? I don't like you, neither, but I wouldn't think of leaving for that."

Christine, however, managed to remain firm, and Mrs. Dunn, in her turn, went.

Thus Christine struggled with her new problems. Then something else happened to add to the strangeness and confusion.

"I think I'm going to have a baby," she said suddenly one day to Nicholas at lunch.

She had kept it to herself for some time, but now she told it suddenly, as she was eating salad. She looked at him with a scared expression over the piece of tomato on her fork, and when she finally put the tomato into her mouth, she couldn't swallow it, but kept it bulging her cheek while she waited for him to speak.

"Good Lord," he said, his own fork arrested.

"I think I am," said Christine on a rising note of alarm.

"Oh, what bad luck," said Nicholas. "D'you feel rotten, darling?"

"No."

" You're not frightened, are you ? "

" No," lied Christine. " But I feel kind of queer."

" So do I," said Nicholas, pushing his plate away.

" Oh, Christine," he said, going round to kneel on the floor beside her and put his arms round her. She held herself stiffly within them. Absurdly ignorant, she had moved cautiously ever since she suspected about the baby, in case she should injure it by lolling, or doubling up or dangling her legs over the arms of chairs as she used to.

" It's too soon," said Nicholas.

" It's very soon," agreed Christine. " It's bound to make an awful difference."

When Christine some weeks later wrote to tell Penelope, Penelope threw the letter across the breakfast-table to her aunt in disgust.

" Everybody's having babies," she said. " Everybody."

" Women do have babies," remarked Victoria. " Even in these days. You'll find as you go through life that your friends are all doing the same thing at the same time."

She buttered more toast.

" First they're all going away to school, then they're all being presented, then they're all getting engaged and married. Then they're all having babies, then they're all attending their children's weddings and by and by you'll find they're all actually being buried. If you're not doing the same things yourself, you notice it more. You'd better hurry to join the series, Penelope, or you'll feel out of it."

" Did you feel out of it, Aunt Victoria ? "

" No, my dear, but I don't think I ever wanted to be in it, particularly," said Victoria, helping herself liberally to marmalade.

" Perhaps I shall be like you," said Penelope.

" Oh, no, you won't," said Victoria complacently.
" I have my art, but what, in that nature, have you ? "

Christine in her letter urgently invited Penelope to
come to stay with her.

" Do, do come," she wrote.

But Penelope wrote to say she couldn't. Not at
present. She expected to be going into an office any
day now. Paul Kenworthy had no vacancy in his, but
he was trying to find a place for her in someone else's.
In the meantime, he took her out to tea and the
pictures, and he had been to Saunby several times on
Saturday and Sunday and she had been to Brockington Grange (a lovely house) ; so things were not so
bad as they had been.

Once Penelope had been in need of help, but
Christine was otherwise absorbed and did not see.
Now it was the other way round.

CHAPTER XXIV

PENELOPE knew Paul Kenworthy would propose to her as soon as she would let him. She interpreted quite rightly his nervous silences, his looks of appeal, but so far she had steered him dexterously from what he longed to say. She was quicker than he was and could do it. Also he was deeply in love with her and at her mercy ; he behaved as she wished him to.

She considered the subject as she lay in bed in the mornings or as she rowed herself about in the old boat on the lake. She thought it out, calculating but candid, and if she did not think it all out, it was more because some of her reasons were submerged too deeply in herself for her to know about them, than because she shirked the admission of them.

Penelope was subconsciously seeking a form of life that would be pretty much like the old. A life where she would *matter*. She had mattered considerably to Christine, who had spoilt and given into her since childhood. The girls had both mattered at Saunby. In their little world, they ruled. No one said them nay. They were waited upon, yet they were independent. They behaved like princesses ; neglected princesses, but princesses all the same. But with the departure of Christine and the ascendancy of Anthea and Nurse Pye, Penelope's power was broken. She was nothing in the house. She had to fit in as best she could. No one considered her, or indeed took any notice of her. She didn't like this. Youthfully, she thought if she didn't do something about it, it would go on for ever. She was determined to break away and re-establish herself somewhere else.

The point she made clear to herself, her first point, was that she was not going to stay at Saunby. That was very certain.

She wasn't going to stay at Saunby, but she couldn't go out into the world to work, because she wasn't trained for anything, as Paul had pointed out, and because her education, as Christine had realized long ago, was extremely inadequate. There was only marriage for her. But she could not make an ordinary marriage, because she was determined never to have children.

"Never," she said vehemently to herself.

She could therefore only marry someone who was willing to agree to her conditions. She thought Paul would be willing. But perhaps no one else ever would. Perhaps Paul was her only chance. She felt she could drive this bargain with Paul, if with nobody else, because, if she wasn't the perfect kind of wife, neither was he the perfect kind of husband. Not what she considered perfect, anyway. He was too fat and too humble. He seemed to her not to have a personality of his own, but always to be adapting himself anxiously to someone else, principally to her. (Here she was hard on poor Paul, who was so much in love as to be almost abject when she was about.) But he was very sweet-tempered, generous, and comfortable to be with, and if she felt no passion for him, she certainly felt no repulsion.

She decided to bring him to the point, tell him candidly and let him decide.

They were having tea in a restaurant in the city. An orchestra was playing dance tunes. The leader made eyes at the women who had secured the tables nearest to him. He had his following. These were his fans

281

who came regularly for morning coffee and afternoon tea to receive his *œillades* and to return them. The fans were mostly in the forties and had what Penelope called " football faces," blank, blown-up faces, liberally powdered, rouged, mascared, lipsticked, under jaunty hats. They liked pearls, pink lace, and cream cakes. The band-leader was coy and conscious among them, rolling his eyes round on them all.

" Do watch him doing his stuff," Penelope implored Paul.

She could look about and laugh, but Paul couldn't. He could only look at her. He gazed at her, with her curls turning up over a little turned-up hat, her deep blue eyes, so clear and yet so beautifully shadowed that you almost had to exclaim at them at times, and that delicious mouth smiling, smiling at the leader of the band. Her cheeks were faintly hollowed, her throat was hollowed at the base. Hollows were very attractive to Paul who was himself all curves and creases.

Penelope turned to look at him. Seeing an expression almost of anguish on his face, she leaned halfway across the table to him.

" Well ? " she said.

" Penelope," he said hoarsely.

A waitress approached their table with a wheeled trolley of cakes. Paul waved her off.

" Oh, but I want one," said Penelope.

" I beg your pardon," groaned Paul, horrified to have so forgotten himself. He beckoned the waitress back and Penelope took a chocolate éclair. Paul breathed unevenly. He'd almost said it then. He'd almost got it out.

" Well," said Penelope, when she had the chocolate éclair on her plate. " What were you going to say ? "

" Oh, nothing," said Paul heavily.

" Say it," said Penelope.

Paul clasped his hands on the table and leaned forward contemplating them. His heart beat so hard he was glad to press his chest against the table.

" It's only that I adore you," he brought out. " And I know it's no good. I don't suppose you'd ever marry me. No, of course you wouldn't. You must think I'm mad."

" No, I don't," Penelope assured him. " I thought you'd be asking me soon."

He looked up from his hands, his eyes alight with hope. She'd been expecting him to ask her and yet she hadn't choked him off.

" But I must say something to you," said Penelope.

" Oh, what ? What is it ? " he asked eagerly.

" I don't want any children," said Penelope. " Ever. You must understand that right from the beginning. I never want children. And if you don't think that's fair, you mustn't marry me."

An expression of incredulous joy had come into Paul's face. She was talking about marrying him ! She would marry him.

" Penelope," he said breathlessly, moving the sugar basin aside to get nearer to her across the table. " It's you I want. You ! You ! Blow children. You must please yourself about that. Penelope, I adore you."

" But will you like not having any children ? " persisted Penelope. " How will you like it when we're old ? "

" But we're not old, thank God," said Paul vehemently. " Darling, do you love me at all ? "

" I'm very fond of you," said Penelope, looking at him with her clear eyes. " I like being with you very much indeed. I'm very, very comfortable with you. Will that do ? "

" It'll do to go on with," said the ecstatic Paul. " I

say, can we get out of here? I shall make an ass of myself if I don't get out."

"Half a minute," said Penelope. "I haven't finished my éclair."

She licked the cream oozing from the sides delicately like a little cat.

He watched her with what was, in spite of his fat, a haggard devotion.

"Penelope, I'll do everything in my power to make you happy," he said earnestly.

She smiled kindly at him.

§

At Saunby, although it was Bessy's afternoon off, Nurse Pye was taking a constitutional. Anthea's mother had called, and when Mrs. Sumpton came in, Nurse Pye generally went out.

The babies were sleeping and she could leave them. A pair of perambulators stood almost permanently now at the foot of the majestic west front of Saunby, because that was the most sheltered place.

"It screens them from the wind," said Anthea.

"Poor Priory," said Victoria. "Its sole remaining function is to shelter the twins in their prams."

Nurse Pye instructed Doris, who took Bessy's place when Bessy was out, to keep her eye on the babies, and in her new spring mushroom hat, her long grey coat with her State Registration medal pinned to her breast and her white gloves, she set off to have a look round. Major Marwood was out of the way in London for several days and this was a good opportunity.

Nurse Pye had within her an inexhaustible spring of interest and energy. This inner fount kept her going where other people, though they might start, would flag and give up and say to themselves that after all it was nothing to do with them. Nurse Pye hardly ever came to such an inert conclusion. She hardly ever felt that there was anything that had nothing to do with her.

Her interests and energies were now fastened upon Saunby. There was such stuff here for her to get her teeth into. So much that needed management. Major Marwood up to his eyes in debt and yet spending so much money every year on a silly business like cricket. Young Miss Penelope Marwood hanging about all day with nothing to do ; she ought to be encouraged to hook that rich young man she was going about with. Old Miss Marwood who had no right in the house at all, unless she paid for her keep, which she didn't. And poor Mrs. Marwood, struggling against them all to get some provision for her children before everything went smash.

All Nurse Pye's sympathies were with Anthea and the babies. She had made their cause her own. Protective and pugnacious, she wanted to fight for them. She felt she couldn't leave them, she felt they couldn't manage without her. She stayed on and on well aware that this devotion was unpractical. She knew it was foolish to let her large nursing practice go so that she could remain indefinitely with someone who might, in time, be unable to pay her at all. But she would do it. She would stay as long as she could, and if she had to turn out again, well then, she would. Nurse Pye had complete confidence in her ability to earn a living.

She also liked the life at Saunby. She liked the little kingdom in the nursery. She liked this space and beauty better than the little street up by the Castle. And though she did not approve of any of the family except Anthea and the babies, she was not averse to being associated with them. She always had a weakness for what she called the upper ten. Not for them, perhaps, but for being with them.

She looked at Roger, small and fair, in his perambulator, and at Veronica, dark and robust, the image of her mother, in hers. Then she walked off into the sunshine of the spring afternoon, looking about her with her small, lively eyes.

Only the lawns round the house were kept in order. More and more of the garden was going to the wild for want of care. Mrs. Marwood said they couldn't afford the necessary number of gardeners, but Nurse Pye would have put Thompson on to it, if she'd had her way. What did he do but live like a gentleman? Nurse Pye had a grudge against Thompson. She felt he was her opposite in the game. She felt the Major played Thompson against her and Mrs. Marwood her against Thompson. Nurse Pye felt it was much more important that she, as compared with Thompson, should remain at Saunby. She was some use, she knew, but what was he?

She went into the warm walled garden where the old medlar grew. In the middle of one walk there was a round stone basin, cracked and empty now, where, on a pedestal in the middle, a stone swan with a crown round its neck, curved in melancholy grace.

It made Nurse Pye feel sad to look at it. She didn't know why.

She went on to look at a sundial where the old copper disk had burst from the encircling stone.

'A bit of mortar would soon put that right, but nobody does it,' she thought. 'I could do it myself.'

'Tyme tryeth Troth,' she traced on the dial.

'My hat it does,' she agreed with fervour, and walked on.

In the kitchen garden an acre of fruit bushes and

strawberry beds had once, at much expense, been roofed and sided and divided into compartments by wire-netting. But the netting had gaping holes in it now and already the birds were busy.

'The netting isn't keeping the birds *out*, it's keeping them *in*,' noted Nurse Pye in exasperation. 'If that isn't just like these people. I've no patience with the Major,' she thought, stumping on.

Greenhouse with no heat. Stables with no horses.

"It's too big," said Nurse Pye, looking about her.

Nurse Pye liked reasonably sized, compact, manageable places. She began to feel as she went over it that perhaps Saunby was too much even for her to manage.

What was the use of all this if you couldn't keep it up in style? The Major was simply letting the place fall to pieces.

'He shouldn't be allowed,' she thought with indignation. 'He should be made to get out and pay his bills.'

Pay as you go, was Nurse Pye's maxim, inculcated in the little house in one of Oldham's back streets. If you can't pay, do without, was another, and she thought the Major would be better for a few such principles.

She left the kitchen garden by the small beautifully wrought iron gate with an 'M' worked into the scroll design. There were many such gates made in the prosperous days when Saunby had its own smith.

Half-way across the cricket field she paused. She considered whether to go down the elm avenue and past Thompson's lodge, or whether to go into the wood and have a look at the lake. She decided for the wood; you couldn't go there with the prams, so she would take the opportunity while she was without them. She struck off sideways and went through the gate into the wood. The green alley between the crowded trees received her, a stumpy figure in white gloves.

The deeper she went into the wood, the more the brambles caught at her skirts, the more the trees dislodged her hat. But she pushed on. The more Nurse Pye was impeded, the more she didn't give up.

'Eh, what a neglected place,' she thought with disapproval. 'Why doesn't somebody haul these fallen trees out and get them sawn into logs for the fires? Or why don't they sell the timber? I would.'

She reached a small clearing and sat down on a stump to pick the burrs off her coat. The sun shone warmly upon her, and when she had cleared her coat, she sat on, her short legs extended, her white gloved hands on her knees, relaxed from efficiency into primitive enjoyment of the sun's warmth.

Suddenly she was alert again. What was that?

She listened sharply, waiting. The sound came again. A man's laugh, a low, lazy kind of laugh from somewhere quite close at hand. Nurse Pye got noiselessly to her feet. Who could be laughing in this private wood? She must find out, she must see to it.

There was a murmur of voices now. Low, but distinct enough to make out that one was a woman's.

Nurse Pye tiptoed into the thicket, swimming the air with her white gloves to balance herself. She paused to locate the voices. The unseen persons helped her by speaking again. Her tongue between her teeth, Nurse Pye cautiously parted the leaves of a beech tree and peered through.

At once, she withdrew her hands and face.

Bessy! Bessy Palmer. Lying on the ground with a man.

Nurse Pye trembled violently from her discovery.

She held to the trunk of the tree to steady herself, to grasp the implications of the situation. She was filled with a strange, palpitating excitement.

When she could trust herself, she peered again. Longer this time.

The abandoned girl was lying on the ground, with one arm thrown out, her head turned aside, while the man, lying on one elbow beside her, leaned above her. Even as Nurse Pye looked, he kissed Bessy.

Nurse Pye fell back, breathing fast. The man was Thompson. Thompson. And he was married. Nurse Pye's excitement became almost unbearable.

She peered again.

There was Thompson kissing Bessy's neck, while Bessy lay with her face turned away. Nurse Pye, from her tree, could see Bessy's strange expression. She had a faint, sad smile on her face. She looked almost beautiful, but it was a beauty that outraged Nurse Pye. Lying like that. Looking like that. It was dreadful. Dreadful. Disgusting.

Nurse Pye suddenly broke from the tree and went blundering away through the wood, tearing her stockings on the brambles, knocking her hat on the trees, soiling her white gloves. Hurrying, almost running, she got out of the gate, crossed the cricket field, the kitchen garden, the gravel sweep and gained the house. She hurried up to the nursery. Empty, thank heaven. She hurried into her room and shut the door. No one must see her so upset.

Her hair straggled in wisps. Her face was like sodden tissue-paper, crumpled, crimson. She wiped her forehead and under her eyes. That girl. With that man. It was disgusting ; that was why she was so upset, because it was so disgusting. It was all she could do not to burst into tears. Because it was so disgusting, she repeated, stifling a terrible wild regret that no man had ever lain like that with her, that she had never looked like that for any man.

"It's the shock," she said, plunging her hands into cold water, throwing cold water over her face.

CHAPTER XXV

SHORTLY after six o'clock Bessy was putting her collar on before the little swing-glass on top of the yellow-painted chest of drawers in her room, when the door opened and Nurse Pye came in. Bessy, her hands at her neck, stared through the glass at Nurse Pye. Her coming in like that could only mean one thing. She knew. White in the face, Bessy turned slowly round.

In the low attic-room where the light was fading, Nurse Pye seemed to loom upon her. Bessy put out one arm behind her to steady herself against the chest.

"You may well look like that," said Nurse Pye in a voice she could scarcely control. "I saw you this afternoon, you madam, you. Under that tree with Thompson. Ah—you disgusting creature," she stammered, her face twisted. "You make me sick to look at you. Sick."

Bessy panted against the chest as if she had been running. Her mouth hung open, her eyes implored Nurse Pye.

"You!" Nurse Pye burst out again. "Trusted with innocent children and carrying on with a married man. For shame! Shame on you."

Her voice vibrated and rolled round the attic and came back multiplied to Bessy. She slipped down against the chest of drawers, lower, lower until she was huddled on the floor.

'It's come out. I'm found out,' she clamoured

silently. 'What shall I do? Where shall I go? What will they do? Will they bring my father to me?'

"How long has this been going on?" Nurse Pye was demanding.

Bessy made no answer. She rolled her forehead against a white china knob.

"Well, if you won't answer me, you'll answer your mistress," said Nurse Pye. "Wait till she hears about it. After all she's done for you, you to behave like this. Oh, you wicked girl, what end d'you think you'll come to? You'll be on the streets before you've finished. And what'll your father say? You'll have him to face. Mrs. Marwood'll send for him, you see if she doesn't."

"Oh, no," cried Bessy, clutching Nurse Pye's skirts. "Oh, don't let her do that! Don't bring my father to me. Don't let him know. He'll kill me. Oh, I'll do anything. I'll go anywhere. I'll go right away now, if only you won't tell my father."

Nurse Pye wrenched her skirts from Bessy's grasp.

"You don't think we're going to let it rest here, do you?" she cried. "Your father'll be told, and either you or Thompson'll have to go, that's certain." One way of getting Thompson out, she thought. He'd played into their hands. Serve him right.

"Oh, I'll go. Not Bill. I'll go," said Bessy, clambering up from the floor.

"You'll stay where you are till Mrs. Marwood's dealt with you," said Nurse Pye. "So you know."

Suddenly she remembered unconnected incidents, tears, sick headaches, that had occurred while Bessy was being, as she had put it, knocked into shape for a nurse-maid.

"Here," she said, seizing Bessy by the shoulder. "Are you pregnant?"

Bessy put her hand to her mouth and stared with

292

terrified eyes at her inquisitor. All, all had to come out. There was no help.

" Ah," said Nurse Pye. " So you are."

She let Bessy's shoulder go and dusted her hands together as if she could wash them of the affair now. Her desire to punish was appeased. There was nothing beautiful or enviable here, only the usual sordidness.

She walked to the door.

" Well, you'll both go now," she said coldly. " There'll be no doubt about that. I'll go and see what Mrs. Marwood has to say about it. You stop where you are. We don't want you in the nursery again, thank you. Doris can take your place."

She went out, closing the door behind her. Her firm steps died away in the hollow-sounding passage. The house, up there, was quiet.

Bessy stood at the chest, her face on her arms. The stillness of despair was on her. From the beginning she had known it would all end badly. It couldn't end any other way. What they had done was wrong, wicked, and sometime she would have to pay. She knew it and accepted it. But she didn't want Bill to pay. She wanted him always to be happy. She loved him and she had kept her secret. When the end came, she would manage, she told herself. And the end was here. She had thought she would be able to get away before they found out. But they'd found out and soon everybody in the house would know. Soon they'd do something with her ; they'd bring her father, or they'd send her home to face him. Soon she'd have no chance to take her own way ; they'd take charge of her.

Bessy clutched the sides of the chest for a moment, her head bowed. Then she walked to the door, and listened. There was not a sound. They'd all be busy downstairs with the dinner and the table.

She went noiselessly down the back stairs. She

could hear voices now in the kitchen and the servants' hall, as she had heard them on the night she had first stolen out to meet Bill in the wood. They'd never meant any harm. He'd meant to protect her, she knew. But love was too strong for them both. Well, they'd been happy. This was the hour her father had threatened them with, the hour of reckoning. She'd meet it, because she'd have to in any case, but meeting it this way, she would save him, her love, her darling, born to laugh and be happy.

She went out into the grey spring evening. Her thoughts ran very light and fast and jumbled now. They said there was the ghost of a woman in the avenue there, of a woman disgraced like herself. But one of the gentry. You'd think it would be different for them. But they'd let her die, her family. Just as her father would have let her die and thought it the best end for her. Better so, he would say, letting them put her in the ground, glad to see the last of the daughter who'd brought shame on him. Her name would never be mentioned in her home again, she knew. Not after to-night.

She reached the wood she had left only a little while ago. She made her way to the lake. When she came to the sandy edge, her fluttering thoughts stood still. A cold horror filled her and she stood peering into the water. If only she could have thrown herself in a moment ago, while she was wild, unthinking.

The heron, which frequented the wood, flew up and flapped slowly away. He landed in a tree on the other side of the lake, and with his long neck sticking out of it, he waited for the figure by the water to be gone.

Bessy looked round in terror, trying to urge herself. She must do it. There was no other way. She stepped into the water, among the thin little bulrushes at the edge.

" Oh, it's cold," she whimpered. " It's so cold."

She advanced a little way. The water crept up her stockings. She lifted her skirts out of the water, weeping, her face distorted ; but she walked deeper in. She wailed, in pity for herself. The water filled her skirts, swelled them, stained them dark to her waist.

" Oh," she cried in terror. " I can't. I can't."

She took a step farther and fell face forward. She gulped and thrashed the water wildly. She struggled to her feet and floundered back to the shore. Wild duck on the other side of the lake rose from the water with a great commotion and wheeled in the grey sky.

Bessy, streaming with water, gulping, choking, dragged herself on to the grass and lay there. She was terrified. Her heart beat madly, strongly. It would never die, she felt. How could she kill her heart ? She rolled face downwards on the bank in despair.

The wild duck settled to the bosom of the lake again. The heron still waited.

Bessy sat up. " I must," she said with grim purpose. " I've got to do it."

She clambered in her streaming clothes to her feet and took a rush into the water. She drove herself on. Deeper, deeper, till the water reached her chin. She was like an animal, silent, drowning, her eyes terror-stricken. Let me die. I must die. She shut her eyes and lowered herself into the water. It closed over her. But instantly she was up again, gulping, choking, thrashing about her as before. She thrashed her way back to the bank. She dragged herself out of the water, covered with mud and slime and green weeds. Dark and streaming, she lay on the bank, moaning with her face in the grass.

She couldn't die. She was as hard to kill as the cat her father had once drowned in the tub. She had seen him do it and had hated him ever since. Her father's face as he thrust the cat back and back into the water returned to her now. If only he was here to do the same to her. If only someone would hold her under.

"I can't do it," she moaned. "I want to, but I can't. I can't let myself die."

By and by the ducks settled again. The heron flew over, but he saw the figure moving on the bank and returned to his tree.

Bessy struggled to her feet, her wet clothes impeding her. She turned from the water. She knew she could not drown herself. She knew she couldn't kill herself. And it was worse to live. If she could have died, it would all have been over. Now she had worse to face.

She got out of the wood, dragging every step. She was heavy and deathly cold, her teeth chattered. But her head felt light, mazed. Which way, she thought, standing in the field like a stricken tree. Not to the house. Not that way. The other, she must pass the lodge. A light showed at the window. She crouched low to pass the house. The gate creaked and Thompson, turning his paper, wondered idly who was going through but was not sufficiently interested to get up to see.

Bessy reached the lane, but a violent ague took her, and she sank to the ground, clasping her arms round herself, trying to still her shivering body. Water from her hair dripped over her face. She rocked herself. I shall die now, she thought with hope and fear.

"I'm so cold. I'm so cold," she kept moaning.

She dragged herself into the hedge in search of warmth. Moaning and shuddering, she moved about restlessly. She rubbed her arms, her legs. Suddenly she became aware that someone was going along on the other side of the hedge, in the field. With a cry she clambered out of the ditch into the lane again.

She was standing there when Johnny Spencer, looking at his sheep, came through a gap in the hedge to see what was the matter.

He fell back at the sight of the dark, wild, dripping figure as if it had been an apparition. Then he strode forward to look closer.

" Bessy ? " he said.

Bessy was moving off, wrapped round with her wet clothes like a shroud. She moaned and stumbled forward down the lane. A terrible pain had begun to grip her. She bowed herself over it.

" Bessy ! " shouted Johnny Spencer, striding after her to seize her by the shoulder. " What's up ? What's happened ? "

" Oh, don't." She doubled up, sinking to his feet. The pain stabbed her like a knife.

He gathered her with difficulty into his arms and struggled upright. She was heavy.

" Let me down," gasped Bessy, struggling fiercely. " Let me alone."

" Keep still," said Johnny. " You're coming home with me. What've you been trying to do to yourself? Keep still."

" Let me down." Bessy put her hand under his chin and thrust his head back, forcing him to drop her.

" Leave me alone," she said, standing before him shivering violently. " I've got myself into trouble and all I want is to be let alone."

" Stop talking and let me carry you quiet," said Johnny, making to pick her up again.

Bessy stepped backwards.

" You let me alone."

" You'll catch your death standing there," shouted Johnny furiously.

" That's what I want to do," said Bessy grimly. " That's what I tried for. I tried to drown myself," she said, beginning to weep. " But I were too strong for myself. Oh, what shall I do to myself? What shall I do ? "

The pain came on again and she pressed her hands over it and groaned.

Johnny snatched her up and strode down the lane.

" Don't take me to your mother, Johnny," implored Bessy. " Don't. She thought so well of me."

She put her arms round his neck to support herself, and he braced his head against them to bear her weight better. Sweat broke out on his forehead ; his heart laboured.

" Oh, Johnny, don't try and be kind to me," wept Bessy. " You'll only be sorry later."

" Be quiet with you," gasped Johnny. " D'you think I haven't known all along as you were going with that chap ? "

" Oh." Bessy writhed in his arms.

" Can't you keep still ? " breathed Johnny.

" I can't," wailed Bessy. " I've got such a pain."

" We're nearly there," comforted Johnny.

He got her to the farm kitchen at last.

" Mother ! " he shouted.

Mrs. Spencer came in from the dairy.

" Whatever . . ." she exclaimed.

Johnny gave her a warning look.

" Sit you down on the settle, Bessy," cried Mrs. Spencer, running forward. " Off with those clothes. Johnny, get me two blankets out of the press."

" I didn't want to come. I didn't want to come," wailed Bessy.

" Be quiet and no nonsense," said Mrs. Spencer, peeling off the wet clothes and rubbing briskly.

" Where's that brandy I had for the mare, Mother ? " asked Johnny.

" Back of the cupboard."

John held a cup to Bessy's lips, but her teeth chattered it away. He put a hand behind her wet head and tilted the brandy into her mouth.

"Fill the aluminium bottles, Johnny. The kettle's boiling," said his mother. "I'll put her into my bed and make up the other later."

"Oh, don't keep me here." Bessy stayed the rubbing hands. "Hasn't he told you? I've brought shame on myself. I'm going to have a baby. You don't want me here."

Mrs. Spencer's hands stopped for a second, but resumed as briskly as ever.

"Come on upstairs. Can you walk? Or shall our Johnny carry you?"

Bessy, weeping, shook her head at Johnny. Clutching her blankets, she stumbled up the stairs, protesting.

In a few moments, Mrs. Spencer was half-way down again.

"Johnny! Johnny!" she called. "Get your bike and go for Doctor Carter."

Johnny, alarmed, sprang up the stairs, but his mother pushed him down again.

"Go on, quick! Quick with you!"

§

Towards half-past nine the next morning, in a red straw hat, a rain-coat and light cotton gloves—a mercy they were clean, for she hadn't had gloves on her hands since goodness knows when—Mrs. Spencer hurried, as fast as her best shoes would let her, down the lane to the park-gates. It was an unheard-of thing for her to be dressed up and abroad at that time in the morning, but it was an unheard-of errand she was on. She was going to the House to tell the Family what she thought of them.

As she went through the lodge-gates, Bertha was cleaning her front-room windows. She sent a malevolent look at Mrs. Spencer, though she did not know who she was. Mrs. Spencer knew her and tightened her lips. Why couldn't she keep her husband at home instead of letting him harm a good girl like Bessy?

She hurried on up the avenue, clutching her brown leather hand-bag with cherries done on it in poker-work. She was breathless with haste and her face was almost as red as her hat. Her work was waiting and she must get back to Bessy. She had hardly dared to leave her, but Johnny was keeping about, and after all Bessy was too weak to move. Poor, poor girl. A good lass like that brought to such a pass as to try and drown herself!

'And our Johnny's just as set on her as ever, I can see,' she thought. 'Funny, you'd have thought it 'ud have turned him. Still, it hasn't turned me,' she marvelled. 'There must be something about the girl that you can't help yourself loving her.'

She crossed the field and went in at the iron gate. She made her way to the back of the house.

Mrs. Marwood, she was told, was always busy in the nursery at this time.

"Then I must wait," said Mrs. Spencer firmly. "But I hope it won't be for long. Let her know Mrs. Spencer from Top Farm is here, if you please."

She was put in the morning-room and closed in. She had time to cool down. She fanned herself with her handkerchief and her face slowly resumed its normal clear tan.

At last the door opened.

"I'm sorry to have kept you waiting, Mrs. Spencer," said Anthea. "But I am always busy with my babies in the morning. Do sit down. You wished to see me about something ? Or is it my husband ? He's away just now."

" No, it's you I want to see," said Mrs. Spencer, sitting. " It's about Bessy Palmer."

" Oh," said Anthea, her face clouding. " You know, do you ? "

" Yes, I know," said Mrs. Spencer.

" It's a terrible thing," said Anthea. " I'm most grieved. I trusted Bessy completely. I haven't made up my mind what to do about her. I'm most distressed. I haven't seen her yet."

" Well, you won't see her now," said Mrs. Spencer grimly.

Anthea opened her eyes in surprise.

" Not see her ? " she said.

" Bessy's with me," said Mrs. Spencer. " And there she'll stop."

" Bessy's with you ! Surely not. Bessy's in this house ! " cried Anthea, rising from her chair and going to the bell.

" You can ring, but you'll not bring her," said Mrs. Spencer. " Bessy's in bed at Top Farm. She tried to drown herself last night, Mrs. Marwood."

" No ! " cried Anthea in troubled protest.

" Aye," said Mrs. Spencer. " That nurse of yours frightened her that much she went out and tried to drown herself in the lake. If it hadn't been for my Johnny she'd be dead by now, for she had a miscarriage last night, Mrs. Marwood."

" Oh." Anthea reached for a chair in distress. " This is terrible. It's terrible."

" I must say I'm surprised at you, Mrs. Marwood," said Mrs. Spencer, doggedly getting in what she had come to say, " for you not to have gone to that poor girl when you knew what a state she was in. You knew she was terrified to death of her dad, you knew your nurse had threatened to turn her out, but you never went near her. And now it turns out you never even knew she was missing. I don't call that Christian, Mrs. Marwood, if you'll excuse me. Nay, it doesn't matter if you excuse me or not. That's what I think.

"And as for that man, that Thompson," went on Mrs. Spencer. "I'm surprised you kept him in a place where there are so many young girls. He's got a very bad reputation, has that man. They say his wife had to force him to marry her. Bessy's never mentioned his name, nor won't, I don't suppose, neither ; but my son knew about it. A good girl like Bessy doesn't give in to a man without a struggle, Mrs. Marwood." She looked sharply at Anthea, whose face was conscience-stricken as she remembered Bessy's attempt to get away from Saunby. "Aye, I can see you know something about it too," said Mrs. Spencer sternly. "You shouldn't have let that nurse of yours deal with things as you should have dealt with yourself. She doesn't know her place, that woman. And if I ever see her, I'll tell her so. Who's she to go frightening Bessy to her death? However," Mrs. Spencer rose, "if you'll please to have Bessy's box packed, my son'll come for it this afternoon.

"And there's another thing while I'm here, Mrs. Marwood, for I don't want to come again. Me and my son have been talking since last night and we want to buy our farm or leave it. Our farm's been connected with this house since the Priory was built, they say, but we can't help that. We don't want to be connected no more, and Major Marwood, if you'll excuse me, though as I'm speaking my mind I might as well speak it all, Major Marwood isn't what you'd call a good landlord. We can't get nothing done. It's uphill work getting so much as a gate out of him. We'd rather have the place to ourselves. Or else we'll move.

We'll take Bessy and we'll go somewhere else, unless we can buy. Put that before him, if you please, and my son'll come and see him. Now I'm going. Good morning."

" How is Bessy? " asked Anthea, getting it in at last.

" She's as well as can be expected after what she's gone through. She's a strong girl, but it's her thoughts as is making her suffer. Broken up, she is. Proper broken up. It makes your heart ache to see her."

" Will you tell her how distressed I am? " asked Anthea.

" I shan't mention you," said Mrs. Spencer, going out of the door. " Without she speaks of you first, which I don't suppose she will. It's not you she's bothering about, poor girl."

" May I come and see her later? " asked Anthea.

" Nay, I'd rather you didn't, thank you," said Mrs. Spencer. " Let her forget the past. It's the only way."

" I'm so very sorry this has happened," said Anthea humbly. " I never thought she'd take what Nurse Pye said so much to heart."

" Well, you've had an escape as well as Bessy," said Mrs. Spencer. " If she'd drowned herself, there'd have been an inquest and you and Nurse Pye, as you call her, wouldn't have showed up so well then, Mrs. Marwood. Good morning."

CHAPTER XXVI

IN agitation, Anthea hurried to the nursery in search of Nurse Pye. Mrs. Spencer had upset her. She felt humiliated and in the wrong. She must find her friend and ease these uncomfortable emotions by sharing them. But Nurse Pye received the news of Bessy's attempted suicide in a very different fashion. She was indignant.

"Fancy going and doing a thing like that," she exclaimed, pausing in her measurement of the twins' food. "The stupid creature! She never intended to drown herself, not she! She was just trying to make trouble and get her own back. I know that type. I've had a lot to do with girls, Mrs. Marwood. I wasn't ward-sister for nothing."

Standing waist-high at the table, Nurse Pye lifted the blame from where Mrs. Spencer had just laid it, on herself and Anthea, and put it firmly back on Bessy and Thompson.

"That's where the blame belongs," she pointed out. "And don't you be persuaded it doesn't. You've nothing to reproach yourself with, dear, and neither have I. Why, most folks 'ud have turned the girl out there and then. The law allows it. But what more did I do but tell her to wait till morning? She got off very lightly, I can tell you. Besides, it's all turned out much better than she could ever expect. She *didn't* drown herself, but she made enough mess of herself to get pitied and taken in by her friends. She got rid of the baby into the bargain and I daresay she'll end up by marrying that Mrs. Spencer's son. So what is there to be upset about ? We'll have a cup of tea. The kettle's boiling."

They always had tea in the middle of the morning, sitting together and enjoying each other's company and the pause from work.

" Mind you," resumed Nurse Pye when she had her strong, steaming cup in her hand, " I don't think Thompson ought to get off scot-free."

" Neither do I," agreed Anthea with fervour.

" Oh dear me, no," said Nurse Pye, snapping her eyes over the edge of her cup. " Going and getting a girl into trouble and sending her nearly to her death without losing so much as a night's sleep about it, it isn't good enough. It's always the way ; women *will* protect men. I've seen it over and over again. Thompson wants telling a thing or two, but I don't suppose Major Marwood will ever do it. Men always hang together in these things, and I think women ought to, too. What about you seeing Thompson this morning, before your husband comes back ? "

Anthea looked at Nurse Pye. She didn't like the idea of speaking to Thompson, but it might serve a purpose she had long had in mind. The two women looked at each other ; then they looked away. They were thinking the same thing.

" Perhaps it would be better if I saw him," faltered Anthea. " Though I don't much like the idea of it."

" We all have to do things we don't like at times," said Nurse Pye. " I'll go down and find him, shall I ? Will you see him in the morning-room ? "

" I suppose so," said Anthea without relish.

Thompson, having put on his jacket and smoothed down his upspringing hair with both hands, presented himself in the morning-room where Anthea, seated at the table for support, waited. He came in, vigorous, handsome, confident, with his fine distended nostrils and his smile.

Anthea looked up at him with discomfort. Must she dash all this away?

" I was just going to give the ground its first cut and I've been fiddling with the old mower. It's fairly falling to pieces. That's why my hands are so bad," he apologized, exhibiting them. " I got the worst off, but I didn't like to keep you waiting any longer. Was there something you wanted to see me about, Madam? " he asked cheerfully.

Anthea rolled a pencil between her fingers, looking at it, not at him.

" It's something very unpleasant—very painful that I have to say, Thompson."

Thompson shifted his weight, looking keenly at her.

" It's about Bessy," said Anthea.

His face changed. The look of pleasure fell away, leaving it set, wary.

" You were seen with Bessy in the wood yesterday," continued Anthea.

Thompson flushed a dull red and made a muffled sound of anger and dismay.

" Nurse Pye had to speak to Bessy, of course," Anthea went on, looking steadily at the pencil. " And Bessy took it so much to heart that she tried to drown herself in the lake last night."

" She . . . Bessy! " cried Thompson. " Drown herself? " he repeated in horror. " What for? "

" Because she was going to have a baby, I suppose," said Anthea.

There was such a silence after this that she looked up from the pencil. Thompson was staring at her, his eyes black in his white face.

" You didn't know, then? " ventured Anthea.

" Where is she ? " he brought out.

" She's with the Spencers at Top Farm. She's ill. She's had a—a miscarriage."

" How did she get there ? "

" Johnny Spencer found her in the lane by your house last night."

" By my house." Thompson groaned. " I was there and she never came to me."

He strode to the door.

" Thompson ! " Anthea sprang from her chair. " Wait ! I haven't finished what I want to say to you."

He turned to look at her.

" I'll come back for that later. I must go to her. She told me nothing. I knew nothing, poor lass. I'll come back, Mrs. Marwood. But I must go and see her now."

" Thompson, I don't think you ought to," said Anthea, reaching him. "No. I don't think you ought to. You're a married man."

" Ach," said Thompson, shaking that off and seizing the door-handle.

" I think you've done Bessy enough harm as it is," said Anthea, speaking very fast and getting it all in. " I think you ought never to see her again. The only thing you can do for Bessy now is to leave this district, and let her make a life for herself where she is. She'll never do it if she knows you're within a stone's throw of her. She's going to stay with the Spencers. Mrs. Spencer's been to see me and Johnny Spencer's been in love with her a long time and wants to marry her. If you let Bessy alone, I daresay she will marry him in time. What can you do for her but drag her down ? You ought to go away from her and keep away."

Thompson listened to her. She had made him pause. The fire had died out of his face, the determination to get to Bessy at all costs. He leaned heavily on the door-handle, his face grey, thoughtful.

Anthea waited. What would he do?

Thompson opened the door and went out. She heard him striding away. But she thought, from his face, that she had won.

She felt very disturbed again and hurried up to the nursery to be reassured and restored by Nurse Pye.

§

Thompson rose at last from where he had been sitting by the lake and made his way out of the wood. It was dinner-time, and when Bertha saw him coming down the avenue she dished up the potatoes. But he did not come in for them.

He strode down the lane and turned up to Top Farm. They saw him coming, and before he could reach the Dutch barn outside the yard Johnny Spencer had come out to meet him. The two men approached each other, Johnny like a farm dog coming to warn another off his premises. They stood in silence, in strong contrast to each other : Johnny, his lint-fair dusty hair blowing, his fingers in his front breeches pocket, thumbs outside, slow, solid, strong ; Thompson, supple, keen, alert, but defeated now and hurt.

" What d'you want here? " asked Johnny.

" I want to hear how she is."

" She's as well as can be expected," said Johnny, repeating his mother's formula. " But no thanks to you."

" I knew nothing about it," said Thompson. " She never told me. D'you think I wouldn't have taken her away if I'd known? We'd have gone, her and me, and to hell with everybody else. Why didn't she tell me? "

Johnny laughed bitterly. She'd have gone with this chap, he knew that.

The wind blew the straw round their boots.

" I suppose you won't let me see her ? " said Thompson.

Johnny shook his head.

" Nay. She's got a high temperature and you'd only make her worse. You've done enough damage as it is. The best thing you can do for Bessy is to get out and keep out."

" Don't bother yourself," said Thompson. " I'm going."

Hope showed in Johnny's eyes.

" D'you mean you're leaving these parts ? "

" Yes," said Thompson heavily. " I'm going."

" When ? "

" Soon as I can get off."

They stood in silence again.

" We'll look after her," said Johnny in a minute. " She'll be all right with us."

Thompson lifted his head, and looked at the house where she was. He smiled at Johnny, a strange smile so that Johnny could not tell whether he blessed or cursed him. Then he turned away and strode off down the rutted track to the lane.

§

By the time Bessy came to take her first walk, he was gone.

The Major, beseeching him in one breath to listen to reason and in the next swearing at him for a fool, had been able to do nothing with him.

The Major urged his own cause : " How the devil d'you think I'm going to run the season without you ? Who am I going to get to replace you ? "

He urged Thompson's cause : " What sort of a job d'you think you're going to get ? Jobs as private professionals aren't to be had for two a penny, you know. And by God, Thompson, if you must have it, your game's not as good as it was. You'll have difficulty in getting yourself taken on in any but a private team."

" I know, sir," said Thompson, tight-lipped.

" Well, don't be such a damn fool, then. Why should you give up your living, because that's what it is, your living, simply to get out of the girl's way ? "

Anthea had told him about Bessy, though she had not told him the part she herself had played in bringing Thompson to his decision.

" Your notions of chivalry are exaggerated," the Major told Thompson. " It's always fifty-fifty in these cases."

Thompson shook his head.

" No, it isn't, sir. It costs a woman more. A good one, anyway."

" Well," sighed the Major. " Women have been the ruin of you."

Thompson listened to all the Major had to say, but he went. At the month's end, the carrier's van came for the three-piece suite and Bertha's other household goods. Bertha superintended their removal from the house to the van and then begged a lift from the driver. She climbed up into the front and was borne away, her goods behind her, her husband following on a bicycle, up the avenue under the elms.

From her perch, she viewed the last of Saunby. She looked as if she was going to put out her tongue at it as if it had attempted a personal injury and she had got the better of it. She'd won. She'd waited and she'd won. Bill had been delivered, bound, into her hands. He'd got the sack, or so she thought, for carrying on with Bessy Palmer. Bertha had been told nothing, but she had put two and two together and if she added incorrectly, she did not know it. Bill had been taught his lesson, and now he should go *her* way. They were going to her sister's at Telby, since they had nowhere else to go. Bill hadn't been able to find anywhere for them, if he'd tried, which she doubted, since he didn't seem to try at anything these days. Bertha had made the arrangements. They were going to her sister's and he didn't need to think he'd be able to keep himself to himself there, because there was no room for nonsense of that kind at her sister's. Man and wife were supposed to live together and nothing else would be or could be arranged for.

Bill hadn't been able to get himself taken on anywhere. Everybody was fixed up for the season.

" But same as I says to him," Bertha told the driver when they had gone several miles towards Telby and got to talking. " I says : ' You've no need to starve. You've been a miner before, you can be a miner again, can't you ? ' "

" That's right," said the driver.

" Of course, Telby's a mining village," said Bertha. " All the men are in the pit there. He'll come to it."

" Aye," said the driver. " That's right."

So, by the time Bessy came to take her first walk, Thompson was gone.

Johnny, who accompanied her, thought she had gone far enough when they reached the place where the track from the farm joined the lane from the lodge.

" I reckon you've done enough for the first time out, Bessy," he said.

But she said she'd like to go a little farther.

Half-way up the lane he tried again.

" I think we ought to be turning," he said.

" No," said Bessy persuasively. " Let's go on a bit."

He realized that she was leading him to the lodge. Well, let her look, he thought. Let her realize he'd gone. Perhaps she'd settle better then.

Bessy reached a place where she could see the lodge through the gates. Talking of other things, only glancing towards the lodge now and again, she reached the place where she could see it. She hardly paused in her talk. Hardly paused as she saw the chain and padlock on the garden gate, the windows blank. He had gone. It was all over. There was nothing left. All these weeks she had never dared to ask about him, never dared to ask if he had come, or tried to see her. It had been terrible, knowing that other people knew what you longed to know and dared not ask them to tell you.

It was as if he had died, and as if she had died too. The life she had lived, before that dreadful night, was over. She was numb, weak, empty in a new world, where there was nothing yet but the kindness of Johnny and his mother.

" We'd better be turning, Bessy," said Johnny, suffering for her.

She turned obediently now. There was nothing to stand there for. She would do as he wished. She owed him that. She owed him everything.

" Would you like to take my arm ? " said Johnny, offering it.

" I'm not tired," said Bessy wanly.

" Right," said Johnny, dropping the rejected arm.

Compunction seized Bessy. He was so good.

" P'r'aps I'd better," she said.

Johnny walked carefully with her hand through his arm.

" You've not done so badly," he encouraged her.

Her heart was sick, but she smiled.

Soon she was working, doing her share, taking over the bottling of the milk and the care of the fowls. She was busy, she was tired at the end of the day, she hardly had time to think.

One sunny afternoon, as she stood in the field where the scarecrow woman was, throwing split maize to the hens, something wheeled in the blue sky overhead and with a strong flapping of wings, two fantails alighted and hungrily began to pick up maize round her feet.

She knew them. They were the birds that lived in the stable-loft, the ones that had come to him every day to be fed. Now that he had gone and no one fed them any more, they had found their way to feed with the hens. They had come from him to her. They were like a message from him.

She knelt on the grass beside them. They were not afraid of her. She remembered how he had trained them to eat out of his hands. Weeping, she poured maize into her own and offered it to them. She stifled a sob in case it should shake her hands and startle them. Biting her lips, she waited. She had not to wait long. The fantails raised their wings to lift themselves a little into the air and alighted on her hands, one on each. They pressed her palms with their strong, nervous red feet. Bessy, tears running down her cheeks, smiled to see them. This was what he used to do, hold them like this. He had taught them to trust him and through him to trust her.

She knelt there on the green field under the high blue sky, a girl holding two white birds on her hands.

From that time the fantails came every day and no one knew the anguish and delight they were to her.

CHAPTER XXVII

NURSE PYE was now established at Saunby and she made her presence felt. Her activities were no longer confined to the nursery, but extended to every corner of the house and beyond it ; as far, in fact, as the last stick of rhubarb and the last gooseberry in the kitchen garden.

At Saunby, rhubarb and gooseberries, like rabbits and bracken, flourished to excess. Hitherto no one had realized how much rhubarb and how many gooseberries Saunby produced, but now everyone realized and deplored it, for both appeared endlessly at table in pies, puddings, stews, fools, jams and other guises, thanks to Nurse Pye. Tinned foods were no longer admitted to the kitchen. Golden Peaches in Heavy Syrup were replaced by rhubarb and gooseberries, and Nurse Pye catered for the staff on the take-what's-provided-or-do-without principle.

Life behind the green baize door was changed. Nowadays, the servants were kept on the alert. They never knew when Nurse Pye would walk in or where the attack would be made next.

"What d'you want with all this olive oil, cook ? " she would inquire, throwing open the cupboard doors. "It's ridiculous. Don't order any more until this is done and then ask me."

"You must make your own scouring powder," she said to the kitchen-maid. "It's nothing but powdered pumice and dry soap. I'll give you the recipe. And collect all those bits of soap and make them into a jelly for the laundry."

" Don't leave the lids off your tins like that," she said to the under-gardener. Since the house-boy had been dismissed, he cleaned the shoes. " It dries the polish up," said Nurse Pye. " And don't let me have to tell you again."

Several servants gave notice, but Nurse Pye did not mind and cheerfully engaged more. She was good at choosing her subordinates.

After overhearing a conversation between husband and wife, Nurse Pye also appointed herself chauffeuse to Anthea. Since Thompson's exit, the Major had been obliged to drive the Daimler himself, and nothing would induce him to get the car out of the garage unless he wanted it himself. Anthea, at first, had tried.

" Francis, I have so much shopping to do. Could you take me into the city sometime to-day ? "

" Oh, God," groaned the Major, over his *Times*. " What on earth do you want to go into the city for on a day like this ? "

If it was a fine day, who wanted to leave the country ? If it was a wet day, who wanted to go into the town ?

" I've so much to do . . ." said Anthea anxiously.

" What, for instance ? "

" I want silk for the twins' smocks, and a great many things for cook, and I want to go to Black's and to Morton's . . ."

" My dear girl, there's nothing there that can't wait. You really can't drag me out ten miles for silk for smocks and things for cook. Besides, what do you think I'm going to do while you do all that in the shops ? Hang about outside ? Damn it all, I'm not a chauffeur."

" Come along, Mrs. Marwood," said Nurse Pye,

walking in on them like a bantam-cock. "I'll take you myself."

"Oh, will you?" cried Anthea, hurrying gratefully away with her. "Thank you so much."

The Major did not analyse his feelings, but as he turned his *Times* and bent his beautiful face above it, he muttered: "Damn that woman."

Thereafter Nurse Pye and Anthea made their excursions to the shops and elsewhere in Nurse Pye's baby car, and, bowling over the roads with her friend, having secured the things she wanted, a feeling of great satisfaction invaded Anthea. She remembered a phrase from one of her old books on happiness, in which the necessity for effort was dwelt upon. "'Everything worth while,' said Nietzsche, 'is accomplished *notwithstanding*.'" Anthea acknowledged it; notwithstanding Francis, it was in her case.

Nurse Pye and Anthea contrived to pay the running expenses of the car out of the housekeeping money. The petrol they bought, and paid for, from the little man who had two pumps on the high road not far from the main gates of Saunby. They bought and paid for it to make up to him, Anthea said, for having had to wait so long for the payment of his nine-pound bill by the Major. The bill had at last been paid, with other bills, with money from the sale of Top Farm.

"But we shall soon be in debt again, I suppose," sighed Anthea to Nurse Pye, who by this time knew all.

"Well, what can you expect?" asked Nurse Pye. "When more money goes out than comes in? It stands to reason. At least, it does to mine. All the same, we're cutting down expenses; there's no doubt about that. Things are better. Thompson's gone, Miss Christine's gone, Miss Penelope's going. Of course, there's cricket and Miss Marwood left. I don't know how Miss Marwood has the face to stop on without paying a penny for her keep. I don't know why you put up with her."

"I put up with her because I've no alternative, I suppose," said Anthea. "She's been here since she was a child, you know."

"She's not a child now," said Nurse Pye. "Far from it."

"But about cricket, I don't *think* there's going to be the usual fortnight this year," said Anthea almost roguishly.

"Well, I should hope not indeed," said Nurse Pye. "Talk about fiddling while Rome burns, the Major's on a par with his cricket."

Anthea was right. There would not be a cricket fortnight ; not because Anthea didn't want it or because of the expense, but because the Major was lost without Thompson. Good servants, good secretaries, good subordinates of all sorts make life smooth ; they also make helpless those they serve and the Major was helpless now.

Everything went wrong. Thompson had always rounded up the team, but now the Major had to do it and he had never realized before how awkward they could be. They seemed bent, he told them, on giving him trouble with their holidays, their family illnesses, their damaged knee-caps or thumbs or one thing or another.

"I hate slackness and inefficiency," he fumed to the surprised team.

"Everybody wants to leave everything to me, and, by God, it isn't good enough," he told them.

They left no more to him than before, but without Thompson it was far too much.

He was defeated by small things. If, for instance,

the cover wouldn't come off the typewriter at his first attempt to remove it, he didn't struggle with it, he left it and didn't do the letter. And the fact that there was no ribbon in the second typewriter was enough to ensure that it would never be used again. Thompson had always put the ribbons in.

He made an attempt to coach Stead to take Thompson's place, but he soon gave it up. Stead was a fool, he said, only fit to cut grass.

With Thompson to do the work and share, even double, his enthusiasm, all had been well. Without Thompson, he had all the work and none of the enthusiasm ; the one cancelled out the other, he found. He gave up the idea of holding the cricket fortnight this year because there would be so much to do and he would have to do it.

The day matches, however, were to be held as usual at Saunby, and the Major wrote to ask Nicholas to play for him against Lord Barwell's side. Christine replied that Nicholas would come and she with him. She would stay until Penelope's wedding and probably afterwards too, because Nicholas was away a great deal for cricket and she didn't much like being at Mansbridge by herself. "Not when I can be at Saunby," she wrote.

So, one evening as the May dusk was falling, Christine returned. Stiff after the long drive, she clambered out of the car and stood once more on the gravel sweep before the Priory. The air passed like a cool hand over her eyelids and round the back of her neck. In her creased suit, her figure distorted, she stood, letting her eyes visit every feature of the West Front. It was always the West Front you looked at first at Saunby. The birds were nesting, as usual, she noticed, in the Virgin's crown. What a relief to look up at something, she thought, throwing her head back. In Mansbridge there was nothing to look up at or look up to. When she had gazed her fill at the West Front and the house, she turned to look at the lake, gentle in the evening, and at the Mound beyond it where the tallest beech trees stood. Her eyes followed the sweep of lawn and wall and walk, and Nicholas saw her look of pride and pleasure.

'This is my home. This is what I love,' she was thinking, and her thoughts showed in her face.

Nicholas, who had been slumped at the wheel, unwilling to move, now got out, sighing unconsciously. Very creased himself at the back of the jacket, his hair rough, he followed Christine into the house. No one had heard them arrive, so no one came to meet them. Their return was very different from their departure as bridegroom and bride ; but it did not occur to them, mercifully, to compare.

In the hall, Christine sniffed up the familiar smell of the house with pleasure.

" What is it ? " she said, more to herself than to him. " You only notice it when you come back to it after an absence. It's like age and incense—the ghost of incense after all these centuries."

Nicholas didn't speak. He couldn't smell anything but what he thought was mustiness from the tiger-skins and buffalo-heads. He stood in the hall like a child that has wakened up cross from its afternoon sleep ; one is apt to feel and look thus after a long drive.

" Where is everybody ? " said Christine, crossing the hall to pull the bell.

She went towards her father's room, but before she could reach it the door opened and he appeared.

" Hullo, hullo, Christine, my dear, how are you ? " He bent his cheek to receive her kiss and gave her a kind pressure on the elbow, which was as much as he could manage. "Nicholas, I was never so glad to see anybody in my life. Come in here and have a drink. Staveley's fallen out and I don't know what the devil to do."

A maid now appeared, and Penelope came running down the stairs. The sisters threw their arms round each other.

"Oh, darling," cried Christine, holding Penelope off to look at her. "I'm so glad to see you. You do look lovely. Look at *me*! Aren't I a sight?"

Penelope protested, but half-heartedly. She did think Christine looked a sight. The change in her sister embarrassed her; she almost felt she didn't know her, she looked so different.

In their reunion, the sisters were a little constrained. They could not be completely candid with each other. Penelope didn't want to be made to pretend to raptures she did not feel, so she avoided talking too much about Paul and her marriage. But sisters do not need to be told about each other; they know. And in a very short time Christine knew all that Penelope didn't wish her to know; she knew that Penelope was not in love with Paul. Penelope, for her part, knew that things were not right with Christine and Nicholas, and when, later, Christine ventured to say what she felt she must say to Penelope, Penelope was ready for her.

"You're so young, you know, darling," Christine said, very anxious to protect. "I wish you could have waited a bit longer. Until you know your own feelings better. I mean, Pen, do you think this is the *ideal* sort of marriage?"

Penelope looked at her.

"Is yours?" she asked.

Christine flushed and was silenced. She could not say it was meant to be. That was the difference. It

320

was meant to be. But it had so soon gone wrong, and Penelope had every reason to object to a lecture upon marriage from one who had failed in her own.

But Penelope didn't know, thought Christine, withdrawing from her sister, how difficult it all was. She didn't know Nicholas's friends. It was they, thought Christine, deeply resentful, who were responsible for the trouble ; Cicely Hoyle, the Bainses, the Marchants and the rest. Nicholas, she considered, was ruined by them and made into someone she did not like. He was at his worst when he was with them ; he was like them, reckless, noisy, trivial and drinking too much. He had soon given up his water-drinking at the parties ; he felt himself falling too far behind in gaiety when he drank only water. So he waved Christine's proffered glass aside and got up to mix his drinks himself and the results were frequently lamentable.

Finally, Christine, fretful and out-of-sorts, struck. She said she couldn't have his friends bursting in on her the way they did. So Nicholas fell into his old habit of going to the club. He fell into all his old habits, among them that of playing golf with Cicely. He had offered to stay in with Christine, but she refused his offers. " Oh, no, you must go," she had said, but was hurt when he did. She was hurt at first, but gradually she withdrew herself so that she should not be hurt. She implied that she could always amuse herself by herself, that *she* didn't have to drink and gamble and run to sit in a different hotel every night to be happy, and this attitude, which began by being a pose adopted in self-defence, became almost a reality, and although it was broken by moods of regret and sadness and loneliness, Christine did, at this time, become rather self-congratulatory.

Nicholas, man-like, took her at her word. He thought she didn't want him and flung off. Women may be too subtle for men, but as it is probable that they suffer most from this very subtlety, it seems a pity they should have been endowed with it.

Christine was too inexperienced and intolerant to make a plan for getting Nicholas away from his friends. She alternated between trying to put up with them and leaving him to them in disgust. She was far from feeling that she was her husband's keeper. Such an idea never occurred to her.

She was too taken up with trying to find her own bearings to be able to deal as well with his. Too much had happened to Christine in too short a time. She had fallen violently in love and had been swept from the peace of Saunby and girlhood into marriage and a strange new life among strange new people. Before she had time to adapt herself to any of these experiences, she was plunged into the still stranger experience of having a baby.

Perhaps it was the baby, as well as Nicholas's friends, that estranged them, she thought. Perhaps marriage, instead of being a union, is a separation. Perhaps it is the parting of the ways for lovers, she thought sadly. She had to follow her own path now, to turn off from being a lover and become a mother. It was a natural development, but she had left Nicholas behind. He was still doing as he had done before. The baby made no difference so far, to him, except that it removed her from him. And he didn't seem to mind much about that, she thought.

She was wrong. Nicholas felt her loss deeply, but he thought he had to put up with it. Ever since the baby started she had been moving away from him. While they were lovers, they had been able to understand each other and keep together. Now they seemed to have no meeting-place. He was driven back on himself and he couldn't bear that. He couldn't stand himself. He knew Christine didn't like his friends, but he thought she ought to realize that the only way he could get away from himself was to lose himself in drinks and poker and rush and noise. That was the way he was used to getting rid of himself, and that was the way he had to do it still. Christine didn't understand, he thought resentfully, that when he kept quiet, all the unrest he felt broke loose and goaded him beyond bearing. He dared not give way to unrest now. He must lie low and bear it, at least until the baby was born and grown a bit.

When he had played in the match against Lord Barwell's side, victorious this year to the Major's disgust (" We should have won," he fumed, " if Thompson had been here to bowl for us "), Nicholas left Saunby to play elsewhere. He was glad to be going to a fresh place, glad to keep on the move, and always have company. The " crowd," Cicely and the Bainses and Doreen Wood and Bob Marchant, were coming down in their cars to Burley Parva to watch the match there. They were good fellows like that, he thought ; they supported him almost everywhere. Cicely came down with the Bainses, but went back with him when he was going back to Mansbridge. He preferred her company on the long drive to no company at all.

" And are your friends going down to Burley Parva ? " Christine asked evenly as he got into his car to leave Saunby.

" Yes. Yes, I think they are," he admitted reluctantly.

It seemed too bad to be going off to play in a match and make up a party afterwards at some hotel or other on the road, while she couldn't go anywhere. All the same, he thought, she didn't *like* matches and parties and would certainly have preferred to stay at Saunby even if she had been able to go with him. So what was there to be done about it? His eyes asked her this in rather wistful bewilderment, but she had her head turned sideways to the lake and was smiling in faint contempt. His friends, she thought, he has to have his friends.

" Well? " said Nicholas, his hands spread on the wheel.

" Well? " said Christine, turning back to him.

" I'd better be going," said Nicholas.

" Yes," said Christine.

" Good-bye, then, darling."

" Good-bye."

Both hurt, but both perversely smiling, they kissed and parted.

§

Christine was now mostly alone, but being alone at Saunby was very different from being alone at Mansbridge. There she had been like a fish out of water, gasping on the asphalt, but Saunby was her natural element, her home.

Penelope was too busy to spend much time with Christine. She had her trousseau to see to. This was no small collection of cheap home-made things. Penelope was a tougher young woman than her sister and determined to get what she wanted. She horrified and alarmed Anthea and Nurse Pye by her expenditure and delighted in doing it. The boxes that arrived by van down the drive and by Pidcock on his bicycle caused the greatest consternation in the nursery.

" There's something *else* coming now," Nurse Pye would announce, looking, like Sister Anne, from the high windows.

" I've just been into Penelope's bedroom," Anthea would say, returning to the nursery. " She's got a

white tulle evening dress—a most unpractical thing—
and how much do you think it cost ? How much ? "

The two looked deeply at each other.

" Twenty-two guineas ! " announced Anthea.

" Twenty-two . . ." whistled Nurse Pye in outraged amazement. " Twenty-two guineas ! It's scandalous. It's downright scandalous. You must speak
to the girl. It can't go on. Where shall *we* be ? What
about the children ? "

" Oh, darling," said Anthea, taking Roger from
Nurse Pye's knee and covering him with kisses to
console him for the money that was being taken from
him by his wickedly extravagant step-sister. " What's
Mummy going to do ? What can she do ? "

" You must speak to her. That's what," said
Nurse Pye firmly.

But when Anthea spoke to Penelope, Penelope
went to her father.

" Get what you want," he told her. " You must
do things properly, of course."

He still felt full of money from the sale of Top Farm.
Besides, turning one's daughters out properly on their
marriage was one of the things one had to do ; like
educating one's sons.

So vans and boxes continued to arrive.

Everything was being made pleasant for Penelope.
Paul's mother was retiring from Brockington Grange
to her London club. She was passionately fond of
bridge and happy, even eager, to go where there
would be plenty of it. In Brockington it was sometimes very difficult to make up a four. She was
leaving a staff of well-trained maids for Penelope and
the house was being entirely done over to Penelope's
taste. Mrs. Kenworthy was amiably putting up with
all the upset so that Penelope should have none of it.

As for Paul, he poured all he had and was at the

feet of his beloved, and to make himself more seemly in her sight, he refused every day at luncheon at the club the baked jam roly-poly pudding of which, like most fat men, he was extremely fond.

CHAPTER XXVIII

AFTER Penelope's wedding, Christine stayed on and
on at Saunby, putting off her return to Mansbridge as one puts off the leaving of a warm bed on
a cold day. She kept giving herself just a little longer,
much to the indignation of Nurse Pye.

Nurse Pye, firm in her middle-class conviction that
if you look after the pence the pounds look after themselves, pointed out to Anthea that an extra mouth to
feed cost extra money.

" I know," said Anthea, with the harassed expression
that came into her face when the question of money
cropped up, which it frequently did. " I quite realize
that. But what can we do ? "

Nurse Pye said that, without actually putting it into
words, they must let Christine see that she wasn't
wanted. Christine soon began to feel unwelcome in
the nursery and she mostly kept out, but it never
occurred to her that she was unwelcome at Saunby.
That would have been incredible to her. Saunby had
been her home long before Anthea or Nurse Pye came
to it, and she looked upon them as the interlopers, not
herself. Saunby had always been her home and it was
her home still.

She was, in fact, rather alarmed that it should be
still so much her home. The house in the Drive at
Mansbridge, even though she had lived in it with
Nicholas and would live in it again with him, meant
very little to her. She was ashamed to admit to her-

self how little. And Mansbridge meant less. She disliked Mansbridge; principally because it wasn't Saunby. If she had not had Saunby for comparison, Mansbridge might have seemed quite a good sort of place, but as it was, she actively disliked it and was reluctant to go back.

There were some black and yellow striped caterpillars that covered the tansy plants at Saunby in the summer. The girls used to call them tigers, and listened with interest when Thompson told them that they could only live on the tansy. If you moved them to another plant, he said, they either died or made their way back to the tansy. Christine, noticing them again now, wondered if she was going to be like that about Saunby; unable to live anywhere else.

She wandered about, relaxed and at ease, and more conscious of Saunby itself than ever before. Many a morning, she sat on the fallen tree in the avenue, looking across to the Priory and thinking about it and the relation of her family to it.

She saw for the first time that the history of Saunby was a sad one. It had been diverted from its purpose; it had been narrowed from a great purpose to a little one. It had been built for the service of God and the people; all people, but especially the poor.

'And now it serves only us,' she thought.

In the old days, the people from all the villages round about had come to Saunby for help and advice. They had brought their sick and their children. They had come up the avenue and down the drive and the back drive and in at the side from Byford and Munningham. Travellers had broken their journeys at Saunby, and pilgrims rested on their way from the north to Canterbury and on their way back.

'I wish I could have seen the monks going up the

drive with bread and beer,' Christine said to herself. ' They used to sing as they went, the book says, and stand on the high road till the pilgrims came and the bishops and priests. I wish I could just for one moment see Saunby as it was then.'

She stared with concentration at the ruins and the house, trying to reconstruct them and make them into the picture of what they had been, but she could only see the unaltered gables and chimney-stacks, and the fretted screen of the West Front with the birds flying in and out of the arches and the trees of the Mound waving beyond the gap of the great west window.

At the dissolution, Saunby had passed to the Perwyns. But the people, she supposed, would still come into the park and use their right of way, which went under the very windows of the house, she knew. It was not until her own family came to Saunby in 1793 that they enclosed the park with a wall and put up the gates and lodges, and even after that the people had their right of way and could cross Saunby whenever they wished. It was her great-grandfather who finally excluded the people and secured Saunby entirely to himself. He waged a fierce war with them over the right of way. He said he'd be damned if he'd have people passing before his drawing-room windows and looking in on him. The people came in a procession, headed by the village bands, and tried to make their way past the house as they had done for centuries, but the owner of Saunby came out with his whip and his dogs and his men and turned them back. The case went to court in the city, but when he declared that if he lost the case he would leave the Priory—leave it, but not let it, so that the village should be deprived of the material benefits that resulted from having a large establishment installed at the house—the case was settled and the right of way lost to the people. Thus

Saunby was withdrawn, and withdrawn from life and brought to its present state.

'We're not fit to have it,' thought Christine. 'We can't do anything for it. We just let it rot.'

She looked around her almost in fear. How nature strove to cover and efface ! Its silent work was going on, going on, all the time at Saunby. Look, for instance, at the bracken, she thought. The tide of bracken crept farther and farther through the park. Each winter it lay so dead-brown, brittle and broken-spined you'd think there was no life left in it, but every spring, bending its neck to push through the hard ground, it came up again in hoops, stretched its antic arms, unfurled and waved in a wider sea than the year before, to sink, break, couch again, and come up again in the spring to spread farther than ever. It had quite defeated the heather. Christine remembered the time when the slopes of the drive were purple with heather, but now there was hardly a sprig to be found in the whole park. The bracken had engulfed it.

And out before the bracken ran the willow-herb, always keeping ahead. It bloomed magnificently at the moment, but soon it would send its seed like snow in summer over the neighbouring fields and make the farmers curse it. So it was with the thistles, which stood in great dark green patches in the very field Christine looked over to the house. Since Thompson had gone, the thistles went unspudded even round the cricket field.

The woods decayed silently. Trees fell and lay prone, or rested slantwise on their still upright fellows. In every space the ubiquitous little birches pushed up in crowds together. They were pretty in themselves, but they had no right to be there.

Nettles choked the fences, and the land was riddled with rabbits. Rabbits were pretty creatures and charming to watch at play in the evenings, when they leapt in astonishing arcs over each other and played a recognizable game of Tig. But there were far too many of them at Saunby. They rayed out before you at every step you took, and the fields were blotched with the sand they threw up and pitted with the holes they made in hundreds.

The farmers and farm-hands no longer came at the Major's invitation to clear off, with guns and ferrets, as many rabbits as they could in a day. That was another thing the Major had dropped.

'Poor Saunby,' brooded Christine.

It suffered at Marwood hands and yet she could not bear the thought that it might some day belong to someone else.

'Suppose someone else lived here?' she said, making herself face the unwelcome possibility. 'Suppose I couldn't come here? Suppose I couldn't walk in this avenue or sit on this tree or go into the woods or even so much as look at Saunby?'

She stared round in a fierce effort to fix it all indelibly in her mind's eye and her memory so that it would be there for ever.

'If only you could hold on to something,' she thought. 'Everything fleets past you. No, it's you who are fleeting past the rest. Saunby has been here a long time and will be here a long time still. It's I who pass across it and pass on.'

This thought disturbed her and broke her mood of reflection. She could not hold on to Saunby, she could not hold on to one moment of fleeting life. She could not hold on to so much as her own moods. Like everyone else's they were always changing, hurrying her from one aspect of life to another. Now she was suddenly lonely. She wanted to grasp at someone subject to transitoriness like herself. She wanted to make some contact, however trivial, with another human being. If she only said " Good morning " and was bidden " Good morning " in return, she would hear the voice of someone going the same way, imperceptibly passing, as she was.

She got up from the fallen tree, determined to make for company. She looked regretfully towards Top Farm. Although Mrs. Spencer was just the person to make her feel safe again, she couldn't go to see her. Christine had heard the tale of Bessy and of Mrs. Spencer's indignant determination to have nothing further to do with Saunby.

Christine turned towards the house, although she hadn't much hope of help from anybody in it. She wouldn't ask for it, of course ; she would just take some comfort from their indifferent presence.

As she dawdled rather disconsolately in the hall, her father came out of his room with a large red book in his hands.

" I say, Christine," he called out with unusual animation in his voice. " Look at this."

He strode towards her, holding up the back of the book for her to see.

" *Until Now*," she read the title, and underneath the name of the author, " Charles Barwell."

" Oh," she cried on a high note of surprise. " He's got it published after all. And you thought he never would, didn't you ? "

" Yes, but look here. Look," said the Major in a warm voice of pleasure. He turned back the stiff crimson board and exhibited the fly-leaf.

Christine read the printed dedication : " To my friend, Francis Marwood."

" Oh, he's dedicated it to you ! " she cried.

" Yes, he has," said the Major, smiling down at the page. " And I've only just found out. When the book came this morning, I chucked it to one side. Then five minutes ago, I picked it up, idly, you know, and saw this. Thank God I did. It might have been years before I opened it. It might indeed. Isn't it decent of him ? By God, I appreciate it very much," said the Major with feeling. " And I daresay it will be a very good book too. He was always a clever fellow, old Badger. Damned clever, really. I'd forgotten."

He smiled warmly down at his daughter and returned, clasping the book, to his room.

Christine smiled, but with affection and sudden insight. The change worked by the dedication in her father's attitude to Lord Barwell's literary activities was almost ludicrous on the surface, but she could see below it. Her father had heard a voice on the road, a voice such as she had wished to hear, but more directly friendly ; he had had an assurance, from an unexpected quarter, that he was not travelling alone, and she understood the warmth of his response.

This brief revelation stirred Christine to a more conscious affection than she had ever felt for her father. He hadn't any very noticeable virtues, but he was lovable. You had to smile at him, unless you were Anthea. But no wonder Anthea found him infuriating. He just sat down and let things go to pieces. At times, during Christine's years at Saunby, when he had been brought up so hard against the chaos he created or allowed that he couldn't do anything but face it, he always said, " Damn it all, I'm a *soldier*," as if no soldier should be expected to cope with civilian life, or that it would be somehow derogatory to a soldier to make anything but a mess of it. He was probably saying it still, thought Christine with amusement. He was not a very good husband, or a very good father, or a very good owner of Saunby, but, she concluded again, he was lovable. That was perhaps all you could say of him, but it was nevertheless a good deal.

You cannot feel a glow of affection for anyone without being warmed by it yourself, and Christine's sense of loneliness was now quite dissipated. Indeed, she felt a kind of general friendliness which prompted her to go up to the nursery and see how the babies were getting on. The babies were nice, except that Roger was small and fair and Veronica was large and dark, and Christine thought it would have been better for them if it had been the other way round. Christine would have liked to assist at the bathing, dressing and feeding of the twins so that she could learn how to do these things for her own baby, but Anthea and Nurse Pye had never been encouraging.

In fact, Christine suspected Nurse Pye of hiding operations from her. It seemed to her that Nurse Pye deliberately got between her and the baby in the bath, and that when she got the baby out of the bath on to her towelled knee, she turned sideways, away from Christine, so that Christine couldn't see. Christine was always craning over shoulders or peering under elbows and dodging about somehow to get a glimpse of what was going on. And Anthea and Nurse Pye talked so hard to each other and the twins that Christine couldn't get a question asked or answered. That was how it seemed to her ; though of course, she admitted, she might be wrong. Perhaps they were just bent on being efficient, and that always made people rather tiresome.

She went up to the nursery now, nevertheless, full of amiability and ready to try again. The twins had just been brought up from their perambulators and were being divested of their outdoor things for lunch. Their bottles waited, their measurements of orange juice, their clean feeders. Anthea and Nurse Pye, their hands busy, looked up as Christine entered, and a guarded expression came into their faces. Christine suddenly remembered how she and Penelope used to receive Anthea when she came to the nursery in their day and blushed at the recollection. She was only getting what she deserved. It was tit for tat, really, she admitted.

How things had changed ! How things were always changing !

Her friendliness rather damped, she hovered uncertainly round the twins.

" When did you say you expected your baby ? " Nurse Pye asked, tying Veronica's feeder.

" October," said Christine.

" Getting near," said Nurse Pye.

" Yes," said Christine.

" You really ought to be getting home," said Nurse Pye.

Christine looked at her.

" Well, you never know," said Nurse Pye.

" Don't you ? " asked Christine, alarmed.

" No, you don't," said Nurse Pye, bridling as if she herself did. " Mrs. Marwood, could I trouble you for that spoon ? Thank you. I think we'll knock off Veronica's oil for the present, but keep on with Roger's. She doesn't seem to need it, does she ? The children are going to have their bottles now, Mrs. Ashwell, so we won't talk any more if you please. That's one of our rules, isn't it, Mrs. Marwood ? "

" It is," said Anthea.

Christine went away, looking thoughtful.

" That's done it," said Nurse Pye, with a wag of her head at Anthea. " She'll go now."

" You *are* awful," said Anthea, pretending to be horrified. " I don't know how you think of such things."

" Well," said Nurse Pye. " If I can't manage one way, I try another. Besides, she ought to be getting back to her home and her husband. She oughtn't to leave a young man like that all this time. He's too good-looking. How does she know but what there's some other woman after him while she's mooning about down here ? "

" Oh, I hardly think that," protested Anthea, genuinely horrified this time.

" Oh, go on," said Nurse Pye. " You don't know human nature like I do. But sh ! " she cautioned. " Veronica's dropping off."

A few days later Christine went back to Mansbridge. The house in the Drive was closed because she had no maids, but it had been arranged that she and Nicholas should stay at Red Lodge until she engaged more, and there she went. Nicholas was away when she arrived, playing cricket.

Sarah had given Christine the largest, sunniest bedroom overlooking the sea, and there, tired from her long hot journey from Saunby, Christine lay on a couch before the windows, waiting for tea to be brought to her and surveying the summer scene from under the sun-blinds.

The sands seethed with children darting about, digging, jogging on the donkeys, running, screaming, sucking ice-cream horns and sticks of rock, perpetually on the move in the first burst of human energy. Their parents, their energy somewhat diminished by the production and maintenance of these very children, sat in deck-chairs behind them, the fathers sprawling, the mothers sewing and keeping a sharp eye on their offspring, or here and there sleeping with their mouths open and their toes turned in. Above these on the asphalt promenade, the older people, the generation of grandparents, their energy still further diminished, sat in stolid rows on the seats, observing as much as they could without moving. Behind these again, on the roadway immediately beyond the garden wall of Red Lodge, a constant stream of cars like beetles in migration bore young girls with bare legs, bare arms, bare backs, and young men with bare arms only, to tennis, to drinks, to dancing or the baths. This stream of youth separated itself from the children, the middle-aged, the old, as if it had nothing to do with them, and could not bear to be reminded of them.

Looking out at the crowds, Christine wondered why Nicholas's parents stayed at Mansbridge during the height of the season. Why didn't they go away from it for a few weeks, she wondered. It did not occur to her that they had remained behind to keep their house open so that Christine need not trouble to open hers, so that she could stay at Saunby as long as she wished and not worry about what was happening to Nicholas in her absence.

None of this occurred to Christine, nor did it occur to her, when Sarah came in with the parlour-maid bringing tea to Christine on her couch, that Sarah would very much have liked to be invited to have tea with her, but would not invite herself in case Christine preferred to rest and be alone. Christine did prefer to be alone, so when the tea-table was arranged beside her, she smiled at Sarah and said, " You're so kind," and let Sarah go.

Sarah sighed as she went downstairs. She felt she had not made much headway with her daughter-in-law and she felt it was her own fault. She felt she was too dull and old for a young girl like Christine.

" What does she want with an old woman like me ? " she frequently asked herself. " She needs companions of her own age, of course."

She knew a good deal about the young *ménage*. She

knew things were not quite right between Christine and Nicholas, but she could not ask about it and neither of them told her anything. Christine wasn't used to making confidences. She had never had anybody to tell anything to but Penelope, and was not at all used to the idea of seeking help from older people. The older people at Saunby, her father and her Aunt Victoria, would not have been able to give any help about anything. As for Sarah, she was the last person to invite confidences. She could not bring herself to ask the most tentative questions. So that these two, while affectionately disposed to each other, were rather at a deadlock with each other, which was a pity.

Sarah's hopes were now all centred on the baby. The baby would make a great difference to them all, steady Nicholas, occupy Christine, and give her and James something to love. The baby would bring them all together. Sarah yearned for her grandchild even more fervently than she had yearned for her children.

'They say you always do,' she thought.

So she waited hopefully, going about her usual occupations : ordering her house, keeping James company, walking with Peke on the front, knitting endlessly for the baby, fitting in the knitting of socks for James, who liked her socks better than any he could buy in a shop, golf stockings and pull-overs for Nicholas, and fleecy bed-jackets in preparation for Christine. She sent her usual parcels of clothing, her own, James's, Nicholas's, to Birchley to the Arkwrights, the Greenhalghs, the Blackledges, the Steads, and made surreptitious visits to a wardrobe-dealer at the back of the town to sell clothes that would be unsuitable for them and send them the money. She had done this ever since she left Birchley. These families were on her conscience and in her heart. She never forgot the need that James and the times had brought them to.

338

Christine had not let Nicholas know that she had left Saunby and would be at Red Lodge when he arrived. She wanted to surprise him. In absence, her thoughts had turned to him with tenderness, as always. No matter how hurt, angry, disappointed she was with him when he was there, no sooner was he not there than love began to rehabilitate in her heart. She had been away from him for some time and now she was eager to see him, eager to begin again, to make everything better. She waited her few days for him in happy anticipation.

But on the day he was expected, he did not come. Sarah said there was nothing unusual in this. They hardly ever knew when he was going to turn up, she said ; it depended on the length of the matches. Christine sat up late, waiting for him, and went to bed at last very disappointed.

The next afternoon, sitting in a striped deck-chair on the lawn, a sea-side lawn where the grass came up coarse and sparse out of sand, but where it was beautifully warm under the sun, Christine heard the familiar throb of an approaching car.

" He's coming," she cried, and began to extricate herself with care from the low chair. She could not move quickly now and the slightest exertion made her breathless.

She stood up, smiling, as Nicholas swung into the drive, but when he brought the car to a halt before her and got out, she was chilled by his expression. Her surprise was not a pleasant one to him. He looked as if she were the last person he wanted to see. Christine's smile faded. She felt he couldn't love her if he looked at her like that. She thought it was because she looked ugly, and her heart contracted. Couldn't he wait with her, even so short a time ?

Before they met on the red sand of the drive, she had withdrawn, in pride, from him.

"Christine," he said, with no smile. "How did you get here? I thought we'd arranged I should come for you in the car next week?"

"I thought I'd come," she said, lamely.

He even seemed to pause before he kissed her. But he did kiss her at last, and holding her arm, went with her into the house.

"Nicholas, you look very tired," exclaimed Sarah.

And what had happened to Christine, she wondered.

'Eh, dear,' she sighed inwardly. 'These young people.'

"We expected you last night," she said aloud.

"Yes," said Nicholas, wandering about the room. "But I had a slight accident. Oh, nothing much," he reassured them. "I ran into a heap of stone chippings at the side of the road and did the car a bit of damage. I had to wait for it to be put right, so I—er"—he went to the window and looked out—"I spent the night on the road," he finished.

"On the road!" exclaimed his mother, who took it literally.

"In a hotel, of course," he said impatiently. "Now I must go and wash."

CHAPTER XXIX

NICHOLAS'S daughter had been half an hour in the world before he knew about her.

He had been to London to see his tailor, be measured for shirts and have his hair cut. He always went to London for the two first and for the third, too, if he could.

"Would you believe it, my son goes to London to get his hair cut?" said James sometimes at his club. He pretended to be quoting an instance of the extravagance of youth, but it was a boast really. James Ashwell, late half-timer, was secretly proud to have got on so well in the world that he could afford to let his son go to London to have his hair cut.

Nicholas wanted to escape from the house. The atmosphere of waiting was too much for him. The nurse had now arrived and he felt increasingly apprehensive and helpless. He decided to go and do something, move about a bit, see something different. When Nicholas felt any emotional discomfort, he sought to distract himself from it. This habit had grown on him increasingly. Other people had indulged him so long, he now indulged himself.

"Do you think you ought to go away just now, dear?" his mother asked him.

"Nurse says it's quite safe for me to go," he said. "Besides, what can I do, hanging about the house? If I could do anything for Christine it would be different. And after all, I'm only going for two or three days."

Sarah said no more. She was divided in her feelings herself. She didn't know whether she wished Nicholas to be spared anxiety, or whether she thought he ought not to be spared. She didn't want him to suffer, and yet she thought he ought to *know*.

Nicholas went to London, and enjoyed himself, but he had an unpleasant shock when he arrived at Euston for the return journey. Cicely Hoyle was on the platform.

The day before he had left for London, Cicely, at the golf club, had proposed a game for the following day.

" Sorry, I can't. I'm going to London to-morrow," he said, only too glad of the excuse. He never played with her now if he could help it.

" Oh," said Cicely, considering him narrowly. " Well, I have to go up myself soon. I may as well go to-morrow. Shall we travel together ? "

" I don't know what train I shall be able to take," said Nicholas, moving towards the door of the Common Room, where the only other occupant, a woman reading the papers, had looked up with interest when Cicely spoke. Why must Cicely shout about the place like that, implying that he was in the habit of travelling to London with her ?

Cicely followed him out of the room.

" You know you can damwell take any train you like," she said. " So why not be sociable ? "

" I may not be able to go at all," he said coldly. " It depends entirely on Christine."

He got into his car and drove away from her. Why did she make such a nuisance of herself? She used to be so decent, never bothering him or forcing herself upon him, but now she waylaid him and stuck to him at every turn. This dated from the time they had been held up on the road home from Thaneford in the summer. What made him have that accident, he wondered, swerving into a heap of granite chippings and ploughing through it to butt into a telegraph pole ? Was it fatigue or too many drinks ? Whatever it was, it had landed him at the Bearded Barley Inn on the Great North Road with Cicely and time on his hands, waiting for his car to be put into enough shape for him to drive home. It was a mistake to wait for it. He should have hired a car and taken Cicely back to Mansbridge. But he had been dog-tired at first and later he'd been rather drunk. He and Cicely had sat on and on in the hotel lounge, he, at any rate, in a state of haze and indetermination induced by successive whiskies. He had been extremely depressed before and after the match, but now he was in the mood not to care about anything. Nothing seemed to matter at all.

" We can't possibly get home to-night now," Cicely said.

" Well, let's stay where we are," he said, and walked rather uncertainly with Cicely behind him to the hotel office.

There he was startled to find the hotel proprietor knew him. He was a cricket enthusiast and had seen Nicholas bat many a time. He had, in fact, been at Thaneford that very day.

" I may say I've followed your career with interest, sir. And not only on the field," said this amiable man. " I knew about your marriage," he said, bowing to Cicely. " And I'm delighted to welcome you and Mrs. Ashwell to my hotel. You shall have the very best we can offer."

Beaming, he thrust the hotel pen into Nicholas's hand and turned the hotel register round for him to sign. Nicholas held the pen poised, filled, in spite of whisky, with a violent distaste for what he was about to do. Then with Cicely pressing warningly on his elbow and the proprietor bending benevolently over the other side of the register, he wrote : " Mr. and Mrs. N. Ashwell."

" Number twenty-four," said the proprietor, taking a key from a hook.

" China tea at eight in the morning, please," said Cicely.

" Certainly, madam," said the proprietor.

When Nicholas woke, cold sober, the next morning, he suffered an extreme revulsion of feeling. He never wanted to see Cicely again, but he had to endure her company for the long drive home.

Separated from Christine in body and spirit, he had drifted back and back into his old relations with Cicely, but he had never meant to return to this final relation with her. Never. He felt the most sickly disgust of himself and her ; and when he got home and ran straight into Christine, he felt a worse moral discomfort than ever in his life before. He began to be haunted immediately, too, by a dread that she would find out. He used to sit sweating behind his paper, fearing that every time she began to speak she was going to say something about it. He was afraid every time she went out that somebody would tell her. He looked for danger from the most unlikely quarters, but it did not come. He began to breathe freely again. So long as Christine never knew he told himself there was no harm done, except to his nerves ; the affair itself had meant nothing to him otherwise, nothing at all.

As for Cicely, she had been gay and rallying all the way home.

" Oh, forget it," she kept saying.

He had dropped her on the bus route to Mansbridge

and she left him, light-hearted and reassuring to the end. Why, then, had she gradually become menacing? Nicholas couldn't understand her. He had accepted her for what she had made herself out to be, a girl who was out to have a good time and take what she wanted.

" ' Take what you want, said God. Take it and pay for it,' " she often quoted with bravado. " I don't mind paying," she said. " If I get what I want first."

He had avoided her whenever possible, and now when he saw her coming towards him down the platform at Euston, picking her way with conscious grace among the porters and the luggage, a cigarette in her mouth, he swore between his teeth, and when she reached him his teeth were still clenched and his eyes steady with anger.

" Found a carriage? " asked Cicely lightly.

" I'm dining on the train," he said, looking coldly down at her.

" Right you are," said Cicely. " I'll dine too."

There was no escape. He had to sit opposite her in the dining-car, but he didn't talk. She had forced herself upon him, but she couldn't make him be pleasant, and he wasn't.

" We might have been married for years," she said, passing Rugby.

' Thank God we haven't,' he thought.

" Has the baby arrived? " she asked after another silence.

" Of course not," he said shortly. " D'you think I should be here if it had? "

" Why not? " asked Cicely, raising her newly-plucked eye-brows. " You've always done as you liked, regardless, haven't you? "

Nicholas compressed his lips the more firmly and said nothing. Restive under her eyes which seemed to implore him haggardly while her lips darted sarcasms, he turned sideways to the window. But it was made into a mirror by the night, and there she was again, bleached hair, white face, lined brow—far too lined for her age—beautiful arched nose, narrow upper lip and full lower one. She was never still ; the hand that was not occupied with her cigarette felt for her pearls, her curls, her coat buttons. She turned her head from side to side, she lifted her chin to blow smoke into the air, and all the time she was darting at him, he could see, her anxious, imploring looks. Nicholas felt a sudden impulse of pity for her, which he strove to suppress. He mistrusted these impulses ; they only put you farther into the clutches of people like Cicely. If you decide on a course, he told himself, you should stick to it. A struggle went on in him between pity and a desire to keep free of her.

But, at last, with a sigh he reached for his cigarette-case and offered it to her. Cicely at once understood. She relaxed, and a look of happiness came into her face.

" Thanks," she said, inserting her fingers with their deep red and very pointed nails into his case.

Her hands put him off again. He didn't like them. He used not to mind Cicely at all. Now he could hardly bear anything about her. But he mustn't show it. It would be too bad, unsporting ; by which he meant unkind. He never used words like kind or unkind, even in his thoughts. He shied from words like that.

They had passed Manchester and were nearing home.

Cicely leaned over the table with a smile.

" Since you're so respectable these days," she said. " I'll get out at the Junction and taxi from there. I won't compromise you by arriving at Mansbridge with you."

"I can't offer to do that myself," said Nicholas. "Because I've left my car in the station-yard."

He helped her into her fur coat, pressed her shoulder by way of thanking her for going, and sank into his corner with relief when she had gone. It was as if a weight had been lifted from his head. He whistled under his breath and looked sideways to the dark window, empty now of her. When the train drew into Mansbridge station, he sprang out, called a porter up and sprinted, because it was raining, to his car. He drove home through the empty, wet, lamp-lit streets, and when he let himself into his house, there was his mother standing in the hall to tell him his daughter had been born half an hour ago.

"Mother!" he cried, seizing her by the shoulders. "A girl! Christine will be so glad. So am I. How is she? Christine, I mean? Did she have an easy time?"

"Easy?" said Sarah, rather grimly. "I should never call child-birth easy. No, she didn't have an easy time, but she's all right now. You can't see her yet, but you can see the baby, if you like."

"Oh, let me," said Nicholas, springing up the stairs.

Christine's door was fast closed and there was silence behind it, but in the adjoining nursery the nurse had the baby naked on her knee. Nicholas was strangely moved by the sight of his child. He had not expected a new-born child to look like that. Her eyes were wide-open, she turned her head from side to side. Nicholas bent down and looked into her eyes.

"She can't see anything much yet, you know," said the nurse indulgently.

But Nicholas thought she could. He never forgot the look of life, of awareness in the newly-born child's face. When he saw her again two or three hours later, it had gone. She was nothing but a baby then, years younger than when she was born.

Later in the night, Christine awoke and asked for
him. She was very tired and only smiled without
speaking. She put out a hand, and he took it and sat
down beside her bed. She fell asleep again, and he
was alone in the quiet, warm room where there was
peace after pain. Christine slept, her curls damp and
straggling, her lashes dark on her pale cheeks, her lips
pale, and he sat there, holding her hand, his eyes
pricking with tears.

Deep feeling was painful to him. He didn't know
what to do with it, how to give it expression. In this
he was almost like his friends. The only expression
the " crowd " gave to their finer impulses was to treat
drinks all round.

Nicholas liked to feel confident, with hands everywhere applauding him, clapping him on the back,
reaching out to grasp his own. He didn't like to feel
all cracked up like this, aching with tenderness and
remorse, filled with most uncomfortable yearnings to
do better, to make a better thing of life. He didn't
like it because he didn't know how, situated as he was,
to make a better thing of life. What was the use of
having these aspirations when his feet were tied down
by circumstance ?

He was dependent on his father and until he got a
job he would continue to be dependent on his father.
He couldn't get a job. Not the sort of job he wanted.
None of the employers he knew, the friends of his
father, would take him seriously.

" Nay, Nick," they said, shaking their heads at him.
" We have to give what jobs there are to men that
need them."

He also felt that they feared they would be asked to
give him time off for cricket. They didn't want a
well-known cricketer on their staff ; they wanted hard-
workers whose whole interest was in their work. Yet

when Nicholas assured them that he was willing to give up cricket, they strongly protested.

" Eh, you mustn't do that, lad," they said. " That would be a shame."

In times of desperation Nicholas had gone to Labour Exchanges in distant towns, he felt he couldn't very well go to the one in his own. But he couldn't hear of anything but the smallest, most distasteful kinds of jobs. In dress agencies, for instance. Imagine him, Nicholas Ashwell, going about the country with the back of his car full of women's dresses ! He wanted a job, but he hadn't come to hawking women's dresses, he told himself.

Subconsciously, he wasn't willing to break away from the comfort and adulatory atmosphere of his present life. He thought he was. He thought he was ready to do anything to get away from it, but he wasn't. At moments like this, he became almost ready. But by the time the nurse came in and whispered that he must go, he was back at the stage of deciding that he couldn't do anything for the present. At any rate, not until Christine was up and about again.

He put her hand carefully under the eiderdown so that it should be warm, resisted a temptation to kiss her in case he should wake her, and stole from the room.

§

And now the Ashwell family entered, in the wake of the baby, into happy waters. The baby was christened Angela. She was very fair, very good and from the first showed, or so her doting relatives thought, a decided personality and sense of fun. Nicholas was in a constant state of surprise. It had never occurred to him that babies could be interesting ; he had thought

349

that was a figment of the mother's imagination, but *his* baby was a most fascinating little creature. The way she came on amazed him. He often stole, out of hours, to look into her perambulator and in no time at all she was turning her head to look at him, getting her bonnet over one eye in a way that tickled him immensely. He used to step out of sight to laugh, but by and by she was laughing with him ; gurgling at the joke of not being asleep when she ought to be. No other kid would have done that, he thought proudly. And her energy in her bath was astounding ; she could splash the water right into her father's face.

Sir James was never prouder in his life than when he accompanied Christine and the perambulator along the promenade. He had something else to boast about now, and boast he did. But Christine didn't mind this kind of boasting ; she felt it had every justification.

Sarah was happier than she had ever been since Rupert's death. When she sat on the front, getting Angela off to sleep by the out-of-date method of gently jigging the pram, Sarah felt drawn back into the stream of life, healed and comforted. And Peke was so sensible, which pleased her. He never barked at the wrong time. A " Sh " and a sign with the finger was enough for him.

Christine glowed with health and happiness. It was so good to feel well, to be able to fly up and down the stairs, to have her hair curling, her eyes shining, her body slender and strong again ; but above all it was good to have Angela's pram to run with on the promenade, to look into the pram to see if Angela was enjoying the joke of scudding over the asphalt which she always was, to have Angela to occupy her hands and her thoughts all day long and to fall tired and happy into bed at night.

She had refused, almost with horror, Sir James's offer of a nurse for Angela.

" Oh, no," she said. " I must look after her myself."

She had quite good maids now and could rely on them for help if she wanted it. Angela kept her very busy, however, and she had not much time for Nicholas. But she had no need to be anxious about him, she felt. He never seemed to drink, he never seemed to see the " crowd." If Christine sometimes felt a slight sense of triumph that she was no longer dependent on Nicholas alone for company and happiness, it was all that was left of her old resentment.

Nicholas, at the bottom of his heart, felt rather relegated to the background. He felt humble and unlike himself at this time ; superfluous, but pleased all the same to hang about and watch Christine handling Angela with what seemed to him amazing efficiency considering she had never done it before.

He was engaged, almost automatically, in keeping himself fit for next season's cricket. He motored to distant links to play golf, so as to avoid Cicely. He saw nothing of the " crowd " now because, to avoid her, he had to avoid them. Since he had become a family man they seemed resigned to his desertion ; at any rate, they did not invade his house. He suspected Cicely of stalking him, but he generally managed to evade her. If he had to speak to her, he said as little as possible and got away as soon as he could.

He searched, spasmodically, for a suitable job, but so far he hadn't found one. In moments of desperation, he considered the idea of asking Christine to go farming with him to Canada. He wanted to work, but he wanted an open-air life too, and that seemed the best way to get both. When Angela was in bed and he had Christine's attention for the moment the words sometimes trembled on his lips ; but he never got them said. How could he ask her to give up the security and comfort of her present life, not only for herself but for Angela ? There was Angela's health and upbringing to be considered always now. She must be kept near doctors, play-fellows, schools. And how could he ask Christine to leave England, she who loved England so much through Saunby ? It had seemed at times almost as much as she could do to live as far away from Saunby as Mansbridge was ; how could she want to go to Canada ? He kept shelving his problems and going on in the same old way. Sir James had increased their allowance, and Nicholas bought a new car, which gave him quite a lot of pleasure for a week or two. And after all, cricket would, in time, come round again.

After Christmas, Penelope and Paul came for a week-end to Mansbridge. They stayed at the Grand Hotel because Penelope liked staying in hotels ; she had, as yet, stayed in so few. She arrived, trim in a navy blue suit from Paris. Christine had had a navy blue suit from Paris, so Penelope had one too. She followed in Christine's wake when she could, a younger sister whose admiration for her elder was tempered by a little jealousy, which was really an inverted form of love. She admired Christine so much that she wanted to be like her, to have what she had and, if possible, more.

She was now ready to survey her sister's world. With her possessions behind her, she came to look at Christine's. While she had nothing, as before her marriage, she had not wished even to see what Christine had, but now she was eager to compare, almost certain beforehand that she had the best of everything.

Christine had no idea of this. She didn't know Penelope had got up a competition and was congratulating herself on winning it. So when Penelope, on arrival, cast a scornful eye over Mansbridge lying flatter than ever, cowed by the winter, and said, " What a place to live in ! " and on seeing Number 19, The Drive, for the first time said, " What a house ! It looks as if there ought to be a card in the windows : Apartments, or Vacancies," Christine only smiled in equable agreement.

Penelope might feel a scornful amusement for the place and the house, but when she came to Angela, taking her tea-time exercise on a play-rug spread on the nursery floor before the fire, Penelope forgot competition and became her old self, completely at one with her sister. Kneeling on the floor, their hair swinging forward, they were as absorbed and united in Angela as they had been in the old days in their fledgling bird, George.

" The darling," breathed Penelope. " See how she holds my finger."

" Hasn't she got lovely little feet ? " said Christine, catching one in her hand.

" She's like you," said Penelope.

" She's like *you*," said Christine.

Angela took part in the trio by blowing a chain of ecstatic and very wet bubbles. When one of these burst in her face, her look of surprise was so comic that the sisters laughed out loud. After considering the faces above her with deep gravity, Angela laughed too. Thrashing the air with her arms and legs, crowing, blowing, she worked herself up into such a frenzy of giddy joy that the girls collapsed on the floor beside her, where she clutched their curls and held them captive while they laughed themselves out.

Nicholas, coming into the nursery with Paul at this moment, suffered a strange pang. At the sight of Christine lying on the floor, laughing with her baby, he had a sudden piercing realization of love for her, a love quite unlike his first blind passion. This love was deeper far, but filled with a sense of loss that frightened him ; he felt as if he had lost her long ago without knowing it and was prohibited from finding her again, kept from her by his own secrecy, his sense of having something to hide. He longed for absolute truth and candour between them, and it was impossible. And somehow she was conscious of it and had hardened herself against him, and was finding happiness without him. No good pretending, he told himself ; it was so. For one moment, with everybody in the room laughing but him, Nicholas was acutely unhappy. Then the moment passed as such moments do, and they all, Angela included, went down to tea.

Thenceforward Penelope was Angela's slave. Every morning immediately after breakfast at the Grand Hotel, Penelope appeared at the house in the Drive and sat on the nursery table in her checked coat and skirt, her bright hair uncovered to the morning, her long legs swinging, waiting for Christine to get Angela ready to go out. When the careful toilet was completed, the sisters emerged upon the promenade pushing between them the pale grey perambulator, wherein Angela, fresh as a rose, babbled contentedly to herself on the way to sleep.

During one of these morning walks, the girls met Cicely Hoyle. At this time of the year, the promenade was almost empty. Only a few residents strolled upon it or sat, if the sun was warm, recessed among the tamarisks. In the general flatness and emptiness people stood out distinctly, and Christine saw Cicely coming from a long way off.

" Now this is the girl I told you about," she said to Penelope. " Take a good look at her. She was the bane of my life once, but I don't bother about her any more now."

With lively interest, the girls came on, two slim young creatures secure in youth and beauty, Christine secure too in maternity and in marriage with the man Cicely wanted herself. Christine had very much the advantage and Cicely hated her for it. Cicely, conscious of the encounter she was about to make, kept her gaze steady with difficulty, drew from the cigarette she was holding, threw it away and said good morning coldly as she passed.

" Good morning ! " Christine called out briskly.

" What a hag," said Penelope, turning to have another look at Cicely's narrow back. " Her hair's dry with peroxide, her skin's like chalk, her bones are thin enough to snap. She looks as if she's no juice in her."

" I don't suppose she has," said Christine. " I should think her heart's like a dried pea, too."

They giggled and propelled the perambulator with pleasurable vigour, while Cicely proceeded in the opposite direction with bitterness.

Sitting in the sun during these few days together, the girls discussed Saunby. Christine's attitude was one of wistful anxiety, Penelope's of acceptance of facts.

" Oh, Anthea and Nurse Pye completely run Saunby now," she said. " Father's nothing. He spends his time in his room listening to the wireless and reading the papers or walking about the park. Those two have ten times as much energy as he has, so no wonder they win."

Christine sighed. She felt the management of Anthea and Nurse Pye was somehow a danger to Saunby itself.

" I wish Angela could have spent her childhood at Saunby," she said. " I wish she could have had all we had. Collected those perfect polished chestnuts, d'you remember them? And had tea-parties with acorn cups. D'you remember the absolute silence of Saunby in the snow? And how the wild duck cackled in the night on the lake? And d'you remember how silver the grass was in the autumn mornings with dew, criss-crossed with green tracks made by the rabbits? D'you remember all the tiny flowers in the grass, the sweet wood-ruff and that tiny red sorrel like little towers, and the tiniest of all, the wild geranium? You know, it was Thompson who taught us the names of all those flowers. He taught us a lot."

"He's a miner again now," said Penelope.

"Oh, *no*," protested Christine, deeply shocked.

"Yes, he is," said Penelope calmly. "He did get a job as a chauffeur after he left Saunby, but he was always a reckless driver, you know, and he had a slight accident. That did for him, poor chap. Then he and Bertha took a place as man and wife, but I expect the people didn't like Bertha. Who would? Anyway, they left and went back to her sister's, and now he's in the pit again, so father says."

"Oh, it's a shame," said Christine indignantly. "He loved the open air and birds and wild flowers. It's awful to think of him spending his days in a pit. You know how he hated it. He was so happy at Saunby."

"Well," said Penelope. "He shouldn't have got himself mixed up with Bertha. It's Bertha that's ruined him."

"Has Bessy married Johnny Spencer yet?" asked Christine.

"I don't know," said Penelope, comfortably indifferent.

When the time came for the return to Brockington, Penelope was sorry. She had meant to spend some of her time at least in being fashionable at the Grand Hotel, in wearing her newest frocks, dancing to the orchestra, being admired, doing things she had not done during her years at Saunby, but she had spent her whole time with Christine and Angela, doing nothing but push the perambulator, sit on the front, and watch Angela being bathed, fed, dressed or undressed, and she had been happy in doing it.

Paul, on the other hand, had not enjoyed the week-end. He had played golf with Nicholas, but Nicholas was a scratch player and Paul's handicap was twelve. He felt inferior going round, and worse afterwards when Penelope laughed at his score and said " Poor Darling " with a gay commiseration that showed she didn't care in the least about it.

After leaving Christine and Angela, Penelope was silent for a long time on the drive home, and Paul's plump brow was puckered with anxiety. Didn't she want to go home ? Was she bored with him ? Didn't he make her happy enough ? Did he look very fat beside Nicholas ? Was that it ? Did Penelope wish he was handsome and athletic like Nicholas ? Did she wish she had a baby like Angela ?

But as Mansbridge receded and Brockington approached, Penelope turned from the one and readapted herself to the other.

" Of course, darling," she said ruminatively. " I could never live Christine's life."

" Couldn't you, sweetheart ? " said Paul eagerly.

" Oh, no. I could never stand Nicholas for a husband. He's too restless and discontented and too lazy. You work so hard, darling, and I do admire you for it. And I couldn't stand Mansbridge itself. Or the house. When I think of our lovely house, and our lovely things . . ."

She laid her hand on Paul's knee as he drove and he was happy. He could only be happy when she was happy, and he didn't care what it was that made her happy so long as it did.

CHAPTER XXX

ONE bright February morning, Nicholas and Christine were out with Angela on the front. They walked with the perambulator between them, hatless, Nicholas's tawny hair rough, Christine's curls kept tidy by a dark-brown ribbon ; Nicholas wore a yellow sweater under his jacket, Christine an attractively skimpy coat and skirt with a vivid scarf tied at her neck ; Angela, no longer recumbent but propped up at an angle suitable to her advancing age, wore a soft, warm coat of pink lambswool and played with a silver bell on an ivory stick. They made, between them, a charming domestic group as they proceeded along the promenade to call at Red Lodge.

Suddenly from one of the cement grottoes two people, a young woman and an old one, emerged directly in their path.

" Damn," said Nicholas under his breath. " Cicely and Mrs. Hoyle. Let's turn round."

" We can't," said Christine, under hers. " Too obvious."

She was glad that Nicholas was as anxious as she was to avoid the odious Cicely, but she pushed on towards her.

Cicely rarely walked abroad with her mother, but this morning, for lack of something better to do, she had accompanied her as far as the front. She never had the patience to adapt her pace to the old lady's and hurried her along with no regard for her years. She thought her mother could certainly go faster if she tried, especially in traffic. She thought she ought to be able to hurry for buses better, get off them quicker and altogether be more spry and less irritating. By the time they reached the promenade, Cicely was fuming and poor Mrs. Hoyle was breathless and distressed.

" Now you go, dear," she panted, coming to a standstill at last. " Thank you very much for coming with me, but I shall be quite all right by myself now. I won't detain you any longer."

But Cicely was staring at the oncoming Ashwells and paid no attention to what her mother was saying. Mrs. Hoyle turned to look too.

" Good morning," said the Ashwells and would have passed on, but Mrs. Hoyle, now that they had come near enough to be recognized, halted them with a black-gloved hand.

" My dear," she said to Christine, " I've never seen your baby. Never. Isn't that disgraceful? You must please allow me . . ."

Smilingly, Christine wheeled Angela towards her and Nicholas had to follow. He nodded briefly to Cicely and stood apart, his hands in his pockets, his eyes on the sea.

" Well, now," quavered Mrs. Hoyle, poking her black bonnet under the hood of the perambulator. " You are a pretty little girl, dear. Yes, you are. You're like your pretty mother. You are indeed."

Angela considered the black bonnet with intense gravity.

" Pooh, pooh, pooh, pooh," said Mrs. Hoyle.

Angela considered these sounds. She liked them better than the bonnet.

" Pooh, pooh, pooh, pooh," said Mrs. Hoyle again. Angela smiled.

" There," said Mrs. Hoyle in triumph. " She smiled at me. I always think, you know, dear," she said, emerging from under the hood and laying her hand on Christine's, " that babies and old people understand each other very well."

" Yes," agreed Christine, thinking of Sarah. " I think they do."

" They do," affirmed Mrs. Hoyle with pride. " I'm sure of it."

Cicely stood apart, her face set, her heart throbbing painfully. This was his child. This was the child another woman had borne him. Not that she herself wanted children, but she wanted Nicholas. She burned with wanting. She was in anguish. To be so near him and unable to speak to him. To be unable to show her claim to him. For she had a claim. This smug, smiling girl didn't know, but she had a claim to him.

" I could wipe the smile from that face," she thought. " My God, I could."

She dropped her cigarette to the asphalt and ground it with her sharp heel. She looked at Christine with a grin that was no smile, nor was it meant to be, stretching her lips.

' She's got lipstick on her teeth again,' thought Christine. ' It looks like blood. It's most repulsive.'

Cicely was impatient with her mother's babblings at the baby, she fumed and fretted standing there, but when Nicholas put his hand on the perambulator to urge Christine on, Cicely was seized with rage. Trying to get away from her. Trying to take his precious wife away, to go off with her and leave Cicely behind. She stood there trembling, staring at him, and Nicholas saw and was more than ever anxious to go.

" Come along," he said to Christine.

" Good-bye," said Christine, smiling to Mrs. Hoyle.

"Good-bye, my dear. You're a lucky girl with your fine husband and your pretty baby. You are indeed. But you deserve them. Yes, you do. Bye-bye, baby," said Mrs. Hoyle, waving her black gloves at Angela, who agitated her silver bell very aptly at this moment, probably more by accident than design, though it immensely pleased old Mrs. Hoyle.

"What a sweet child !" said Mrs. Hoyle, turning to Cicely.

"Oh, shut up," said Cicely.

Mrs. Hoyle's face changed. She sighed.

"Well, dear, you go," she said. "I'm going to sit on this seat for a little while. You go off now and enjoy yourself. Will you be in to lunch, do you think ?"

"I don't know," replied Cicely, disappearing through the cement grotto.

Old Mrs. Hoyle made her way to the seat among the tamarisks. Cicely was in one of her worst moods to-day, but she must try not to be upset by her, because it made her tremble so. She must try to think of something pleasant. Of that sweet baby. She had made the dear little thing laugh. She was proud of that. Even at her age, too old though it was for Cicely, she hadn't forgotten how to make a baby laugh. To think that Cicely had been a baby like that once. As sweet, too, in her way.

Old Mrs. Hoyle sat in the sun, remembering.

§

The following morning, Christine, carrying Angela rolled cocoon-like in a blanket, was as usual first down to breakfast. She always brought Angela down to the dining-room and barricaded her with cushions into an armchair while she herself breakfasted with Nicholas.

362

Afterwards, she took Angela back to the nursery for bath and breakfast in her turn.

This morning all was as usual, except that yesterday's sun had not reappeared and the prospect from the windows was a cold one : cold grey sky, cold grey sea, cold grey promenade. But the room was warm and cheerful with early daffodils on the breakfast table and a fire leaping and glowing in the grate. Christine, busy with Angela, could see that there were some letters, but she did not hurry to look at them. The only letters she cared about were the ones from Penelope, and as she had had one a few days before there could not be another yet.

She settled Angela, rang the bell to let Dora know she was ready for breakfast and sat down to table. Then she reached for the letters. There were three ; two bills and an envelope addressed to her in a square scrawling hand.

Angela caught her attention again.

" Don't suck your blanket, my pet," she said, removing the pink ribbon edge Angela had just succeeded in conveying to her mouth.

Dora brought in the bacon and the coffee as Christine ran her finger under the flap of the envelope. She brought out two sheets of paper. On the first she unfolded was written : " Thought you might be interested, Cicely Hoyle." What could possibly interest her that interested Cicely ? wondered Christine.

" Darling, don't suck your blanket," she said, removing it again. Angela kicked protestingly, but suddenly found her bell and became absorbed in that.

Christine unfolded the second piece of paper. It was a hotel bill headed : " The Bearded Barley Inn." Christine looked casually at it and put it down. She picked up Cicely's note again.

' Funny girl,' she thought. She thought Cicely

was trying to be friendly by recommending the Bearded Barley Inn as a good place to stay. The " crowd " were great at telling each other of what they called possible pubs.

' She saw us yesterday, so I suppose that reminded her of us. I suppose she wants to start coming here again, but I really can't have her. I've nothing in common with her.'

She poured out her coffee and wished Nicholas would come before it went cold. She put her hand in a housewifely way round the jug. Then she got up and put it in the hearth. She wished it would occur to Sir James to give them a hot-plate. She knew she had only to mention it to get it, but she wouldn't do that. Still, it would be nice, she thought, on her way back to the table, if it should occur to him to give them one. Nicholas was always so late for breakfast.

She sat down again and looked idly at the bill. Funny thing to do, she thought, sending it.

Coffee-cup in hand, she looked at it again. She put down her cup and picked the bill up. It was made out to Mr. and Mrs. Ashwell. No. 24.

' But I've never stayed there,' she thought.

Mr. and Mrs. Ashwell? She looked at the date. July 3rd. But in July she had been at Saunby.

She held the bill in both hands and bent over it. " Mr. and Mrs. Ashwell. No. 24. Room, 18s. Dinner, 9s. Wine, beer, spirits, £1 5s. Morning tea, 2s. Breakfast . . ."

Christine went over each item. What did it *mean* ?

Angela, conscious of lack of notice, reared herself up to look for her mother and fell back red in the face. She kicked off her blanket, but no one replaced it and she felt cold and neglected. When Nicholas came into the room she was beginning to whimper.

He hurried to soothe and sympathize.

" Hello, my pet, are you all uncovered ? "

He tried to cover her, but it was difficult because her arms and legs went like flails in her frantic plea to be picked up.

" Err-err-err-err," she jerked imploringly.

He bent down and rubbed his nose against her cheek.

" I can't," he whispered. " Mummy's here."

The blanket again offered itself as a consolation to Angela, and she began to suck it with audible satisfaction.

Nicholas poured out his coffee, helped himself to bacon and had started on his breakfast before Christine spoke.

" What's this ? " she asked, holding out the bill in shaking fingers.

Nicholas, his mouth full, looked at it. He stopped chewing. Staring at the bill, he went white. He swallowed the food in his mouth with difficulty and put down his knife and fork. Then he raised his eyes, dark with apprehension, from the bill to her.

" I know what it means now," said Christine. Her voice trembled, her whole body trembled. She was as white as Nicholas, even to her lips.

" You slept with her at this place. While I was at Saunby. Didn't you ? *Didn't you ?* " she demanded, jumping up from the table.

Nicholas rose slowly to his feet as if to face a charge he had long expected. He looked old, careworn and as if he had no fight in him.

" Burn it," he said, making a clumsy gesture at the bill. " Burn it."

" Burn it ! " cried Christine, whipping it behind her back. " I should be a fool. She's sent me evidence for a divorce. That's what she wants. She shall have it. Both of you. You slept with her when I was

365

having a baby. D'you think any woman would forgive that? No woman would, and I never shall. Never. Never."

At the strange loudness of her mother's voice Angela began to cry with fear. But no one heard or comforted her.

"Christine," said Nicholas heavily. "Don't let our lives be ruined by a thing like that."

"A thing like that!" echoed Christine, her eyes blazing. "I suppose you think it's nothing. To a man like you it's nothing."

"It is nothing. It was nothing," said Nicholas. "It meant nothing to me."

"So I suppose you think it means nothing to me?"

"I was drunk," said Nicholas. "I'd stayed with Cicely before—once or twice—before I knew you, before . . ."

He stammered, his tongue and brain were clogged, he couldn't say the right thing.

Christine had turned her back to him, her hands were over her face, her elbows out square. Nicholas stood helplessly at the table. Angela wept with abandon in the chair. It was past her bath-time and she wanted her breakfast.

"Christine," said Nicholas, moving suddenly to try to put his arms round her. "Forgive me."

Christine twisted away from him.

"Never. I'll never forgive you," she said through her hands, which she kept tightly pressed over her face though tears came through her fingers.

"Christine, listen. Cicely is absolutely nothing to me. Long before I met you we went away together a bit. I was never in love with her and she was never in love with me. We got stranded at the Bearded Barley. I'd had an accident and I drank too much

—and—I suppose having stayed with her before—
and you know, you and I were kind of separated—
and I was desperate about everything."

She was standing quietly, her back still turned, her
hands over her face so that he thought she was listening
to him and he began to speak more easily.

"You know, Christine, a thing like this means
absolutely nothing to a man. Men aren't like women.
A thing like this means nothing. If a thing means
nothing to your heart or your soul or whatever it is,
it's just a physical incident. It means nothing . . ."
he pleaded.

Christine dropped her hands and turned a white,
streaked face on him.

"It means this," she said with deadly quiet. "You
knew that if I found out, it would ruin our happiness,
but you were willing to risk it. You were willing to
risk ruining our happiness. Well, you've ruined it.
I've been afraid many a time that you were cheap and
smart like your friends and that you'd do cheap
dreadful things—and you've done them. Now I know
you are what I was afraid you would be. You thought
you could have everything, Cicely Hoyle and all she
meant as well as me and all I meant. Well, you can't.
You can have her. But not me. I shall do as she
wants. I shall divorce you."

"Christine, listen, listen !" He seized her wrists and
held them to her sides. He held her in a vice, but her
face was implacable.

"Let me go. You'll never change me," she said.
"While I was having a baby ! D'you think any
woman would forgive that ? "

"Christine ! "

"Let me go. D'you think you can keep me by
holding my arms down ? "

"Christine ! " He couldn't get anything else out.

Angela thrashed wildly in the chair. Nobody would come. Nobody.

" Let me go," cried Christine, freeing herself by one fierce wrench. " Angela's falling."

She ran to the chair and snatched Angela. Angela stopped crying at once and looked in woe-begone fashion, wobblingly, above the cowl of her blanket, tears stuck on her cheeks.

" Well," said Christine, with conscious cruelty, folding Angela close and looking over her head at Nicholas. " You've lost us. And now you can go to Cicely Hoyle."

She went out of the room and climbed the stairs to the bathroom, talking reassuringly to Angela. Nicholas stood frozen.

Passing between the bathroom and the nursery, Christine was calling out to Angela as usual : " Mummy's coming, darling. Be a good girl, because Mummy's being as quick as she can."

Dora came into the dining-room with her tray, but fell back at the sight of the master standing at the table, his bacon uneaten on his plate.

" I'm sorry, sir. I thought you'd finished."

" I have," said Nicholas, plunging from the room.

Their lives were crashing about them, but Christine had to give Angela her bath and Nicholas could not suffer in the dining-room because Dora wanted to clear away.

CHAPTER XXXI

NICHOLAS walked out of the house and stood at the foot of the steps. The wind from the sea rushed through his hair. He put up both hands and held it down with a distracted gesture. He wondered what he had come out to do. Then he remembered and strode like an avenger in the direction of the Hoyles' house in South Road.

The maid was startled by the sight of such a wild-looking young man at the door.

" Miss Cicely's not up yet, sir. She doesn't get up while gone eleven when she's not playing golf."

" Ask her to get up, then," said Nicholas shortly. " I'll wait."

He strode into the hall and was put into a sitting-room, furnished to Cicely's taste in a colour known as " off-white," though it was really more the colour of cold-porridge. The armchairs were deep and low ; the sort of chairs an old lady could not sit in. There was a concession to Mrs. Hoyle in the shape of a high winged chair, faded and out-of-place like herself which was pushed almost out of sight into a corner behind the jut of the mantel-piece. There was a wireless cabinet in the room, a gramophone cabinet and piles of fashionable magazines, the sort of magazines that when you had looked through them once you had finished with.

Nicholas did not notice the room. He paced it, his emotions divided between rage against Cicely and apprehension as to what Christine would do.

After a few moments the door opened and old Mrs. Hoyle came in, holding out her hand.

" Good morning, Mr. Ashwell," she said, coming to do the honours of the house until Cicely should appear. It would be an unheard-of thing to leave this young man to wait by himself in the sitting-room. " How are you to-day ? " she said, making for her own chair and drawing it a little forward to the fire before she sat down. Not very far, because when Cicely came it would have to go back to its place again. " And how are your dear wife and your little daughter ? It's a long time, Mr. Ashwell, since I have seen such a pretty child. Won't you come nearer the fire ? It's such a very cold morning, isn't it ? It is indeed," she said, answering herself, since the young man seemed unwilling to answer her. She had not been alone in his company before and she feared he was going to be a little difficult to entertain, but she did her best, tapping her hands together on her black lap. Mrs. Hoyle had been a widow for many years, but she still wore her weeds because Cicely made her. Sternly suppressing innocent wishes for hats with purple pansies, Cicely kept her mother in a coif and crêpe veils because she thought she looked better, or rather less bad, like that.

" Your little girl is the image of her mother. They make a beautiful pair. I always think there is some-thing particularly touching about a young mother and her baby, as I said to Cicely," said old Mrs. Hoyle, who had done nothing of the sort. She imagined that by reporting fictitious conversations with Cicely she was keeping up the appearance of being on excel-lent terms with her daughter. The conversations always sounded too cosy for anybody knowing Cicely to believe in them.

" I am glad to see you so happy in your home life,

Mr. Ashwell," went on Mrs. Hoyle to the tortured Nicholas. "It really did me good to see you and your wife and baby yesterday, making such a picture. A happy marriage is God's greatest blessing, isn't it? And as I say to Cicely, happy though we are, the two of us together, I tell her she won't know what real happiness is until she finds a good husband and has children of her own. That's what I tell Cicely, Mr. Ashwell, and I am sure you agree with me."

Nicholas made some sound Mrs. Hoyle was bound to take for agreement, though she thought he was a very restless young man and not half as nice-looking as he had seemed yesterday.

"Ah, here's Cicely," she said as the door opened and Cicely came in wearing a long white house-coat over scarlet pyjamas.

"Here's Cicely," said old Mrs. Hoyle, and putting her chair back, she stole from the room like a well-trained servant.

Cicely, her head high, blew smoke down her nostrils and invited attack.

"Well?" she said as the door closed.

"What did you do it for?" asked Nicholas chokingly. "What possessed you? What devil? What good could it do you to ruin my life?"

"I turned," said Cicely with an assumption of lightness. "I may be a worm, but I turned. You thought you could take no notice of me, didn't you? You thought you could brush me aside as if I didn't matter, you and your precious wife. Well, I made you notice me, didn't I? I certainly did."

Nicholas thrust his hands into his pockets out of the way. He longed to seize her, hurt her, vent his hatred on her.

"It's the dirtiest trick ever played," he said in a tense voice. "The lowest. Damn the day I ever saw you. You're rotten. You got hold of that bill after I paid it and you kept it. I suppose you thought you'd blackmail me sometime and then you changed your mind and thought of something worse. You sent it to Christine. Because you saw that we were happy. All these months you've been lying low, waiting to use that bill."

" I haven't," said Cicely petulantly, standing on the fender and rearranging the things on the mantelpiece. "I didn't keep the bill for that." She added sullenly, "I kept it as a souvenir."

" A souvenir ! " exclaimed Nicholas in deep disgust.

" A souvenir for me," said Cicely with a kind of pride. "I kept it to remember by."

" But you didn't keep it," he said contemptuously.

She was silent, fiddling with the candlesticks and the clock. The bill had been at first a souvenir, then it became a weapon to be taken out and turned over and held ready. Yesterday, on a sudden impulse, she had used it. She had thrown the bomb primarily to destroy, but she also hoped that when the smoke cleared there would be something for her in the ruins. Nicholas had come back to her once, he might come back again. When his wife turned him out, as Cicely was sure she would. Little prig, she thought.

" If you were a man," said Nicholas, " I'd know how to deal with you, but you're a woman and I'm stumped. You're a dirty fighter. I can't say worse. I'll never willingly speak to you again as long as I live."

" God, what a threat ! " said Cicely lightly.

He made for the door, and his face, as he passed her, made her realize suddenly that he meant what he said. He was going and he would never come back. She stumbled from the fender and fled after him, her long coat blowing out and catching on her fashionable armchairs, impeding her.

" Nicholas, wait ! I did it because I love you. I love you far, far better than she does. I'll *die* without you," she said violently. " Nicholas, please, please . . ."

But Nicholas had gone through the front door and closed it behind him. She rushed out and stood at the top of the steps, calling after him.

" Nicholas ! Nicholas ! "

Her white coat streamed away from her scarlet figure, her hair streamed from her white face, her cries streamed away on the wind.

" Nicholas ! Nicholas ! "

Two women, strangers to each other, halted on the pavement to look at her.

" Have you *ever* ? " said one to the other, deeply, deliciously, shocked. This sort of thing didn't often happen on the way to the butcher's. " Fancy coming out in pyjamas to shout after a man like that ! "

They observed the receding male figure with avid interest.

" It's young Mr. Ashwell, the cricketer."

" What does she want with him ? Isn't he married ? "

" Yes, and got a baby too."

" Oooh, isn't it disgusting ? "

They turned to look again at the girl on the steps, but she had gone, weeping convulsively, back into the house, and an old lady in black, herself much distressed, was just closing the door.

§

Nicholas made for the sandhills. He ploughed his way for some time through the sand, but it was difficult going and at length he flung himself down in a hollow.

373

The fine cold sand flowed instantly into his shoes, over the edges of his trousers and his jacket. There was something deathly and menacing about the swift greedy sand. The sharp sea grass whistled in the wind. He had no overcoat, no cigarettes, none of the comfort he was used to. In misery he lay there, the collar of his jacket turned up to his ears, his hands sifting, sifting the sand.

Christine's face had been implacable. Would she never forgive him ? He thought of Deering, a familiar figure in Mansbridge. Deering's wife had discovered him in just such a minor infidelity and had never forgiven him. For ten years, poor Deering had been disconsolate, living in rooms, buttonholing people when he was in drink and telling them : " My wife's left me, you know. And she's as unhappy without me as I am without her, but she won't come back. She'll let us die, separated like this." Would it be like that for him ? Would Christine condemn him to a life like Deering's ?

He got up from the sand and stood irresolute. He must go back and plead with her. But not yet. He must give her time. Time and absence would work for him, perhaps, as often before. Often he had come back after a quarrel to find that she had forgiven him. This was the worst thing that had happened between them, but her own generous heart was his best advocate and he must trust to that, if to anything. He could do little for himself, he felt so tongue-tied with her, her justifiable anger was too much for him ; he could not meet it.

Shivering, he made his way to Red Lodge, because there was nowhere else to go.

At Red Lodge, Sarah was hovering about trying to get James to move, of his own accord, his papers from the dining-room table so that lunch could be laid. She would not *ask* him to move them. She was so glad he should find something to do with himself that she would not interrupt until she was absolutely obliged to, that is, until the housemaid had appeared and disappeared at least three times with her tray of glass and silver.

So James walked round and round the table on which a great number of docketed papers and cuttings from financial columns were set out. He read here, marked there, took elastic bands off, snapped them on again, and exclaimed aloud in concern or self-congratulation. He had taken to speculation as a hobby. The bulk of his fortune was kept strictly safe, but he allowed himself a margin to play with, and since he played with his usual shrewdness and thoroughness, the margin grew broader and broader and James was vastly pleased with himself. Whatever he touched, succeeded, he boasted to Sarah, who believed him, but wished she could get hold of some of the money these financial manœuvrings brought in. All the Arkwright children were down with measles, even the new baby. Sarah wished very much that Mrs. Arkwright, middle-aged, underfed, overworked as she was, could have avoided this last baby. But there it was in the world, and with measles, so Sarah pawned a ring James had given her long ago and had most likely forgotten. At least she hoped he had. He had a most disconcerting way of remembering when she didn't want him to.

When Nicholas came in, his parents exclaimed with pleasure and surprise.

" I've come to lunch," he said.

" That's very nice," said Sarah. " But you look chilled to the bone, child. Come to the drawing-room fire while Ellen is laying the table."

" Here, hold on," cried James, bustling to the sideboard. " Let him have a whisky and soda to warm him up."

"Er—no, thanks," said Nicholas, thinking rapidly.

"No ? " said his father. " What's up with you ? Have one. It'll do you all the good in the world."

" No, thanks," said Nicholas, going out of the room behind his mother.

Christine didn't like the smell of whisky. She said she could always tell as soon as he came into the room if he had been drinking it. He had mocked at that, but now he would not let the smell of whisky come between him and reconciliation. If she forgave him, and if she let him kiss her, she should not smell whisky on his breath. He made this small, hopeful sacrifice, but his mother was worried. She knew at her first glance that something had gone wrong, but since she had never known him refuse a drink before, she felt it must be something serious. She sighed as she poked the already blazing fire, and went away to tell Ellen to lay another place at table.

At lunch, attending unobtrusively to his wants, moving salt, pepper, sugar, cream, towards him in a way that invited or reminded but never forced acceptance or refusal, she learnt from his face the measure of his distress. The pallid look of cold he had come in with had disappeared, but his lips were folded and he looked as if he saw and heard with difficulty, so absorbed was he in his trouble.

His mother yearned over him. Although he was twenty-six years of age, to her he seemed young and inexperienced. It was a great pity, she thought, that all the violence of life should fall on the young, before they have acquired any resistance to it. What could have gone wrong now ? Some trouble between him and Christine, since he hadn't gone home for lunch. She had hoped these troubles were over, because they had all been so happy since Angela was born. Angela had made a focus for them ; they had all met in loving her.

Nicholas wouldn't tell her what was wrong, of course, and she couldn't ask. They sat at the table, conveying food to their mouths and making conversation. James made the most. Sarah wondered if he noticed that something was wrong. Sometimes when she thought he hadn't noticed anything, his remarks afterwards showed her that he had.

After lunch, they sat in the drawing-room, where James soon fell asleep. Sarah usually took a nap at this time too, but to-day she could not " lose herself " as she put it, because she was worried about Nicholas, who sat behind a newspaper.

Peke dozed at her feet until the time arrived for his customary walk. He knew the time as well as anybody, and at half-past three he rose, stretched himself against his front legs, stretched himself against his back legs, and sat up with forepaws crossed in silent reminder that it was time to go out.

" Not this afternoon," whispered Sarah. " Not yet."

Peke growled slightly and jumped into her lap, where she explained further. He accepted her explanations, but he was not pleased. He jumped down, and going to the farthest corner of the room he flung himself down and kept resentful eyes upon her.

After tea, Nicholas rose.

" I think I'll be going now," he said.

He kissed his parents. Sarah thought it was one of his most lovable traits, that great young fellow though he was, well-known cricketer and all that, he should still kiss his father.

' Poor boy,' she thought, watching him go. ' I hope they'll make it up quickly.'

Nicholas went out into the wet, windy dark. He turned up his collar and ran all the way home. After the vigorous action, his heart beat fast, he felt more hopeful, stronger to plead for himself.

When he opened his own front door, he found Cook and Dora standing in the hall with round eyes. At the sight of him they went, jostling each other in their hurry, back to the kitchen. But when he had gone upstairs to the nursery, they came out again and stood at the back of the hall, their eyes turned upwards, listening intently.

" Eh, it's a nice how-d'you-do, isn't it ? " said Dora in a stage whisper. " What ever will he do ? "

" Shut your mouth," said Cook tersely. " How d'you think I can hear ? "

They heard him go from room to room. He did not call out. He went from room to room, and from room to room again. Then there was silence from his dressing-room.

" He's found that there letter," whispered Dora, unable to resist communication of this dramatic information.

CHAPTER XXXII

THE middle-aged spinster across the carriage, emboldened by Angela's response to her timid advances, now ventured farther.

" Could I hold her ? " she asked, as eager and uncertain of permission as a child asking to hold a globe of spun glass, or something fragile and rare.

Christine smiled mechanically and transferred Angela from her own knee to the stranger's. The woman curved her hands carefully round Angela's body ; it was an event in her life to hold a baby.

Christine, her arms empty, sat slackly, her face turned to the darkness beyond the window. Her lips were tight, her eyes bright, she was like someone in a fever. She was absorbed, drawn in to her own trouble ; it throbbed in her like a pain, making her unconscious of other people. She was conscious only of herself and in some degree of Angela. All the way people had helped her with her baby and her luggage and she had let them, sometimes without noticing, sometimes remembering several minutes later to thank them.

Now that Angela was out of her arms she could look at the bill again. She opened her bag and took it out. It was limp from constant handling, and she had to unfold it carefully so as not to tear it.

" Mr. and Mrs. Ashwell," she read, poring over it as if she had not seen it before. " Morning tea."

She folded it up and put it back into her bag. She turned her face to the window again. If she could think, as for a flashing moment now and then she did think, like telling oneself in a bad dream that it is only a dream, if she could think for a moment that it wasn't true, that it couldn't be true, the morning tea convinced her that it was true. It was true. It had happened. And the morning tea made it deliberate and callous.

She shuddered suddenly and put her hands to her face. Then she remembered where she was, and dropping her hands saw the heads in the carriage turned towards her in interest and alarm.

" Hello, darling," she said, plunging towards Angela.

Her behaviour was unco-ordinated, incalculable. She sank back from Angela into her corner again and bit her fingers. Oh, to reach Saunby, to arrive at Saunby ! She yearned for Saunby as for the bosom of a mother. Wounded, she was making blindly for home. If only she could get there, be folded in.

" Are we nearly there ? " she asked the red-faced man beside her.

She had asked him many a time already. She had never made the journey from Mansbridge by train before, and it was dark and she could not tell where she was. So she kept asking the man beside her, and though it was quite an operation for him to get his large watch out of his little tight waistcoat pocket and still more of an operation to get it back, he performed it again and again with patience, because she was so pretty and seemed in such trouble.

" About another thirty-five minutes, I make it," he said.

Christine sighed and fell back to her corner. The time, the time it took to get away.

In some highly illuminated place in her imagination, Nicholas and Cicely were together in the hotel bedroom. They were fixed there like a peep-show and she had to keep looking at them. Against her will she was dragged back and back to look at them.

"You can be getting your things together now," permitted the red-faced man, working his watch into place between his cushioned ribs.

Christine took Angela and rolled her into a fish-tail of shawl, while the woman looked on. 'If I had a baby like that,' thought the woman, 'I'd be happy.'

With Angela's head bobbing beneath her chin, Christine reached round her to take her ticket from her bag. Her fingers came into contact with the bill again and it sent its now familiar sickening message along her nerves. She closed her bag on it, and, holding Angela and her ticket, sat on the edge of the seat waiting for the train to draw into the station and let her get out.

When the train stopped, she got blindly out and left her luggage to the red-faced man, who hauled it all to the platform while she looked urgently for her father. She had wired asking him to meet the train and had not doubted that he would be there. But the train went out, the alighted passengers dispersed, and on the cleared platform there was no sign of him.

The great dome of the station was yellow with sparse lamplight and imprisoned smoke. A few porters stood about, a few travellers paced a little this way and that, sighed and stood still again. The whole place seemed bemused in gloom and ennui. Christine, with Angela in her arms and the luggage at her feet, felt suddenly frightened. Her father had not come. There was nobody to help her. She felt alone, cut off from all she knew, threatened, and very afraid of exposing Angela to discomfort and danger. Angela had lived up to her name all the way, but now she was rubbing her small smutted nose with her fists, which was a sign,

381

her mother knew, that soon she would begin to cry. Christine pressed her lips to Angela's head with passionate tenderness and strained through the station murk for her father.

"Oh, come," she urged him mutely. "Come and get us to Saunby. I want to put Angela to bed. I want to get to the end of this day."

If only she could get to Saunby. But she had a nightmare feeling now that Saunby might not be there. She felt as if she had stepped into a void. All that she had hitherto relied on was destroyed behind her, and before her there was nothing. She turned from side to side, looking for help.

Suddenly there appeared on the platform steps a small female figure descending, a figure all mushroom hat and great fur driving-gloves. With a cry of relief, Christine hurried towards it.

If she had encountered Nurse Pye on alighting from the train, Christine would not have been pleased to see her in the place of the father she expected. But she had had to wait, she had been brought down considerably by anxiety, and Nurse Pye was very welcome to her. She greeted her like a friend, like a deliverer.

"I didn't expect *you*," she chattered, voluble from relief, as she hurried, Angela slipping in her arms, to accompany Nurse Pye along the platform to the luggage. "I was looking for my father."

"He's away," said Nurse Pye shortly. "So I had to turn out. There was nothing else for it."

"It's very kind of you," said Christine. "I was getting so worried."

"Is all this lot yours?" asked Nurse Pye, standing over the luggage with extreme disapproval. However long did the girl think she was going to stay?

"Yes," said Christine, looking anxiously from the

luggage to Nurse Pye's face. " Can't you take it ? Is there too much ? "

" Well, I'm in my own car, you know," said Nurse Pye, both injured and indignant. " However," she sighed loudly and summoned up a porter, " I suppose there's no help for it."

Christine relapsed into silence. She was too tired to resent anything ; all she asked was to be taken to Saunby.

She was silent all the way there. Angela had gone to sleep and lay warm and heavy in her arms. Nurse Pye drove like a little Jehu. She liked driving a car, she liked to manage it, to conquer the road. The worse the road, the more the car bumped and rattled, the better Nurse Pye liked it. It gave her a satisfactory sense of effort and achievement. So she bumped and rattled Christine and her baby over the ten miles and brought them up abruptly at the door of Saunby.

" You can go in," she said. " I've got to put the car away now."

She made it sound as if that was another tiresome thing she had to do on Christine's account. But Christine did not notice it, any more than she noticed Nurse Pye's permission to enter Saunby. She went into the hall and found Anthea there.

" I suppose you wonder why I've come," Christine said wearily, dragging off her hat and dropping it to the chest. " But could I tell you in the morning ? "

" Oh, your father will be back to-morrow," said Anthea hastily.

Christine could tell him. If there was anything wrong she didn't want to hear about it. She didn't want to be involved, or asked to help. She was too busy ; the twins took up all her time. No breach must be made in her life with the twins and Nurse Pye. Christine must really manage for herself.

"May I look at your baby?" she asked in a voice that managed to be both interested and chilly. She wanted to see Christine's baby so that she could compare her with the twins, and she wanted, by the courteous formality of the request, to put Christine in her place. Christine was a guest, an uninvited guest at that, and she, Anthea, was her hostess, albeit an unwilling one. All this Anthea managed to convey, since we generally do manage to convey what we wish so successfully sometimes that we are alarmed and have to disclaim and withdraw.

Anthea, bending to look at Angela, felt a pang. Here was the Marwood beauty she had failed to convey to her own children. But the pang was brief, and she straightened up from her inspection of Angela loving the twins only the more passionately.

"A pretty child," she admitted.

"I should like to put her to bed, please," said Christine.

"Yes, of course," said Anthea with some of her old empressement. "I've put you in the room you shared with Penelope before you were married. I suppose your baby can sleep in a bed for the time you're here. We haven't a spare cot, you know. I suppose you dined on the train?"

"No," said Christine, who hadn't thought of food.

"Oh," said Anthea uncertainly. "Well. I must see what the servants can get for you."

A frown appeared between her dark brows. She did so hate any interruption of the routine worked out in such detail by herself and Nurse Pye.

"It's late, of course . . ." she murmured, going away.

"Will you go up?" she remembered to say, calling backwards.

Christine climbed the familiar stairs. Her feet

384

dragged, Angela was heavy in her arms. She went along the passage, opened the door of the bedroom, felt for the switch. The room was dim and cold, there was no fire, and some of the chairs were still shrouded in dust-sheets. But again the inhospitalities of Anthea and Nurse Pye were lost upon her. She put Angela down on a bed and set about getting things ready for her bath and her supper.

And now she had to ask for first one thing and then another ; boiling water to mix food, a spoon, a plate, a basin, a night-light, a box of matches, a hotter hot-water bottle, a lower pillow, and every time she asked for these things from the maids, who were all strangers to her, Anthea appeared looking more and more per-turbed because everything was being upset.

When Angela was wakened to be undressed, she protested so loudly that Anthea came running to say she hoped she wouldn't wake the twins. Christine rushed Angela into the farthest bathroom and shut the door. It was warm there, and when Angela was bathed and put into her comfortable nightgown and given her bottle she recovered her good humour, and after sucking with much earnest vigour for some time, she began to play her usual game of letting the teat go and laughing at the resultant fizz. She expected her mother to join in this game, and Christine did her best. But the sight of Angela wanting to play when everything was changed made the tears start to her eyes. She seized the sponge and pressed them sternly away. No crying.

" Come on, darling," she said, jogging the teat in Angela's mouth.

Thus urged, Angela put play aside and set to again, to such purpose that she simultaneously sucked her bottle dry and fell asleep with the last drop. Christine carried her to bed, the bed against the wall in which she used to sleep herself. The last time she had slept in that bed was the night before her marriage. She smiled bitterly to remember that. Poor deluded thing that I was, she thought, propping a chair against the unprotected side so that Angela should not roll out.

She went down in search of supper. She was hollow with hunger because since morning she had forgotten to eat.

Anthea was still hovering about the hall, a disturbed housewife unable to settle. She conducted Christine to the dining-room where the great table was set out small-ly with a boiled egg, a dish of bottled goose-berries, a dish of junket which had been broken into and was in consequence very wet ; Nurse Pye's idea of what would do very well for one who chose to arrive at Saunby without an invitation and at that time of night.

" We thought you'd better just have something light to go to bed on," said Anthea, who could not help mitigating her inhospitality in this way. Her up-bringing would not let her be as rude as she wanted to be. She wholeheartedly admired the uncom-promising behaviour of Nurse Pye, but she could not manage to imitate it. She tried, but it didn't quite come off ; unless Nurse Pye was there, and then she was more successful.

" You don't mind if I leave you now ? " she asked Christine. " I have so much to do."

She escaped to the nursery to make the latest report to Nurse Pye. They had discussed Christine's sudden descent upon Saunby ever since the arrival of her telegram, and they found endless matter for discussion in it still. Nurse Pye and Anthea were by this time, from long encouragement of each other, as addicted to discussion as other people might be to drugs or drink.

Christine, left to herself, devoured the boiled egg and

a good deal of bread and butter. Then she remembered the bill, and took it out of her bag. The sight of it deprived her of what appetite remained. She got up abruptly from the table, leaving the pale green gooseberries and the pale blue junket and leaving also, to Anthea's indignation when she came down later, the lights on.

When Christine, after standing unhappily about in the bedroom, got at last to the stage of going to the bathroom to make her toilet for the night, she found she had forgotten her toothbrush. She had left it hanging beside Nicholas's in the porcelain rack in the bathroom of the house in the Drive. Leaning on rigid arms above the basin at Saunby, she saw the bathroom at Mansbridge, warm, white, brilliantly lit, with Nicholas going in and out in his red dressing-gown with the white spots. The sight of him did not move her. She visualized him coldly. She would never forgive him. Never go back.

" Never," she said aloud.

Pride, bitterness, jealousy, resentment stiffened her. The weakening emotions, regret, self-pity, sadness for loss, she did not feel.

She straightened up from the basin and wondered where she could get a toothbrush at this time of night. She wondered if her Aunt Victoria had a new one in her stores. With surprise, she realized that she had not thought of her aunt until this moment. And there was, of course, Penelope. She hadn't thought of Penelope, either. To-morrow she would telephone ; although, when she telephoned, when she got into communication with Penelope, she would have to explain everything, and she dreaded that. If only she need never say a word about what had happened !

But the toothbrush, the toothbrush, she thought wearily.

387

She went to knock on her aunt's door. When there was no answer, she opened it and turned on the light. The room was emptied of her aunt's things ; the familiar litter was gone. The bed was shrouded, the carpet rolled up.

' She must have changed her room,' thought Christine, and went down the passage into one room after another. But there was no sign of her aunt's occupation in any.

Puzzled, she went up to the nursery. Light, warmth, talk flowed forth as soon as she opened the door there. But the talk ceased at once, and Anthea and Nurse Pye looked up, sewing suspended.

" Is there something else you want ? " asked Anthea, emboldened by the presence of her ally to put a slight emphasis on the " something else."

" I've been looking for Aunt Victoria," said Christine, standing in her dressing-gown, with her hair dragged back from her white face.

Anthea looked at Nurse Pye. Then she looked back to Christine.

" She isn't here now," she said.

" Not here ? "

Anthea pinched the narrow hem she was making between finger and thumb. She gave it her attention.

" Where is she ? " asked Christine.

" She left last week," said Anthea primly. " She has rooms in the village."

" Rooms in the village ! " repeated Christine. " What for ? "

Nurse Pye and Anthea exchanged glances, but said nothing.

Christine stood by the table, puzzled.

" I don't understand," she said. " Why has Aunt Victoria gone ? "

Anthea made no reply. Christine thought suddenly that they must have had a row.

" Is she coming back ? " she asked.

" I don't think so," said Anthea with finality.

" Where is she ? " asked Christine.

Nurse Pye made an impatient sound and bit off her thread.

" I said she had rooms in the village," said Anthea.

" There aren't any rooms in the village."

" There are rooms in the hotel," said Anthea.

" The pub ? The Three Pigeons ? " cried Christine, astonished. " But it's a dreadful place."

" *May* I trouble you for the scissors, Mrs. Marwood, please ? " interrupted Nurse Pye with significance.

" Is Aunt Victoria at the Three Pigeons ? " persisted Christine.

" I have already told you : yes," said Anthea.

Christine looked at her. But Anthea sewed on and Nurse Pye with her, and Christine, puzzled by their mysteries and machinations, had no choice but to go away.

Once back in her room, where the night-light threw fan shadows to the ceiling, and Angela made such a small hump in the bed against the wall, the brief relief of thinking about something else forsook Christine. Bill in hand, she flung herself down on the top of her bed in her dressing-gown as she was. How could he do such a thing ? She had told him in her anger that she expected it of him from the first, but of course she never, never had.

She lay there. She heard the surge of the trees in the garden, the sound of falling water, suddenly loud when the wind fell, she heard the krak-krak of the wild duck on the lake. These were the familiar sounds of her childhood. She thought with sudden defiance : ' Well, I'm at Saunby. I'm here. I've left him.

What's to prevent me being as I was before I knew him?
And I've got Angela.'

She took off her dressing-gown and got into the
bed. She would survive. She would go on.

In the middle of the night, she realized she had
forgotten Angela's perambulator ; it was still standing
in the garage at Mansbridge, a dust-sheet protecting
its immaculate pale fawn. How could she have been
so stupid as to forget it, she asked herself, sitting up in
bed. How could she get hold of it ? She couldn't
ask anybody there to send it on. She had cut herself
off from them all for ever ; she couldn't ask favours
from them now. She had no money for another. But
how could she manage without one? How could
Angela continue to be happy and healthy if her good
habits were broken ?

The coldness of the room made her lie down again.
She turned this way and that in the bed, wondering
what she should do without a perambulator. The
night passed like that ; the sundry inconveniences of
having left home kept floating up, like spars from a
wreck, to the surface of her sea of desolation.

CHAPTER XXXIII

CHRISTINE had spent most of the morning pacing the garden with Angela in her arms. In the afternoon she went farther afield, into the park, down the elm avenue. Her arms ached from Angela's weight, and she had to keep sitting down, on a bench, on the fallen tree, anywhere she could, to rest. She could not sit long because of the cold, but she kept on, walking a little, sitting a little, keeping Angela out in the open air. Angela had always spent a certain number of hours in the open air, and Christine was determined, in spite of the lack of the perambulator, that she should do so still.

This difficult, but determined promenading of Angela was merely one manifestation of the curious stubbornness Christine showed at this time. Her inner self was dislocated, bewildered, but her behaviour was stubborn ; she went on, almost stupidly, from one thing to another, overcoming each obstacle as it presented itself as if it was something put in her way by Nicholas and Cicely.

When she reached the lodge that used to be Thompson's, she sat down again. There were railings on the top of the low wall and there was not much room to sit, but she sat, her feet braced against the ground, her back pushed forwards by the railings, Angela asleep in her lap. In this uncomfortable posture she looked about her with eyes swollen from lack of sleep, a flat misery in her face.

Snowdrops were out on the grass-plot to the right again, but they gave her no pleasure. Nicholas had destroyed her pleasure even in the sight of snowdrops. Nicholas and Cicely had *got into everything*, she thought bitterly.

She turned her head and looked over to Top Farm. The scarecrow woman walked no longer with a dog at her feet and an umbrella in the crook of her arm. She lay prone, face downwards in the grass, but in an awkward position as if she was always trying to get up and could not. Christine found an obscure satisfaction in that.

She sat looking about her. Everything was bleached again from the winter. Bleached fields, bleached bark of trees, the wooden palings round the grass-plot bleached and silky.

From the left, from the lane, she became aware of the sounds of an approaching horse and trap. She turned her head without much interest, to watch, and presently there came into view the light milk float from Top Farm, coming from the village, not with its usual load of giant milk kits, but with three people in it ; Johnny, Mrs. Spencer and Bessy, she could see. As the float turned up the lane to the farm, she saw the flash of something white on the whip that Johnny never used but to lay like a caress on the horse's back. A white bow on the whip, thought Christine, could only mean one thing. They must have just been married.

' So she's given in to circumstance, has she ? ' she thought. ' Well, I shan't.'

It was Johnny who had tied the white ribbon to the whip. He made the celebrations Bessy did not make. She was quiet, but she smiled whenever he looked at her and he for his part was satisfied. It was enough for him, as much as he could get anyway, that she would be happier with him than without him, happier at Top Farm than anywhere else.

When she reached the farm, Bessy went upstairs to take off her best hat. She tied an apron over her best frock and went out to feed the fowls and the fantails. The fantails were domiciled at Top Farm now. Seeing that she was fond of them, Johnny had built them a cote, and painted it white with a red roof. It stood on a tall prop, very clean and clear in the green field, making a picture that pleased Bessy every time she looked at it. The fantails had settled in it and produced a family. Once they had come like messengers from Bill to her, standing on her hands as they had stood on his. Now she had no time for them to stand on her hands and the four fantails were so alike she could hardly tell any longer which had been his. They were older, they were settled, they were merged in their family. She would be like that too. You would hardly be able to tell, someday, that she had once been his, either.

Throwing the last grains of wheat from her apron, Bessy went back to the farm-kitchen where the wedding tea was waiting.

As Christine walked up the avenue, a maid came running from the house, across the cricket field towards her.

" Please, madam, will you come ? " she panted from a distance. " There's two gentlemen to see you. I couldn't find you anywhere. In the drawing-room, madam. Shall I take the baby ? "

Christine halted.

" Who are they ? " she asked suspiciously. Who could they be ?

" I don't know, madam. It was the mistress who sent me to look for you. I've been looking ever such a long time. Shall I take the baby ? "

They must be lawyers, thought Christine, whose ignorance led her to wild conjectures. But they'll never make me go back, she thought. Never.

"Can I trust you with her?" she asked, looking sternly into the maid's face.

"Oh, yes, madam. I often help in the nursery, and I'll be ever so careful," said the girl. "I'll take her to the nursery till you come."

Christine went slowly to the house, wondering what to say to the lawyers, wondering what they would say to her. But when she opened the drawing-room door, she found Sir James and Nicholas standing in the room. She shut the door sharply behind her and stood leaning against it, unwilling to go a step farther towards them. White in the face, with all the emotions of yesterday crowding upon her, making her feel sick, she stood there without speaking.

"You've come at last," said Sir James. "D'you know we've been here nearly an hour? Get your things together, now, and let's be off. It's a long way home and Angela'll be late to bed again, which is very bad for her. So come along."

Christine looked steadily at him. She wouldn't look at Nicholas, though she was acutely conscious of him, standing white and silent, somewhere to the right.

"I'm not coming back with you," she said.

"Don't talk silly," said Sir James. "And don't waste any more of my time."

"It's you who are wasting your time," she corrected him. "I've said I'm not coming and I mean it."

"Christine." Sir James dropped his brisk, dismissing manner and spoke sternly. "You must come to your senses. Admitted Nick's behaved abominably. He knows what I think of him. But he's had his lesson. He doesn't care a pin for that girl. He never did. You leave her to me. I shall have something to say to her, I promise you. But you've not got to let her do what she wants to do. She's out to break up your home. You've not got to let her do it. It's too precious to you and Nick and his mother and me, and, above all, to the baby. Come back with us now, before anybody gets wind of this trouble. You should never have gone off like that. It was a right down silly thing to do, upsetting us all, yourself included, and coming down here letting everybody know what's wrong. Always wash your dirty linen in private, my girl. Don't you know that ? "

" I don't," said Christine. " I've never had any before. Not until I married your son."

" None of this back-chat," said Sir James. " It's too serious. Get your things on and get the baby and come along home."

Christine shook her head.

" I can't," she said. " I couldn't be in the same house with him. I never want to see him again. To go back would be . . ." She shut her eyes and with revulsion in her face, said : " It's like asking me to eat something that's just made me sick."

That was too much for Nicholas. With a smothered exclamation he strode forward. Christine, opening her eyes, thought he was coming for her and stiffened to meet him. But it was the door he was seeking, the way out.

" Stand away," he said, with a jerk of his head, and when she obeyed, he went past her, his lips set. He opened the door, went through, and closed it sharply behind him.

" You shouldn't have said that," cried Sir James, aghast. " No man can stand a thing like that. You should never have said it. Never."

Christine stood fiddling with her waist-belt.

" I wish you'd go," she said in suppressed desperation. "It's no good your talking," she said, turning on him. "I shan't change my mind. I shan't come back and I shall divorce Nicholas."

"Ah," said Sir James, narrowing his eyes at her. "So that's what you've been telling yourself, is it? Well, you might as well discard that notion once and for all, my girl, because it's no use to you. Divorce indeed. Not only will there be no divorce, because for one thing you've no money to bring an action, and unless I'm very much mistaken your father hasn't either and wouldn't provide it if he had. Also there would be no alimony for you because Nick hasn't a penny but what I give him and on no account would I pay alimony for him. There's no law to make me do it, and if there was, I wouldn't. So what would you live on? Not only will there be no divorce," resumed Sir James, remembering that that was how he began, "but there's another thing." He paused to make what he was going to say the more impressive, and Christine, white, taut, her head up, listened. "There's another thing," said Sir James. "I will not contribute one single penny to the upkeep of either of you, either Nick or you, unless you continue to live together in the house I've provided for you. You're a pair of young fools. But I've seen young fools before and I know this will blow over. God bless my soul," said Sir James, going, in his unwisdom, far too far. "Nick's not the first man to be unfaithful to his wife and he'll not be the last. It's happening all the time, but are homes broken up for it? You're being a fool to yourself. This'll blow over and you'll be able to make a go of your marriage if I hold you to it. You haven't the sense to hold it together yourself, so I'll do it for you. Not a penny for either of you, unless you live together. I hold the reins, my girl, and you'll go the way I want, the way I *know* is best."

Christine looked steadily at him, her face bright with anger. Anger swept her across the polite distance youth mostly keeps from age. Now she could say anything. Now she hated him, saying what Nicholas had done was nothing, thinking he could compel her with his money, calling her " my girl."

" Now I see," she said ringingly. " I see where Nicholas gets his morals from. From you. Like father, like son."

Sir James, his bushy white brows drawn together in stupefaction, opened his mouth to speak, but she spoke before him.

" You may drive your wife and son," she said. " But not me. From this time on, you've nothing to do with me. What Nicholas has done has freed me and Angela not only from him, but from you, and thank heaven for that, because I've hated taking from you. You give to acquire power and you hold back from giving to acquire power. That's what you're trying to do now. You're a bully and you're a bad father. You've bullied Nicholas and you've spoilt him. What he's done is your fault. You gave him every-thing he wanted before he'd time to want it. He didn't have to work or wait for what he wanted. You gave it him. He's used to getting what he wants even if he doesn't want it very much, and that's what hap-pened about Cicely Hoyle. Threaten me as much as you like," she said. " It makes no difference. Angela and I can manage without your help."

Sir James, breathing heavily, stared at her as if he could not believe his ears. A bully, did she say? Ruined his son? Threaten her?

Before he could get a word out in protest, in self-defence, the door opened and Anthea came in, agitated and apologetic.

" Tea's coming in a moment, Sir James."

" Tea," he exploded. " I want no tea. If Christine doesn't withdraw what she's just said to me, I'm leaving this house, and I'm not giving her another chance, either. Will you withdraw, my girl, or won't you? Are you coming back with me, or are you not? Think well before you speak, because I'm not going on my bended knees to you to consider your own interests. Are you coming or aren't you?"

" I'm not coming," said Christine, moving towards the door.

Anthea stepped into her path.

" Wait," she said. " I'm sorry to interfere, Sir James, but this is my affair too. Christine is refusing to go back with you, I understand, but she can't stop here, you know."

Christine turned in swift inquiry.

" You can't, Christine," said Anthea. " You can't stop indefinitely. Sir James," she said, appealing to him, " her father can't do any more for her. He has other responsibilities now. We simply cannot afford the extra expense of Christine and her baby. It may sound incredible, considering the size of Saunby and the whole establishment, but if you knew . . ." Anthea almost wrung her hands.

" I can guess," said Sir James grimly. " Well," he turned in triumph to Christine. " You'd better change your tune now, young lady, hadn't you? You can't stop here, so you'd better think again about coming back with me. I'll give you one more chance. Are you coming?"

" No," said Christine.

They stared at her.

" Don't worry, Anthea," said Christine coldly. " I shan't stop at Saunby. You drove Aunt Victoria out. You shall drive me. You forget I have a sister."

Passing between them, she went out of the room and,

switching the telephone through from the hall to her father's room, she went there to ring up Penelope.

Sir James mopped his brow with his handkerchief. He was red in the face and breathing heavily.

" She's bested me," he said. " Eh, Mrs. Marwood." His Lancashire accent was suddenly very evident. " I tell you what, but the young people are hard to-day. Hard."

" They are indeed," agreed Anthea, without inquiring too closely into his meaning. All she knew was that she was on Sir James's side. Whatever had happened, Christine ought to go home.

" You must have some tea, Sir James," she said, ringing the bell.

" I don't want any, thanks," he said wearily. He was beginning to feel tired. He was very hurt. A bully. A bad father. Surely Nick didn't think that ? He must go and find the lad and ask him. Put it to him straight. A bad father. Him. Why, he loved the boy better than anything in the world, together with Sarah. He thought of Sarah with sudden longing. He wished he'd brought her with him. She might have managed better.

" I won't wait for tea, thank you, Mrs. Marwood," he said heavily. " I'll get out to Nick. He'll be sitting in his car, poor lad. He would come in his own car, though I don't know why. Didn't want to travel with me, I suppose. Or else he thought there'd be more room for her and the baby and all the baggage going back. And now she's not coming. I don't know how I'll face my wife without her and that baby, Mrs. Marwood. My wife'll break her heart if she's parted from that baby."

" But surely, Sir James," said Anthea, going with him to the door, " surely she'll see reason soon. She can't go on like this. She simply can't. I mean, there is no place for a woman with a baby but her own home, is there?"

"I wish her father had been here," said Sir James. "Perhaps he'd have made her see sense. Tell him he can tell her from me that if she wants to come back the house is open for her. But what I've said I stick to. Not one penny does she get from me unless she comes back to her husband."

"I'm sure her father will agree with you," Anthea assured him earnestly.

By this time Sir James had come out to the broad shallow step before the door of Saunby. He stood peering through the dusk of the February afternoon. The Rolls-Royce stood alone under the West Front.

"Gibbs," he called sharply. "Where's Nick?"

"He must have gone," shouted Gibbs, who, unlike a southern servant, never thought of coming near to speak. "He weren't here when I came back from having a walk round and that were half an hour ago."

"He's got a long start, then," said Sir James. "D'you think we can catch him?"

"Nay," said Gibbs, bringing the car up. "I don't. But we can have a good try."

"Well, good-bye, Mrs. Marwood," said Sir James, sighing as he offered his hand. "I suppose we shall just have to wait for that girl to change her mind. I'd like to have had a look at the baby," he said, turning his hat in his hands and pausing uncertainly on the step. "But better not, I suppose. Yes," he said, getting into the car, "better not."

CHAPTER XXXIV

PENELOPE swooped to the rescue. Within the hour, her coat flying, her curls on end, she burst into Saunby followed more soberly by Paul.

"Come away at once," she said indignantly. "Don't stop another minute. To think that one of *us* should be told we can't stay at Saunby. But don't mind about it, darling, you'll be all right with me."

She began at once to run up and down the stairs conveying things from bedroom to car.

"Don't bother to pack," she cried to Christine, running with her arms full past Anthea, past Nurse Pye. "Cram them in and let's get away.

"Couple of cheese-paring lodging-house keepers that they are," she said, banging the car doors when they were all in. "That's what they've brought Saunby down to. Lodging-house standards."

Paul laughed. He loved Penelope's vehemence. He had little of his own.

"Angela'll have to sleep in a bed to-night, Christine," said Penelope, twisting from her seat in the front to her sister at the back. "But she shall have a cot to-morrow."

Cot, perambulator, play-pen, toys, all that had been left behind, Angela should have again to-morrow. Paul would provide them. He would do whatever Penelope wished, and she knew it. She was very pleased with Paul to-night. He was so much better than

Nicholas. He would never do a thing like that. He would never look at another woman, she knew. She put a hand on his knee as he drove and a wave of happiness and relief went over him.

Lately he had been worried. That day, for instance, at intervals during his work at the office—and Paul in his office was a busy, efficient lawyer—he had wondered what was wrong, what it was lying heavy at the back of his mind, and after a second's search had found the answer in Penelope.

Penelope, he feared, was beginning to be bored at Brockington, with the house, the garden, the village that had so delighted her at first. He didn't *think*, he assured himself, that she was bored yet with him, since when he kissed her good-bye in the mornings, she always complained that he was leaving her. But boredom was an insidious thing. If it wasn't checked, it spread to everything within radius, and any day now he might find himself included. When that day came he would be miserable indeed. He had feared ever since she said she would marry him that he would not be able to hold anyone so young, beautiful, gay and in every way so different from himself as Penelope.

This business of Christine's, he thought, driving through the dark while the sisters talked, sad though it was for Christine, and of course it was very sad, might nevertheless prove to be a godsend for Penelope. She would have company now, and the company she liked best. He had felt quite out of it during that week-end at Mansbridge when Penelope spent all her time with Christine and the baby, and he feared it was going to be the same now. But he would put up with it, if Penelope was happy. That was the essential thing ; that she should be happy.

He listened to Penelope's eager plans for all she and Christine and Angela were going to do together,

and he smiled indulgently. Penelope was dismissing
Nicholas as if he had never been, and implying that
Christine could do the same. But that, thought Paul,
would not be so easy for Christine as for Penelope.

" Here we are ! " said Penelope, and felt, as the car
swung into the drive, what a good house Brockington
Grange was to come home to, to bring the homeless,
like Christine and Angela, to.

Rectangles of lighted windows showed warmly in the
long, low house-front. A fan of light shone downwards from the lamp above the solid white door, which
opened as if by magic as the car drew up, and showed
massed flowers and a leaping fire in the hall.

" Come in," cried Penelope, warmly welcoming.

" How lovely it looks," said Christine, who had never
felt more tired in her life. Weary and battered, she felt
beaten quite flat.

" Yes, it is lovely, isn't it ? " said Penelope. " But
come upstairs."

She led the way to a room where firelight glowed
on white walls.

" Harrison's seen to everything," she said with satisfaction, turning on the lights and revealing delicate
furnishings of coral pink and blue.

" Oh, it's too nice," said Christine, hanging back
from the padded silk quilts, the coral carpet. She was
beset with the fear of mothers who take their babies
visiting. Babies are no respecters of other people's
spare rooms. " It's much too nice, Pen. Can't you
put us somewhere else ? "

" Nothing's too nice for you," said Penelope.
" Besides, it's all like this. But come on. Your bathroom's through there. Let's get Angela to bed."

" She's so tired," said her mother. " But can you
wonder ? After these two days."

" Never mind," said Penelope rallyingly. " That's

all over now. Give Angela to me while you get her things out."

Angela, transferred from mother to aunt, turned down the corners of her mouth. Looking at yet another face she didn't know, she began to cry, not loudly, but in a small piteous way. The world was full of strange faces and nothing was what it had been.

" It's all over," said Penelope, making her voice rise and fall in an attempt to distract Angela. Angela was successfully distracted. She stopped crying and looked hopefully at the mouth whence this nice noise had issued. Penelope did it again. Angela smiled. She bobbed towards her mother as if to say " Did you hear that ? " and bobbed back to Penelope, waiting for more.

" She is a lamb," said Penelope.

" Yes, she is," admitted Christine thankfully. After all, she had Angela. " It will be nice when you have a baby like her, won't it ? Because I expect your baby will be like her. Just as sweet, anyway," she conceded.

Penelope's face closed in a sudden proud, cold look. Don't interfere, her face warned.

But Christine didn't see it. She was busy with the bath-water and didn't know she had touched on a dangerous subject.

" I'm ready for her now," she called.

When Angela was in bed, the sisters went down hand-in-hand to dinner. Christine was comforted by the feel of Penelope's hand in hers. She was grateful that Angela had a warm room to sleep in and a maid to listen for her. She was glad to sit at the candle-lit table between Penelope and Paul. They talked and she talked ; all the time. But she felt that nothing that was said had any bearing on reality. She must talk, she must eat, she mustn't disturb anyone else in any way, but her thoughts ran in a dark current away from all this.

It was like paying a visit on a dark night to a house where there were lights, fires, friends, and knowing that sooner or later you would have to go out into the dark. The knowledge that the dark waited, haunted the visit and prevented pleasure. Christine felt that no matter how kind the hosts, it would always be like that for her now.

§

The following day, Major Marwood came to Brockington. He tried first to deal with the matter by telephone, which was always, in his opinion, the best way.

" I say, Christine," his voice came over the ten miles. " What's this absurd story of Anthea's that you've left your husband ? What's happened ? Eh ? What is it ? Speak up. I can't hear you."

But Christine could not speak up. The words she would have to use to speak of Nicholas's unfaithfulness stuck in her throat. She could not utter them into the celluloid receiver. She stood stammering and holding back, until her father lost patience.

" I can't make head or tail of it," he said testily. " You'd better come over."

" I'd rather not," said Christine. " After what Anthea said yesterday."

" Good God, you don't need to take any notice of that," said the Major dismissingly. " She's mad, Nurse Pye's mad. They're both mad on economizing. I suppose she told you you couldn't stay here ? I thought as much. But you should just have sat tight and stayed. You shouldn't take any notice of Anthea. I never do."

"Couldn't you come over here?" asked Christine, not labouring the point as to whether she could have stayed at Saunby or not. It was no good pursuing such subjects with her father. He made no attempt to see another person's point of view ; he simply said it wasn't there, couldn't be there, it was so silly.

"Could you come over?" she asked.

"Well, I suppose I'll have to," sighed the Major.

He had to overcome his disinclination to get the car out and drive himself over, because he had his own reasons for wanting to get this affair settled.

The Major's visit to London had revived him. More and more frequently nowadays did he seek refuge at his London club, since all he did and spent at Saunby was noted and disapproved of by Anthea and Nurse Pye. The bustling, organizing atmosphere generated by these two did not suit the Major. He found it more and more difficult to sit in his room in peace with these two on the prowl, as he put it, so every now and then he went to London to sit in peace and have a glass of sherry when he felt like it without Nurse Pye finding out about it.

It did him good to get away from Saunby, he told himself. At a distance things did not seem so difficult. Always, when he got away, he felt a recrudescence of energy and optimism, and this time these had taken the form of an intention to revive the cricketing glories of Saunby. The last year had gone by like lead without the cricket fortnight. He felt he couldn't face another year like that, with nothing to look forward to. Thompson had gone, it was true, and couldn't be got back. He had to admit that he could not afford Thompson, though he would probably be only too willing to come back now, after the bad time he'd had and was still having. A miner ; with a child ; he was properly tied up to that woman now, poor fellow.

He couldn't have Thompson to help him, but what was to prevent his having Nicholas Ashwell ? Nicholas was the ideal help. He was his son-in-law, he had nothing to do, he was a first-rate bat. He could run the cricket fortnight as it had never been run before. He could make all the arrangements, do the clerical work and all that from Mansbridge, then come to Saunby in good time beforehand and see to everything, all last-minute arrangements and all that, and then play in the matches. It was a grand plan and the Major couldn't imagine why it hadn't occurred to him before. He came home eager to put it into immediate operation and Anthea met him with the news that Christine had left Nicholas, that Nicholas and Sir James had come to fetch her back, that she had refused to go, that Nicholas had flung out of the house in a rage and that later Sir James had followed him, also in a rage. It was all very, very tiresome, thought the Major, and most inopportune.

He arrived at Brockington full of an irritated desire to settle the silly business as quickly as possible and get on with his plan. But confronted by Christine, he became at a loss. He sat in the bright flowery morning-room where Penelope had tactfully left them, with his long legs crossed, his long hands extended on the arms of his chair and said practically nothing, except to murmur, " It's a very bad show." " Young pup ! " " I'm very surprised. A good bat like that."

Christine was hardly more explicit than she had been on the telephone, but her distress convinced the Major that the breach was serious.

By the time he stood up to go, he had relinquished his plan. For the time being at any rate. Consciously, and with a feeling of respect for himself, he put family sentiment before the cricket fortnight.

He laid his hand on his daughter's shoulder as they

walked to the door. Poor child, he didn't like to see her lips tremble like that.

"Father, I've no money," she said.

"But neither have I," he assured her, alarmed at this turn in the conversation.

"I know. But could you let me have a very small amount to go on with? For Angela's patent food. Penelope's so good, but I can't ask her for everything."

"You can have what I've got on me," said the Major, turning out his pockets and counting it up. "Thirty-two bob. Will that do you? But you know, Christine, I'm in a very awkward position. Anthea put it much too crudely yesterday, but she is right in the main. I can't afford to do anything for you, my dear."

"I know," said Christine. "I'll manage somehow."

"But what are you going to do?" asked her father.

"I don't know. I don't know yet," said Christine, opening the door so that he would go and cut short the interview. She couldn't talk about what she was going to do ; she didn't know. She might approach the idea of divorce in her own mind, steal to it as to the edge of an abyss over which one has to throw oneself sooner or later, but she couldn't talk to other people about it. She couldn't talk about her life with Nicholas, her life and his ; it was impossible to let other people into it. Dumb, numb, she did nothing but skirt and avoid the subject, turning anxious eyes on people when they opened their mouths in case they were going to begin talking about her and Nicholas.

§

Penelope said they must go and bring their Aunt Victoria to Brockington for the day. Now that Christine was with her, she could undertake a duty she had hitherto put off. When one is bored the

408

prospect of a visit from an aunt does little to enliven ; at least, the visit of such an aunt to such a niece. But now that Christine was there to share the visit, Penelope could invite it.

Christine, though she said nothing, was reluctant. She shrank from having to explain yet again, even though it was only to her aunt, that she had left her husband. She thought badly of Nicholas, but somehow she was not ready yet for other people to think badly of him. Her pride winced every time she had to tell how he had preferred another woman to herself. She also disliked being an object of curiosity and commiseration. She felt everybody knew. Even in the shops, when Penelope was choosing things for Angela, Christine, standing by with Angela in her arms, felt sure that everybody must know why Penelope and not she was buying them.

" We can go through Saunby, if you like," said Penelope, driving her own car with conscious pleasure. " In at one end and out at the other."

" Oh, yes, let's," said Christine, sitting beside her sister with Angela in her lap. Angela was a modern baby ; she liked being in a car and was always very good in one. When the car stopped, she urged it to start again with exhortatory noises and imperious nods of the head.

The girls were hurrying immediately after breakfast to pick up their aunt and get back in time for Angela's morning sleep. This adherence to time-table was curiously appeasing and satisfactory to Penelope, who had lately found all the hours the same and hardly ever knew what the time was.

March was coming in this year like a lamb. The morning was mild and the sun gained moment by moment on the mist. The swathes of mist in the hollows of the park were moving and the trees seemed

409

to swim. Saunby seemed to be materializing from a dream.

" It's like a dream that we ever lived here," said Christine. " D'you remember how happy we were ? "

" Yes, I realize it now," said Penelope.

The West Front was appearing now through the mist like a vision.

" It's so beautiful," said Christine. " It soothes me to look at it. It reminds me that there are other things, enduring, great things that we keep forgetting. Doesn't it you ? "

" Oh, I don't know," said Penelope. " Anthea spoilt it. I was very glad to get away, once you'd gone."

" Oh, I daresay," said Christine. " People come and go and use Saunby for their own purposes, but Saunby itself doesn't change. It's serene and aloof, and yet it's subject to the treatment of human beings, and since the monks went they've treated it very badly. I have a terrific wish to preserve it, haven't you ? "

" I don't know that I have," said Penelope, glancing at it. " It's very beautiful, of course, but I always feel that it has nothing to do with me now."

" Do you ? " asked Christine, amazed that her sister should feel so differently about Saunby. " Oh, I never do. I feel as if my life is bound up with Saunby, somehow. I feel I'm the spiritual heir to Saunby."

" Do you ? " cried Penelope, equally amazed. " Well, how funny ! "

They left Saunby by the north gate, a mere wooden affair this and hanging from its hinges so that Penelope could hardly get it open.

" I do think father might see to things like this," she complained, getting back into the car. " Because he can't do everything, he doesn't do anything."

The Three Pigeons thrust itself forward in the middle of the village with a projecting gable and a swinging sign. It had been rebuilt when it was taken over by the brewery company ten years ago and brought up to date by half-timbers above and stained-glass windows below. The largest of these windows, the pride of the village, served the dual purpose of screening those having a drink within and entertaining those without by the presentation of a scene which showed up very well when the lights were on in the bar behind it. This scene had something of almost everything in it : a landscape in the foreground with cows, cottages, sheep and trees, a seascape in the background with a ship in full sail, a setting sun and a rock with a lighthouse on it, where the light winked most realistically until closing-time.

" It's just like one of Aunt Victoria's own pictures," said Penelope, seeing and remembering this window again. " So perhaps this is her spiritual home as Saunby is yours. Perhaps we don't need to pity her for being here, after all."

She knocked on a front door that was studded with such a determined attempt at the antique that there was hardly any room anywhere for her knuckles. She had to knock many times before the bolts were shot back and Mrs. Pink, the landlady, peeped out as if she suspected somebody of trying to get a drink out of hours.

" Oh, I beg pardon, I'm sure," she said, throwing the door wide at the sight of the young ladies from Saunby. " Have you come to see your Auntie? Step inside, please. But do excuse me. I'm not dressed yet."

She seemed fully clothed, nevertheless, to the girls, in a green georgette too *passé* now for the bar, but with some wear in it yet for the mornings. She wore a pair of white kid slippers very withered at the toes.

"What a lovely baby!" she cried, bolting the door behind the girls. "Bless her, she is a little beauty, Miss Christine. Oh, excuse me, I did ought to have called you by your married name, didn't I? But I've forgotten it. I haven't had time to get used to re-membering it, have I, seeing you've only been married such a short while?"

Christine smiled with constraint. Short indeed, but over already. Mrs. Pink led the way inwards.

"Now can I offer you a little glass of something?" she said, pausing in the passage.

She was exceedingly proud of her lodger and anxious to do honour to her guests. "Just to warm you up after your drive. No? Very well then," said Mrs. Pink, disappointed but disguising it. "Come this way."

"We've only just had breakfast, you see," said Christine, to soften their refusal.

"It's all right," said Mrs. Pink, leading the way upstairs through the curious deadness that reigns in a public-house during closing-hours.

Crossing a landing, with red-distempered walls, Mrs. Pink laid her ear to one yellow door, highly varnished and violently grained to resemble no known wood.

"Miss Marwood?" she inquired.

Then smiling conspiratorially to the girls, she tip-toed to the stairs and disappeared.

Miss Victoria came to greet them with wet white stockings in her hands.

"Ah, here you are," she said, offering a ruddy cheek to one and then to the other. "Ah, and how are *you*?" she said to Angela. The only time Miss Victoria showed any embarrassment was when confronted by a baby. She simply did not know what to say to babies. " Come in here, girls, I must finish these," she said, turning back to the bedroom.

The girls looked round with wondering eyes. The room was chaotic with clothes, canvases and oddments from Saunby. The walls were red like the landing, a highly varnished sticky-looking linoleum was on the floor, a short lace curtain as yellow as the yolk of an egg dangled shrunkenly at the window. The room looked dreadful to the girls, but Miss Victoria seemed quite happy. She went on washing stockings in the bowl on the wash-hand stand.

Christine had no need to dread making explanations to her aunt. Miss Victoria did not ask for any. She talked about herself and her own concerns.

" Yes," she said. " Anthea wanted me to pay to stay at Saunby. So I left. I wasn't going to let her have the satisfaction of getting money out of me. So long as I have the run of the park, which is full of subjects for me still, I don't care where I sleep and eat. I'm quite comfortable here. The advantages of accommodation at Saunby were more than outbalanced by the presence of Anthea and Nurse Pye. Now I'll just hang these stockings over my easel and then I'll be ready to go with you. Quite bohemian, isn't it ? " asked Miss Victoria, looking round as if she liked it and oblivious of or indifferent to the dismay in her nieces' faces.

She spent a cheerful day at Brockington, eating hearty meals and sitting in the garden, muffled to the eyes, painting a picture of the house, which, she said, she would present to Penelope.

" Unless Paul will buy it ? " she said.

" Paul shall buy it," promised Penelope, suppressing a smile.

After dinner Paul was to drive Miss Marwood back

to the Three Pigeons. He came into the drawing-room with his coat on.

"Would you like to come with me?" he said wistfully to his young wife sprawling in a bucket chair with her legs over one arm and her curls dangling over the other. He didn't mind taking her relations home if she came with him, but it was not a thing he could enjoy without her.

"No," said Penelope. "No, I wouldn't. You'll be all right, darling. You won't be long. Bye-bye."

"Isn't Aunt Victoria amazing?" she said, plunging into discussion with her sister when Paul and Miss Marwood had departed. "She staggers me. She's as devoted to her art, as she calls it, as if it were really real. And fancy changing over from Saunby to the Three Pigeons without turning a hair! My goodness, she's tough, isn't she?"

"I expect she got tough early," said Christine. "Living with Grannie and Grandpa and that old governess who stayed until she was seventy, I expect Aunt Victoria had to be tough. Nobody did anything for her, she never had any fun or any occupation except what she found for herself. She owes nothing to anybody and she pays nothing to anybody. I don't blame her. Let her live and die tough," said Christine wearily. "It's the best way."

CHAPTER XXXV

THERE was a letter at Christine's place when she
came down to her solitary breakfast. At Brockington she bathed and dressed Angela while Paul and
Penelope had breakfast, then she gave Angela into
Penelope's charge while she herself breakfasted. This
arrangement suited everybody; Christine was glad
to keep out of the way by not making a third at the
breakfast-table; Paul was glad to have Penelope to
himself, and Penelope looked forward to having Angela
entirely to herself. She liked, above all things, to get
Angela to herself. She also found breakfast much
more enjoyable now that there was something to do
after it. She had to hurry as much as Paul now; he
had to get off to his office and she had to get off to
Angela, so she ate cheerfully and fast with Paul, able
to interest herself in his plans for his day now that
she had plans for her own.

Christine hesitated to open her letter. She recognized the writing on the envelope. Nicholas's mother
wrote in this fine angular hand. Christine had seen
Sarah at her letters, and holding this one, saw her
again now. She sat very upright, a long way from the
paper and wrote, not with a fountain pen, but with a
long thin penholder fitted with a long stiff nib. The
pen scratched audibly, and when Sarah paused, everybody knew. She paused a good deal, thinking gravely
over what she wished to say.

With a pang of regret for the loss of the writer and

415

a dread of what she was going to read from her, Christine opened the envelope.

She drew out two sheets of paper, a large white one enclosing a blue one, folded small. She opened the white one and her face changed as she read.

My dear Christine,

Although, as I understand, you do not wish to have anything further to do with Nicholas, I think you ought to know that he has gone away. He has disappeared, taking with him nothing but some clothes, his car and ten pounds in money. We have no idea where he is. He wrote a letter to me, which I am sending for you to see. Will you please send it back ? This is a great sorrow and anxiety to us. We have lost one son and now the other has disappeared. We never saw him again after his visit to Saunby. His father says you said something which made him rush out of the room and away. I am very sorry for what my son has done and very ashamed. But I wish you could have seen your way to give him another chance. He is not bad at heart, and I think he has been much steadier since Angela was born. I wish you could have helped him. No doubt you feel very bitter towards us all. But my husband, although he has made mistakes, always meant to be kind. He was very hurt by what you said to him at Saunby, and since Nicholas went away, he seems quite broken up. I sent your maids home ; they both went to Alice's home and this morning I received notice from both of them. You and Nicholas have walked out of your home and left it empty. I suppose there is nothing for it but to close it. It is all a great pity. I hope little Angela is well. Her grandmother sends her a loving kiss. I hardly know how to sign myself. Per- haps you wish to cut yourself off from me as you have cut yourself off from my son. But for my part I remain,

Yours affectionately,
SARAH ASHWELL.

Christine fumbled blindly with the blue paper. Her eyes were full of tears from reading Sarah's letter, but she dashed them away to read Nicholas's. She smoothed the sheet out and ran her eyes rapidly over the familiar handwriting.

MY DEAR MOTHER,

I am going away. Christine doesn't mean to come back. I knew that as soon as I saw her. I've got to do without her and Angela now and I can't face that in Mansbridge. I've got to get a job somehow now and I can't do it here. Nobody will give me a job round here. When there are hundreds of men after a job, why should it be given to a man whose father turned hundreds of men out of employment, including his son? So I'm going. You will understand, Mother, but I'm afraid Dad won't. He'll want to do everything for me, buy me a job somewhere, and I can't have that. My life's been too soft. I've been too soft. I'm ashamed of myself, but too late. Don't worry about me, Mother, and please don't try to find me and get me home. I'll find means of knowing how you and Dad are, but you just leave me alone, will you? I'll come back some day—different.

With love to you and Dad,
Your loving son,
NICHOLAS.

Be sure not to worry. I'll always carry your address on me in case anything should happen, so remember no news is good news.

The housemaid came into the room with her tray,

but at the sight of Christine at the table the girl backed hastily out again.

" I can't clear yet," she said, returning to the kitchen. " Mrs. Ashwell's in there, crying. I did feel a fool, barging in."

" Poor young thing," said Cook, rubbing lard into flour for the pastry. " She's fairly in trouble and I bet you ten to one it's her husband. Well, it goes to prove what I always say : you're better single. But you girls won't be told, I suppose."

" Not likely," said the housemaid. " Besides, we might manage better, what say, Hester ? "

Christine had not noticed the housemaid, but when the clock struck ten, she heard it and got up hastily from the table. She folded her letters small and hid them in her belt and went out into the garden. She had kept the maids from their work a long time, and when you are staying in other people's houses you shouldn't do that.

She struck quickly into the side garden away from the house, where she could be alone. She walked unseeingly, clasping herself with her arms, between the tiny box edgings behind which the earth in the beds was tidily dug over, waiting for things to come up. Later the sun would be strong, but at present the morning was silver with wetness. The air shimmered with suspended moisture ; each blade of grass had its scabbard of dew. Drops of water slid along the branches of the trees at even distances from each other as if they were in a bucket-conveyor and every now and then a terminal drop fell icily on Christine's bare head, or through the mesh of her woollen jumper to her shoulder, making her shiver and clasp herself closer.

Nicholas had gone. Life was a dream that went from bad to worse. The sense of unreality was the most dreadful part about it. If only she could wake up, she might find it wasn't true. But she couldn't wake ; she struggled as if in a nightmare. It *must* be a nightmare. These things couldn't have happened to Nicholas and her.

She knew she had thrust him to a distance and kept him there, but somehow that had been unreal too, something that she hadn't really meant, almost a part she was playing to pay him out for getting drunk and running about with his friends. She hadn't meant it to be serious, she told herself. His betrayal had come with as much shock to her as if they had always been on the best of terms. She had felt that, fundamentally, all was well between them. But, she told herself, she had been deceived. She had been living in a fool's paradise. No, not living in it, but keeping it to her hand with the idea that she could go into it whenever she chose.

She couldn't believe, again, that Nicholas had really gone. Gone where ? Where could he go to ? Had he gone to Spain to fight, like so many other young men ? He had such strange ideas, he might do that. Or had he gone to Canada where he always wanted to go ? But he couldn't, she remembered, go there because he had only taken ten pounds. Oh, it was cruel, she cried, beginning to weep again, to leave them in such anxiety. Cruel to separate himself from her. She had separated herself first, but that was different. As long as he was in Mansbridge, it was different. And it is so much easier to go than to be left. Now she was the one to be left.

She could never go back now ; there was nothing to go back to. Not that she had ever intended to go back. Oh, no, she wept, she never had. But to make it so that she *had* to stay away for ever ! How cruel to make her hold for ever to her decision, to give her no option.

That ought to show her, she reasoned, that he didn't love her, that he had never loved her. She must realize it, she told herself, she must face it. She stood still, her hands clenched, and said aloud, to make it more real :

"He doesn't love me. He's gone. He's left me. Now I must look after myself and Angela."

She waited under the dripping trees to let the bitter truth sink home. Then drying her eyes, she walked on, up this path, down that, casting about for a way to live without Nicholas.

Penelope came out into the garden, carrying Angela. Angela's round head, as fair as flax, as smooth as silk, bobbed against Penelope's cheek, one small hand lay trustfully at Penelope's neck, her blue eyes were round with interest in the world.

Penelope walked about, showing things to Angela. She pulled down the twig of a tree to show the crystal drops, but one splashed Angela in the face, startling her comically. Penelope laughed and kissed her, so Angela laughed too, assured then that the cold splash was a joke.

Penelope crouched to the grass to let Angela see the blue of the squills. Penelope maintained, without a wobble, a position an older person would have found difficult : knees bent, heels raised out of her court slippers, arms encumbered. She rose from it without effort and walked on, talking to Angela in the warm, loving voice she used for no one else.

She saw Christine in the rose-garden.

"I wondered where you were," she called gaily. But coming near enough to see her sister's face, her own changed. "Christine ! What's the matter ? What's happened ? "

"Nicholas has gone," said Christine, standing with her tear-blotched face like a lost child whom no one can tell how to find the way. "He's disappeared. I've had a letter from his mother. He's gone and he never said a word about what Angela and I were to do."

"But, darling," Penelope reminded her, "you told him. You said you were never going back, didn't you?"

"Yes, I know." Christine was too distressed to defend her inconsistencies. "And I wasn't going back. But now I can't."

Angela jerked vigorously in her aunt's arms, implying that she would like to be walked on. Penelope said, "Yes, darling," and continued to look anxiously at Christine. She didn't know what to say to her.

"I've been trying to think what I can do," said Christine.

"Do?" Penelope was puzzled.

"I must do something. I must find some way to keep Angela and myself."

"But why? You're staying here," said Penelope.

"I can't stay here for ever."

"Of course you can."

"No, I can't, Pen. You're very good, darling, and I know you would let me stay for years, but it isn't fair to Paul."

"Oh, Paul doesn't mind at all. Paul's only too glad . . ."

"He would mind, in time," said Christine, who was a mixture of wisdom and inexperience. "And it would work no better for me than it would for him. No, darling, I'll stay for the present and be grateful, but in the end I shall have to find a job and make enough money to get a home or a room or something where I can have Angela. But there is something you can do for me, Pen, if you will. Will you have Angela until I get settled somewhere?"

Penelope's face changed; like a child who, about to cry because one thing is taken from him, finds himself presented with something he wants still more. Her face cleared of distress for her sister and showed nothing but eagerness for Angela. This was certainly more than she had ever dreamed of.

"Oh, Christine, can I really have her?" she breathed, clasping Angela close as if she were already hers. "I'll take the greatest care of her. You know I can look after her nearly as well as you can already, and I'll have Hester to help me. She's so good with her, isn't she? And I daresay, darling, that you'll be able to come here for lots of week-ends, so perhaps it won't be so bad for you after all," she finished, wishing to console.

"Perhaps it won't," said Christine, trying to smile because Penelope wanted her to, and taking Angela while she could. The sooner she got work, she told herself, gathering the small, comforting body into her arms, the sooner she would be able to earn enough money to have Angela altogether.

As she walked to the front of the house where Hester was getting Angela's perambulator ready for her morning sleep, Christine's head was already full of the swift, rash plans of youth. Penelope, hurrying behind her, was full of her plans too.

For the rest of the day, Penelope suppressed her excitement as well as she could out of consideration for Christine, but she was impatient to gain the privacy of the bedroom she shared with Paul. The worst of having anyone to stay, even a sister, is that you have to wait until you go to bed to say anything in private to your husband.

As soon as she had said good night to Christine on the landing and closed her own pale green door, Penelope burst out with her news.

" Paul, listen, Nicholas has disappeared . . ."

" What ? " he exclaimed.

" Yes, he's disappeared and Christine is going to look for work in London so that she can make enough money to get a room or a flat or something so that she can have Angela——"

" Well, she can't do it," said Paul bluntly.

" Oh ? " said Penelope, halted. " Why ? "

" Well, what can she do ? She's not trained for anything, and her education, like yours, my pet, is decidedly sketchy. I was never more embarrassed in my life than when you asked me to get you into an office."

Laughing, he tried to kiss her, but she held off, eager to come to the most important part of her news.

" But listen, Paul—oh, well, kiss me and be quick ! Christine says I can have Angela here until she finds somewhere to have her in. We shall have Angela all to ourselves."

He could see that she was very happy at this prospect.

" Oh, good," he said warmly. " That'll please you, won't it ? I know you're awfully fond of the kid."

" I am. I adore her," said Penelope. " But, Paul, do you think it will take Christine a long time to make enough money to have Angela with her ? "

She was torn between wanting it to take a long time for her sake and wanting it not to take a long time for poor Christine.

" Take a long time ? " repeated Paul with good-humoured callousness. " She can't do it, I tell you."

" But, then," faltered Penelope, seeing her plans threatened. " Ought we to let her try ? Oughtn't we to tell her ? "

" Oh, no," said Paul easily. " Let her try. It'll take her mind off things. I say," he said, going through to his dressing-room, " I wonder where

Nicholas has gone to. It is a queer business, isn't it ? "

" I shall have the room we're using for a nursery made into a real nursery now," said Penelope, sitting down at her dressing-table to brush her hair. " It wasn't intended to be a nursery, so it doesn't look like one, but now we must make it into one."

It wasn't intended for a nursery, but she had a baby in it, one she was sure she loved as much as if she were her own, as much as the one she would never have. Never, she thought, staring at herself in the glass and seeing her eyes dark and strange in her face. She had only to look at her fear to look like that.

§

Every morning now Christine scanned the advertisement columns of the daily papers, of which large numbers were delivered to the Grange. There were papers for Paul, papers for Penelope, papers for the maids, and Christine collected them all and went down the columns with her finger, while her coffee went cold beside her.

The sun of these March mornings flashed on the silver of Penelope's breakfast-table and fell warm on Christine's bent head. Her hair straggled out of curl, her face bore the marks of anxiety and lack of sleep. Sitting in the breakfast-room, which compared in simplicity and elegance with an illustration to a Jane Austen novel by Hugh Thompson, Christine went, with decreasing hope, through the jobs in the papers.

Among the hundreds upon hundreds of advertised posts, there was hardly one for which she could apply. She was appalled by her own inefficiency.

What did women in her position do ? What did they *do* ? If there was only marriage for girls brought up in the way she and Penelope had been brought up and marriage failed, what then ?

It was a question parents, in her world, did not ask themselves.

'All the money goes on the sons,' thought Christine. 'They just trust to luck about the daughters, hoping they'll be pretty enough to make a good marriage. If they're not, they just have to exist like Rosamund Hunter and the rest, and end up like Aunt Victoria. She lived for twenty years in a home that wasn't hers any longer and then had just enough money to go and live at a place like the Three Pigeons.

'No wonder Anthea pinches and scrapes,' she thought with sudden light on the situation at Saunby. 'She's afraid of finding herself thrown on the world with two children. Like me with one. Of course I know someone would keep me. But I don't happen to like being kept. I hate it,' she said vehemently.

She turned over the pages of the papers.

'People say : " Oh, it's not like that for girls *now*." But it is, and it's going to be more like it than ever, it seems to me. According to these papers it is. Women are being pushed back into homes and told to have more babies. They're being told to make themselves helpless. Men are arming like mad, but women are expected to disarm, and make themselves more vulnerable than they already are by nature. No woman is going to choose a time like this to have a baby in. You can't run very fast for a bomb-proof shelter if you have a baby inside you, and a bomb-proof shelter is not the place you would choose to deliver it in. No protection against gas is provided for children under three, this paper says, so presumably the baby you have laboured to bring into the world must die if there is a gas attack. Look at this,' Christine directed herself. 'In this paper, the headlines

425

are about the necessity of preparation for war and the leader is about the necessity for an increase in the population. " The only hope," they say. They urge women to produce babies so they can wage wars more successfully with them when their mothers have brought them up.'

What a world ! For herself, for everybody, what a world !

' Well, this has taught me one thing,' she thought wearily, picking up another paper and turning to the advertisement columns. ' If I've to scrub floors or eat the bread of dependence all my life, Angela shall be educated to earn her own living. She shan't find herself in the hole I'm in now if I can help it.'

§

One morning, as sunny and as warm as a morning in June, she picked up the still unopened *Daily Telegraph*. At the head of the Personal Column her eyes fell at once on the name that meant more, though painfully, to her than any other.

" Nicholas," she saw.

" Nicholas. Come home on your own terms. Will agree to anything. Dad."

Off her guard, Christine clasped the paper and echoed that. " Oh, come, come . . ." she called from her heart.

Standing on Penelope's hearthrug, she summoned him with all her might to come. Then she stopped herself.

" No," she said, shaking her head, putting the paper from her.

What she wanted was the Nicholas who had not had morning tea with Cicely Hoyle, the Nicholas before that. And she knew she could not have that Nicholas again. What had happened had happened and could never be wiped out.

She picked up the paper again. She was out of it, she took no share in this appeal. But poor Sir James ! She found the two lines of print unbearably touching. She didn't want to be sorry for Sir James. She wanted to remember him as she had seen him last, a bullying old man. She wanted to keep herself stiff and hard so that she could go on and do as she had to do.

But she could not keep herself from writing two days later to ask Sarah if there had been any reply.

No, Sarah wrote back, not yet. Nicholas might not write, though ; he might come. They were always looking for him.

" Should I send Angela's pram ? " wrote Sarah in this letter. " It seems such a pity to let it stand in the garage."

" Angela has a pram, thank you," Christine replied. " Penelope bought her one some time ago."

CHAPTER XXXVI

" THERE'S a more promising advertisement here,"
said Christine, arriving, paper in hand, in the
nursery where Penelope was getting Angela ready to
go out.

" Oh ? " said Penelope, trying to get to the button
under Angela's chin, which was difficult because
Angela was doubled in deep interest over her own toes.
" There you are, pet. Now. What is it, Christine?
Is it anything you can do ? "

" You may well ask," said Christine and read out :
" ' Young lady, eighteen to twenty-four. Wanted for
West End Beauty Parlour. Experience not essential.
Good figure, smart appearance essential.' "

" The very thing," said Penelope. " Your figure's
very good and you can make yourself look very nice
when you want to. And you're the right age. What's
the address ? "

" No address. A box number."

" I should write then and get the address and go
and apply in person," said Penelope briskly. Nothing
had come so far of the many letters Christine had
written. The stamped addressed envelopes she had
enclosed had either come back with the news that the
post was filled or had not come back at all.

" I should have to go to London for the day,"
demurred Christine.

" Well, why not ? "

" I haven't got the fare."

" Goodness, *I* have," cried Penelope. " Write now and say you'll come as soon as you get the address. And send a snapshot of yourself and then they'll see how good looking you are. Hester ! " she called. " Bring me that little pink bonnet. I think she ought to have a bonnet on this morning, Christine, don't you ? "

" She never does wear a bonnet," said Christine.

" But it's frightfully cold this morning," said Penelope, with anxious maternal glances at the windows. " I really think she ought to, Christine."

" Very well," said Christine. If she was to leave Angela in Penelope's charge it was better that Penelope should be too careful than not careful enough.

She wrote the letter, she sent a photograph, she suggested she should come for an interview, but she hoped she wouldn't get a reply. She got one, however, and promptly. It arrived on the Thursday morning, asking her to call at the Vannette Salon, off Regent Street, on that same afternoon between two and three o'clock.

" Come on ! " cried Penelope. " We've only just time to get you to the train. You get ready while I get the car out. Hester ! " she called, " come and take baby. Put on your navy-blue suit," she said, following Christine into her bedroom. " You look so nice in it. I say, darling, are you getting short of silk stockings without ladders ? How awful of me not to notice. Why didn't you tell me ? I'll get you a pair."

She flew back with a new pair of stockings.

" Paul will meet you to-night," she said, thrusting her sleeves into her coat. " Will you catch the six train ? Unless you'd like to stay the night and go to a play ? "

" Oh, no," said Christine, shrinking.

" Well, catch the six train and Paul will meet you.

I may come too, but I shall have to see how Angela settles, of course." She was like a little girl playing importantly at house. "Do hurry up, darling, and don't look so dazed."

Penelope was brisk and bustling, but Christine was cold with nervousness and uncertainty. She sat in the train almost resisting its bearing her away. She felt so unwilling. I'm stupid, she told herself. Either I want a job or I don't. If I do want it, I must go out after it. If I don't, I should leave it alone. I must get a job, she told herself, because if I stayed at Brockington long I should get jealous of Penelope monopolizing Angela or Penelope would get jealous of me. I must get this job. But I feel it's another step farther away. And I don't want to leave Angela, she thought miserably. I'm frightened. I don't know what it's like to work. I dread all the strange people.

She was back at Brockington soon after nine o'clock that night, eating a late supper, while Penelope sat at the table to keep her company and hear about the day. She had been appointed to the Vannette Salon in a rather vague capacity at two pounds a week.

"Two pounds a week!" Penelope kept exclaiming. "It's splendid."

"I knew you'd get it," she told Christine. "It's your looks."

"I don't think it was my looks," said Christine. "I think it was your address. Miss Vanne—she's married really—asked what I was doing at Brockington Grange, and when I said I was staying with my sister, she seemed impressed."

"Why didn't you bring Saunby in and impress her still more?" said Penelope gaily. She was highly cheerful now that it was certain that she was to have Angela practically for her own. "Angela's been so sweet all day," she said. "But go on."

Christine went on, but she did not say, because she always avoided speaking of Nicholas, that she thought she had got the job because Miss Vanne had discovered that she was, like Miss Vanne herself, a deserted wife. At least that was what Miss Vanne termed her.

Miss Vanne, in private life Mrs. Porter, had an absentee husband and a son now at Cambridge as a result of his mother's hard work. Miss Vanne was forty-five years of age, with a good head of hair she could dress in any way that happened to be fashionable at the moment, a good skin that had also been a great asset to her in her business and a figure whose generous proportions were sternly quelled. She was kindly, coarse, practical and cheerfully dishonest on the Robin Hood principle of taking from her rich clients to give to her poor son, or rather to the son who would have been poor if she hadn't.

The clients of the Vannette Beauty Salon were not drawn from the fashionable women of Mayfair, but from middle-class, middle-aged, plump, plain women who daren't go anywhere else. These women were frightened of the smart *salons*, but ventured into the Vannette. Miss Vanne bullied them and they liked it and came back regularly for more. She hardly troubled to disguise her contempt for them, but remarked in justification for taking their money that she kept them clean and tidy and kept their fat down which was as much as anybody else could do for them.

" They'd look a lot worse if they didn't come," she said.

Miss Vanne, with her questions, hooked out Christine's tenderest feelings and let them squirm in the open, like poor small fish laid out still alive on a slab. Miss Vanne handled Christine's feelings as if they were nothing out of the ordinary, and as if, though they might be squirming a bit now, they would soon be dead and nobody, including Christine, need bother about them.

"Let's hope your husband stops away. You'll do better without him. I don't want mine back, I can tell you. It was good riddance for me. I'd never have been able to send my son to Cambridge if his father had stopped about the place spending my money on booze and bitches. You cheer up, medear. You don't know when you're well off. I've managed. Why shouldn't you?"

Miss Vanne, though she never allowed it to interfere with business, had romance in her nature. As soon as she saw Christine she was sure she would do; she was pretty, she dressed well, and she was "a lady." All Miss Vanne's girls were lady-like, but this girl, Miss Vanne told herself, was the goods. While Miss Vanne was putting her brisk, brutal questions, romance was making pictures in which Christine appeared as an impoverished aristocrat, like someone Russian or out of the French Revolution, a young and lovely girl deserted by a young husband, equally aristocratic, but full of wild oats, a girl left with an infant child and forced to earn her living and coming to Miss Vanne to help her to do it. It was this combination of suitability and romantic appeal that led to Christine's subsequent appointment.

When Miss Vanne asked for a reference, Christine was at a loss until she remembered that she had a brother. She looked him up in the telephone book and rang him up from Miss Vanne's desk while Miss Vanne waited. But Guy had gone to the West Indies on a Mission, she was told, and would be away for several months.

"Never mind," said Miss Vanne. "I don't need a reference with you. It's only a matter of form. You

can come on trial. At first you'll have to be odd girl
about, learning the ropes and the clients and arranging
the show-cases and so on. Deidre, my receptionist, is
getting married in September, the fool, and it's her
place I intend you to take. So if you find you're at
everybody's beck and call at first and don't get any
tips or commission, put up with it for the sake of what's
coming, see ? "

" I will," said Christine. " And thank you for
taking me," she stammered.

" Now, what shall we call you ? " said Miss Vanne.
" Oh, you can't be ' Mrs.' anybody here, and you can't
wear that wedding-ring, you know. So let's find a
pretty name for you. I always find pretty names for
my girls."

She liked pretty names so that she could call them out
in the *salon*.

" Delphine, the patter ! " she would flute from one
cubicle to another. " Valerie, the drier, dear ! "

" Let's see, what's your Christian name ? " asked
Miss Vanne.

" Christine."

" Oh, very Christian indeed," said Miss Vanne.
" But it won't do. Now, what can we call you ? "

She considered Christine with her head on one side,
while Christine waited meekly to be named.

" Sonia," announced Miss Vanne triumphantly.
That was the name for this Russian ballet look.
" Now, Sonia, where are you going to dig ? "

" Dig ? " Christine was puzzled.

" Live, get a room," translated Miss Vanne.

" Oh," Christine, enlightened, blushed. " I don't
know," she faltered.

" Well, I'll give you an address," said Miss Vanne,
searching in a drawer. " I'm particular where my
girls stay. I'm like a mother to my girls. In fact,

they call me 'Ma' behind my back. But I don't mind. There's lots worse names they could have called me. You'll be all right here, Sonia, and you can thank your stars it was my advert. you answered. You're that green you might have got anywhere. But you'll be all right here. No men here," said Miss Vanne sternly. "Oh, no. I could make a lot of money if I'd take men for treatments, but I won't. No hanky-panky here, thank you. Keep it clean is my motto for other things besides skins, and you can't do that if you let men in. You and I know that, medear, don't we? Now, here's this address. Mrs. Gaws, Manchester Street. Valerie's just moved out, so you'll probably get in. When the girls get a raise they move to a bit pricier digs, you see. I should go and get it fixed up right away, if I were you. Take a bus to Selfridge's and go up Baker Street. You turn at George Street, I think, on the right. But anybody'll tell you."

"I've got a bed-sitting-room," Christine told Penelope over supper.

"Well, you've managed beautifully," said Penelope admiringly. "And you know it really sounds very exciting."

Christine smiled. The bed-sitting-room might sound exciting to Penelope. She hadn't seen it. But to Christine who had, the thought of sleeping in the room had filled her with such dread and nausea that she had almost gone away without taking it. But she had realized that if she didn't sleep there she would have to sleep somewhere else, and Mrs. Gaws seemed a kind woman. So she said she would take it, and escaped from it while she could.

During her last days at Brockington she would not let Angela out of her sight or out of her arms. Penelope kept coming upon her looking bleak and desperate

434

while Angela sat in her lap and played happily with her own toes.

"I don't think you need take it *quite* so much to heart," said Penelope at last. "After all, you'll be back on Saturday."

"I know," said Christine. "But I've never left her before. Not for a single day since she was born, except for last Thursday."

"Well, think of the people who go to India and leave their children for years," said Penelope.

"I know," said Christine. "Penelope, you will see that she has her orange juice every day, won't you? And that her bath water is warm enough? Hester never runs it quite warm enough. I always have to warm it up."

"I'll buy a thermometer and see that it's exactly right, so don't worry about that," said Penelope briskly. "Don't worry about anything. I'll look after Angela all right. I don't need to be told to be careful with you, do I, my pet?"

Christine packed her things for Sunday. She had to go to London on Sunday night to be in time at the *salon* on Monday morning. In her blotter she put all the snapshots of Angela that Nicholas had taken; none had been taken since. In another place in the blotter, she put the bill, to preserve it. She could no longer carry it about in her bag, it was too worn. It was falling apart. She unfolded it carefully and read again: "Mr. and Mrs. Ashwell. Morning Tea." She had played on one note too long; it was almost mute. Nothing came from it now but a dull realization that this was the cause of everything, the cause of her having to leave Angela.

On Sunday evening she travelled to London. In her corner of the compartment, she kept her face turned from her fellow-passengers, who thought, having seen Paul at the window bidding her good-bye, that she was crying because she had left her young man.

She reached the house in Manchester Street, and Mrs. Gaws, large in a flowered frock for Sunday, admitted her to the narrow passage where an immensely tall, ancient, fly-pocked pierglass glimmered on one wall with a marble slab beneath it, an altar to Mrs. Gaws's idea of what was what for a hall.

" Father ! " called Mrs. Gaws to the basement, and a bald, kindly looking man in shirt-sleeves and a dangling waistcoat appeared to carry Christine's cases up the three flights of stairs to her room.

" You should have put your coat on, Father," reproved Mrs. Gaws, following him with Christine. " Or you should at least have buttoned yourself up."

Father made no reply, and Mrs. Gaws was driven, like so many wives, to apologize for him herself.

" Of course, it's Sunday," she said in extenuation.

Father deposited the cases, and without a glance at Christine went nimbly and good-humouredly down the stairs again.

Mrs. Gaws stood in the room looking round with proprietary satisfaction.

" I hope you'll be comfortable," she said. " The gas-ring in the hearth is a bit broke, but it lights all the same. The meter's under the dressing-table. The bathroom's down one flight and the double-yew's next to it. Reeny—that's my daughter—will bring your breakfast up at half-past seven. Is there anything you want to-night ? We only do breakfasts here, as I told you, but you being a stranger I can let you have a pan and drop of milk to hot up if you like ? No ? All right. You must just please yourself," allowed Mrs. Gaws. " Well, I think I've told you everything, and we've got friends in so I'll say good night. Good night." Mrs. Gaws said it with a smile that was unabashed by the fact that there were several teeth missing from her upper plate. What looked like the heads of pins gleamed where the teeth should have been.

"Good night," said Christine, closing her door.

She was alone. She stood in the middle of the room, unwilling to let it receive her. It looked worse by night than by day. Under the single electric light, the purple artificial silk of the curtains and bed-cover gave off sudden bloody gleams. The thin hard carpet was so stained that Christine determined never to let her bare feet touch it. Under the window stood a gaunt wicker-chair, wrenched sideways, like the skeleton of something that had had a stroke. The dressing-table and wash-stand were of stained deal with long white splinters off the edges. There was no wardrobe ; only a curtain of the bloodshot purple stuff. The room smelt of gas and long occupation.

She threw up the window and looked out. A London night scene was there : dark cliffs of houses, pierced by lighted windows ; sharp angles of roofs, crazy chimney pots outlined against the suffused sky. There was a deep steady underlying hum, overlaid with the sharp sounds near at hand of cars passing in the street, footfalls, someone calling out, the bang of a door, faint sounds of music.

This was a London Christine did not know. She had only been to London for fun before. Mostly with Nicholas. They used to do themselves very well on Sir James's money, trying the luxury hotels one after the other and revelling in everything. She remembered morning tea at the Dorchester. Morning tea. There it was again.

She unpacked her things and laid them in the rickety drawers. She could not bring herself to accept

437

the room. She touched things with distaste and when at last she got into bed, she lay stiffly in it, refusing to relax.

She thought of Angela and stifled a rising sob. She mustn't cry and make her eyes red for her first morning at the *salon*.

She couldn't sleep. The curtains blew inwards, parting to reveal London standing dark, crowded, menacing, in the sky. The hum seemed to swell to a roar. Steps approached her door and seemed to pause. She started up in terror. Who was there? The steps passed on. She lay down again. A cat began to miaul somewhere near at hand. She almost wept, she was so tired. She was cold. Mrs. Gaws's covers were too thin. She got up and spread her coat over the bed. A door banged down below. Steps receded in the street. The roar diminished to a hum, the hum sank to silence. The glow faded in the sky. She fell asleep.

She dreamt she was with Nicholas. There had been some dreadful trouble between them, but they could not remember what it was. They kept saying to each other : " Why have we been away? Why did we go? We must never, never leave each other again," they said, lying in each other's arms. The dream was so real she could feel the slight prickle of Nicholas's unshaven night-time cheek on hers.

A thump on the door woke her. She started up bewildered. Nicholas wasn't with her. She was alone. She couldn't think where she was. The door was thumped again. The damp murk of a London morning showed between the curtains. She sprang out of bed and ran over the sticky carpet to admit Reeny with her breakfast.

CHAPTER XXXVII

CHRISTINE, sitting on a high stool in a white overall filling jars with face-cream, could see herself in a small looking-glass hanging on the window-frame. At the *salon* there were mirrors everywhere ; there was even a mirror in the toilet-paper holder in the lavatory. The Vannette girls were intensely preoccupied with their personal appearance. As they hurried about, doing Miss Vanne's bidding, or working on the clients, they threw incessant glances at themselves, living a looking-glass life, a life quite unconnected with, and infinitely more exciting than the one they lived in reality. They looked at themselves, and when they looked down again, they saw no warning, no death to their hopes in the ruined, middle-aged faces under their fingers.

When Christine raised her eyes from the jars and encountered her own face in the glass she wondered, for a flash, who she was. Her eyebrows were thinned almost to nothing, her lashes were stiffened, her lips redder than they had ever been before, but the greatest change had been made by the arrangement of her curls on the top of her head by Miss Vanne herself. Now her ears were cold, and she looked, she thought, as if she was just going to have her bath.

'Angela wouldn't know me,' she thought. 'If I tried to take her, she'd hide in Penelope's neck.'

She was without husband, baby, wedding-ring, name, and now she was without her own face. She seemed to have lost everything. Her very self was missing. It wasn't here. It was wandering unhappily, trying to get to Nicholas and Angela. She had to keep dragging herself back to the present.

The place she worked in was as narrow as a cell, with an uncurtained window and the walls taken up by shelves on which were ranged ready-prepared bundles of white overalls, towels, gauze, cotton-wool, head-bands, chin-straps. When the bell rang, Christine had to take one of the bundles to the indicated cubicle and prepare the client for hairdressing or massage as required. For hair-dressing the overall had to be tied at the back, for massage at the front.

" And don't you forget it," warned Valerie. " Ma goes off the deep end if it's on wrong when she comes in. But the first time you have to get anybody ready, the one who's there will show you how to do it, so don't look so scared."

Christine felt scared. She watched the girls' faces with the anxiety of a lip-reader in her attempts to find out what she was expected to do. She was apt to forget, too, that the bells were summoning her. So far in life she had only rung bells ; she had never been rung for. Now she was anxious to remember to jump to the bell. She felt she must look like Bessy when she appeared in answer : eager, afraid that she had kept someone waiting. Poor Bessy, she thought, filling jars with face-cream in a *salon* off Regent Street. What things have happened to us lately at Saunby. In the old days people used to live such long, slow lives there, but now everything is changing. She paused over the cream, and in her mind's eye Saunby itself stood in the Spring morning, sunlit, serene, enduring.

The bell rang. Seizing a bundle from the shelves, Christine hurried out to number seven. By good luck, it was Valerie who was there, with a large client in camisole and bloomers.

"Massage," said Valerie, and Christine put the short starched overall correctly front to front.

Towel under the head, band round the hair, towel over vast bosom and pink blanket over bloomers. The client closed her eyes and sighed with anticipatory pleasure. Valerie gestured "Get out," and Christine returned to her cell.

On the table stood the giant jar of face-cream looking as if it had spawned the dozens of little jars of different shapes and sizes which had to be filled, labelled, covered with cellophane and tied up with ribbon. The same cream went into all the jars, but it was called by different names. It was "Cleansing Cream," "Nourishing Cream," "Night Cream," "Massage Cream," "Tissue Crême," "Special Crême," "Anti-Wrinkle Crême," or "Skin Food," according to the shape of the jar. The prices varied accordingly.

Christine had filled and labelled many jars. She now tried covering one with cellophane and tying it up with ribbon to see if she could do it properly. She had to be very careful. She had never been able to tie things up well. She and Penelope had always made up the most unsightly parcels. To think, she said, fumbling clumsily, that such a small thing as tying up a jar properly should matter. She had never had patience for such things, or considered them worth doing. It had always irritated her to fiddle ; but now she had to suppress her irritation.

The bell rang. She rushed out to number four. Miss Vanne was there, terrifying a client about her hair.

"You're going bald," said Miss Vanne, fingering the client's scalp. "You'll have to do something

441

about it and quickly too. I'll have to give you a course."

" Give " was one of Miss Vanne's euphuisms.

" Does it *show* ? " asked the client in anguish.

" Of course it shows," said Miss Vanne unfeelingly. " And it'll spread. Hairdressing, Sonia. Where's your frill ? "

Christine looked helpless. Miss Vanne indicated a pleated paper frill and directed Christine to fix it round the anxious client's neck.

" I suppose I'd better have a course, then," said the client.

" Well, I won't answer for your scalp if you don't," said Miss Vanne. " That's all, Sonia."

Christine went back to her cell. The window was uncurtained and she could see directly into a work-room across the street, a big room filled with girls bent over sewing-machines. A woman went about among them, inspecting. Close against the window was a young girl, hardly more than a child, with a pale face and pale straight hair caught up with a slide. Christine watched her running material through her machine, expertly, unceasingly, her back bowed, her head bent so that she must almost be sewing her hair in with the stuff, thought Christine.

The air in the *salon* was scented and too warm. It was tempered to the clients who were partially un-dressed. Christine wondered if there was any air in London that did not smell of something. If only she could breathe the pure air of Saunby on this April morning ! Oh, Saunby, she thought, you've spoilt me. I'm so used to breathing pure air I can't breathe foul. I'm so used to beauty I can't bear to look at ugliness. I'm so used to freedom I can't bear to be tied.

She averted her eyes in disgust from the pot of cream and they fell again on the girl opposite. The sight of the little industrious girl at the machine taught her a sudden lesson. She realized that she was only breathing the air that other people had to breathe, that she was looking at the ugliness other people had to look at, that she was no more tied than other people were.

The girl opposite, lifting her material to put it again to the machine, looked directly at Christine, and Christine, on an impulse, leaned forward and smiled. The girl, arrested with her material uplifted, stared for a moment and then smiled back.

The bell rang and Christine, snatching a bundle, hurried out.

The day came to an end at last. She was so tired at the end of her first working day that she was astonished at herself. She was so tired when she opened Mrs. Gaws's door that she could not draw back and go out again as she had the impulse to do as soon as she saw that hall once more, so dead with its marble slab like the top of a tomb and its great, ancient glass. There was a terrible melancholy about this glass, reflecting a dim void. It had a surface, from age and fly-blow, like a stagnant pond, and you swam into view in it like a fish coming to the front of a dark aquarium.

As Christine, held by the glass, stood in the hall, the door opened again and in came a middle-aged woman carrying cardboard boxes of prepared food. With an indifferent glance at Christine, she passed and climbed to her own life in a room upstairs.

A young man came running down, passed across the mirror and banged the door behind him. Christine had turned to watch the woman coming in and the young man going out. Now she went upstairs in her turn and closed herself in for the evening, for the night.

The week passed between the *salon* and the back-bedroom. It was better at the *salon*. She was kept busy, there were people there. In the back-bedroom she was alone. When you are happy, you can be alone. When you are unhappy, you need other people. Christine, who had always escaped from other people, now longed for them.

She dreaded the closing hour at the *salon*. At six o'clock, the girls, having made up their faces at the mirrors, put on their hats, thrust their arms into their new spring coats, seized their handbags and their gloves and rushed away. Miss Vanne had driven herself off in her own car at five. The girl across the street stood up at last and stretched her arms. Christine felt her relief in her own bones. They waved to each other ; and that was the last friendly signal for Christine until morning.

Christine put on her things and went in her turn. She was always the last to go. Other people seemed to have somewhere, someone to hurry to, the streets were full of people hurrying. But she had nobody, nothing ; only the back-bedroom.

She sat as long as she could over dinner, a cheap meal in a cheap restaurant off Manchester Street. She sat on at the table, looking at the other diners, wondering about them. She walked to Mrs. Gaws's through the streets where daylight lingered longer every evening, watching the children darting about at their games. If a child ran into her, she was glad ; glad to catch it and keep it from falling, glad to exchange smiles, to feel for an instant the impact of a young eager life on her own solitariness. But linger as she might at the *salon*, at the restaurant, in the streets, she had to come to the back-bedroom at last.

' I know now,' she thought, ' why people take to drink and aspirin and jig-saw puzzles and the pictures.'

She had no money for these. She had no money for anything. She was in a state of terror at the way money went in London. Penelope had made her take five pounds, but when this was done, how was she to manage on two pounds a week, since she had to pay twenty-two shillings and sixpence of it to Mrs. Gaws? How do people manage, she asked herself, appalled, looking down the grim vistas of other people's lives. She was always making anxious calculations on paper. Bus fares must be stopped ; she must walk to work. Lunches must be cut down to bread and cheese and coffee. She must see if it was cheaper to bring food in like the woman on the second floor, than to eat her evening meal in the restaurant. She must wash her own stockings, handkerchiefs, underclothes, all she could. The half-pint of milk she had rashly ordered for supper must go. But how, in spite of these economies, was she to get to Brockington to see Angela at the week-ends? The fare was nearly as much as a week's lodging. She must see Angela at the week-ends. That was what she lived for. She terrified herself so much by the thought of not being able to see Angela at the week-ends that she had to stop thinking about it. This week-end at any rate was safe because she had Penelope's money. She would not look farther. She sat in the back-bedroom, saving her money, mentally clutching her purse.

She wondered sometimes, but dully, what made her do as she did. She was surprised, in a muffled sort of way, at the pride and stubbornness that made her refuse the comfort other people would have given her.

She wondered what Nicholas was doing. He was probably living in much the same way as she was herself, she thought.

"Well, he brought it on us both," she said, hoping

445

at the moment that he was paying as dearly for what he had done as she was.

Her feelings towards Nicholas were still a muddle of anger, bitterness, anxiety, love and hate. First one came uppermost and then another. Her feelings hadn't settled. She didn't know, in her waking hours, what she felt. But in her dreams, she knew. In her dreams, she was always looking for him, and when sometimes she found him, the happiness was so great that she woke crying with relief.

Saturday came at last. At the end of the morning she waved ecstatically to the little machinist across the street and the girl waved back, indicating by rubbing her hands that she also had something nice to do.

" Have a happy week-end," said everybody at the *salon* to everybody else. This, Christine discovered, was the Saturday farewell formula.

At a quarter past three she was running up the steps from the platform, outdistancing Paul, who had come down to the train, by half the flight. She ran out into the front of the station and stood looking eagerly for the car. She found it, ran, wrenched open the door and snatched Angela from Penelope's lap.

" Darling . . . darling . . . Mummy's little girl."

Angela blinked in astonishment at so many hard kisses. She hung between her mother's hands, blinking.

" Oh, Pen, she doesn't know me," cried Christine in distress. " She's forgotten me."

" You startled her," said Penelope. " And you look so different. What have you done to yourself? It's your hair."

" Oh, that's what it is," said Christine, clambering into the back of the car with Angela. She snatched off her hat and combed her curls down with her fingers. " See, darling, do you know Mummy better like that ? " she asked, waiting eagerly.

446

Angela smiled. Her mother's voice woke pleasant recollections. Christine lifted her up again so that she could press her face against the vigorous little body.

" Now you know Mummy, don't you ? " she said, comforted.

Angela cheerfully beat her on the head with both fists to show familiarity.

" You shouldn't have spoilt your hair," rebuked Penelope. " It was very becoming. When I can leave Angela, I shall come up to London and have mine done like that."

" Has she had her orange juice every day ? " asked Christine. " These slippers are getting too short for her. How she does grow ! D'you know, my pet, Mummy's brought you a pink plush rabbit ? "

" Oh, Paul bought her one the other day," said Penelope. " She loves it."

Paul got into the car and drove them away. Penelope sat beside him, her lap cold without Angela. Her lovely long legs were carelessly disposed, her knees together, her feet turned in. There was something childish and touching about the way she sat, looking over her shoulder at the other two, and Paul's fond heart felt a pang. He knew at once when things went even slightly wrong with her.

Penelope was already feeling flat and out of it. She had had a lovely week with Angela, she'd felt responsible and busy and as if she was really doing something in life, but now Christine had come all that seemed to have been make-believe. Christine was so very much Angela's mother, and now she had come Penelope had to take a back seat.

Christine, having walked with Angela in the garden, having bathed her and put her to bed, felt a little guilty as she dressed and did her hair again. She had been so absorbed in Angela she had hardly noticed

447

Penelope or Paul. Now she would go down and make up by telling them all the amusing things she could think of about the *salon*.

But Penelope was in a difficult mood and would not respond. She looked very like her father, thought Paul, observing her with anxiety. She would say the most cutting things in this mood and not care how she hurt anybody. In the old nursery days, Christine had been able to bring her sister round, but it was not the same now. Penelope was not so amenable as in the days at Saunby. So Christine and Paul treated her carefully during dinner, avoiding all provocation.

It was in the drawing-room after Harrison had handed coffee and withdrawn that Penelope, sitting on the sofa, turned her head sideways to Christine and said carelessly :

" Saunby's up for sale, you know."

She had been wondering during the week how best to break the shock of this news to Christine, but now she wished to hurt and brought it out brutally.

Christine was successfully hit. The look of happiness she had from being under the same roof as Angela was dashed away. She looked in horror at her sister.

" Saunby for sale," she repeated. " *Saunby !* "

" Paul, throw another log on the fire. They're at your side of the hearth. Why do you always have to be *asked* to put one on ? " complained Penelope.

" Saunby for sale ! " Christine turned to Paul.

" I'm afraid so," said Paul. He was sorry for Christine. " Your father rang me up at the beginning of the week to know who were the best agents. He says he can't afford to live there any longer. In fact, I think it's worse than that. I think he has to realize on Saunby to get his debts paid. He's only one farm left, you know. The way that estate has dwindled is truly awful."

448

" Oh, it's Anthea who's doing it," threw in Penelope.
" And that Pye woman. Just think of the difference
those two have made to Saunby. And to us. If they
hadn't come to Saunby, I might be there yet. I
mightn't be here," she said, swinging one slipper at
the end of one slim foot. " I couldn't stand them,
so when Paul offered, I accepted."

She looked at him unkindly, and Christine was angry.
' She's getting worse,' she thought. ' She's more and
more spoiled.' And poor fat, humble, adoring Paul
sat by and put up with her.

" Tell me more about Saunby," she said to Paul,
ignoring Penelope.

" I can't," said Paul. " I don't know any more.
Penelope and I went over at once, but your father
wasn't very communicative. He'd seen Guy in
London, it appears, before he went to the West Indies,
and Guy had agreed that there was nothing for it but
to sell. Guy evidently doesn't want Saunby for
himself."

" He has never wanted it," said Christine sadly.
" But he's never really been there since he was about
eight years old, except for holidays, so how can he love
it as we do ? As I do," she corrected, feeling she was
alone in her love for Saunby. " Guy never came to
Saunby much after he left Cambridge. It can't mean
anything to him, but I can't believe that he and father
will really let it *go*," she said incredulously. " I can't
believe it."

This was somehow the end. Her roots were in
Saunby ; she had grown there. When things had
been very bad, the thought of Saunby had brought a
kind of peace. In the back-bedroom at Mrs. Gaws's
she had gone in loving detail over and over Saunby,
remembering everything. And she had always felt
that she would go back there and somehow be happy

in the end. Now that was proving to be another of her delusions.

" Penelope, I can't bear the thought of Saunby being sold," she said, turning to her sister in distress.

" Oh, Saunby's nothing much," said Penelope, belittling it. " Hideous inside and vilely cold in the winter. I'd rather be here. Besides, Anthea's got it. I'd sooner a stranger had it than Anthea."

" But we shall never be able to go there. We shan't even be able to *look* at it," said Christine. " It's not the inside of the house, it's Saunby itself and the West Front and the way it stands in that clear space with the lake beside it. It's all that's gone on there and what it stands for. How can you take it so calmly, Pen ? "

" Because I feel calm," said Penelope. " Besides, who left it first ? "

She turned accusing eyes on her sister, saying without words : " It was you. You were in such a hurry to get married to Nicholas, and look where it's landed you. Look where it's landed me." In her own mind now, she was landed in a dreadful place. She was hating Paul now, hating everything and everybody.

Christine had been looking forward to going to bed in Penelope's spare room, which was a haven of comfort and beauty after the back-bedroom in Manchester Street. But when she went up to it, she couldn't sleep. An aching regret for Saunby kept her awake.

There was no trace, next morning, of Penelope's bad mood. She came in while Christine was having breakfast in bed with Angela, in a minute dressing-gown, sitting up in the curve of her mother's arm. Angela had a finger of toast from Christine's plate. She turned it over and over in her small fumbling fingers. She bent over it absorbed. She attempted to put it into her mouth, but hit her nose instead. She got it

450

into the right place at last and sucked the toast soft. She took it out again and turned it over a little more. Then with sudden generosity she reached up and planted it on her mother's mouth. The more Christine laughed, the more Angela urged the sopping toast upon her.

" Pen, help ! Help ! "

Penelope rushed to the rescue with a sponge and towel and expertly removed the toast from Angela's fingers.

" Would you like to go to Saunby this morning ? " she offered, when both were clean. " Paul will drive us over if you'd like to go."

" Oh, I would," said Christine eagerly. " I'll get up at once."

They drove to Saunby through the sweet spring morning. Everything shone ; the grass shone in the fields when the breeze went over, the new leaves shone on the trees.

From far off, approaching Saunby by what Christine thought must be one of the loveliest stretches of road in England, they saw a great green board reared up beside the gates, painted glaringly in white. Swiftly they came near enough to read.

SAUNBY PRIORY
HISTORIC MANSION
FOR SALE

" He hasn't lost much time," remarked Paul, " getting that up."

The girls were silent. Even Penelope, who had made out that Saunby was nothing to her, felt a painful shock when she saw the board. Christine's eyes swam with tears as they were borne down the drive.

The beeches were whorled with golden buds. The chestnuts had put up their tender crumpled umbrellas.

451

The green slopes rolled back on either hand from the drive, like the sea leaving a passage for the Israelites.

When Paul drew up before the house, Christine got out at once and, carrying Angela, made straight for her father's room.

" Father, must you sell Saunby ? Is there no other way ? " she said, bursting in on him as he sat reading the Sunday papers.

" Hello, Christine," he said, rising and coming towards her in extreme surprise. " What are you doing here ? Anything up ? How did you get here ? Oh, Penelope and Paul are here too, I see. This is just a family visit."

" Father, must you sell Saunby ? " persisted Christine in distress.

" By God, I must if I can," said the Major, laughing to Paul as one man to another.

" Why ? Why ? "

" Because I haven't a bean," said the Major, standing very handsomely on his rug. " Not a bean. Ha, ha," he laughed as if it was a good joke.

He can be very maddening, thought Christine. I should think Anthea almost hates him at times. You can't get hold of him somehow.

" But tell me, Christine," said the Major. " How are you getting on ? "

" Quite well, thanks," said Christine. It was no good saying anything else. She knew he had no idea how she lived and would still have no idea if she told him.

" Sherry, Paul ? " invited the Major.

" Not yet, thanks."

The Major became more communicative.

" I've put Saunby in the market," he said, " while there's some remote chance of selling it. When the war starts, there'll be none."

" War ? " cried Christine, startled.

"There'll be war before long," said the Major calmly. "Good thing, too. They've twisted our tail long enough. Time we ate 'em up, eh, Paul?"

Paul looked grave.

"War's a terrible thing. I hope we keep out of it."

"Bah," said the Major. Fellow's too fat, he thought. Do him good to join the army. Rich, though, he thought wistfully. I wish I was. "We can't keep out of war," he said. "Man's a fighting animal. There have always been wars and always will be. Everybody's getting ready for wars. Even your bloody pacifists. Look at 'em. They clamoured like hell for England to disarm. They made us disarm, but now we're threatened, they're running about sobbing louder than anybody for us to hurry, hurry, hurry with the guns. Soldiers may be of no account in peace time, but by God as soon as there's a threat of war, they know who to turn to. I only wish I were a young man."

"I'm going to see Anthea," said Christine, who could not listen to this talk.

"I'll come with you," said Penelope. "Don't take any notice of him," she said, hurrying after Christine to the staircase. "It's only Father. It's all talk."

"Oh, good morning," said Anthea in the nursery. "I didn't know you were here. How well Angela looks, doesn't she, in spite of being without her mother? How are you getting on in London, Christine?"

"Quite well, thanks," said Christine. "This is dreadful about Saunby, Anthea. I can't believe it's not going to be ours any more."

Anthea cast a glance at her ally, but Nurse Pye was just disappearing into the night-nursery and Anthea had to manage without her.

"We're obliged to sell it," she said, compressing her lips. "It's not only because we can't afford to live

453

here, but because we have nothing to live *on* but the money we hope to get from the sale of Saunby."

Christine was silenced. She knew what the lack of money meant now and could not blame Anthea for wishing to provide for her children.

" Have you had any offers yet ? " asked Penelope coldly, looking without admiration at Anthea's children. Veronica was exactly like Anthea must have been, and Roger was too girlish looking.

" No," said Anthea. " But then it's only been up for sale a week. Nurse Pye doesn't think the agent is doing enough about it. She's going to speak to him. We're hoping a financier or somebody like that will buy Saunby. Some such person bought Claughton the other day, did you notice ? I believe financiers are going about the country simply snapping up estates like this. In fact, the sale of Claughton gave us the idea, didn't it, Nurse ? "

The girls went down again. Penelope went to release Paul, who was never very comfortable with his father-in-law. Christine hurried outside to look at Saunby while she could. She stood beside the lake, she stood under the West Front where the birds were flying in and out of the arches as always and where the little Virgin stood with her Child in her arms as she had stood for six centuries.

" Perhaps I shall never come here again," said Christine, as she got into the car with the others.

" By God, you're hopeful," cried her father. " I wish I could think Saunby would sell as quickly as that. Well, good-bye to you all. Good-bye . . ." He waved a newspaper at them and went inside.

In the evening, Christine relinquished Angela to Penelope and returned to London and the back-bedroom.

CHAPTER XXXVIII

THE sky, which had been a candid blue and white all the May day, showing the colours of the Virgin whose month it was, began now to take on the splendour of evening. Over the sea the sun still stood in a blaze of gold, drenching all other colours within range, but over the town it looked, from the great sweeping shapes of rosy wings, as if an angelic host was moment by moment assembling. The sea ran in like thin shining gold over the dark gold sands. Mansbridge was transfigured. The glory, the compensation of such a flat place is the vast uninterrupted view it affords of the sky.

Full in the path of the sun, Sarah and James Ashwell sat on the promenade with Peke at their feet. Peke nosed about, sat in resignation, nosed again, sat again and exchanged glances with his mistress. Sarah and James were mostly silent. Their bodies gave every indication of being well-fed, well-clad, well-housed, but their faces were strongly marked by age, anxiety and sadness.

James carefully took his slippery watch from his waistcoat pocket. Nicholas had made him stop wearing a chain, and though Nicholas was gone and his watch never felt safe to him, James did not put a chain to it again.

" It's going on for six, Mother," he said. " D'you think we ought to be moving ? "

" It's a pity to leave this sky," said Sarah.

" Well, so long as you're warm enough," said James.

" I am," she said, and put her arm through his. He squeezed it with his own to welcome it.

They were close together in these days. Each felt a great need of and a great wish to comfort the other. They were alone. Nicholas had gone and Christine and Angela. The young do not know what they do when they withdraw themselves from the old. Life, light and hope seemed to have gone with these three.

Other people, their former friends, were no good to James and Sarah now. James no longer went to his club, Sarah no longer called anywhere in the afternoons. There had been so much gossip.

People said Nicholas had been the wildest young scoundrel. He had been seen leaving the Hoyles's house in the early hours of the morning, people said, with Cicely Hoyle screaming after him in her pyjamas from the steps. She'd gone abroad afterwards. Switzerland, people hinted, and everybody knew why young women went to Switzerland. And Cicely Hoyle hadn't been the only one. Far from it. People reminded each other that young Mrs. Ashwell could never keep a maid. The drunken orgies, people said, at the house in the Drive were indescribable, and they knew *that* was true because some friends of theirs had a maid who had been with the Ashwells for a time. Young Mrs. Ashwell hadn't been able to stand it any longer. She had walked out with her baby, and who could blame her ? Although she was a fearful snob and Mansbridge had never been good enough for her. She came from some old ruin in the Midlands and thought no end of herself for it, probably. Sir James had sent Cicely Hoyle to Switzerland, people said, and turned his son out. Told him to go away and make good and not dare to show his face until he had. But Sir James himself was dreadfully to blame. He'd

456

ruined the boy, spoiling him, encouraging him to play cricket instead of putting him to a decent job, simply so that he and Sir James could get in with the right people and go about staying at country houses. Of course, people said, that title had completely ruined the Ashwells.

This talk, as talk always does, came home. It came to the ears of James and Sarah, and they felt they could never like the people of Mansbridge again. They avoided them. When they saw anyone they knew passing on the front, Sarah would occupy herself with Peke and James bury himself in the newspaper. They would have left the town, but for the hope they had that Nicholas might come home at any time. They could not entertain the idea that he might come back and find the house empty.

One result of the scandal was that the " crowd " found themselves looked at askance everywhere. Once they had been proud of the effect they created, proud to be thought of as good fellows going about together bringing gaiety and custom to the places they chose to frequent, setting the fashion. They had always assumed that any hotel managers would welcome them, but now it appeared that the hotel manager was much more afraid that they would give the place a bad name. The " crowd " had to be more careful of their behaviour now. Cicely was seen no more in Mansbridge. After an interview with Sir James, she had gone abroad taking her mother with her, dragging the old lady from place to place.

" Perhaps it is getting rather chilly," said Sarah after a time.

James was up at once, glad to move on. He could not sit still for long ; his thoughts bothered him like gnats. If only Nicholas had told him . . . let him see into his mind . . . There was that job at Jackson's . . . it would have been the very thing for him . . .

" I'd like to call round and see how the Arkwrights are getting on," said Sarah.

" Right," said James, welcoming the distraction.

They left the sea-front, exclaiming at the sight of the sky when they turned towards the east. Peke, delighted, ran before them with his fringes flowing, his plumed tail proud. He waited for them at the edge of the pavement. They looked to right and left for traffic and all three crossed together to number nineteen the Drive.

" I can never understand," said James, climbing the steps, " how they could just walk off and leave all this. I thought I'd made it so nice for them, you know."

" So you did, love," comforted Sarah. " Try not to bother yourself. And the house isn't being wasted."

One good thing that had come out of all the evil was the fact that her activities on behalf of the Birchley families need no longer be kept secret. In their new closeness, she wanted to make a clean breast of everything, to keep nothing back from James, so she confessed about the Arkwrights, the Blackledges and the rest. To her astonishment, she received a return confession from him that he had been doing pretty much the same himself ever since he left Birchley for Harper and Simpson and Walmsley, his former overlookers.

Their plans for these families could be combined now and made more useful. Moreover, they formed a bond of interest between them. Sarah had hit upon the idea of putting the Arkwright family as caretakers into the house in the Drive. James had at first objected, saying the children would spoil everything. But Sarah stored away the most fragile things and trusted the rest to the vigilance of Mrs. Arkwright.

It was while she was going through the house in

preparation for the Arkwrights that Sarah sent to Brockington a box of summer things Christine had left behind. "I thought you might be wanting these, dear," she wrote, and though Christine was glad to have them, since they saved her from buying others, she felt subdued and sad, as if Sarah had now closed the door and gone to sit by her own fireside, accepting the fact that Christine was never coming back.

James, brought into contact again with the Arkwrights, sturdily making the best of their bad lot, kept making half-hearted plans for their re-establishment and the re-establishment of the other families in some new industry.

"Not cotton," he said. "Cotton's done for."

The plans were half-hearted because he had not the energy to carry them out. He was paralysed by the absence of his son.

"If only Nick would come home," he kept saying. "We could do something.

"I can't do anything without Nick," he said. "He mightn't like what I decided upon. We must be in it together."

Carrying in a paper bag a present of a fresh oven-bottom cake—Mrs. Arkwright was a grand baker when she had anything to bake with—Sarah re-emerged from the house in the Drive and called to the whole Arkwright family to come out to look at the sky. They all stood together on the steps with their faces tilted, saying they had never seen anything like it.

Christine, making her way up Oxford Street, was thinking the same and wishing she could see more of the sky than the narrow strip that showed above the street. If only she had been at Saunby now! The faces of the crowds were rosy in reflection and everybody was looking up. Complete strangers smiled at each other.

It was a little after six o'clock and the pavements were crowded. Christine had almost to fight to get along. From the back and side entrances of the big stores, employees, released, flowed to swell the main stream surging in Oxford Street. Pushed a little way round the corners of the side streets, to be out of the way of traffic but not of custom, were handcarts piled with spring flowers, daffodils, narcissi, jonquils, wallflowers, hyacinths, and the cool sweet smell of these came suddenly through the petrol vapours to Christine and reminded her of Saunby again, and of all the flowers that had bloomed there this spring that she had not seen and would, in all probability, never see again there.

She didn't want to think of Saunby. It made her too sad. Saunby had become another thing she mustn't think of. She was always turning her thoughts from one thing or another in these days. Nicholas. And now Saunby.

But she had Angela, she reminded herself. Though even the thought of Angela brought anxiety now. Penelope was going to take her all the way to Cornwall for the month of August. She and Paul had taken a house there. Christine could not blame them for wanting to spend their holiday in Cornwall, but she did wish they had chosen somewhere nearer so that she could get to them for the week-ends. She had not been long enough at the *salon* to be entitled to a holiday ; she would only get Bank Holiday Monday and she could not travel to Cornwall for that. It meant that she would not see Angela for a month, and that meant not only deprivation, but anxiety. She needed to see her constantly so that she could assure herself on a dozen points about her health and growth, points that she felt no one else would watch.

Penelope scoffed at this idea.

" I admit I've never brought up a baby before," she said. " But, then, neither have you. We start level, and I think I'm every bit as careful as you are. In fact, I think I'm *more* careful."

' I ought never to have left her,' thought Christine wearily, crossing the road. ' And now I can't go back.'

She could go back periodically, but not for all of the time. Penelope would not want her there all the time now. She liked to have Angela to herself.

' Well,' thought Christine, ' it was I who separated myself from Angela in the first place. I don't suppose they would ever have thought of my going away to work if I hadn't insisted on it. I did it myself. And it's been a miserable failure and there's no hope in it. But I can't tell them that. And I can't see what else I could have done.'

The traffic flowed in the roadway, flowed, stopped, banked up and flowed again in obedience to the lights. Christine, deep in her own thoughts, never looked at it and Nicholas, deep in his, looked straight before him as he drove down Oxford Street in his own car, considerably the worse now for wear and piled up inside with small square cases of the samples of apple-juice and vegetable-juice he was peddling through the length and breadth of England. He had had an unprofitable day, and at six o'clock had still almost two hundred miles to go. His neck ached at the back, his eyes were stiff and he remembered with astonishment that he had once driven a car for fun.

Nicholas and Christine passed each other and did not know it, though Christine, in spite of herself, was thinking again of him. She was thinking that she knew now what he meant when he used to say he must have a *decent* job. He'd been quite right when he said that so much work simply wasn't worth doing. " What's the good of doing work," he used to say,

" if you can't take a pride in it ? If you can't throw your heart and soul into it and *like* it ? " She wondered what he would think of the work she did at the *salon*. She knew what she thought of it herself. Silly rubbishy waste of time. And not even honest.

' Angela shall be trained to do good work,' she thought.

According to this young mother, everything was going to be different for Angela. Angela should profit from her mother's misfortunes and mistakes. Angela should be educated, Angela should be equipped to earn her own living, Angela should never be obliged, like her mother and other unfortunate women, to drift about among relations because their parents had treated them badly in the first place and their husbands in the second.

' I won't accept from Sir James for myself,' thought Christine, walking up Baker Street. ' But I'll accept for Angela. I'll beg for her when the time comes.'

A man accosted her. The first time a man accosted her in the streets of London she had stopped courteously to listen, only to start forward with a flush of mortification and horror. Now when this man planted himself before her she said, " Oh, get out ! " with fury.

" O.K., sister," said the man. " Don't get sore. My mistake."

She walked on, forgetting him. You can get used to anything. She was going to the back-bedroom to get her enamel mirror to pawn, and if the mirror wouldn't provide her with the fare to Brockington, the brush would have to go too. The first time she pawned anything, she had walked about before the shop for more than an hour not daring to go in. Now she was used to it. But she wondered what people did who had nothing to sell and what she herself would do when she had nothing left to sell. Two pounds a week for a girl living alone in London was an appallingly inadequate wage.

" And yet I'm not worth more," she admitted.

" But Angela shall be," she promised herself.

§

The week-ends were half pleasure, half pain. The Saturdays, beginning with the supreme moment when she ran up the steps and found Angela in the car, the Saturdays were pure, unmitigated joy. But at some time on the Sunday morning, about the time when Hester came to take Angela after breakfast in bed together, the peak was passed and the shadow began to fall over the day, growing darker with every half-hour. Every Saturday afternoon, Christine felt she was put together again, and every Sunday evening torn apart. She could not get used to leaving Angela and suffered on every successive Sunday as much as on the first.

" But you're only leaving her for five days," said Penelope, not wholly to comfort but to remind Christine that she was really making rather a fuss.

" I know," admitted Christine, and from that time tried to hide her feelings, unwilling to expose them to an unsympathetic eye. It wasn't Penelope's fault that she didn't understand, she told herself. You have to experience to understand. I was like Penelope once.

As the elder sister, she was used to making allowances for Penelope, but the time was coming when she would abruptly give that up.

As soon as she arrived, on this Saturday in June, Christine realized that Penelope had some plan she had set her heart on. Christine knew all the signs. Penelope couldn't keep still ; she walked about tugging at her waist-belt, she perched herself on the arm of one chair after another, swinging her legs and making herself extremely charming.

'She's prettier than ever,' thought Christine admiringly. 'And more like father every day. But what's she up to?'

She expected Penelope to burst out with it every minute, since she could not keep back anything for long. But the afternoon passed as usual. Angela was promenaded by her mother in the garden, slept for a little in her pram (" She never sleeps quite so well when you're here," said Penelope), had her milk and her rusks and was then dressed by Penelope in a new dress that had just come from the very expensive baby shop where Penelope bought Angela's clothes. Christine looked on while Penelope guided Angela's unwilling arms into the puff sleeves of an exquisite pink organdie and tied a sash of watered silk ribbon in the right shade of nattier blue.

" Now, doesn't she look lovely? " asked Penelope proudly.

" Very," agreed Christine. " But it's far too good for now. You ought to save it for a party."

" Oh, we can get her another for a party," said Penelope.

Christine, looking at Angela in Penelope's lap, thought she had never seen anything so enchanting in her life. Angela was nine months old now, and though slightly troubled by two teeth, she never lost for more than a moment at a time the gay good humour she was born with. Her energy, thought her mother, was terrific. Her arms worked, her fingers worked, her toes worked. She signified that she wanted to stand up. She stood up and stamped and abruptly sat down again. Then with great seriousness she began to blow backward and forward in an attempt to whistle. This was her latest trick and she had learnt it from Penelope.

" Darling," said Penelope fervently, kissing the top of her head. Then it all came out.

" Christine."

Christine turned her eyes from Angela to her sister. Penelope's eyes were bright with excitement, her nostrils were slightly dilated.

" Er . . ." began Penelope again.

" Go on, darling, what is it ? " Christine helped her.

" Well," said Penelope, plunging. " Christine— suppose Nicholas never comes back ? "

A flush rose slowly to Christine's cheeks. Her eyes went dark at this hand laid on her wounds, but she looked steadily at Penelope, waiting.

" Well, suppose he doesn't," Penelope said, almost defiantly. " It's much better to talk about it and you never do. We must face facts, after all."

Christine waited.

" If Nicholas never comes back, I don't suppose you'll go back to the old people without him, will you ? You can't very well, after what Sir James said, can you ? "

" What are you trying to say ? Have I been here long enough ? Is that it ? "

" Oh, no," Penelope protested vehemently. " You can come here as much as you like. You *know* that. But your future is very uncertain, isn't it ? And Paul's sure you'll never be able to make enough money to keep Angela as well as yourself. And after all, London's no place for a baby, and who are you going to get to look after her during the day while you're at work ? There are so many difficulties, aren't there ? So wouldn't it make it much easier and relieve you of a lot of anxiety, darling, if Paul and I adopted Angela ? I mean, legally."

Christine's face stopped her. It had become Medusa-like, fixed, stony. Now she swooped forward and took

Angela from Penelope's lap. The hoop of pink organdie with a pair of small bare soles showing on one side and a round fair head on the other passed through the air from one sister to the other. It was all the same to Angela, who continued to blow backward and forward in her mother's arms as she had done in her aunt's.

Christine stood up clasping Angela.

"You must be mad," she said hoarsely, looking down on her sister, who flinched as she looked up at her.

"Mad," repeated Christine. "To think I'd ever give her up to you or anybody else. *My* baby—that I made and bore. D'you know what it is to have a baby? No, you don't or you'd never think of suggesting such a thing to me now. You have a baby and let someone try to take it from you and then you'll know what I feel now. Your suggestion is absolutely childish, Penelope. It's a child's suggestion. It shows you don't understand anything. Or you don't want to."

Penelope's face closed. She folded her lips tight.

"And unless you put the idea out of your mind once and for all," said Christine sternly, "I must find another place for us to go to. I can't stay here with you thinking you're going to get Angela one day, because you never, never are."

Penelope got up and walked out of the nursery, leaving the door open. Christine ran to it and locked it.

Penelope went through the house in search of Paul. She found him in the drawing-room reading in an arm-chair drawn up to an open window. He looked up from his book to watch her come towards him. Everything about her was endearing, even the fact that her face was sullen and her court slippers were rather loose and threatened to come off as she walked. She came up, took his book from him and flung it aside. She flung herself on his knee and lay on him as if he had been a sofa or something equally inanimate. Paul held her carefully. If he made any demonstration of his love for her, if he kissed her or held her close, she would get up and leave him, he knew.

For some time, she did not speak. Then she brought out :

" She won't let us adopt Angela."

Paul threw his head back in a movement of amused exasperation.

" Penelope, why can't you *wait* ? You can't wait for anything. You only thought of this adoption plan yesterday, but you must rush in and put it to Christine almost before the poor girl's got her hat off. You've entirely ruined your chances. You should have waited weeks, months, years if need be," said Paul the lawyer. " You should have bided your time."

" Oh, I couldn't," said Penelope. " Besides, it would have been too underhand. I couldn't do a thing like that."

Paul burst out laughing and could not keep himself from kissing her. She was so funny. She was such a mixture.

" Oh, if you're going to laugh," said Penelope with dignity, making to get off his knee.

He tightened his hold.

" I'm not," he assured her hurriedly. " But you are rather swallowing a camel and straining at a gnat, aren't you ? "

" How ? D'you think it's mean to want to adopt Angela, then ? You didn't say so last night when we were talking about it. I thought you were as keen on it as I was. You pretended to be," she charged him.

" Darling, I want you to be happy. I'm quite selfish. I want to be happy myself and I can't be happy unless you are. I want you to have what you want, mean or not. But if I'm to tell the truth, I do think it's rather too bad to try to take Angela from Christine when Christine is down and out as she is at present."

He waited nervously, expecting Penelope to leave him at once for daring to pass judgment on her. He thought it was the first time he had ever done it. But she lay still.

" I really love Angela," she said, looking at him gravely with her dark blue eyes. " Christine thinks I'm only playing at it, but I love her and I long for her to be mine. I want to make plans for her. I want to be able to look forward to a future with Angela always in it."

" I daresay. Who was the chap that coveted Naboth's vineyard ? I've forgotten. Besides, you can do all that without taking Angela from Christine ; you can see more of her, you can do more for her than Christine."

" Yes, but it's not the *same*," objected Penelope.

" Of course it's not the same. How can you expect it to be ? It won't be the same until you have a baby of your own."

" Are you beginning about that ? " asked Penelope angrily, attempting again to get up.

" No, no, I'm not," Paul said hastily. " I'm not really. Tell me how Christine took it."

" Very badly." Penelope sank again to his shoulder.

" Dear me," said Paul.

" She's furious," said Penelope.

" Perhaps I'd better go to her," she said in a moment.

Christine had unlocked the nursery door. She was getting Angela ready for bed. No matter what happened to Christine, she did the right thing at the right time for Angela. Her eyelids were red in her white face, and she had such a look of being at the end of everything that Penelope was smitten with remorse. She knelt down by the nursery chair and rubbed her face against her sister's.

" I'm sorry," she murmured awkwardly. It was hard for Penelope to apologize. " I'll never speak of it again."

Christine smiled and kissed her and accepted what she said. But the damage was done. She would never be able now to rid herself of the idea that Penelope wanted to take Angela from her, if not legally, then in other ways. She was quite as aware as Paul that Penelope could see more of Angela and do more for her than she could. She felt now that Penelope did not mean to share Angela, but to monopolize her. Penelope was greedy about Angela as she had been greedy about other things during their life together. Christine remembered suddenly a favourite paint-box she had once had to give up to her. But those things had been small and immaterial ; this was serious and it made her sad.

There is no happiness like loving someone with complete trust, like being able to feel : whatever happens, there's always so-and-so. The young love like that, with complete confidence, but in return they demand that the object of their love should be well-nigh perfect. The young can't allow for flaws. No flaws, they say, forgetful of their own, and if they find flaws, they take their love back and turn sadly away.

Christine had loved Nicholas like that and had been disillusioned in him. She had loved her sister like that and was being disillusioned again. She was not so bitter this time, because she felt older and less expectant. The older we grow, the less expectant we are, and the less expectant, the less we suffer. We gradually settle down to the fact that we are all disappointing each other almost all of the time.

Penelope tried hard to make amends. She made herself humble over the bathing of Angela, proffering sponge and soap and towels to Christine in a most aunt-like and second-fiddle way.

" But you will let me take her to Cornwall just the same, won't you ? " she said, anxiously.

" You should remember," said Christine with the mordant bitterness that had so routed Nicholas, " that I have no alternative."

Penelope looked uncomfortably into the bath-water. She didn't know what was happening to Christine. She could make you feel such a worm.

" But you don't mind about Cornwall, Christine," she said wistfully. " You said you didn't, you know. It's only for a month and it will do her so much good. And d'you know what I've been thinking ? " she went on, leaning persuasively over the edge of the bath to see into her sister's face. " You know, Paul's mother's coming here in August. That's why I want to go to Cornwall then. I don't like having her to stay. You can come here for every week-end just as usual of course, but I suddenly thought you might like to go to Saunby for Bank Holiday week-end. Wouldn't that be rather nice for you, don't you think ? You'd like to stay there again for one last time, I'm sure. And I don't suppose it will be sold before then. Paul says no one's jumping at it. Do go, Christine, will you ? "

" I'll have to think about it," was all Christine would say.

CHAPTER XXXIX

SHE went to Saunby for Bank Holiday week-end. Penelope arranged it, and Anthea sent a surprisingly cordial invitation. Nurse Pye came to the station on the Saturday afternoon to meet her and jolted her over the roads in the little car much more amiably than on the March evening which seemed so long ago now to Christine.

When she got out of the car, where her knees had been almost under her chin, she stretched her arms, took off her hat and felt the air cool on eyelids tired from London. She drew in a long breath and looked round on the grass and the water and the West Front. However the people in the house might receive her, she thought, Saunby itself welcomed her. There was a deep bond between her and Saunby, a bond—another—that would have to be broken when Saunby was sold.

She went into the house, smelling again what she always insisted was incense. Anthea came to meet and kiss her and conduct her, much astonished, to the yellow room. Christine could not think why she was being treated so well. She did not know that, having discussed her between them, Anthea and Nurse Pye had come to the conclusion that Christine was much improved of late. Misfortune, uncomfortable though it may be to those who suffer it, often improves people. Christine, however, did not know she was improved and continued to puzzle about the warmth of her reception.

Anthea had another reason as well for feeling more friendly to Christine. She had realized, when the girls called on the Sunday morning after Saunby had been put up for sale, that though Penelope judged her harshly, Christine did not. Christine understood, although it meant the loss of her beloved Saunby, that Anthea had no alternative but to do as she was doing ; and Anthea was grateful to Christine for that.

When she left Christine in her room, Anthea invited her to tea in the nursery.

" Your father will probably be in for tea, but you know how he likes to have it alone in his room. He'd be very surprised if anybody attempted to have it with him, wouldn't he ? So come up when you're ready, will you ? "

Christine, left to herself and still marvelling, went about the room putting her things away. It was strange to come to Saunby and be treated like a visitor. This was the room Nicholas had slept in the first time he came. She opened the door and looked up at the nursery stairs, remembering how she had stood there longing for him that moonlit night. 'Well,' she thought, turning away from the stairs and the memory, ' life is too uncertain for anything. I don't know how we stand it at all.'

She went up to the nursery and entered a world where all was simple and orderly and innocent. The children, washed and brushed, were in their high chairs with their bibs tied on. There was honey and bread-and-butter and sponge cake for tea. Puffed white clouds sailed serenely past the windows. Nurse Pye was fresh in starched linen, Anthea was large, matronly, healthy and happy, and the conversation was honest and cheerful.

It was strange to be admitted behind the scenes and allowed to see Anthea and Nurse Pye as they really were. They were so comfortable together and with the children. That was the word : comfortable. It was a state Christine, now that she herself was not comfortable anywhere, could appreciate and envy.

There was no doubt that Anthea was happy, in spite of the fact that she seemed to see little of her husband and in spite of anxiety about money. Nurse Pye seemed to have almost transformed this anxiety into optimism and a determination to get rid of the causes of the anxiety. Nurse Pye liked living with effort and seemed to have inspired Anthea with the same liking. They probably thoroughly enjoyed skimping and scraping, thought Christine, and would not have been half so happy if they had no need to do it.

Of course, thought Christine, Anthea was still her fundamental self. She didn't think Anthea would get on any better with other people in general than she had ever done. She was too intense or something. She didn't think she herself would ever *love* Anthea. But she could quite like her, she thought, if Anthea went on treating her like this.

Anthea talked about what she and Nurse Pye intended to do when Saunby was sold.

" Have you had any offers ? " asked Christine.

" Well, none that have come to anything yet," admitted Anthea. " But people are always coming to look."

Admission to view Saunby was supposed to be by card only, but all sorts of people got in and were allowed about by Anthea. They had no need to feel nervous or guilty when they were seen in the park, because Anthea welcomed them all and smiled encouragingly at them, with difficulty restraining herself from pointing out the beauties of the place.

Like Sister Anne, Anthea was always looking from

the top of the house for somebody to come. Unlike Sister Anne, she frequently saw somebody coming who never, so to speak, arrived.

Every stray man seen from the nursery windows was taken to be a financier. By Anthea ; Nurse Pye was not so sanguine. Anthea's hopes and plans were rather wild, but Nurse Pye was indulgent with them. The upper classes, Nurse Pye felt, had this difficulty in getting down to brass tacks. She pricked Anthea's balloons with her tacks as kindly as possible, and if it so happened that there was one occasionally that she could spare and allow to soar, Anthea was delighted ; most happy to have blown up something Nurse Pye could approve of.

To the excitement of the nursery, a financier did come, preceded by a courier in the form of the agent.

The Major came out of his apathy.

" You leave this man to me," he commanded Anthea.

The financier arrived, an affable man in a striped suit and a diamond ring. He was taken over the estate by the Major and over the house by Anthea, who opened and closed a great many doors and pointed out a great many advantages. The financier looked affably on, listened and said nothing. He went away and did not come back. Anthea told Nurse Pye she had gathered from the agent that the financier did not consider that Saunby would cut up well.

A woman-promoter was heralded, a Mrs. Jay. The Major would not concern himself with her ; he had no faith in women-promoters. But Anthea was all excitement. Women were so wonderful these days. She ordered tea to be ready in the drawing-room.

Mrs. Jay arrived, a tall, stout woman with hair so realistically coppered as to have verdigris gleams in it and a handbag so bulging that it looked as if she was prepared to pay for Saunby in bullion on the spot. She was the sort of woman, thought Nurse Pye, who had probably started in cast-off clothing and had now got on to estates. She had come to consider the possibilities of Saunby as a pleasure-ground.

" I'm looking for the ruins of something," she said, clutching the handbag and examining the West Front with a business-like eye. " They like an Abbey or something like that to come to, you know."

" I can understand that," said Anthea, standing and looking up with her.

" These lakes would be useful for boating," said Mrs. Jay. " And I could make a paddling pool too. I'd have a putting green on that lawn. But let me see," she said thoughtfully. " Where could I put the ladies and gents ? "

Anthea was puzzled, but anxious to help.

" Must you put them anywhere ? " she said. " Can't you just leave them free to go about ? "

" Go about ? " Mrs. Jay was outraged. " Mercy on us, there must be decency."

" Decency ? " Anthea was bewildered.

" It's the conveniences I'm talking about," said Mrs. Jay sternly.

" The . . . ? " Anthea was momentarily as bewildered as before, then light dawned upon her. " Oh. I'm so sorry," she said. " I didn't understand."

' Well-bred, perhaps, but not all there,' thought Mrs. Jay. " I'll have a look at the house, now," she announced.

" Oh, certainly," said Anthea, leading the way.

She pointed out all the advantages of the house, and Mrs. Jay said " That's right " so often that Anthea thought it was. She told Nurse Pye she was sure she had sold Saunby at last, and was very disappointed to learn later from the agent that though Mrs. Jay had liked the place, she hadn't liked the price.

Since then, no one had appeared at all. But the agent said August was a slack month and Anthea had set herself to hope for September.

" Are there no matches here this week-end ? " asked Christine in surprise.

" No matches," said her father, and implied by continued attention to his paper that he did not wish to discuss the subject.

' No cricket at Saunby,' thought Christine. Things had changed indeed. She wondered if her father had lost interest in cricket as he seemed to have done in everything else. But she noticed that his paper was open at the cricket scores, and as she watched, he took out his penknife, cut an account of a match from the paper and put it carefully into his pocket-book. He was still interested in cricket.

" We couldn't arrange for play here when the house might be sold at any time," he said. He often re-opened a subject he himself had closed.

" D'you ever hear anything of Thompson these days ? " asked Christine.

" Bah." The Major's expression was one of deep disgust at the fate that had overtaken Thompson. " The poor fellow works in the pit and that little shrew has got him tied up to her by having a child. I'm sorry for Thompson. When I think how he loved fresh air and birds and flowers and all that, by God, I'm sorry. But the war will get him out."

Christine determined that if her father began again about war she would get up and go out of the room. She couldn't stand talk about war. It filled her with nervous horror. It made her desperate to think that Nicholas was still missing and that war might break out and sweep him away before she could see him again.

The Major liked talking about war, about the machinery, the actual waging of it. He gave Christine a long exposition of the seven points of war.

" These remain as true to-day as they were in the time of Alexander the Great," he explained, as if he were explaining a game of chess. " But the method of warfare will be very different in the coming war, you know. The object of the attacker will be to paralyse, to destroy the morale of the people so that they will force their government to agree to peace at any price."

" Oh, don't," said Christine, hurrying away.

" Hi ! " he called after her. " Don't be so squeamish. You're a soldier's daughter and don't you forget it."

Life was a nightmare, thought Christine, rushing out into the park. She was walking with her own personal disaster in a world of disaster. Everything was black, within, without ; there was no hope anywhere. If only she had Nicholas and Angela. If only they were all together and could hide from this looming terror. Angela was so little and helpless, she thought, torturing herself. Those children in the dreadful photographs from Spain had been like Angela . . . But she must refuse to think ; refuse, because she could do nothing and must keep sane.

She pressed down a rising sense of panic. She wanted to rush into the city and take the next train to Cornwall. She thought of Angela as she had last seen her in Penelope's arms, her blue eyes rounded in surprise at her mother's hat, her bare feet, shoes and socks gone as usual, showing beneath the muslin frill of her dress.

The sight of a figure in the avenue mercifully changed her thoughts. She remembered that she had intended to visit her Aunt Victoria this morning and here she was. Christine ran down the avenue in pursuit of the square figure with a folding stool under one arm and a black-japanned paint-box at the length of the other.

" Aunt Victoria ! Aunt Victoria ! "

Miss Marwood turned.

" Hullo, Christine," she said without much surprise. " I'm just going to paint that group of particularly nice birches behind the lodge. How are you ? "

She always told you about herself before she asked about you, thought Christine, as she kissed her aunt's cheek. And she never kissed you ; she let you kiss her.

" I'll walk along with you," said Christine, taking the folding stool. " But I won't stay with you, because I know you don't like to be watched while you paint."

" No, I don't," said Aunt Victoria, stumping cheerfully along. " I'm very busy just now. I'm painting all I can while I've got the run of the park. Although the next owner will probably be quite glad for me to paint here as usual, you know. Unless he is a complete vandal, of course."

They went down the avenue together. With really nothing to say to each other, thought Christine. Impervious or Spartan, Miss Marwood neither asked for communication nor offered it. Christine went with her to the trees, helped her to settle herself and left her.

She walked on into the open ground behind the lodge. The warm air was laden with the smell of sweet-woodruff which was spread like lace everywhere over the short fine turf. There were companies of little birch trees, no higher than Christine, glittering softly in the sun. They had no right to be there, they should have been uprooted, because in time they would entirely cover the ground ; but they were very pretty. Over the old dry-built wall, the boundary of Saunby, Christine could see Top Farm, across a dusky-gold wheat-field and a bright green pasture. She could see the white dove-cote in the field with white birds standing on its red roof. Two red-painted carts were sticking out of a shed, with a neatly sliced hay-stack beside it. It all looked very toy. But a print-clad figure, which must be Bessy going about, thought Christine, was a reminder that existence at Top Farm was no more toy-like than anywhere else. And the scarecrow struck a grim note ; it was a skeleton in rotten rags now.

Christine climbed to the woods covering the low hills. There was a deep steady insect hum ; the song of August. In the dimness of the woods where the light struck, gnats rose and fell, rose and fell in thin shining fountains without source.

In her two days, Christine revisited every haunt of her childhood and girlhood, and on Monday night, averting her face, she left Saunby and returned to the back-bedroom.

§

It was hot in London. At the *salon*, the blankets to cover the recumbent clients were replaced by sheets of pale pink linen. Electric fans whirred all day long. Miss Vanne dyed and double-dyed submissive heads of hair, repeated permanent waves before they had grown out, insisted on expensive and hitherto unheard-of treatments ; her son had gone fishing to Norway for the long vacation and she needed the money to pay for it.

Summer came to Mrs. Gaws's in the form of smell. A smell of cat pervaded everything. Christine had

479

not known there were cats in the house, until one evening, coming in, she saw two great black ones dozing on the area steps, with Father cleaning the basement windows behind them.

Christine did not go to Brockington for the week-ends ; she would not spend her precious money in going when Angela was not there. She had no money at all in hand now and was putting off the pawning of her engagement ring as long as possible. It would have to go in the end, but she would keep it until the last minute, not for love of the ring itself—she had never liked jewellery—but because Nicholas had given it to her.

She spent the week-ends walking and sitting in the parks, watching the children rolling on the sparse London grass among the eager dogs and sleeping men. These men were a terrible sight in their utter exhaustion, and, looking at them, she was cured of self-pity.

She put on time. She waited for August to be over. She was sunk in passive unhappiness. Then suddenly she was jerked into active pain.

In the middle of the hot day, after her lunch of coffee and cheese sandwich at a Lyons, she walked down Oxford Street to put on time before going back to the *salon*. The pavements were crowded as usual. Christine waited until the lights arrested the traffic, crossed half-way to an island and stood there. Traffic swept thickly past her. It piled up and slowed down, and as she stood there, a car in mid-stream caught her attention. Nicholas was sitting in his own car within a few feet of her. She saw him, saw his face, thinner, paler, saw his familiar striped tie, saw cases piled up in the back of the car—saw it all and stood transfixed on the island, and the car was gone. It jerked forward, was swallowed up, was gone.

Christine plunged into the traffic.

" Nicholas !   Nicholas !   Nicholas ! "

A furious honking broke out, brakes screeched, cars closed in on her.   Drivers leaned out to shout at her. She stood in the midst of them all for a moment, then, her face convulsed, she went back to the island.

" You didn't ought to have done that," said a woman deeply shocked.   " That's asking for death, that is."

Christine turned, not knowing what she was doing, and went blindly back to the side of the road she had come from.   Nicholas had swept far away with the traffic.   He had never seen her, never turned his head. She went down a side street and walked about a mews, crying openly like a child, twisting her hands. Chauffeurs cleaning their cars stared after her.   She didn't see them.

Suddenly it struck her that he might come back the same way.   She ran into Oxford Street and stood on the pavement, trying to see all the cars that went past. Then, with a gesture of despair, she gave up.   He wouldn't come back.   He had been going somewhere. There were those square boxes piled up in the car. He must be a commercial traveller, she thought, with a laugh and a sob.   To think of Nicholas being a commercial traveller !   Though it was no funnier, really, than her being in a beauty *salon*.

The *salon* !   She looked in alarm at her watch and began to run.   She would be late and have her money docked.

That afternoon the little machinist across the street got no response to her smiles.   Christine did not see her.   She saw only Nicholas staring before him in his car.

When the *salon* released her she went back to stand on the island in Oxford Street, trying to make herself believe that he had been within a few feet of her there.

She went on to Manchester Street and sat for a long time in the twisted chair, doing nothing. It made her more despairing than ever to feel that he was near, going about an everyday life, and making no attempt to seek her out.

Suddenly she reached for her blotter and took out the bill. Without looking at it again, she tore it into small pieces and dropped it into the waste-paper basket. After a moment she picked the pieces out again and set a match to them on the hearth.

She unscrewed her pen and began a letter to his mother. She gave the bare facts of her sight of him, but no account of her own feelings, and she headed the letter : " Brockington Grange." They must not know she was working in London ; they might think she was hinting for help if she told them that. They must think she had been in London for pleasure, as they would unless she expressly told them otherwise.

Three mornings later, there was a reply, redirected from Brockington.

My dear Christine,

Your letter has brought us great relief and happiness and we thank you very, very much for letting us know that our dear son is alive and well and in this country. Lately we have been afraid that he had left it. We are so happy to know what you tell us. We feel he might walk in any time now. His father is going to put appeals in the papers again, but I don't fancy they are much good. I think Nicholas is working out his own salvation. He will come when he is ready. I feel much more hopeful and able to wait since I had your letter. It was kind of you to write at once, dear.

How is little Angela ? I suppose she will be quite a big girl now. If you could bring her on a visit to us, how pleased we should be. But perhaps you don't care to come to Mansbridge ? Perhaps that is too much to ask. If so, I quite understand.

With love to you both,

Yours affectionately,

SARAH ASHWELL.

This letter touched Christine. Sarah's resignation to other people's behaviour touched her. She thought sadly of her. She wished she had been better to her. She could have done so much and had done so little ; nothing, in fact. At first she had been so absorbed in Nicholas that she had hardly taken any notice of his mother ; later she did not want her to know that things were going wrong. After Angela was born, she had begun to admit Sarah, but tolerantly, not warmly as she should have done. It was too late now. She had a wild desire never to go back to the *salon* or the back-bedroom, but to rush to Cornwall, get Angela and fly for refuge to Red Lodge. Oh, kindly, comfortable house, what a haven, viewed from London, it seemed. But she couldn't go there. She couldn't face Sir James, she could hardly face Sarah. It was she who had driven away their son.

She wrote again to Sarah for the sheer comfort of writing to her and for the expectation of a reply. It was rarely that a letter for her lay on the marble slab in Mrs. Gaws's hall. Penelope, in Christine's opinion, did not write half often enough. She sent hasty scrawls from time to time to say that Angela was splendid, Cornwall marvellous, the weather mixed, and she herself just going to bathe, or going for a picnic, or was too sleepy to write any more.

Christine had been straining towards the end of August, towards the thirty-first. Two days after that her long wait would be over and she would see Angela.

But Penelope wrote to say they could have the house

for a few more days and had decided to stay until the Sunday. "I hope you won't be very disappointed not to see Angela this week-end, darling," she wrote. "But it is only for a few more days, isn't it? And it is doing her so much good. You'll hardly know her. She is so brown."

CHAPTER XL

WHEN Christine opened the door of the house in
Manchester Street on the Tuesday evening,
she saw that there was a letter on the marble slab.
Without waiting to close the door behind her, she
hurried to see if it was for her and from Penelope. It
was. She seized it and went back to close the door,
to close in the smell of frying that rose fiercely from the
basement. The Gaws family were very fond of fried
food.

In the dim light of the hall, she made out the post-
mark. It was Brockington ; they were back. She
would see her darling in four days.

She threw her hat on the bed and went to read her
letter by the window. Her eyes ran through it picking
out the references to Angela. The rest could come later.

"Lovely time . . ." she read. " Angela so sweet
in her sun-suit on the shore. Everybody noticed her
. . . the loveliest brown, like a peach . . . unfortunately got a slight cold . . . such a pity to end a
holiday with a cold . . . blame Hester for putting
her into her pram in a damp suit, the fool . . . I was
so angry with her I made her cry . . . better to-day,
sleeping herself well . . . am keeping her in bed."

Putting her into her pram in a wet suit ! It was
madness. She might get pneumonia. Didn't they
know ? How could Penelope leave her to Hester ?
But, worse, how could she herself leave her to Penelope ? Her latent fears, once they were given an

485

outlet, rushed out and clamoured beyond her control. She read the letter again.

" A slight cold."

Could Angela be really ill and Penelope dare to conceal it ?

' I should be there,' thought Christine. ' I should look after her. No one else can.'

She must know how Angela was. There was a telephone downstairs. It was almost seven. She would wait until the cheap calls could be made. She stood at the window, waiting, her heart beating fast with foreboding.

" I want to speak to Mrs. Kenworthy," she was calling out a few minutes later.

The voice of the maid came faint : " Who is it, please ? "

" Go and tell Mrs. Kenworthy quickly. It's her sister."

Maids could be too polite, and it seemed ages before Penelope came to the telephone.

" How is Angela ? "

" She's asleep now. She's got a bit of a rattle, poor lamb. But she's quite all right, Christine. Don't worry. I'll have the doctor out in the morning to be on the safe side. But I've kept her very warm in bed all day. It's only a cold . . ."

Three pips sounded.

" Your call's up," cried Penelope faintly. " Don't worry. It's only a cold . . ."

The telegram came in the middle of the morning at the *salon*.

" Think you'd better come Penelope."

Christine ran out into the middle of the *salon*.

" Where's Miss Vanne ? " she called out loud in distraction. Only undertones were allowed from the assistants in the *salon*.

486

Miss Vanne came, outraged, to see what the disturbance was.

"I must go," said Christine, dragging her overall off. "My baby's ill. They've sent for me. I must go. I'm sorry."

Miss Vanne was talking, protesting, but Christine did not hear what she said. She ran, white, breathless, into the street. She had not enough money on her to take a taxi. She had to take the tube. She felt everything was in her way, everything preventing her from getting to Angela.

'Why did I leave her? Why did I?'

Mrs. Gaws and Reeny were making her bed and gaped to see her come in.

"I've been sent for. My baby's ill. I'm going, and I don't suppose I shall come back. I shall never leave her again. Have I enough money to pay you, Mrs. Gaws? No, I haven't. I must have what I've got for my fare. See, I'll leave you my travelling clock. It's worth more than twenty-two-and-six. And I'll send you the money later and you can send my clock back to me. Will that do? Is it all right?"

"Well, I suppose it'll have to be," said Mrs. Gaws. "Not but what I'd rather have my money. But I can see you're in a fix and I'm sorry for you. And I'm ever so sorry you're going. I said to my husband as soon as you come here, I said that's a lady that is, didn't I, Reeny? I'm sure I hope your baby will be better. I never knew you had one, though of course I've seen photos about. Reeny was terribly bad when she was one year old, but look at her now. You keep your heart up, it mightn't be as bad as you think. What time's your train?"

"I don't know. I shall go to the station and take the first there is. Have I got everything?" She whisked the curtains aside. The corner was empty.

"What about this good butter and this cocoa and stuff?" asked the shocked and thrifty Mrs. Gaws.

"Throw it away or you have it and the pan and the kettle. Take them. Good-bye," she said, shaking their hands.

"Father," shouted Mrs. Gaws to the basement. "Father, where are you? Come here and carry these cases down!"

§

A few days before, in Cornwall, Penelope had witnessed a revelation of the nature of maternal love. The village shop was always crowded in the mornings. The summer visitors, coming for sandshoes, ice-cream, cigarettes, bathing-caps, picture postcards, papers, added themselves to the local housewives in such numbers that half the would-be purchasers could not get in and had to wait outside. Nobody minded waiting outside when the sun shone and the sea showed blue and glittering beyond the edge of the grassy cliff as it did on the morning Penelope waited outside for Paul, who was wedged against the counter within.

A woman came up, propped a perambulator against the wall and worked her way into the shop. A moment later the baker drove up in his motor-van, braked it, and, taking his basket of bread, went round to the back of the shop. The holiday-makers chattered on. Suddenly someone gave a loud cry. The van was moving backwards, moving towards the perambulator against the wall. The groups broke, ran, frantic hands were laid on the van. Lumbering, swaying, it came to rest, cracking the perambulator like a nutshell against the wall. The hands strove with the van, moved it. The women clustered, a dozen hands tried to lift the jammed hood where the baby's legs showed

488

kicking through the splintered wood. Nobody could move the hood. Women groaned, weeping, struggling; others standing by covered their faces. Suddenly the crowd was cleaved apart. The mother had come. She flailed them aside with her arms, and what they could not do, she did. She took the structure of iron and leather in her hands and tore it apart as if it had been matchwood and paper. She snatched her baby out, crying and unhurt. The crowd fell back before her splendid face. She went apart and with her back turned bent over her baby. Many of the women had to go into the shop to sit down and have drinks of water. Not the mother. No water, no sitting down for her. She carried her baby away up the lane. No one went after her. Kindness had no place here.

" She was like a tiger," said Penelope to Paul.

Penelope was to see the same thing again now and close at hand. Christine arrived, and putting Penelope and her explanations aside, ignoring Hester's tears, went straight to Angela. She knelt down by her cot and looked at her. She neither touched nor kissed her, only looked.

" Have you got a nurse ? " she asked, stern and pale.

" The doctor's trying. He says there's a fearful shortage of nurses. He's going to bring one out as soon as he can get hold of one."

Christine got up and went out of the room. Penelope, frightened of this new Christine, stole after her and heard her telephoning in the hall. She was telephoning to Saunby. She heard her speaking to Anthea, speaking to Nurse Pye.

" Can you come ? Will you come at once ? Angela is very ill. Please help me. Please come."

She came back, passed Penelope without seeing her and knelt down by the cot again.

Penelope went into her own room. Her illusion that Angela was as good as her baby was shattered. There was no doubt who was Angela's mother. Penelope was displaced, as the women round the broken perambulator had been displaced; by the mother.

After Nurse Pye had come, after the doctor had come back and the children's specialist been sent for, after he in his turn had come and gone, pronouncing the dreaded word, pneumonia, Penelope wept to Paul in their bedroom. She sat up in bed, weeping with her head on her humped knees.

"After all I've done . . . she might let me do something . . . she might realize that I love Angela too . . ."

Her fair hair hung down childishly over the padded pale green quilt as she wept. Paul was distressed.

"You know, darling," he said, stroking her hair. "You really ought to have a baby of your own . . ."

Penelope turned on him like a wild-cat. Her tear-stained face was distorted.

"Don't you dare to say that," she cried, putting her wet hair out of her eyes. "Don't you dare. I told you I wouldn't. I *told* you. You shouldn't have married me if you wanted children. I warned you . . ."

"Penelope darling," he said. He put out a hand to stroke her hair again, but she wouldn't have it stroked. She tossed her head away from him, and drawing the clothes up she lay down.

"It's for your own sake, darling," he said. "You're quite enough for me, but I'm not enough for you."

Penelope put her hands over her ears. He was stupid, stupid.

In the hushed nursery there were three distinct

sounds, the flickering of the fire, the tick of the clock and the baby's rough, rapid breathing.

Christine stood at the foot of the cot, looking in anguish at the piteous little face whose nostrils were pinched, whose mouth had a terrifying bluish tinge.

" Look at the way she lies," she whispered, turning desperately to Nurse Pye.

" I like to see a baby lying like that," said Nurse Pye. " If grown-ups would lie like that when they're ill, they'd get better quicker.   Babies are the best patients ; they don't fret or fume and they get better the quicker for it."

Hope flickered in Christine's eyes as she listened.

Nurse Pye drew her away from the cot into the room adjoining the nursery.

" It's going to be a fight," she said.   " And you must help me."

" How ?   How can I help ?   I will.   I will if I can."

" I believe in influences," said Nurse Pye.   " Try not to fear.   Try to hope.   Fear's bad.   It weakens not only you but the ones you fear for.   At least that's what I think.   Hope's good.   It helps you and it helps them.   Things are very mysterious.   Love some-times has a wonderful power.   I nursed a man once, who was in fearful pain, but every time his wife came and held his hand the pain went off and he fell asleep. What do you make of that ?   And I've seen a child die of fuss.   His parents kept coming to stand at the bottom of his bed and ask him if he would like a drink, or if he'd like his mother to sing to him, or if he felt just a little better.   Poor things, they were so anxious, they couldn't stop themselves.   And I couldn't stop them, because the father was a doctor and I daren't tell him what I thought.   I was young then.   I'd tell him now.   But you mustn't be like that."

" Oh, I won't," said Christine. " But let me stay. Don't send me away."

" You shall stay," promised Nurse Pye. " I don't want another nurse here. We'll share the nursing between us."

She did not say that the crisis would soon be over, the issue soon decided for good or ill. Four or five days, at most. She could last out unrelieved for that length of time. She would trust to no one but herself.

They kept vigil. Life outside that quiet room ceased for Christine. Once or twice, she looked out and numbly felt it strange that the world should be the same : flowers blooming in the garden, a cat sunning itself, a cart rumbling through the village. She turned back to the bed, noting every change, every shadow on the small face. Her eyes moved between Angela's face and Nurse Pye's, trying to read both. She prayed all the time.

" Oh, God, save her. Let her live. Help her to breathe better. Help her, God."

In the back-bedroom at Mrs. Gaws's, she had thought about God and prayer. She had not been able to think that God, or Nature, or First Principle or Mind behind Matter, needed praise or prayer. What was the good of prayer in the face of incurable disease ? What was the use of prayer in war ? It seemed to her that God had made immutable laws, and if man went against them, man had to pay. If she had reasoned now, reasoned about someone else whose baby was ill, she would have said that because a maid had put a baby into a pram in a wet suit, a law of health was violated and a fight set up between disease and the baby's own strength. She would have said it was nothing to do with God. But it was her own baby who was ill and she did not reason. She prayed instinctively and all of the time. She prayed desperately. Whether God needed prayer or not, she needed to pray.

The hours dragged on. It was night and day. Doctors came and went away. Penelope looked in with a white face, found no place for herself and went out. Trays of food appeared. Christine and Nurse Pye took it in turns to lie on the bed in the adjoining room. From the bed, Christine could see Angela in her cot, and she lay facing that way, her eyes on Angela until her lids dropped from exhaustion. When she woke, she sprang up and hurried to see if there was any change. But it seemed to her that the breathing was always terrifyingly fast, that there was the same whiteness round the mouth, the same pinched look about the nostrils, and all she could do was to pray.

When Nurse Pye took Angela's temperature, Christine's eyes were raised in agonized question. But Nurse Pye never said anything ; she shook the thermometer down very quickly, rinsed it and put it back into the jar of surgical spirit. Christine dared not ask what the temperature was. Her eyes returned to her baby's face.

Once or twice other thoughts pierced her consciousness. If she dies, she thought, Nicholas will never forgive me. His mother will never forgive me for taking her away and leaving her. But these thoughts did not come often.

There came a day when Nurse Pye seemed less grave. Every time she came to look at Angela, Christine held her breath in case Nurse Pye was going to say something ; something hopeful. But Nurse Pye said nothing.

At last, when she had taken Angela's temperature in the evening, her eyes met Christine's. For the first time since they had been together in that room, they almost smiled. Nurse Pye turned away with the thermometer. They said nothing.

The night wore on. The fire flickered, the clock ticked, but it seemed to the listening Christine that Angela's breathing was easier, more regular. Nurse Pye came in from her brief rest, stooped low over Angela, took her temperature again. She held the thermometer to the light under the shaded lamp. She turned and looked at Christine. She smiled openly.

" What ? " said Christine breathlessly.

" She's better," whispered Nurse Pye. " There's no doubt about it. She's better. Here," she warned as Christine struggled up from her knees with a convulsed face. " Don't cry here, love. Sh. Don't wake her. Go outside."

Blindly, Christine obeyed.

§

In the dawn, she crept down through the quiet house. She felt as if she had been ill herself and had to feel carefully for the stairs with her feet in case she should fall. She wanted to make tea for Nurse Pye. She wanted to do everything she could for Nurse Pye, wait on her hand and foot, give her everything she had. Whatever Nurse Pye's failings had been at Saunby or elsewhere, in the sick-room she was an angel, a tower of strength and healing, and Christine would be grateful to her as long as she lived.

A light was burning in the kitchen and Harrison was dozing in a rocking-chair with a shawl round her shoulders. She had been sitting up all night to be ready to answer the nursery bells. She sprang up when she heard Christine and put her cap straight. Harrison, the perfect maid, had been sitting up all night in her cap.

494

"Madam, did you ring and didn't I hear you? Oh, the baby's better! I can see from your face, 'm."

"She is. She's better," quavered Christine, who found she could not speak without crying again.

"Thank God for that," said Harrison fervently. "It has been a terrible time for you. For us all. What with all the anxiety in the house and all the anxiety outside it. I don't know how we've got through the last few days, I don't really."

Christine could not pay much attention to what Harrison was saying. She was still wholly absorbed in the change in Angela.

"I was coming to make some tea for Nurse Pye," she said.

"I'll make the tea," said Harrison, bustling about. "The kettle's on the boil. I'll bring it up, madam. You go and lie down."

"I'd rather walk about," said Christine. "I'm so happy I can't keep still. I'll stay here with you till it's ready."

She wandered round the kitchen table, lifted the blind and looked into the dark garden, came to stand by the fire.

"Oh, madam," said Harrison, more talkative by night than ever she was by day. "It seems as if everything has taken a turn for the better at once, doesn't it? The little girl is out of danger and the Prime Minister's flying to Germany to see Hitler to-morrow—nay—to-day."

"Oh?" said Christine, standing on the hearthrug. "What for?"

Harrison turned in astonishment.

"Why, to talk over this Greeko-Slovonikan business, madam. Didn't you know? Why, madam, while you've been upstairs with the baby, we've been on the verge of going to war. Didn't you know? We've spent our time hanging over the wireless waiting for news. It's been awful, madam."

" Has it ? " Christine had come too lately through a crisis of her own to be able to grasp the significance of the one Harrison was talking about.

She yawned and shivered and Harrison darted, full of compunction, to the kettle.

" Here am I chattering about Hitler and what not, and you so tired you can hardly stand up. See, the tea's made and the tray's ready, now."

" I'll take it up, then," said Christine.

" Allow me, madam," said Harrison, firmly forestalling her.

CHAPTER XLI

THE parlour-maid brought in the tea and the coffee and James's boiled egg. She placed these with the racks of toast on the table and, rustling in her crisp print, went to sound the gong in the hall. The gong at Red Lodge was a comfortable summons, a melodious rumble that suggested rich soup and muffins, though of late the two it brought to table had little appetite for such fare.

James, who had hurried down to the papers and who had already turned the wireless on for the first news bulletin, moved, still reading, to the table when Sarah appeared.

" What's the news, James ? " Sarah asked, sitting down.

" Awful," said James heavily. " The Prime Minister goes to Godesberg this morning, but what he can do, or what he should do, who can tell ? The world's crying shame on us. The papers this morning don't make pleasant reading for an Englishman, I can tell you."

Sarah sighed and put out a hand for her letters. There was one from Christine. She opened it at once and pressed it out flat on the table so that she could read it while pouring coffee for James and tea for herself.

" Your coffee, James." She passed it with her eyes on the letter, then, her own tea steaming unnoticed, she picked the letter up and turned it in her trembling hands. Her hands often trembled nowadays, especially in the mornings. The European crisis was bearing hard on Sarah and James. Nicholas was missing, war seemed inevitable, he might be swept into it and they might never see him again.

Sarah's spectacles slipped down her nose. She read over them. At her feet, Peke sat up on his hindquarters, his forepaws crossed, like a dog in heraldry, waiting for the snippet of toast that did not come. He waited. He yapped sharply to remind. Sarah did not hear.

"James!" she called out, still reading rapidly. "James!"

At the urgency of her voice, he looked up from his paper.

"What is it, Mother? What's the matter? Is it news of Nick?"

"No, but it's Christine. Look, James, what she says here!" Sarah got up and hurried with the letter to James's end of the table. "Look," she said, stooping over him and holding the letter under his eyes. "Look! She's coming back. She's bringing Angela. James, that's what she says! Angela nearly died from pneumonia. She's only just getting better."

"Pneumonia," cried James, seizing the letter for himself. "Oh, I can't read her writing," he groaned. "I never could. You read it to me, Mother. You tell me what she says. But here, sit you down! You're trembling like a leaf."

"I am," agreed Sarah. "I'm so excited. It's a long letter, but I'll just read you the important parts first. See, she says: 'I've been working in London . . .'"

"Working in London!" cried James. "God bless my soul, whatever for? She need never have done that. She knew I'd provide for her if she'd ever given me half a chance. I thought she was with her sister.

They've got plenty of money, haven't they—that fat chap ? "

" Now, James, let me go on," implored Sarah.

" Yes, yes," agreed James. " Go on. Let me hear."

" ' But I can't go back. I can never leave Angela again. I left her and she nearly died. I can't risk that again.' "

" I should hope not," said James.

" ' I didn't want to be dependent on anybody,' " read Sarah, " ' but I find I have to be, so that I can look after Angela, and I would rather be dependent on you than anybody.' "

" Does she really say that, Mother ? Well, that's handsome of her. It means she doesn't hate me as much as she thought she did, and I'm glad of that. Go on," he urged.

" ' I ask you to have us because I know you want us. Only pride has kept me from asking you before and I haven't any pride now. Only relief and thankfulness that Angela is alive.' "

" Poor girl," threw in James. " Poor Christine."

" ' If you could come for us in the car in a few days, Angela will be able to travel. I know I can ask you to fetch us.' "

" She can that," said James. " And you can go, Mother. I won't go. Then it'll be easier for her to come back. You'll manage better by yourselves."

" ' Angela has made a splendid recovery. Nurse Pye is going back to Saunby to-day. She has been wonderful. I don't think Angela could have lived but for her.' "

" I always liked that little woman," said James with warmth.

" ' There's another reason why I want to come back,' " read Sarah. " ' I think Nicholas might come home at any time. Things are so serious and war seems so near that I think he will come home, if not for my sake, then for yours. I want to be there if he comes. I would like to be at Red Lodge with you, waiting for him.'

"There's not much more, James," said Sarah, wiping her eyes. "I'll read it in a moment . . . I'll . . ."

She got up and went back to her place. She sipped her cold tea. James blew his nose. Peke rose again on his hind-quarters and barked sharply.

"Dear me," said Sarah, glad of the interruption. "I'd forgotten you. Here you are, then! And do you know," she said, bending round the stiff folds of the tablecloth to him. "We're going to have that baby back. The one we used to take out."

"Mother," said James, getting hastily out of his chair. "You could telephone to Christine. It's better than writing a letter. She'd have to wait for a letter until to-morrow morning, but you could telephone right away."

"So I could, James," said Sarah, rising too. "That's a very good idea."

"I'll get through for you at once," said James, hurrying out of the room. "I won't speak. I'll leave that to you. But you'll suggest they should come as soon as possible, won't you? Suggest Sunday."

"Eh, I don't know that they could get ready by Sunday," said Sarah, hurrying after him.

"Well, try, anyway," urged James.

§

On Sunday, towards noon, Gibbs brought the Rolls-Royce in an artistic flourish to the door of Brockington Grange and, a hand under her elbow, assisted the sole occupant to alight, backwards. Sarah always got out

500

of the car in this way, and though Gibbs, immensely proud of the Rolls and the title, did not think it a very classy way to do it, he liked Sarah so much that he put up with it, only smiling apologetically if anybody happened to be passing at the time. To-day was such a great day for her and he shared so much in her pleasure, that he would have helped her out through the roof if necessary.

Before Sarah could turn from her backwards emergence, Christine was beside her. They were both so moved that they laughed foolishly because Sarah's hat scraped Christine's nose as they kissed each other. Gibbs shut the car doors smartly, said, " I'll be ready when you are," and went round the back of the house to the kitchen. Sarah, with Christine's hand drawn through her arm, went into the house.

Penelope was in the hall with Paul.

" Christine tells me you can't wait for lunch, Lady Ashwell," she said, very much the mistress of the house. " But will you have coffee and a sandwich or sherry ? Will you come into the dining-room ? "

She led the way, but Sarah hung back, looking beseechingly at Christine.

" Angela ? " said Christine. " She's upstairs, all ready and waiting. Would you like to see her straight away ? One moment, Penelope," she called out.

Sarah, raising her skirt a little in the front, hurried up the stairs with Christine, a flush of anticipation in her cheeks. But when she saw Angela lying in her cot, her lips trembled.

" Oh, darling," she said compassionately. " You have been ill. You are a pale, thin little girl, aren't you ? "

She bent low over Angela and Angela made a sudden, surprisingly vigorous grab at her grandmother's hat. Sarah and Christine laughed then, and Angela stuffed her fists into her mouth and laughed at her own joke.

"The moppet," said Sarah delightedly. "She's evidently better than she looks."

"She gets stronger every day," said Christine.

"We'll soon bring those roses back," said Sarah, beaming with love on Angela. She could hardly believe she was holding those little feet in her hand again.

"Shall we go down?" asked Christine. "We're all ready to start. Angela's going to be carried out and put into the car on this mattress as she is. That was a good idea of yours, Granny."

It warmed Sarah's heart to be called Granny again. She was as excited as a girl and full of joyful haste to get these precious two to Red Lodge to James, who had remained so diffidently at home.

Penelope stood in the dining-room, patiently waiting. She was courteous, but chilly. "Make use of my house by all means," her manner implied. "You have made use of it so long, a little longer does not signify. Forget all I have done, all I have spent. You mean to punish me for what my nurse-maid did, but I am not punished. And though you may forget what is due to me, I will not forget what is due from me. Have another sandwich and let me fill your cup."

'Father all over again,' thought Christine with affectionate amusement, but Paul looked anxious. He would have to bear the brunt of this mood when the others had gone.

"Pen, darling," said Christine, hugging her sister when Paul had followed Sarah out to the car. "Come round! I have to go, you know. I'm not going because Angela got ill. I'm going to wait for Nicholas and make up to his parents if I can and make a home for Angela where I can be, too. I have to go, but I thank you very, very much for all you've done. You've been so good to us. Don't spoil it ! "

" You're knocking my hair down," said Penelope.

" Then you can put it up again when I've gone. I hate to leave you, Pen. I don't want you to be lonely. I do wish you'd a baby of your own. You're so good with babies."

" Oh, shut up," said Penelope.

" What will you do now, darling ? I don't want you to be bored."

" Bored ? " said Penelope. " On the contrary, I may now be able to do many things I haven't had time to do since March."

" Well, good-bye," said Christine, kissing her. " You're rude and unkind, but you can't put me off. I love you just the same. But remember, there might be war next week. We might never see each other again."

" Rot," said Penelope. " There won't be any war."

But she leaned into the car to kiss Christine and Angela again of her own accord and stood forlornly waving in the drive. There was such youth and pathos in the way she dropped her arm and turned away at last, that Christine's heart was wrung. She would always feel, unless Penelope changed very much, that Penelope was an uncertain quantity, that Penelope might fail her when she least expected it, but she loved her and felt responsibility for her. She had a burning desire to make things right for Penelope, and it made her sad not to be able to do it.

The car sped northwards, passing through typically English villages where the church stood among the cottages, with the vicarage alongside and the big house at some little distance in its park.

" You know Saunby's for sale ? " said Christine suddenly to Sarah.

" No ! " exclaimed Sarah. " I didn't know that. I hadn't heard. Oh dear," she said, distressed. " I'm very sorry. I know how you love it."

" Yes," said Christine.

For a moment she sagged visibly. She might have been sitting in the back-bedroom at Mrs. Gaws's from the way she looked.

" Hasn't everything gone *wrong* ? " she said to Sarah.

" Not everything," said Sarah, taking one of Angela's waving fists in hers.

Christine's face cleared. She bent, smiling, over Angela.

" No, not everything. I should have remembered that."

In a few moments, she said : " I'm so frightened of war."

All these months she had kept everything to herself and now she was bringing it all out to Sarah.

" The suspense is so awful," she said. " And where's Nicholas ? If only he would come back while he can. He might not be able to soon. Who knows what will happen to us all ? "

" We must wait," said Sarah. " Wait as best we can. Don't look forward. Live in the moment."

" I can't," protested Christine. " I can't help looking forward. Nicholas was always saying that what was wrong with life to-day was that we couldn't look forward any more. I didn't know what he meant then, but I do now."

" Poor boy," said his mother. " I think he worried a great deal more than we ever realized, and I think he was trying to lead a life that was quite wrong for him. I think he was going against himself all the time."

" So do I," said Christine with a sigh.

They were silent, and in the silence, Angela dropped off to sleep. They smiled to each other with satisfaction, and their hands met as they made unnecessary adjustments to Angela's coverings for the mere pleasure of touching her. They spoke little after that and then only in whispers.

Christine looked out of the windows at the Sunday peace of the villages with their greens and their geese, at the contented cows in the fields, the autumn splendour of the trees : the giant beeches red gold, the silver birches pale yellow gold, the bird-cherry trees coral pink and the hedges burning with scarlet and orange berries. Panorama of a country threatened by war, thought Christine.

James was on the steps of Red Lodge, looking out for them. He approached Christine with some hesitation, not knowing how she would like him to greet her. But she kissed him at once and put Angela into his arms.

" Could you carry her upstairs ? " she asked.

" Certainly," said James, extremely gratified. Fancy trusting me with her, he thought. She never used to. " Grandpa's girl," he said to Angela, whose eyes widened at the vastness of the landing window. " You don't cry any more now than you used to, even though I'm a stranger to you. You're a grand little girl, love, and you don't know how glad we are to have you and your mother here.

" Oh, God, let Nick come home now and let there be no war and I'll do my best for them all, I promise you," he said, kissing Angela while no one was about.

The house was full of bustle and welcome, with willing maids offering all kinds of help. Christine had feared they might look upon a baby as a nuisance, but they welcomed her and envied Emily, who had been appointed nursery-maid at her own request. Angela, as of the first importance, was seen to first. The household in future would turn upon Angela and began at once. She was bathed, fed and got to bed. She soon fell asleep in her original cot, and Christine was able to turn her attention to herself.

As she dressed, she looked out on the scene she used to despise so strongly. She didn't despise it now. Mansbridge looked a most desirable place. She valued it. Everything about the life that had been unthreatened by war was valuable. Threatened by loss, everything seemed infinitely necessary and precious. Christine was realizing as thousands of other people were realizing on this Sunday in September how deeply they were attached to the lives they had led and the people they had lived with.

Christine thought of Cicely Hoyle ; but Cicely had faded into insignificance in her mind. The major catastrophe had crowded out minor ones and Christine found that the affair of Cicely Hoyle was a minor one. You have to be brought to the edge of the abyss to find out what really matters, she thought.

She went down to tea in the drawing-room, where Sarah and James were hovering eagerly. They offered her the chairs they always sat in themselves, but declining them, Christine sought the corner of the Chesterfield near the fire. They took their chairs then and could not keep their eyes away from her. They were so grateful to her for coming to them. Sarah talked more than she used to, coming more than half-way to meet Christine. James talked less and his old tiresome gallantry had gone.

The room was comfortable, even luxurious, with deep chairs and sofas covered with silk damask, a plum-coloured carpet, pale grey walls and flowers everywhere. There was everything Sarah could think of for tea. But there was an unearthly light over the sea and the same strangeness in the hearts of the three who sat together. They talked a good deal, about Angela, about Saunby's being for sale, about the Arkwrights in the house in the Drive, about all sorts of things, because when they were silent, the menace was heavier. And all the time they were talking, Christine was listening. She felt Nicholas might walk in at any moment, and at the sound of every approaching car her heart beat faster and her mouth went dry. But tea was cleared away, the curtains were drawn, shutting out the direful light, the news bulletin was given out, grave, resolved (" We shall fight now," said James. " The whole temper of the country has stiffened "), the gong went for supper, they had to go to bed. Christine was tired, but she went reluctantly ; she wished she could sit up all night. He had not come. But surely, surely he would come to-morrow.

CHAPTER XLII

BUT Monday passed and Tuesday passed, and still Nicholas did not come. On Wednesday Christine had no hope left. No one had any hope. The German Army was massed on the Czecho-Slovak borders and the British Fleet was mobilized.

It poured with rain, the sea was hidden. On the flat wet front bands of children straggled, playing games in gas-masks. Sarah and Christine stared from the windows of Red Lodge at this horrific sight, but James went out and spoke sternly to them. They only laughed and ran off. The schools were being used for the distribution of gas-masks, and a ghastly holiday for the children was thus provided. They added to the sense of confusion and disintegration by trailing about the town.

All morning Gibbs drove parties of people to be fitted with masks. He took the Arkwrights and the Harpers, recently installed, from the house in the Drive ; he took assistants from the shops, anybody who wanted to go, and finally he took James and Sarah and Christine. Christine was appalled to find there was still no protection from gas for children under three years of age. That made the horror complete. She would accept a mask as a matter of form, but she knew she would never protect herself while Angela was unprotected. She joined the queue of strangely assorted people and grimly awaited her turn.

" What's it all for ? " said the woman in front of her,

turning a wan face in question. She was hatless and her hair dripped with rain, she had an old coat pinned across her breast. " I lost two sons in the last war and now they're going to take another off me."

What comfort was there to be offered, thought Christine. She could find nothing to say.

Gibbs drove them home again, and they put down their gas-masks, grotesque, unbelievable, like the snouts of animals, in the hall. From these and from the maids' masks in the kitchen premises a strong rank smell arose and seemed to fill the house. Red Lodge had always smelt of flowers before ; now it smelt of gas-masks.

It was raining so hard after lunch that Christine put Angela to sleep in the nursery, where, with the windows wide open and a fire burning, there was fresh air without dampness. Then she went down to the drawing-room and sat on the rug at Sarah's feet. James had gone out with Gibbs again to take more people for masks. Sarah could not take her customary nap. To please Christine, she tried. But it was no good. She sat in her chair, and Christine leaned against her knees and played aimlessly, endlessly with the poker.

Christine's leaning against Sarah was typical of their relationship. All barriers were gone between them. They were mother and daughter. Sarah was no longer too diffident to put Christine's hair back or take her hand in hers, and Christine leaned on Sarah's knees with complete lack of ceremony, and asked advice and gave it. In spite of the darkness of these days, each found comfort in the other : Sarah had never had a daughter and Christine could not remember a mother, but now this lack in each was supplied.

The rain beat softly on the windows. Occasionally it came down the chimney and made the fire spit. The crystal clock on the mantel-piece ticked time away, chiming every quarter in a sweet, faint, musical box tone. Peke snored slightly as he slept, curled like a whiting, his head on his tail.

Among these soft sounds another inserted itself. Christine turned up her face, listening intently.

" What is it, dear ? " asked Sarah. She saw Christine's attention to something she could not hear herself.

Christine dropped the poker and knelt upright against Sarah's knees. Her eyes widened, her lips parted, she raised a hand. The colour drained slowly from her cheeks.

A car was approaching and she knew the sound of the engine. A car was crushing the gravel of the drive, stopping before the door. She swallowed on a dry throat.

" He's come," she whispered.

Sarah leaned forward in her chair. Her hand gripped Christine's shoulder. They turned their faces to the door. It opened and Nicholas stood in the room.

All three were for the moment transfixed, then Christine scrambled to her feet and ran, knocking against the chairs. She threw her arms wide and was caught in his.

Sarah stood a little way off, clasping and unclasping her trembling hands, saying over and over again : " My boy, my dear, dear boy." She waited her turn to embrace him, she waited to take the second place. She was prepared to stand aside indefinitely, happy in his happiness, but he held out an arm to include her, and Christine put out a hand to draw her in, and all three stood embraced, smiling through tears, asking incoherent questions and giving incoherent answers.

"Where's Angela? Did she really have pneumonia ? Penelope said . . ."

" Penelope ? "

" I went to Saunby for you and when you weren't there I went to Brockington. I came down from Scotland yesterday. I was finishing off what I could for Mills, the fellow I work for. Is Angela really all right now ? Where's Dad ? Where is he ? "

" Oh, he's out, he's going about the town and he doesn't know you're here," cried Sarah in distress for James. " I must go and send somebody to try to find him. Have you had any lunch, dear ? Are you hungry ? Are you sure you're not ? I must go and send somebody to find your father."

With another close kiss to last her until she came back, Sarah hurried out of the room and left them alone.

They stood in each other's arms, smiling, and the smile of each was almost unbearable in its tenderness to the other. Smiles like that, a revelation of the deepest feelings of the human heart, can hardly be borne. They sought refuge from the stress of the moment by pressing cheek to cheek, lip to lip.

" Have you really forgiven me ? " asked Nicholas sadly. He was sad, he would always be sad that he had hurt her so much and brought so much suffering upon her. Remorse was like a nausea ; it had recurred through all these months and was almost insupportable at this moment of reunion.

Christine laid her hand on his mouth.

" Never speak of it again," she said. " Don't say anything. Nothing."

" All right," he said, pressing her head back so that he could look into her face.

" God, I have missed you," he said with a groan.

" Oh, so have I. Would you ever have come home if there hadn't been going to be a war ? " Christine leaned away to ask him. " Would you ? "

" I should have had to," said Nicholas. " I was

about at breaking-point. I should have had to come back to have another try at getting you to forgive me."

" I forgave you long ago," said Christine. " D'you know I saw you once in London? Driving down Oxford Street, and I couldn't make you see me. It was terrible, that, it made me realize . . ."

" Oh, if I'd only known . . ." He buried his face in her neck.

" Darling, what's going to happen now? " asked Christine, clasping his head. " Are we going to be parted again? Will you have to go to the war? "

" That's what I've come home for," said Nicholas. " We'll all have to go."

Christine shuddered in his arms.

" Let's not think of it," said Nicholas. " Not just now. We shall have to soon enough. Let's keep it out of our minds. Let's go up and see Angela."

His arm round her shoulders, her arm round his waist, they went up to the nursery, where the wet wind blew in at the windows and the fire burned brightly in the grate and Angela slept in her cot. Nicholas was awed at the sight of his daughter. He bent over her in wonder, scrutinizing the small face turned sideways in easy sleep on the pillow, one hand flung up against it.

" She's perfect," he whispered. " She's prettier than ever. She's going to be as pretty as you. And was she so ill? She might have died, and you were alone. I wasn't with you. It must have been terrible for you, and all the time I thought you were comfortable at Saunby. "

" Hush," soothed Christine. " Don't blame yourself for everything. You're thin," she said wonderingly. " Your collar's frayed and your tie is very shabby, darling. You look so different."

She ran her fingers over his face, along his sharpened

cheek-bones, the bridge of his nose. How lovely it was to touch him again, to feel the texture of his skin and his thick tawny hair.

" Will it be long before Angela wakes ? " he asked. " I suppose she won't know me ? No, that's too much to expect."

Downstairs the front door was flung open and James's voice shouted :

" Mother ? Where is he ? His car's here. Nick's come home ! Where are you, Nick ? "

Nicholas went swiftly out of the nursery, calling in subdued tones because of Angela : " Dad ! I'm here."

They met at the foot of the stairs, and James propped his hands on Nicholas's shoulders to support himself in his strong emotion. Father and son embraced.

" Eh, Nick, but I'm glad you've come," was all James could say. " I'm glad."

Nicholas stood smiling with affection at his father. Absence riddles relationships : in absence you get to know what you feel for people, so that both the old adages are true ; in some cases it is out of sight out of mind, and in others, absence does make the heart grow fonder. In absence, Nicholas's thoughts had riddled the sand away and he had found gold in his father. His father was pig-headed, tactless, domineering, boastful, but he was, in his own way, immensely kind and, at bottom, immensely sound, and he truly loved, though again in his own way, his wife and his son.

" Come and let's sit down, Nick," said James, taking his son's arm. " Would you believe it, my legs are shaking ? "

Nicholas sent a glance like a lover's to Christine at the top of the stairs. " I'll be back in a moment," his look promised, and he went into the drawing-room with his father.

Behind her, Christine heard faint rustlings from Angela's cot. She went to the nursery and watched from the door. Angela was very solemnly holding up the edge of her blanket as she lay on her back. Then she sat up to it and investigated it further. Then she rolled over with it and looked at it from above ; finally she crawled to the foot of the cot, taking it with her, and investigated it there. When her mother spoke, she looked up with rounded blue eyes and cast the blanket aside with joy. Christine ran to her and picked her up.

" Daddy's come ! What do you think of that ? Daddy's come, and Mummy must be quick and put your best frock on and brush your hair and take you down ! "

She rang for Emily, and carried Angela into the bathroom to sponge her hands and face.

Emily came running. She ran noisily into the nursery, scampered along the landing and burst into the bathroom, amazing Christine.

" Oh, madam, isn't it lovely ? Isn't it splendid ? Oh, I feel I could go dotty with joy," cried Emily, crashing her starched apron together in her hands. " Dotty ! " she cried, drumming with both feet on the bathroom floor. " My young man won't have to go now. He won't have to go ! "

" What is it ? What's happened ? " asked Christine sharply.

" Oh, don't you know, 'm ? It's just come through on the kitchen wireless. Hitler's invited the Prime Minister to go somewhere to-morrow with Mussolini and the man from France to talk things over. It means peace, 'm. It means there's going to be no war. Cook's crying in the kitchen, but I keep laughing. I can't stop, 'm, you must excuse me. I've been that anxious about my young man."

Christine, who had stared at Emily, watching every word come from her lips, now rushed out of the bathroom with Angela under her arm. She scuttered down the stairs into the drawing-room. Gibbs and the maids were there. Gibbs was telling James and Sarah and Nicholas the news.

"Is it true?" said Christine, white-faced. She made her way to Nicholas and put Angela into his arms. "Is it true?" she asked, looking round on them all.

"It's true," said James. "War's averted."

He sank into a chair, his arms hanging.

"Thank God, thank God," murmured Sarah, feeling for a place to sit down.

Gibbs tactfully shepherded the maids out of the room, and Christine fell to her knees on the rug and burst into tears. With her hands over her face she rocked herself backward and forward.

"I can't believe it. I can't believe it," she sobbed.

Nicholas, with Angela in his arms, got down beside her, and James went suddenly to turn on the wireless. The voice of the announcer was heard repeating the news, and Christine stopped crying to hear. She knelt upright, her cheeks wet with tears, an incredulous smile on her face.

"It's true," she said.

Their eyes were on the radio set, but there was no more to come. The announcer gave out that they were now going over to the studio, the spell broke.

Christine went to throw her arms round Sarah. She knew that Sarah knew and shared her feelings. Then she went to kiss James and then Nicholas again and Angela. She was beside herself with relief. She felt reprieved. She felt giddy with joy. She had been a stranger to happiness so long that it was like drinking on an empty stomach. They were all talking at once,

515

and in a moment they got up by common consent and went out to the kitchen where they all talked again. The excitement communicated itself to Angela, who gave short, sharp screams of joy and scrambled ecstatically up her mother's ribs with her bare feet.

"Dear me, Emily, I haven't got her dressed yet," exclaimed Christine.

"Oh, let's go, 'm," said Emily, shocked. "We're forgetting everything."

For tea, Angela's high-chair was taken into the drawing-room, because at this supreme hour they must all be together. Angela squeezed bread-and-butter in her hands to her heart's content and dropped it to the plum-coloured carpet without rebuke. Peke came to eat it up, and Angela leaned over the side of her tray and watched him with great interest, absorbed in her world while the grown-ups talked of theirs.

Life had been given back to them and they were delirious with the gift. The immense wave of hope and goodwill that was sweeping over the world engulfed Red Lodge too. This was the time when miracles could have been accomplished, when, if they could have come at each other, the peoples of Europe would have fallen on one another's necks like brothers and wrung one another's hands with promises of peace.

§

When Angela had gone to bed and dinner was over, they returned to their places in the drawing-room. If anyone had wanted a picture of domestic bliss, he could have found it here with Sarah and James in their chairs and Christine in the corner of the Chesterfield with her legs curled under her; she had never even had enough happiness to sit like that from March until this day. Nicholas's arm was behind her head and from time to time she turned to look at him and say ecstatically : " I can't believe it." She held his hand in both hers and smiled round on James and Sarah. She wanted to smile and stretch all the time.

" If I was a cat, I'd purr now," she said.

" You mustn't expect too much," warned James. " I don't think there'll be war, but I think there'll be a lot of trouble."

" Trouble's bearable," said Christine. " War isn't. What are we going to do now ? " she asked. " We can discuss the future now. Since the afternoon there is a future. What are you going to do, Nicholas ? What *have* you been doing ? We've actually never asked you. That's because so much has been crowded into to-day. What have you been doing, darling ? "

" I've been selling apple-juice and carrot-juice for the Vitameena company, which is a new little concern just started by a chap called Mills."

" Apple-juice ! " Christine was inclined to laugh. She was going to make fun of it, until she saw that Nicholas was perfectly serious.

" It's jolly good stuff," he said. " And I've done a lot to put it on the market."

He looked at them with such modest pride that Christine could not help laughing out. But she kissed him to make up for it.

" Darling, you're so funny," she said.

" Why ? " asked Nicholas, smiling.

" Nicholas Ashwell, the famous cricketer, going about with apple-juice," teased Christine.

" But no one knew I was a cricketer. I called myself Norman Aitken, to keep my initials, because Mother had marked my pants and socks so firmly with them I couldn't get them off."

Christine threw her head back and laughed again.

" Norman ! " she cried. " You were Norman and

517

I was Sonia! We were so *fancy*, weren't we? Oh, thank God, we're Nicholas and Christine again. Thank God we're ourselves! Though I daresay we learnt a good deal as Norman and Sonia that we should never otherwise have learnt. But go on about the apple-juice, darling."

"It's jolly good stuff," said Nicholas. "And Mills is a very good chap. You should hear what sort of people I worked for before I worked for him. You shall later. Mills is a first-rate chap. But there's been no business lately. People have been too worried to drink apple-juice."

"They wanted something stronger," smiled James. "And what about you? You haven't had a drink since you came into the house. Aren't you ready for one yet?"

"No," said Nicholas indifferently. "I'll get one when I want one. I hardly ever have a drink now. I got a shock once when I went in to see the manager of a store. He said to me: 'If there's one thing I don't like it's when a commercial comes in to see me and I smell drink on his breath.'"

Christine was shocked.

"Fancy speaking to you like that," she said.

"Oh, you have to put up with all sorts of indignities," said Nicholas. "It was a revelation to me. I never drank during the day after that and I hadn't much to spare even for drinks in the evening. A bottle of beer now and again got to be about my mark. I only had five pounds a week."

"Five pounds a week!" exclaimed Christine. "Why, it was riches. I'd only two."

"But I'd all the running expenses of my car to pay and my own expenses too," said Nicholas.

"Well, I don't know how on earth you did it," said James.

"I'm sorry for Mills," said Nicholas with feeling. "The Vitameena company will be a good thing in the end, but I don't know if Mills can stay the course. He's very short of capital. If there'd been a war, he'd have gone smash. But everything else would have gone smash too, I suppose. Now Mills will be wondering what to do again. I'd wound everything up at my end. Now I shall have to take it up again."

James had been looking at his son, letting him talk. He had been chewing his cigar unmercifully and it was now almost in rags.

"Nicholas," he said.

There was that in his voice that made them all turn to look at him. He kept them waiting. He sat in the centre of the half-circle, fire-light and lamp-light ruddy on his thick white hair and white moustache. His eyes under their bushy white brows were bright, alert.

"I've been thinking a lot since you went away, lad," said James. "And I made up my mind if you ever came back, I'd go back into business in a different sort of way with you and with some of our old hands from Birchley. I've puzzled my brains by the hour trying to work out what we could do and where we could start. Then this cloud began to come up, this war threat, and I've been as frightened as anybody, I can tell you. This crisis has been like the Day of Judgment to a lot of us, and me among them. I realized suddenly that I'd had my chances and I hadn't taken them, and the time seemed to have come when I'd get no more. I promised God—yes, I'm not ashamed to tell you that—lots of folk have been promising God this, that and the other thing lately. Well, I promised that if I got another chance, if this war was averted and Nicholas came home, I'd really do something worth while with my money."

They stared at him.

"Well," resumed James, holding his audience. "Christine came back and she gave me an idea."

"Did I?" Christine opened her eyes wide in surprise.

"And these last few days," he said, smiling at her, "partly to distract my mind from the war and partly, I suppose, with some idea of showing God that I meant to keep my word," James laughed shame-facedly at himself, "I've been working out a plan."

He paused and looked round on them all.

"I've not even told Mother," he said, enjoying their suspense.

"Go on, Dad, go on," urged Nicholas, taking his arm from behind Christine's head and leaning forward intently.

"It's this," said James, and paused again. He threw his chewed cigar into the fire.

"Shall we buy Saunby?" he said.

There was complete silence in the room. Then Christine shot from the corner of the Chesterfield to the rug at James's feet.

"Oh, d'you mean it?" she cried, clasping his knees and looking searchingly into his face. "D'you really mean buy Saunby? Buy it? Save it? Not let it go?"

"I mean buy it," said James, leaning forward to put a hand on her shoulder. "But not for ourselves alone."

"Who for?" asked Christine.

"The house for us," said James. "Divided into the three. One part for your father and his family, one part for you and Nicholas, and one part for Mother and me."

"Oh," cried Christine, her face radiant as she turned swiftly to Nicholas and to Sarah. "What a magnificent plan. It's wonderful. How did you think of it? It's such a *solution*. Oh, Mother, think of it. Think of Saunby being *ours*!" She was beside herself. She hardly knew what she was doing. She squeezed Sarah's hand fiercely and hunched her shoulders up like a child. Nicholas laughed at her and pulled her back against his knees. He felt a vast relief to see her like this. It meant that though she had suffered, she was not embittered. She was still very young in being able to be so happy.

"Now, listen," said James. "I haven't finished. This is where the plan comes in and this is where our life work comes in. Yes, yours, Nick, if you agree, and mine and Mother's and Christine's. I propose to build a little settlement, a little village as it were, somewhere in the park."

"Oh, at the back," called out Christine. "I know the exact place. There's an awful lot of room, too, in the stable yard and several great outbuildings. But what for?"

"Ah," said James.

They hung on his words.

"For the Arkwrights, the Harpers, the Blackledges, the Greenhalghs, the Steads and the other families we've kept in touch with, Mother and me. About a dozen of them, and if there's room for any more, we'll have 'em; all good sturdy people who've been hard hit and never given in. Now to begin with, Nick, these men are good gardeners. They've all had allotments. It's what's kept them going. They're just the men we need for getting the estate into shape. Those woods are enough to make anybody weep, begging your pardon, Christine. And the hedges and ditches are in a filthy mess. And all that bracken . . ."

"Pigs," said Sarah surprisingly. "There's nothing

like pigs for getting rid of bracken. Nothing else will do it. I read in the paper and thought of Saunby at the time."

"Pigs it shall be, then, Mother," said James. "Then there's the kitchen garden and all those greenhouses to mend up. There'll be no shortage of work. And when Saunby's shipshape, I propose to set up some village industries. Kitchen garden produce, raspberries, strawberries, apples."

"Apples?" cried Nicholas. "Why not set up a juice-extracting plant? Get Mills in. We'd be a boon to Mills."

"There's no end to the possibilities," said James. "No end. We must discuss them all."

"Nobody can bake bread and cakes like Mrs. Arkwright," said Sarah. "She can set up shop and we'll all buy from her."

"Good idea, Mother. And, Nick, I suggest you go to an Agricultural College for a bit to learn something about land and management and that."

"Oh, don't send him away!" implored Christine fearfully, clasping him.

"Now then," said James. "Am I to show that I know more about your district than you do? What about that Agricultural College within ten miles of Saunby? Can't he go there every day and get back to you at night, miss?"

"Oh, yes," said Christine, radiant again. "You're wonderful. You've thought of everything."

"I should think I probably have," said James, with a pleased wag of the head. "When I do a thing, I do it properly. You see, I'm a business man . . ."

"James," warned Sarah, who knew the signs.

"You're right, Mother," said James. "If I don't look out, I'll be boasting. Well, Christine, I thought you might go with Nicholas to the college yourself and learn how to make butter and cheese and cream cheese and all that, so that you can teach others on the place."

" I'd love it," cried Christine. " I've never heard of such a splendid plan."

" Well, Nick ? " said James. " What d'you say to it ? It means risking pretty well all our money— your money. If Saunby fails, we fail. We sink or swim with Saunby. Say the word and stop me now or for ever hold thy peace."

" There's one thing we ought to consider," said Nicholas gravely. " Suppose this peace doesn't come off ? Suppose it doesn't last ? Suppose there's war, not now, but later ? "

" I've thought of that," said James. " And I'm willing to buy Saunby just the same. If there's war, we shall have a good number of women and children safely housed already and we could take a lot more. That park would hold hundreds and we should be growing a great deal of our own food. Saunby would be as good a refuge as the country has to offer any-where. Besides, Nick, I don't believe . . . I no longer believe, I should say, because I've altered a good deal lately and I hope it's not the same man speaking to you now who got out of Birchley in time to save his own bacon. I don't believe in not doing a good thing because a bad thing might happen. Now I came across a quotation the other day in a paper and I cut it out, because it expressed just what I was beginning to feel. In fact, it showed me what I meant. I've got it here," said James, taking out his pocket book, while Sarah stared at him in amazement and pride. Fancy James with a quotation of anything but Stock Exchange prices !

" I'll read it to you," said James, looking round at them all. " It's this : ' Meanwhile, if these hours be dark at least do not let us sit deedless, like fools and fine gentlemen, thinking the common toil not good enough for us and beaten by the muddle ; but rather let us work like good fellows trying by some dim candle-light to set our workshop ready against to-morrow's daylight. William Morris.' There," said James, " that's good, isn't it ? ' Not beaten by the muddle.' I like that. And ' set our workshop ready against to-morrow's daylight.' I like that too. Don't you, Nick ? "

" I do," said Nicholas gravely. " It's good. It's just what we want. ' To-morrow's daylight.' Let's work for that."

He was moved, and looked down at Christine's hair, stroking it, to hide his emotion.

" Well, what d'you say ? " cried James gaily. " To buy or not to buy, that is the question."

" Buy ! " cried Christine. " Oh, buy, buy ! "

" Buy," said Nicholas, reaching out to press his father's hand. " You're a grand chap, Dad. Buy Saunby ! "

" And what d'you say, Mother ? We can't do anything without you."

" Oh, buy, James," said Sarah, twinkling with smiles and tears. She was so proud of him, so immensely proud and delighted that such a plan should have originated from him.

" Right you are," said James, getting to his feet. " I'll buy, and what's more I'll buy now. I've made my inquiries already and now I'll clinch the matter by telephone. The Major likes doing his deals by telephone. He shall do one now."

They all stood up, eager, hampering, but James waved them aside.

" Leave it to me," he said, grandly, pleasurably, and went out of the room to buy Saunby.

" Oh, Nicholas ! " cried Christine in sudden fear. " You don't think anybody will have bought before us, do you ? "

" It's not likely," Nicholas reassured her. " The board was up this morning."

" This morning ! Was it only this morning you were there ? What a day ! This morning there wasn't a speck of hope or light anywhere and look at us to-night ! I've never been so happy in my life. You're here, there's not going to be a war, and Saunby's saved ! "

She clasped her hands under her chin. Her eyes were wide and full of light, her curls flew up like feathers. She looked so radiantly alive and hopeful that Nicholas felt a pang in case life should ever strike a blow at her again. As she went past him on her restless march, he pinioned her in his arms.

" Don't expect *too* much, sweetheart," he warned her. " Life won't change all in a minute. There'll be tremendous difficulties. Where a lot of people try to live together, there'll always be difficulties. I don't say they'll daunt us, but don't hope for too much."

" I shall," said Christine, tilting her chin with defiance. " I shall hope for the best now and always."

He kissed her, laughing.

James opened the door and came in.

" Well, that's that," he said with supreme satisfaction. " Saunby's ours."

Christine flew to hug him. His red face with its white whiskers showed choked, but happy, over her shoulder. He put one hand round her to take his son's, and the other to take Sarah's.

" The Major made one stipulation," he said when Christine released him.

They looked at him in inquiry.

" That Thompson should be included in the settlement. I was a bit touched at that," said James. " Of course, I agreed."

"But what about Bertha?" asked Christine in dismay. " Bertha's not at all the sort of person you'd want in a community settlement."

" Eh, bless you," said James. " We shan't all be angels. Not at first, anyway. Besides, Bertha can't do much damage among Lancashire folk. They've too much horse-sense to be upset by Bertha. We'll have to put up with Bertha for Thompson's sake. Thompson will be a very useful man on the land and he can run the Sports Club with your father. Your father'll have to run a Second Eleven as well as a First now, you know, and with Nick and Thompson to play permanently, Saunby cricket will be worth watching, eh, Nick?"

" I'm so glad Father's going to have his interests given back to him," burst out Christine. " I've been so sorry for him. I'm so glad he's going to be *useful*."

" Oh, everybody's going to be useful," said James. " That's part of the plan. That grand little woman who saved our baby's life, think how useful she's going to be as the estate nurse, running the Clinic ! "

"And Saunby itself is going to be used again," said Christine. " It was built for the service of God and man, and now after three centuries it's going to be used again for what it was built for. You know, it's very wonderful that *you* should have been found to fulfil the purpose of Saunby," she said in an awed voice to James.

§

In the early morning, the grass in the park was silver with dew criss-crossed with green tracks made by the rabbits, the foxes, the hedgehogs, the voles that

526

had been out in the night. Across the faintly blue sky the heron, the same which had watched Bessy's struggles in the water, flew very slowly across to Lake Wood. He had a mate now and a family. There were four herons where there was one before. A family of stoats, a mother and five young ones, rippled head to tail across the elm avenue in search of breakfast. The blackberries behind the lodge hung thick with no Bertha and no girls to gather them. The little birch trees shimmered lightly their remaining heart-shaped leaves. The grove of crab-apple trees in the garden near the house had again their rosy circles of tiny fallen apples. Broad yellow leaves from the chestnuts up the river came floating down the lake beside the Priory, hesitated above the water-fall and were lost. In the autumn stillness the falling water sounded loud. No birds sang, but the starlings chattered and chucked as they flew in and out of the arches of the West Front and stood on the little Virgin's crown, where some had made a nest last spring as usual.

Smoke rose peacefully from the old house chimneys, and by and by the door opened and the Major came out. It was early, he had not yet breakfasted and was still in slippers. He stood smiling round him for a moment, smiling up at the West Front. To continue to live at Saunby without the bother of managing it, without responsibility or debt, to have Thompson again and cricket and some other company than Anthea and Nurse Pye was more indeed than he had ever hoped for. And though he had always expected that something would turn up in time to save him, coal or a legacy or something, he hadn't expected what had come and he was duly elated and grateful. He went round to the stable yard for Rough, who realized at once that he could do as he liked this morning, and began to plunge about him like a mad thing, without rebuke.

The Major, with none of his usual reluctance, got the car out of the garage, and with Rough beside him drove the mile up the drive to the gates. There he got out and with Rough at his heels pushed his way through the tall, dark rhododendron bushes until he could lay his hands to the legs of the board that announced to all and sundry that Saunby Priory, historic mansion, was for sale. With all his might, the Major shook. Rough barked furiously. Above the old wall, the sale board swayed. It reeled sideways, lurched forward, heaved slowly backwards, and went crashing down among the rhododendron bushes, where it lay.

AFTERWORD

****

Dorothy Whipple always had difficulty with the titles of her novels, often settling on one only at the last minute and with some help or insistence from her publisher. Nothing mattered to her except her characters and what happened to them. But she always thought of *The Priory* as being a novel about a large house in the country which, during the three years it took her to write, she referred to first as The Manor and then as Saunby.

The exact location of the house is never precisely revealed but we know that she was partly inspired by the setting for a weekend cottage that she and her husband rented during the 1930s. This was one of the lodges in the park at Newstead Abbey, a 'little clean empty house with a bathroom, a lilac bush, looking into a wood in front – at the end of a magnificent avenue of trees' (she wrote in her working notebooks, later published as *Random Commentary* in 1966). There was no gas or electricity, but even the meticulous Henry Whipple was happy there – Newstead was the Whipples' Petit Trianon. 'It is all so wide here – wide sky, wide view; larch and fir woods on the horizon. The air smelled of almond, from the hawthorns. I could hear the church bells. All was cool, airy, simple and deeply satisfactory.'

Because the Whipples' little cottage was once a lodge 'a number of people came up the lane to the Park and looked upon us as lodge-keepers', asking them to open the gate and so on. This, combined with the romance of living near the thirteenth century Abbey where Byron had lived, was the inspiration for *The Priory*. But Dorothy Whipple's imagination was contemporary not historical – she was only interested in the people around her, not in those in the past; she wanted to know what kind of lives would be led at Newstead in the 1930s. And she needed a family on which to base her characters.

The Priory seems to be in an English county some way from London where the locals speak with undefined 'Mumfordshire' accents. But in fact the most important inspiration was not an English house at all but a Welsh one: in the summer of 1934, just after the publication of *They Knew Mr Knight* and just before the discovery of the lodge at Newstead, the Whipples had visited a house in Anglesey called Parciau. They had gone to spend a month as paying guests with a Colonel and Mrs Lawrence Williams at their North Wales home. This family of vivid, eccentric individuals intrigued her very much, their values, attitudes and way of life seeming from a different age. *The Priory* is the book she wrote about them.

Anglesey, cut off from the mainland by the Menai Straits, was a poor county in the 1930s, inward-looking and slow to change. The landowners were old-established families such as the Pagets, the Bulkeleys, the Merricks and the Stanleys; the islanders were shrewd, chapel-going, hard-working, often extremely poor and, unlike the gentry, were Welsh speakers and were not particularly conscious of their druidical and Roman past, or the glorious days when Cadwallader and the Welsh Kings ruled from Aberfraw. All in all, this flat island (except for the bump that is Holyhead mountain and the old copper mines above Amlwch) was an odd spot for Dorothy Whipple to find her Priory.

A large, square, grey house, comfortable but of little architectural distinction, Parciau had been built by Colonel Lawrence Williams's father William (1805–1892), the younger son of Sir John Williams, the 1st baronet of Bodelwyddan, that imposing castle at St Asaph. However, by the late 1920s Lawrence (1876–1958) and his wife Henrietta (1886–1980), who had married in 1909 when Lawrence was already a widower with four children, were struggling to keep up the aristocratic style of life they had inherited. The expense of running an estate, a family, large house, cricket team and a shoot meant that Parciau had run out of money.

Henrietta's mother was a Sitwell and her father the 4th Bodelwyddan baronet (she and the Colonel were second cousins). A beautiful, spirited woman, unlike the diffident Anthea, Marraine (as everyone called her) believed well-bred behaviour was the key to a sensible and happy life. It did not always work out like that but she was an eternal optimist. Never a snob, she treated everyone with courtesy and interest. Her sense of fun and infectious relish for life made her many friends and admirers from both sexes, but also turned her into an inveterate collector of lame ducks. Always simply dressed, never wearing make-up, she possessed an un-selfconscious but deeply attractive personal style. When her son Lawrence and myself, both aged thirteen, once dined with her at Quaglino's she wore a green felt hat and carried a gardening basket. This was not exactly haute couture – but she was treated like royalty.

In the late 1920s Henrietta decided something had to be done urgently to stop the financial rot. First she turned the house into a girls' school, not very successfully, then she took a giant social leap, opening it as a Guest House. But it was a very upmarket one, attracting visitors who liked the idea of a holiday living with an upper-class family; it was also a holiday home for children like myself whose parents were overseas. When Christine bemoans having to leave Angela, the baby, for a few days, Penelope's rejoinder is, 'Well, think of the people who go to India and leave their children for years': a pertinent remark about the many fathers and mothers who lived abroad and had to send their children to relations or holiday homes and often did not see them for a very long time. There were no aeroplane flights to Britain in those days, and understandable worries about children's health. One summer holiday there were twenty-five children staying as paying-guests.

I was one of them. Born in India in 1929, my happy privileged childhood was spent in the winter months at our family farm, Convillepur in the Punjab, and then in the hot summers up in beautiful Kashmir. In 1937 I was delighted to learn that I was going to prep school in England . . . but the delight did not last long – incessant beatings, horrible food, unhappiness. Thanks to a young master who maybe sensed I had a talent,

I acted in a school play, *Emil and the Detectives*. I believe it was this small success that ignited my love for drama which later turned into a fifty-year theatrical career.

By great good fortune my parents had heard of Parciau, indeed my brother was sent to stay there before me, and it was where I spent all my holidays for seven years (five being the war years when I never saw my parents) before going to Marlborough College. It was a marvellously free existence, almost Blandings Castle style. Marraine became my guardian and substitute mother, a much loved one, and her son, young Lawrence (the twin 'Roger' in *The Priory*) my greatest friend and 'blood brother'.

The Whipples were paying guests at Parciau from July 25th to August 22nd 1934, as the visitors' book reveals (it also shows that the cricket team was staying there at the same time, while amongst the other guests were George and Millicent Oldham, who appear as 'Sir James and Lady Ashwell'). And it was here at Parciau that Dorothy Whipple found the characters for her new novel, visiting once more before the book was finished and, when it was published, giving a copy to the Williams family inscribed: 'Those as others see them'.

The Parciau inhabitants in *The Priory* were hardly disguised, although some ages were changed. For example, Henrietta was 23 when she married the Colonel (Anthea is 37 when she marries the Major) and her stepdaughters Mona and Violet were young children not beautiful 20 year-olds like 'Christine' and 'Penelope'. But there were enough similarities for the Williams family to be far from amused by their paying guest's novel. Dorothy Whipple would obviously have meant well by sending her novel off with such a revealing inscription, but it was naive of her.

The Priory is an Upstairs/Downstairs book for the story of the Marwoods runs counterpoint to the Bessy/Bertha/Thompson story: the millionaire son's illicit affair with his girlfriend is echoed by the housemaid's passion for the chauffeur. And the book is an eye-opener about the often heartless pre-war attitudes of the upper classes to their servants, for the Marwood girls treat their maids with little consideration and the Major fulminates at his staff's inefficiency: 'The house was full of servants, but it was kept like a pigsty, the food was abominable, he'd had indigestion since lunch and now his fire was out.' As a boy I knew the estate and household workers: Hannah the grim housemaid, William the gamekeeper with his lurid tales of French brothels, Hugh Minafon the bailiff, Rowland Owen the rabbit catcher and Polly Amlwch Lodge. But none of these resemble any of the fictional characters in *The Priory*, the only one who does being Sandy McNab, an eccentric long-time resident upon whom Dorothy Whipple based Thompson the chauffeur, changed for the novel from an upstairs 'bounder' to a downstairs seducer. The quality that was immediately recognisable to Anglesey society was his role as the Colonel's court jester and confidante.

George and Millicent Oldham were the most treasured of Parciau's paying guests, not because they were grand but because they were very rich. George was the founder of the famous Oldham's Batteries, a self-made millionaire, with a Lancashire accent, who enjoyed socialising with upper-class society. The Oldhams would arrive in their chauffeur-driven

Rolls Royce, accompanied by their daughter Dinah and Millicent's pekinese. A horse box followed with Dinah's hunter and a groom. The Oldhams visited Parciau many times and became friends (when Dinah was a debutante it was Henrietta who presented her at court). Decent, generous people from a world alien to the Williams, who were sometimes inclined to be snotty about North Country Folk, Dorothy Whipple found them marvellous subjects for her book. They are certainly blueprints for Sir James and Lady Ashwell: Dorothy even gave her readers the clue that they came from Oldham. However, George and Millicent never had a son: handsome, spoilt, athletic Nicholas Ashwell came from his creator's imagination and the second half of *The Priory* describes his near-disastrous marriage to Christine.

Two other Parciau visitors were used by Dorothy Whipple for 'Nurse Pye' and 'Aunt Victoria'. Sister Housby arrived for six weeks in 1925 to nurse Henrietta's first child Penelope; she never left but died there in 1962. Kate Wilcox, an eccentric friend, lived in a rambling cottage perched on a cliff above Benllech, where she painted bad seascapes – one was actually called 'Lead Kindly Light'.

The lynchpin of the house, Colonel Williams (known to us all as 'Old Man') was a good-looking man, a very popular local figure (qualities easily recognisable in the Major), industrious in local matters, who was Chairman of the County Council, a JP, Master of the Hunt and so on – none of which paid him one single penny. His summer delight was cricket, his winter pleasure shooting. Dorothy Whipple must have met him often as he walked round his estate followed by his black labrador (the Major's dog Rough is golden). He was not an extrovert but would preside over the table at mealtimes and then retire to the sanctuary of his study. A paradoxical man, generous but also selfish, hard-working but then idle, he enjoyed a light-hearted relationship with his children but showed little interest in their problems, never involving himself in their education or visiting them at school. However diligent he was about County affairs, he had little business sense of his own.

During the war Anglesey, like the rest of Britain, found things very difficult. The house was turned into a convalescent hospital and the family moved into a farmhouse where paying guests still arrived escaping from the Blitz . The cricket pitch became a vegetable patch. The Colonel ran the Home Guard. German bombers droned overhead at night on their way to destroy Liverpool. Later on, Italian prisoners came to help farm the land.

Life returned to normal, but finally the big house had to be demolished and the family now live in the Farmhouse, Old Parciau. The Bodelwyddan title had leapfrogged over the Colonel, who died in 1958, then his son, my friend Lawrence (now the 9th Baronet) resigned his commission in The Royal Marines and resolved to revive the family fortunes. He had an idea; and with great hard work it succeeded: Parciau Caravan Park (the play on words is intentional) is the best in Anglesey. Just as Dorothy Whipple found a happy ending for the Priory in her novel with Sir James buying it to save Major Marwood from bankruptcy, so Parciau Estate happily survives.

David Conville,
Dorset, 2002